An Illusion of Hell
The Trilogy of the Void Book Two
By Peter Meredith

Peter Meredith

Fictional works by Peter Meredith:

A Perfect America

The Sacrificial Daughter

The Horror of the Shade Trilogy of the Void 1

An Illusion of Hell Trilogy of the Void 2

Hell Blade Trilogy of the Void 3

The Punished

Sprite

The Feylands: A Hidden Lands Novel

The Sun King: A Hidden Lands Novel

The Sun Queen: A Hidden Lands Novel

The Apocalypse: The Undead World Novel 1

The Apocalypse Survivors: The Undead World Novel 2

The Apocalypse Outcasts: The Undead World Novel 3

The Apocalypse Fugitives: The Undead World Novel 4

Pen(Novella)

A Sliver of Perfection (Novella)

The Haunting At Red Feathers(Short Story)

The Haunting On Colonel's Row(Short Story)

The Drawer(Short Story)

The Eyes in the Storm(Short Story)

Chapter 1

12 Shots of Whiskey

"Did we ever kiss or, you know, fool around?" Talitha asked her brother.

"No," Will responded warily.

"What about dad? We did *it,* right?" She shifted in bed, rolling over to look up at him. In the dim light her brown eyes looked like deep black pits. This was heading into dangerous territory. He kept his face carefully composed—even though it was full night out, Talitha could see him as if he were under a spotlight.

"No, not dad either," Will said, then changed the subject, "Hey, it's bedtime and I'm getting pretty sleepy." Will was thankful it was at least partially the truth; now would be a bad time to lie. However, it was no lie that it was exhausting being in her presence.

She ran her hands through her long brown hair and stretched. "Am I sleepy?" She was not at all sleepy. Talitha never became sleepy, hungry, or thirsty.

"No Tal, but your body needs it's rest anyways, so roll on over..." That was a mistake, and he knew it right away.

Talitha had been on that verge between personalities and sometimes just a word would awaken the wrong one.

She'd been lying in her bed, with the silk of her sheets tucked sweetly up to her chin, then in an impossible blur of motion she was up. Her naked body, tan, lean, yet sleek with muscle, was a dreadful weapon. She advanced on Will with the speed of a striking snake.

He *knew* the blow was coming—a right hook that

would level him, and he saw his options were limited to either fighting or lying back as submissively as possible. As usual he chose not to fight and took the heaviest part of the strike on his left forearm. Still there was plenty of force remaining and he was sent sprawling on the old orange and brown shag carpet. Immediately he went to his back, his hands up protecting his face.

To someone peering in through the window of the cabin, the scene would've been ludicrous. Will was tall, strong, and thick with muscle as well as fully clothed. He dwarfed the nude woman, who seemed exposed and unprotected in contrast. In reality it was she who held the upper hand and she jumped full upon the man cowering before her.

"Who the hell do you think you are?" Talitha screamed into his ear. "Insect! You are nothing."

She raked his left hand away from his face and slapped him hard on the side of the head, with her right. Will's head cranked hard over and went deep into the shag. He saw weird orange and brown spots in his vision, and blinked his blue eyes trying to clear them. His face felt as if it had been burned by the force of the blow, but despite that he was happy with the results. He *knew* it would get no worse than being screamed at.

"You don't tell me what to do, damn it! I tell you!" Her anger was real, perhaps the most real thing about her and she unleashed it on him.

"Roll over? You think I'll roll over for you, insect. You're not the Veeerdi...you're not even Ghushkaz! Roll over? Do you think you can make me? What a joke! You can't..." Talitha stopped yelling. With a sudden smirk on her face, she reached out and stroked his thick brown hair from his forehead.

Straightening his head in the carpet, so he could look full up at her, she continued, "Ok, I see now you were not fool enough to challenge me. It was this body you're after. Interesting..."

Talitha had been straddling him. Now she got up, hauling him to his feet as though he weighed no more than a child. Throwing him on the bed, she then crawled up on to him, rubbing her breasts along the length of his body.

He hated this about her.

She had become a creature with a strong sexual appetite and when she was in one of her moods, she no longer cared about social constructs. The terms brother and sister had no meaning for her, and if it had been possible, she would've raped him many times already. She'd tried in the past, but he had fought her to a standstill each time.

Tonight, thankfully, it wouldn't go that way. Will saw it ending soon and helped it along, "I'm so sorry... I didn't mean to presume. I beg your forgiveness."

"I don't like it when you beg. Stop it! You sound like such a fag when you do that." The idea that he was gay seemed to come over her, and she looked down at him with disgust and contempt. "Get the hell out of my bed! Jeez, how does Lisa put up with you?"

Will slipped from her bed, trying not to touch her as he got up. He wobbled slightly as the room pitched first to the left and then way over to the right, and he grabbed her dresser for support. The slap had been harder than he'd thought and his head still rang with it.

It took a moment for the room to steady itself and he almost waited too long to answer her, "She's even weaker that I am; she *has* to put up with me." This was of course only partly true; Lisa didn't have to put up with him at all, but it was the answer Talitha was looking for.

"Yes, I suppose she's just a girl."

Will felt clear headed enough and he turned to face Talitha knowing it would be disrespectful as well as dangerous to keep his back to her. She sat up in the bed with her sheets lying just below her breasts. With her left hand she made gentle patterns in the silk but it was far too dark to see what they were, and with her right hand she was beginning to stroke herself.

"May I retire, please?" he asked and *knew* she would allow it. He knew many things.

"Yeah, get out of here...MMmmhhh." He started to leave quickly but hesitated at the door, knowing what was coming, "Are you going to make French toast in the morning?" she asked sweetly. He hated her sweet voice, it was like icing on dog crap.

If he had to he'd make the French toast, though it was likely she'd be the one to fix breakfast. "Of course, if that's what you want," he replied, struggling to be cheery. "Do you want blueberry syrup or..." he really didn't need to finish the question and his face sunk, "or strawberry?"

"Actually...mmmh...I want chocolate. Mmmmhh." Chocolate meant she would be at this for at least an hour.

"Sure Tal, anything you want...sweet dreams."

"Mmmmhhh...get out."

Will shut the door behind him and went to turn on the lights in the cabin. As tired as he was, there was no way he'd be able to sleep, not with her erotic symphony going on. At the same time he didn't want to sleep, his dreams would be anything but sweet. Tonight he would dream about the rapes. There were so many...seemingly an endless number of them, one after another. An impossible amount, but the void was an impossible place after all.

Poking about in the cupboard he found his Wild Turkey and looked long at the deep amber colored whiskey. There was a formula to getting the right amount of drunk, though he didn't know it. Talitha would be able to tell him he was sure. If he asked her in the morning, she would break it down into charts and graphs and have a gay ole time doing it, too. However, he didn't need a chart to tell him he was going to drink half the bottle in front of him and follow that with a couple of sleeping pills.

He poured himself his first shot; his hands shook as the glass went to his lips. But he paid the shaking little attention; he *knew* it would stop in a few minutes, just as he *knew* there would be some sort of terrible rhino creature tonight. He shuddered at the image that popped into his head and quickly threw back a second shot. The horn of the rhino thing was *not* on its head. Will shuddered again.

"MMMmhhh, yessss."

Have fun, he thought to himself.

That wasn't something he'd ever say out loud. Even with her door closed, she would hear him. Her hearing, her sense of smell, and her eyesight, were all phenomenal. She had spent a day in the void, and it had turned her into some sort of insane superwoman. One moment she'd be taking a bath, something she never tired of, and the next she would break your arms with her bare hands. She was a murderer, but he loved her.

"Number three...down the hatch," he whispered and drained another shot.

The horn was long, over two feet in length and it wasn't smooth as he had first thought, but was ringed every few inches with jagged teeth like barbs.

"Oh jeez!" Will gave his head a vigorous shake to clear away the vision of the horn; it didn't work, it lingered like an early morning haze.

How Talitha had endured it was a mystery he hoped he would never figure out. Nevertheless, she had endured it and a lot more than just the rapes. He knew it because he dreamed it. It was all part of his curse.

Eight years ago, when he was only seventeen and Talitha sixteen, she'd been sacrificed to a demon and her soul had been sucked into the void of hell. It had taken the deaths of two people, one innocent and one guilty to free her, but she had come back changed.

For the most part, she was his sister as he had always known her sweet, funny, smart. Her eyes would still crinkle up when she smiled and she still corrected his grammar at every opportunity. Yet sometimes she'd become a monster, a beautiful killer who enjoyed the pain she caused.

She wasn't the only one that had changed.

He had tiptoed on the edge of the void himself and had seen the demon in its true form, just as she had. The gypsy, Adrina, had given Will her "gift" of foresight...a gift she saw as more a curse than anything. It had passed from her at the moment of her death and had been made permanent when he was cursed by the sight of the demon.

His curse was not nearly such a burden as Adrina's

had been. For the most part she saw visions of death, but she couldn't interfere in any way or she would only make the victim's suffering worse. Adrina would know when a loved one was about to die and yet have no option but to sit and watch.

Will, however, could interfere with the future without repercussion, and had done so on a number of occasions. His visions were of many things; some random, concerning strangers, or even the weather, while others were quite personal. They would come to him out of the blue; he could see what would happen in the next few seconds or sometimes in the next few years.

Seeing the future wasn't the only aspect of his curse. There was another odd talent he possessed, and that was the ability to steal his sister's dreams. When he had pulled his sister from the void they had become linked in way neither fully understood. If they were to fall asleep anywhere near each other, his mind would instantly become flooded with her dreams and for some reason she only dreamt about her time in the torture chambers of the void.

He dreamed what she had experienced for real.

The worst part of this was that once he began dreaming he was stuck in her hellish nightmare until she woke up. Of course, he did have the choice to not fall asleep near her, but Will's conscience, his brotherly love meant he had to do something for her. He knew her pain and it was too great for him to let her experience it a second time.

Therefore, every weekend he'd take the two-hour drive up to her isolated retreat in the woods. They'd spend the day together, sometimes laughing, sometimes crying, and unfortunately when the mood was on her, sometimes fighting. At night he would tuck her in and then get drunk.

It was the only time he ever drank, but it was necessary—her dreams were that horrifying. She'd been tortured in every conceivable way by the most hideous creatures. The rapes, the machines, the blood, the pain were all as real to him as they had been to her, with one huge exception: even while it was happening, he knew it would end, eventually.

She never had that tiny luxury.

For Will, only the earth spinning about measured her time in the void. For him it had been twenty-four hours and forty-two minutes, a total of just under 89,000 seconds. But for Talitha...there was no telling how long it was. More than years or even decades, it could've been many centuries.

"Oh yeah! Oh God!" Her screams of self-inflicted ecstasy jarred him from his thoughts and made him remember he had work to do. He tossed down two more shots in quick succession. "Yes! Yes!" she screamed.

"Oh, jeez!" he mumbled to himself. He was starting to feel the alcohol.

Talitha's place was hardly more than a shack and the walls were thin enough that he didn't need super-hearing to figure out she was nearing climax. She would go at it a few more times, but he figured he still had at least seven shots left to down and he never liked trying to race her to sleep.

On occasion he had misjudged the timing. The last time, her painful shrieks and racking sobs had been almost impossible to bear and strangely when he had finally fallen asleep he'd been thankful when the torturer had turned the flames on him instead.

Will's stomach, angry over the infusion of whiskey, knotted up suddenly and he grimaced. By experience he knew the nausea would pass, yet he also knew it would slow him down in his race to get drunk. He had to concentrate on something and he went out to his jeep Wrangler to get the first of four boxes of books.

Talitha had been a reader of unbelievable appetite before her sojourn in the void, and now it was all he could do to keep up. The fact that she only slept one night out of the week didn't help, either. For the last year, he'd been bringing college textbooks as a way to appease her craving for information. The previous year, she had zipped through three different sets of encyclopedias. To keep her from being bored he would also throw in foreign languages books and sadly, romance fiction.

Talitha loved the romance novels, and would've been quite content if that was the only kind he ever brought. Sometimes she'd read to him from her favorite passages and cry when some shirtless, muscle-bound man finally realized his true love was right in front of him the whole time.

Will would very frequently cry as well, just not in front of her and certainly not over some book. His sister would never be in love again. She had torn out the throat of the only boy who had ever loved her and kicked his lifeless body out into the forest. Her love affair with Brian Galt was over before it started.

There would be no one else.

Coming in from the growing cold, Will plunked the box down heavily in the main room, knowing that Talitha would be able to pick it up one handed if she wished. He then went back to his bottle and despite the queasiness churning at his innards, took another shot.

Thinking about Brian made him long to get drunk even when he wasn't with Talitha. Brian had been an amazing individual and yet there had been absolutely nothing special about him at all. He had been small and skinny, with hair that would become a dense, impenetrable brown thicket if he went too long between haircuts, which would be always. He was cute, Will supposed, after a nerdy fashion, and Talitha had loved him

Will poured a bit too much whiskey this time and it sloshed over the side of the shot glass. He paused with the glass touching his lip, trying to remember if this was number four or five.

"Who cares," he said to the glass and drank it off. Just then he remembered that he was going to drink half the bottle and decided he would mark where he would drink to. There were plenty of pens lying about the place, but the trick was finding one that actually held ink.

Splashing about in the kitchen junk-drawer, he unearthed a pen and began to scribble away at the halfway point on the fifth of whiskey...

The horn was now covered in blood, and shreds of dripping flesh hung from the barbs of it. Will gasped, feeling the horrific pain of his insides being torn out and he pushed the horn away as hard as he could. He looked down and saw a great gory hole.

"Oh, my God! Oh, my God!" Will came back from his vision and felt sudden tears coursing down his cheeks. His breathing came fast and heavy, and the first thing he did was put his hand to his crotch and rub at the lingering phantom-pain. Glancing down, he saw that he had thrown the bottle of Wild Turkey away from him and he thanked God that it hadn't broken.

Crawling to it, he drank straight from the mouth with hands that shook greater than before. The shaking was so profound that he fumbled at capping it, and ended up taking another swig. Placing the open bottle on the counter he gave it a long look, but it suddenly reminded him of the horn and he shuddered convulsively.

"Holy crap! This isn't good, jeez," he whined miserably to himself. It was never good and it was always like this. He'd continue to get a preview of his coming torture until he passed out and then he would get the real thing. With another moan slipping from his lips, he wiped at the tears on his face and shook his head trying to figure out why he was doing this to himself.

At this point he really didn't know. All he knew was that he was supposed to get drunk. He reached for the bottle and took another long pull.

For perhaps the hundredth time Will thought about how he could kill Talitha. "Put her out of her misery, I mean," he said to no one in particular. A high-powered rifle from three-hundred yards might do the trick, but only if it were a head shot. Anything else would just make her angry.

Killing Talitha was not something a person could do with ease. She couldn't be poisoned as far he could tell: if she didn't smell it a mile off, her body would simply break the chemicals down. That same sense of smell would make getting a gun anywhere close to her impossible and the fact that she lived in the thick woods made the long range shot just a pipe dream.

A knife, an axe, a club, or even a sword would be just silly. She could move with blazing speed and it was highly likely that she would take the blade from him and sheath it in his own belly. Still he was the only person with a ghost of a chance of killing her. His ability to see the immediate future had saved him from her on numerous occasions; it allowed him to dodge, duck or block with uncanny precision. However, on the few instances, during their frequent fights, when he has been able to strike her, he had knocked her about quite a bit but it rarely did more than increase her enthusiasm for his blood.

The thought of blood made him remember the horn. "Shun of a bish!" Again, he drank from the bottle and gave it a bleary stare. "Thas better. Ok...pill time." Will got up unsteadily and went for his bag, walking as if on the side of a steep hill.

"Donut take with alcohol ny ass," he said after glancing at the prominent warning label.

There were only two pills in the container and that was by design. Once, he had awoken the following morning from one of his tortured nights, cover in vomit. He discovered that he had taken half the pills in the bottle; deep down he knew he'd been trying to kill himself before he had to face the night.

Will popped his two pills, washing them down with the whiskey. He then looked at the bottle groggily; he was well below the line he'd made for himself. In the background, he heard Talitha's moaning, but it wasn't coming through to his brain clearly anymore, and he sat gazing about, losing focus with each passing moment.

"Ah crappity!" His stomach was going up and

down like a rubber seesaw and he was going to get sick. To stave it off, he had to get up and walk around until the feeling passed or he'd lose the pills for sure. Standing up, he had only a moment of balance left in him and then the cabin heaved over on its side and sent him sprawling.

"Whoa now," he said to the floor, clutching it as though he were on the deck of a rolling ship. Crawling over to the couch, he used it to steady himself, and managed to stand on his own again. "Thas better...what the hell?" he exclaimed to the cover of a romance book staring up at him from the box. "You guys even know what the friggen buttons are for on your shirts?"

Will smirked at his own great cleverness, but in the next second he was despondent, "Oh Lisa, why do I do this? I should be at home wif you an da baby!" Lisa's beautiful face came to him and he sighed heavily with longing. There was no baby just yet. Lisa was seven months along and her belly was only the size of a bowling ball. He loved to place his large hands around the small lump of the baby and caress Lisa's soft skin.

Thinking about her, he plopped heavily down on the couch, his nausea forgotten, and puffed out his own belly. Putting his hands on his stomach, he smiled stupidly and sang, "Gold-en slum-bers kiss your eyes..."

Lisa constantly sang to the baby inside her and it always made him smile to hear her secret voice. As far as he knew, he and the baby were the only ones who had ever heard that magnificent sound. He stopped his own deep, raspy attempt at singing, and it was with a lullaby drifting through his mind that he finally fell asleep. A short while later, Will met the owner of the terrible horn.

Chapter 2

The First Scent

"Good evenin', Sistah."

The words were soft, as if the man who spoke them wanted to disturb the night as little as possible. In the chill of the darkness the unexpected voice startled Sister Mary Agatha. Her hands shot like wounded butterflies to her chest and she gasped. She knew the voice; it took a second for her to remember it and when she did, her fright passed.

Turning slowly, in order to give herself a moment to hide the fact that she been surprised, Sister Mary took in the outline of a police officer framed against the streetlight.

The man's face was unfortunately familiar, he had been snooping around the orphanage off and on for years, but at the moment she couldn't recall his name. It was on the tip of her tongue, however there it stayed. She used to know it. Lately, little things like that would slip from her mind and she had taken to peeking at his nametag whenever he came by. Tonight he would get nothing more than *officer* from her, it was just too dark.

"Hello, Officer."

"I didn't mean to scare ya. I thought ya heard me." The policeman smiled disarmingly and stepped even closer to her. Now she was able to get a better look at his heavily jowled face, but the name danced even further out of her mind and she felt a moment of irritation. Nevertheless, she managed a smile, exposing her teeth, which were crooked and grey with age.

"I heard you, Officer, and you didn't scare me. I was just praying. Probably something I should get back to... if you don't mind." She turned away with a small wave of her hand indicating dismissal and said over shoulder, "So you have a good night now."

There was a time when she was much younger that she liked and respected the police, but that hadn't been for a quite few years. They were always coming down so hard on her boys, using them as scapegoats for any trivial and not so trivial crime in the neighborhood. She wasn't stupid, and she understood that her boys could be a bit rowdy at times but on the whole they were just as good as the neighborhood kids, perhaps even better.

"Well actually, I need a moment of your time," the officer replied in his thick Boston accent, his voice holding a touch of annoyance. With her back turned to him and the black coif of her habit hiding much of her face, he didn't see her rolling her eyes.

Here it goes, she thought. Which one of her boys was in trouble this time, and for what? Her mind ran down a list of the usual suspects, as the officer continued in his annoying accent, "Ya know about the kids disappearin' in the city, right?"

At this a small feeling of alarm crept over her and she turned back to the man. She knew about the children, everyone knew, the news had gone nationwide after the third boy went unaccounted for and in the last three weeks, two more had vanished. It was as if they had wandered into quicksand on a city sidewalk and had been sucked into the earth.

"Yes, yes I know about those poor boys...all very tragic, I'm sure. But what does that have to do with..."

A wild thought struck her. Sister Mary was a big woman, shaped rather like a shoebox, but she still managed to find her hips and she placed her hands squarely on them.

"You don't think any of my boys had anything to do with this? That is preposterous!" She glared at the startled police officer with eyes that were a rheumy wet blue and hard with her anger. "In all my seventy-three years, this is the most..."

"Hold on, Sistah! Ya got me all wrong. I just wanted to know if you had seen anyone lurkin' around in a suspicious mannah. Maybe takin' an interest in your grade schoolahs. Ya see anyone like that?"

She relaxed a little at this, but that feeling of alarm hung on her as if her insides were coated lightly with it. Sister Mary Agatha had never truly considered that the pervert she'd read about would target any of her boys. So far all the other children had been normal, from normal families, living in normal homes. In her mind, her boys didn't fit that description. Saint Thomas' was a home for boys that nobody wanted, not even sex perverts as far as she knew.

"No, I haven't seen anyone like that, Officer Dallins," the name sprang to her mind just as she was saying it and she smiled at this small personal triumph. "If I do, I'll be sure to call." She gave another little wave and the policeman shrugged as if he was satisfied that he'd done all he could do and he headed back to his cruiser, parked up the street.

Sister Mary watched him for a few moments before she walked off into the gradually thickening night and began praying. She'd been praying after a fashion when the officer had given her the fright; that had been no lie.

When she wasn't actively engaged in conversation, prayers ran on an endless loop through her mind. Some people hummed or whistled their day away, she prayed. On average, the Our Father, which was always number one on her top 40-prayer list, would slide from her lips in a low constant mumble up to a hundred times a day.

Tonight she'd been in an Apostle's Creed mood, and she would go through at least four repetitions of it as she went about the grounds making sure the buildings were locked up.

This was part of her nightly routine and was another reason she was not terribly concerned about the pervert. Her orphanage, as she considered it, was one of the most secure places in this section of the city. The two-story building sported only three entrances, all of which were constructed of heavy steel.

Every night she'd walk the entire perimeter of the orphanage, the attached church, and the offices, giving each door a little shake.

When she came to the corner of the first building, she looked back into the gloom to check whether Officer Dallins was still nosing about, but he wasn't in sight. Turning back to her task she paused, startled for the second time that night.

Something had moved among the shadows near the front of the church. A very tall pine stood there, running nearly up the side of the building all the way to the tall steeple. It was just gorgeous in the daytime, but at night it was the perfect place for shenanigans. In her forty-two years of running the home she had cleaned up all sorts of nasty leavings under its thick foliage.

Shadows commanded its base and the idea of the sex pervert sprang to mind. This made her turn to look for the officer a second time. As before, there was no one in sight and her feeling of alarm increased. The shadows moved again and the nun backed around the side of the building, moving as quietly as possible.

This wasn't like her at all. Sister Mary didn't fear sex perverts in the least. She was a large woman, with a loud rough voice, who was used to commanding attention. In her mind, sex perverts were skinny, little greasy-haired men who lacked the self-confidence to ask a girl out on a proper date.

Nevertheless, for some reason she hesitated and it was at least a minute before she chided herself as a coward and was able to waddle toward the dark undergrowth. She wished she could have marched over as she had when she was younger, but a broken hip had constrained her to that unfortunate waddling gait. It was unfortunate because due to her rectangle of a figure and her black and white attire, the waddle made her look very much like the world's largest penguin. She tried not to think about that, especially now that she was going to give a sex pervert a piece of her mind.

Upon nearing the tree, her waddle slowed and her eyes went to each of the shadows in turn, but there was no one to be seen. This should have calmed the odd fear that had her hands shaking, but instead when she finally slipped beneath the branches of the pine, her feeling of alarm grew. There may not have been a person in those shadows but there was a nasty smell, one that awoke long forgotten memories in her.

She had been a nurse's aide in the south Pacific during the war and this smell was the same she had encountered many times back then. It was the gangrenous odor of rotting flesh.

Chapter 3

Every Sunday Morning

"Hey Willy J sleepy-head." Talitha's voice was soft and full of concern.

Thud! Thud! Thud! Will's headache was immediate and nearly debilitating, but despite that, his first action was to reach down and feel his crotch. His second was to breathe a sigh of relief; everything was where it was supposed to be, and more importantly, there wasn't a gaping bloody hole.

The nightmare creature with the horn had been followed by others, and he suddenly remembered that one, a scaly lizard like thing had chewed his left hand off, slowly grinding his bones. The sound of his small bones in its teeth was nasty and similar to a man eating peanuts. He shivered at the memory and brought his hand up; it was whole and the fingers of it wiggled stiffly, but now he saw that his hand was strangely large and hairy.

"Oh right," Will mumbled, his confusion slipping away. In the dreams he stole from Talitha; he would become Talitha, a girl, small and vulnerable and when he screamed, it would be with her voice.

"I have some water and aspirin for you," Talitha said, still using her softest tone. She smiled the sad commiserating smile that he saw every Sunday morning. He knew even without any foresight that she'd been up for a while, letting him sleep a normal human sleep. Moreover, she would have the French toast ready and waiting for him, as well as coffee. He was heartily sick of French toast, having had it every week for the last four years. But, it was what she wanted and it always made her happy, so he'd choke it down if he had to.

"Thanks." He took the aspirin and attempted to smile back at her, but it came across as a grimace of pain.

"Is it bad this morning? I've read that a higher quality alcohol will reduce both the duration and intensity of hangovers. It's a factor of the distillation process..." Will put his hand out to her and shook his head weakly. Her volume had been ratcheting up as it always did when she expounded scientifically. "Oh, I'm so sorry. I'm sorry about everything. Maybe you shouldn't come over..."

"It's ok, Talitha. There's nothing to be sorry for." Will gave her the best smile he could manage with what felt like broken glass in his skull. He swallowed his pills and his stomach warned him against the French toast, at least for a while. "I think I need some coffee." He struggled to his feet wondering if this was what seventy-five would feel like, if he lived that long.

"Can you maybe brush and take a shower first?" she asked shyly. He was certain he didn't smell good and with her heightened senses, his odor was probably equal to that of a dumpster.

"Sure...just one sip and then I'll go." He could feel the pulse in his temple and it felt like it was pushing liquid steel into his brain instead of blood. After a long drink of the coffee, he headed off.

The shower helped as it always did. Talitha bathed three or four times a day and after a night like the last one, he would probably need to do the same. He was far luckier than she was however; unlike her memories, his dreams would fade in time. After a few days...or maybe even after a few hours he likely wouldn't be able to recall the horn or its terrible owner.

He stared dully at the shower wall, trying not to think about anything but the fastidiously clean grout between the tiles. The water was just turning tepid, when Talitha called out, "We have to leave for church in thirty minutes!"

He was done anyway and dried himself off, careful not to touch Brian's towel. Sadly, she would come and check to see if he had. There were little shrines in memorial to Brian all around the cabin. His drawers were still full of his clothing, his coffee mug still sat on the kitchen counter, and his toothbrush lay cockeyed on the sink where he had left it four years ago. These little clues of his life always made Will melancholy.

How he lasted a full year with Talitha was beyond Will.

Will had driven out to visit the two of them frequently and each time Brian sported new bruises layered over the old ones. It must've been hell on him but he hadn't once complained to Will. Quite the opposite; he acted as if he were the luckiest man in the world. In a way he was. There had only been one girl on all the earth, who was perfect for him, and he not only got her to fall in love with him, but he helped save her from an endless half-life of torture and pain.

You couldn't ask for much more than that—except perhaps for a quick death. And Brian's death had been relatively quick. Will unfortunately had dreamed it all in living color even as it happened. It had been like the dreams he endured when he spent the nights in her cabin; he became her.

However, in a reversal of those dreams, Talitha had been the one inflicting pain—and enjoying it. Her victim had been Brian, the love of her life. She savored the blood, hot and coppery, fresh from his throat. It had made her giddy for a short while and then she grew angry; disappointed at how easily the man had died.

"Talitha? I hear the water!" Brian called out.

"And I hear your heart beating, so, fucking what?" Talitha murmured to herself. She hated clothes sometimes, especially if she was angry. The only clothes she liked really were ones made from silk. Her panties were silk and these she pulled off and gently rubbed up and down her body.

"What did you say, Honey?"

Did that thing just call me, honey? Talitha was tired of the thing's insolence...she would have to beat it again.

With that idea, her mood improved and she smiled wickedly cruel and slipped quietly to the bathroom where Brian was just finishing brushing his teeth.

This was going to be fun, she thought and she swore this time she would make him cry. He would normally just grunt which was unsatisfying, but today he would cry even if she had to pull his testicles off. Wait! She liked his testicles. It would have to be an eye then.

"Hey, the pot is boiling, turn it off..." Brian opened the door and froze in place. He looked down at her naked body and Talitha saw the fear in his eyes. She knew all his tricks to keep from being beaten—the cowering, the attempts at fawning, the slave-like

attitude he would wear like a mask.

However, those defense mechanisms depended on him being aware of what she was feeling and how she was coping. But this morning, he had taken too long in the shower, too long to floss and brush his teeth, and he missed it when the blackness had slipped over her, warming her. If he had just come out a few minutes earlier, things might have been different.

But there was no use crying over spilt blood. Brian immediately lowered his gaze and started to say something, "Mi..."

Talitha slapped him casually and Brian's head rocked back, striking the frame of the door. His knees buckled and he might have gone down right there but Talitha reached out her hand and slammed him up against the wall, holding him in place.

"From now on, you'll get down on your knees when I enter the room, do you understand, worm?"

Brian's eyes rolled wildly as he attempted to focus and he said nothing. Talitha felt frisky that morning and letting go of him, she spun in a blur and before his knees could buckle, she sent a spinning back-kick into his mid-section. He went down in a heap and his only sound was a small hitching as his diaphragm attempted to draw in air. He struggled for endless seconds with his face turning a deep red.

Talitha became bored of waiting and picked him up by the hair with a sigh. Brian, who was normally a good fighter, was being so dull and instead of having a good time she was getting angry.

"You're trying my patience. Maybe I'll have you replaced...Will is twice the man you are," Talitha said cruelly. "However you do grovel so much better than he

does...I will just take an eye. Maybe you'll learn proper respect then." She felt suddenly benevolent over her decision, but his response brought her haughty anger to a boil in a second.

"No... uhhhhghh."

This was too much. How could he say no when she being so sweet? Talitha had a grip on his throat with her left hand and she slowly tightened it, so that the color of his face deepened to a wonderful magenta. She liked the color, but it made her just a little crazy. She wondered just how much blood was in his head at that moment. There only one way to find out.

Thankfully, Lisa woke Will up a few moments later. He'd been laughing cruelly in his sleep and it had frightened her. In a state of shock, he had driven up to Talitha's cabin, meaning to bury the body, but she had beaten him to it. As well she had removed all signs of the murder, yet he could still see the wet stains on the walls and carpet, and the smell of bleach was strong in the air.

That had been just over four years before. At first Will didn't think Talitha would last very long. Her dreams and the terrible struggle to stay away day after day seemed to be tearing her apart. As well her intense loneliness grew. The only thing she had to look forward to were his visits. Out of love and pity the weekly sleepovers had begun.

They quickly fell into a regular pattern; he'd arrive sometime after noon on Saturday and they would play games or chat; they'd have dinner and sit on the back porch-swing watching the sunset. But all the while there would be a stiffness about them as if their spines had been replaced with high-tension springs.

By Saturday, Talitha had been without sleep for a week and even though she may not have had the sensation of sleepiness, her body still needed at least a little and her mood could become quickly dark and quite terrifyingly evil.

For her part Talitha couldn't relax because of the great guilt she had over what had happened not only to Brian but to the others as well. There had been quite a few others. Obviously Will couldn't relax because his very life was on the line.

He made sure to keep the conversation light and never brought up anything in the least bit stressful, but he was still exhausted by the time she was ready for bed. Then he'd begin drinking and the visions would come. At some point, he'd finally pass out. This was the only way Talitha could get any proper sleep and on most Sundays, her smiling face and sweet disposition made the pain worth it.

This was not one of those weeks.

The previous night's dreams kept coming back to him and he would shiver with the memories of that terrible horn and the grinding crunching sound his bones had made as they were being chewed.

"It'll fade. It'll fade," he said to himself. His queasy stomach and the re-occurring crunching echoing in his skull made eating an impossibility; so he pushed the French toast around his plate as politely as he could.

"Have you talked with Lisa about the baby? You know...about me, maybe babysitting sometime?" She gave him a shy smile and there was such painful hope in her eyes that it hurt to see.

"For now...I think we may have to limit you seeing the baby. I might be able to talk Lisa into coming out here a few times, but it'll be at Mass only."

Every Sunday morning he'd drive Talitha forty-five minutes to the nearest Catholic Church. It was the one place her cruel side had never showed itself, even for a single moment. "Speaking of church, we better get going if we're going to get a good seat," he added, hoping to change the subject.

The drive into town was beautiful. Western Maine was a treat in October and hell in January and that day was a fine example; the trees were exploding in gorgeous orange and gold, and the pungent aroma of burning leaves was all about them.

Talitha smiled at the sights and Will smiled at her. She was happy, almost carefree, and Will began to think that the pain of the previous night had been worth it. The images were already fading and the pain was not even a memory. It was like the time he broke his arm in the second grade, he remembered it had hurt terribly, but once it was healed, he couldn't recall at all how it felt.

The church wasn't one those great cathedrals with wonderful stained glass windows and an organ the size of a Greyhound bus; it was a little brick affair, rectangular with a low sloping roof. It was in fact nothing special, but Will liked it anyway. It was intimate and cozy and it had rustic warmth that he looked forward to after his hellish Saturday nights.

Before his living nightmare with the demon Ba'al Zubel, he went to church mostly out of curiosity but now attending Mass had become a necessity for him. Deep in his soul, he felt a need to be as near to God as he could and he not only attended this simple church with his sister, he would also frequent one close to his home at least once a week with Lisa.

As they pulled into the parking lot, the bell began to ring in the steeple and Will watched it go back and forth, feeling an odd hint of anxiety. He glanced over at Talitha and the anxiety started to blossom and grow roots deep into his stomach.

She'd just stepped out of the Jeep when her smile froze on her face. Sniffing the air in a gentle fashion, she peered about, her good mood slipping away. Now with curiosity running the same course as his anxiety, Will gave the air a tentative sniff: burning leaves, and under that, the wet earthy scent of the nearby forest.

"What is it?" he asked.

"Someone has brought a gun into the church." She pivoted, scanning each of the cars in turn, and then looked up to building. Her glance pierced every window.

"It could be a hunter...I think it's deer season." He suddenly knew it wasn't a hunter, at least it wasn't a person who hunted deer.

"Don't be stupid," Talitha's smile was gone and her brown eyes had narrowed. "All of the moronic hicks around here use Lucas gun oil. They must sell it by the barrel...scentless my ass." She wrinkled her nose. "This is different, sweeter." He had no idea she knew anything about guns or their oils, and the notion that she knew the name of even a single brand worried him almost as much as the look in her eyes.

"Maybe we should skip church today...or come back later for confession. I'm sure..."

"Shut your stupid mouth," she ordered in a low tone. She bent and picked up a rock that fit nicely into her small palm. The smile came back to her face as she

hefted the rock easily, bouncing it in her hand.
It was a cruel smile.

Chapter 4

The Demon and The Nun

Sitting in the staff kitchen of the orphanage, her buttocks overflowing one the old wooden chairs, Sister Mary Agatha was contemplating sin when the sound of the sirens cut through her partial deafness. She had seen the lights of the police cars a minute earlier and in her younger years she would've heard the insistent wailing a long way off.

Tonight, however, they came to her muffled, a distant sound that was incongruent with the urgent proximity of the flashing lights. Since the police rushed through the neighborhood in this manner almost daily, she was unconcerned and after giving the speeding cars a casual look she went back to her deliberations.

Did the act of taking ice cream that did not belong to her and eating it, constitute a sin?

Four years ago, when he was new to the parish, Father John had told her to help herself to it. Recently, however, there had been looks and sometimes a, "Hmmm" would rumble from his throat at the sight of an empty ice cream container.

Despite her age, her hands were still strong and she stirred the ice cream vigorously. When it was the consistency of soup, the way she most liked to eat it, she took a large spoonful and decided it wasn't a sin after all. She was like a vampire in this way and would need to be disinvited, before she gave up her rights to it.

The lights of the cars flash up the street and around

the block. They ceased to exist for her as soon as they were out of sight and she went back to her contemplations. She had moved on from sin, and was now considering ice cream in general as she worked the spoon into a cold vortex.

How she wished there was some way that ice cream would last in the main kitchen of the orphanage. Currently, there were thirty-six boys in residence, aging from six to nineteen years old. When it came to food, they ceased being boys and became human shaped piranhas.

The boys, voracious as they were, couldn't compare with the two live-in counselors, however. The counselors were very big men and she always had trouble watching them eat. Sean Shay would frequently eat, not with a fork, but with a spatula or serving spoon, shoveling tremendous amounts of food into his huge maw. Despite being only twenty-six years old, Sean wasn't in good shape and Sister Mary Agatha worried for him.

He never exercised and the only time she had seen him sweat was when he was polishing off one of his gigantic dinners. The sweat would start as a trickle in his thick black hair and soon he'd be using his napkin to mop his pale brow, like a surgeon.

The other counselor, Jim Anderson, was taller—practically a giant. Unlike Sean, he exercised quite a bit which always made him the hungrier of the two men. Though his manners at the table were better, he quite literally ate enough for three people. Both of the men were veterans of the orphanage and had been friends, since Jim had been unceremoniously dropped off in the middle of the night twenty-one years before. They'd been assigned as bunkmates and had formed a bond of lasting friendship.

Jim had been hired officially as a handyman/janitor, but he was so good with the boys that he enjoyed counselor status. The two men were a great boon to the orphanage despite the mountainous food bills. Parentless boys frequently require the heavy hand of discipline, but since the two men were so large and intimidating it was almost never needed.

This was a relief for Sister Mary Agatha who had reached an age where she could no longer freeze a child in place with just a scowl.

The nun briefly considered another portion of ice cream. However, a vision of a scowling Father John appeared as she gazed at her empty bowl, so she rinsed the bowl out and headed off for a final check on the boys.

She walked from the small office building through the almost pitch black chapel, pausing on her way to the south wing, where the dormitories were, so that she could genuflect before the altar.

There, she struggled her large body down and touched the floor with her right knee for the barest moment, weaving with her hands a quick Sign of the Cross. As she hefted her bulk upwards, her habit shifted slightly and it was then that she felt the sudden cold.

It slipped down her neckline feeling like icy fingers about her throat. Her world was orderly above all things and the sudden chill that swept over her, felt distinctly ominous. Remembering her silly fright from the night before, she made a conscious decision to ignore the feeling.

"It's an open window," she said loudly, challenging

the gloom of the dark church with her fearlessness. Silence greeted this statement and she gave a smirking, "Humph," as further evidence that she wasn't in the least bit scared. She was very close to convincing herself that all was normal. It could in fact, be an open window, since it had been a cooler than normal, late October day.

Ignoring the unsettling feeling—one that was growing on her—that there were eyes watching her from the balcony, she walked toward the front of the church.

The vestibule of the church contained little besides a pamphlet-filled rack and a large ornate brass font, filled with Holy Water. Ignoring these, she moved in her waddling gate to the tall wooden doors, and gave each a small push, satisfying herself that they were locked. She then went to the stairs leading up to the choir balcony, but paused as a small worm of fear gave a little wiggle inside her. A gentle cold breeze wafted down from them.

She gave the air a tentative sniff and there was a slight nastiness to it, very much like what she had experienced the night before and it caused goose bumps to break out down her arms. Her rational side explained it away; sticking to the theory that it was just an open window blowing in both the cold air and the ugly smell. However, her feelings of foreboding began to overrule rational thought and she toyed with the idea of getting either Jim or Sean to investigate.

But then she pictured the smarmy looks they'd have on their faces when they came down from the balcony to report only that a window had been left open.

Sister Mary Agatha set her jaw firm and started up.

The air on the stairs, saturated with the late autumn cold and the insidious smell, combined to caress the darkness of the church, making it more than it should've been. She thought about the light switches down in the vestibule with sudden regret.

She'd walked right past them without a thought, but now wished that she had turned them on and she felt a sudden childlike fear of the dark springing up from out of nowhere. At the top of the stairs she knew there was another set of switches, but she imagined there could be something waiting in the dark for her and that when the light came on...

"Nothing...there's nothing, Sister," she told herself quietly. However the little worm of fear was now slithering in her belly, serpent-like, and she felt almost nauseous.

It turned out that she was right about the nothing. At the top of the stairs her hand whispered along the wall until it found the switches and she snapped them upright. The choir balcony, save for the pews and the organ, was empty.

With the sudden light, her fears scurried like cockroaches into the dark cracks within her and she let out the breath that she had subconsciously pent up. Since normally she was the most rational of women she stood amazed at how she was acting.

She shook her head at her silliness and looked around. The cause of the cold was immediately obvious; there was indeed a window open, one of the large stain glass ones on the north side of the church. These canted inward to help with cleaning and at the sight of it, she felt relief. Then annoyance.

Someone was going to get a stern lecture—the

homely face of Sean Shay came to mind. This had his irresponsible feel to it. Sister Mary Agatha turned her bulk sideways and began shuffling down the long wooden length of the center pew. Something gold shone dully against the dark blue of the carpet and she saw it was the handle of the window lying there. More annoyance suffused her.

She stuck it back on the device and cranked the window shut. As she turned to leave, the cockroach-like fears that had been watching her from the dark crevices of her mind, strode boldly into the open. They had grown larger and it hadn't taken much.

Just a sound was all it took. A small, sly sound had come from the steeple above. She couldn't describe it, except to say that it seemed purposely made to send a jolt of adrenaline through her old body. The nun stood frozen in place, waiting and worrying but after many seconds had passed with no further sounds, the roaches of her fear gradually shrunk back again.

She told herself that it was nothing, however as she made her way along the pew, she kept her head cocked toward the steeple all the same. When she reached the stairs she felt the cold again, this time streaming unchecked from the steeple above.

The stairs up to it were cramped, steep, and black. Without hesitation or regret, the nun leaned over and swatted the light switch to the up position, but still she hesitated.

She battled internally; her pride against her building fear. Legitimately, she could now admonish Sean and send him up there to check all the windows, only lately he'd been making snide remarks. Remarks, harmless little jokes really, about her age, or her hearing, and recently about senility. If he got the slightest inkling that she was afraid, the not so funny jokes would never end.

With a tired sigh, she again told herself there was nothing up there; just like the balcony, the steeple would be empty.

The decision made, she compressed her large body into the narrow staircase, which had been designed, not for a woman of her bulk, but for a ten-year-old altar boy, and started up. It had been a few years since she had been up there, and she pictured the tiny room at the top. It was a small six-sided area and contained more of the stained glass windows. In the center of the room a velvet rope hung from the bell tower above and in her youth, she had enjoyed calling the people to Mass with it.

Now however, she was beginning to feel claustrophobic, especially as she turned the corner on the small landing. This felt to her like nothing more than a tall coffin and that unsettling image was lingering in her mind when the voice, a voice that was almost human, but not quite, spoke to her from the still unseen steeple.

"Sanctimonialis Mariae Agita...incessus," it was a terrible grating hiss and she jumped, startled by the suddenness of it and let out a small shriek of fright. It was a moment before she realized the words were Latin and another moment before her mind translated them: "*Sister Mary Agatha approach.*"

Her mind was amazingly blank. For seconds, she stood rooted on the landing, her right foot, in its highly polished sensible shoe, on the first stair and her mouth opening and closing pointlessly, devoid of the slightest drop of saliva.

"Incessus!" The voice was angry and demanding. It wanted her to go up to where it waited. The small act of translating the word became a catalyst and her mind ballooned with thoughts, most of them unwanted. She could now picture the owner of that nasty voice; her mind had conjured up a vision of a great, wet, snake.

"Oh dear," she whimpered. The image had her near to panicking and she turned on the cramped landing to flee. However, she seemed to be held in place; the walls hugged her close, keeping her almost immobilized. Her claustrophobia, forgotten at the sound of the voice, came back and the walls of her coffin shrunk in on her again. In vain, she wriggled and squirmed to free herself, so that she could leap down the stairs as her eighteen-year-old self would've done.

The voice now spoke in another language, one that seemed to chill the air around her so that her breath, huffing out of her in great gasps became visible. The words of the fell language were beyond her, but she understood all too well that it wanted her up there with it.

"No," she said in a voice that was not her own. Hers held authority, command, and power. This one was small, that of a frightened child and was barely audible even to her own ear.

Sister Mary Agatha had stopped her struggles at the sound of the weird language, but then there was a small noise from the steeple, the sound of movement. It was coming for her. The very thought was all it took to send her mad with fear.

She exploded into a frenzy, twisting her body in terrific lunges. Her habit pulled back keeping her in place, until a great tearing sound came from right beside her. Her long robe like clothes had been caught on the railing, and now suddenly free, she stumbled down the stairs, a girlish scream ripping from her old woman's throat.

Falling face first; hard on her outstretched hands, she half-crawled, half-slithered down the remaining stairs to the choir balcony. With her breath laboring in her chest like an old draft horse, she had barely got to her knees before she heard the first sound of the footsteps on the stairs above.

They were slow and measured.

She became mesmerized by the sound of her approaching doom; the nun stopped breathing her great fear charged breaths. In fact, she stopped breathing at all.

Chapter 5

An Exorcism in Failure

The sound of the steps descending the stairs was relatively light, but they were magnified in her head, so that Sister Mary Agatha envisioned a great beast coming slowly down towards her. Unknowingly, she had been holding her breath and suddenly realizing it, she let it out in a gush of prayer:

"Hail Mary, mother of God, pray for us sinners..." The prayer was spoken with such urgency that the words ran into themselves, becoming unintelligible in their hurry to be spewn from her mouth.

Finally, the owner of the voice came into view. It wasn't a great beast—just a man of average size with blonde hair that was in need of washing. He wore blue jeans and a grey sweatshirt, the cuffs of which were dark with blood. He held bloody hands out toward her, the palms filled to over flowing with the almost black fluid of his body. His head was cranked down and to his right side, and except for the fact that he walked and talked, the man didn't seem alive.

"Sanctimonialis, you speak in this tongue."

It was not a question.

Sister Mary Agatha couldn't find it within herself to do more than nod. Up close, the man's voice held a dreadful ripping quality and she was sure his vocal cords were being shredded as he spoke. It made her desperately want to swallow, but her mouth was bone dry.

"Nun, deliver unto Ba'al Zubel, the lackey of the foot washer...Alba."

The words were painful to hear and despite being in English with only the single Latin word, sanctimonialis for Nun, it was very difficult to understand. It took her a moment to figure out what he was talking about. "You want Father Alba?"

"Yes! Tell the lackey...Ba'al Zubel is demanding his presence. If he hides again, Ba'al Zubel will kill this...man." As he said this he indicated himself by pointing one dripping finger to his own chest.

Sister Mary was having trouble thinking straight and couldn't get her eyes past the blood. Her own voice was a warbling misery, "I will...ok. Please, don't do it."

"Ba'al Zubel will do as it will with this man." He brought his red hands together briefly and then touching the exposed side of his neck he drew a red line across it with two fingers. Blood instantly poured from a wound that hadn't been there a moment before. "The lackey. Now," he commanded.

"Yes, yes I will, please, don't do that." In order to get back to the stairs she had to crawl towards him and this she did with one hand up, to ward off any possible blow from the man. He took a step back and seemed to take no further notice of the nun, standing just as he had been with his head cocked and his neck glistening a lively red.

There was no taking her eyes off of him and she backed down the stairs until she gained the vestibule. There she turned and fled toward the office building, running in a laughable, waddling rolling gait.

"He's crazy! He's crazy!" she wheezed this over and over, as she huffed up the stairs to the staff quarters, her heart thundering in her chest. She'd stopped running as soon as she had left the church and now she was shaking with fright and unspent adrenaline, and her speed had been reduced to a simple tired plodding.

"Father Alba," she had meant to yell this as she entered the common room, but what came out was only a pathetic, breathy whisper. Squeezing her bulk between the two old leather couches that sat facing an even older TV set, she hurried to the priest's door.

The bloody man was just insane, crazy! That was all there was to this and as she beat at the door, she was quite prepared to tell Alba of the madman threatening suicide in the church.

The priest, with an alarmed look on his face, opened the door quickly at the insistent knocking. He looked to have been in the process of changing and had a green pajama shirt on over his black pants. "Father...Alba." The heavy nun took two huge gulps of air. "There's a man in the church and...he's possessed." She had been lying to herself concerning the man's sanity, but that was forgotten. The truth came rushing out: "Possessed by a demon, I think. He said his name was Bay-al Zoo-bull...I..."

At the look on the priest's face, she couldn't go on. His reaction to what she had said was not helpful to her state of mind. It was clear that he believed her. His normally pale face went paper white. He stepped back into the safety of his room and she thought he was going to shut the door in her face. Instead, he ran his hands over his large abdomen as if he was going to be sick.

Father John Santos, clad in blue and white striped

pajamas, emerged from his bedroom and said, "Possession, really?" He was younger, mid thirties and with his healthy tan and dark hair, he was almost too good-looking to be a priest. "What makes you think it's a possession?"

Sister Mary, amazed that she had to explain herself, spluttered, "Because he is! He...he...spoke in tongues. Latin and uh, some other language. It was a guttural and evil sounding language." She stared back and forth at the two priests, wondering why they weren't rushing off to the church.

With frank disbelief, Father John replied, "It could've been Slovakian. Have you ever heard a worse sounding..."

The nun interrupted him, something she'd never have done if she were thinking straight, "No, Father. It was no language I've ever heard; not even close! Oh, Lord help us! It was terrible and painful sounding...and he had the stigmata!"

"The stigmata? Sister, I'm sorry but I think someone is pulling your leg." Father John smiled and looked to his fellow priest to share the humor, but Father Alba had retreated even further into his room.

The younger priest continued, "The stigmata isn't a sign of demon possession. Also, as you say, he came waltzing into the church? As far as I know demons are atheists...though I think some might be Methodists. If..."

Father Alba interrupted from deep within the darkness of his room, "Was it cold? In the steeple, was it cold up there?"

The nun's old muscles danced a jig all about her body at the thought of the cold. "Yes it was. It was very cold. And he asked for you, Father, specifically. He called you a lackey. He said that if you hid...I mean, if you didn't come, he'd kill the man...the man he was in, that is."

"Maybe we should call..." Father John began, but the other priest spoke over him.

"It asked for me? What did it look like?" He took a step forward. The nun could see beads of sweat forming in his thin brown hair.

"Like...just a man, but he was bleeding from his hands and...he touched his throat and blood came out of it!"

"Maybe we should..." Father John started again.

"Was there a shadow to it...or smoke? Or black clouds around it?"

"No, it was a man. I mean it looked like a man."

"We need to call an ambulance!" Father John spoke loudly so as not to be interrupted again.

"Not yet! I have to see for myself." Father Alba said. "Did you touch it at all?"

"No, thank the Lord!"

"Ok, ok...I need to get dressed," he spoke not to the nun, but to his bedroom door. "Sister, please get James and Sean, but do it quietly. Have them meet me downstairs in the office, in two minutes."

Father John shook his head. "Think about what you're doing! We need to call..."

"And we will! But first I have to see for myself," the older priest responded, and without waiting for any further discussion, he closed his door. The nun could hear the chubby little man scurrying about inside his room and she made to leave, but Father John spoke.

"It's not a real possession you know. There are

thousands of claims per year, and only a couple ever amount to anything. And even those are a bit..." he waggled his hand back and forth to suggest that they were suspect.

"Of course, Father. I'm sure you're right," she said, agreeing with the priest out of habit alone. "But this...I have to go and do as I was asked...excuse me." She left the priest rolling his eyes, something that would normally have had her on the verge of exploding, and hurried to the dormitories to get the two counselors.

Not taking any chance, she crossed to the orphanage through the unseen back hallway that ran behind the main sanctuary of the church. Both Jim and Sean were awake and watching a movie on TV in the dorm common room.

"I need you two! You have to come over to the offices, right now," she ordered breathing heavily. She had held her breath subconsciously as she had passed the entrance to the church and her body was trying to make up for it. The sound of her voice was strangely whiny and pitched high. The image of the blood and how it had turned the collar of the man's grey sweatshirt red at first and then to black, replayed itself over and over in her mind.

"Sure, the show's almost over. It can wait ten minutes, right?" Sean said without taking his eyes from the screen. However, Jim was looking at the nun with a queer cast in his muddy brown eyes.

"No, Sean. We better get going now. Come on get up." Jim stood and stretched, his hands touching the ceiling of the room. With the extra inch on the heels of her black shoes, Sister Mary Agatha stood at five feet, ten inches, and always considered herself big, but she was dwarfed by the immensity of Jim Anderson, and just standing next to him, calmed her down considerably.

"What's going on?" Sean asked as he heaved his bulk, ponderously up out of the chair.

"There's a...a man and he's...just come on!" she cranked at the two men, but instead of leading the way, she gestured to them to proceed. She fell into step on the far side of Sean, using his expansive form as a shield of sorts, as they walked down the hall. As soon as they gained the admin building they came upon Father Alba straining with his collar button.

His hands, wet with sweat, fumbled at his neck, which was quickly turning as red as his face. "Ummph! I give up...Sister would you be so kind." She worked at the button with hands none too reliable, until it finally accepted its position in life.

"What's going on, Father," Sean asked for the second time in two minutes.

"We may be facing a case of demonic possession."

"Wow, just like the movies, cool," Sean gave a big smile to his giant friend.

The priest glared at him. "No, not cool at all. If this is real...and we don't know that it is, then it'll be far from cool." He started off toward the chapel with nothing but a bible in his moist hands.

"It is real, Father. The Lord is my witness, his hands started bleeding right in front of me," she was puffing again and it was a struggle for her to keep up. She had begun to feel a sharp pain running up her back and it was all she could do to stay near Sean who lumbered along placidly.

At the end of the hall, they came upon Father John

leaving the last of the offices. He was still in his pajamas but he had thrown a matching robe on as well and in his hands were two decanters of water, a silver handled sprinkler in both.

"Jim, come take this," he held one of them out. "Now don't spill it. Just walk nice and easy and you won't, ok? Yours is filled with water that I just blessed...this one is just tap water. I think we'll be able to tell if this is a fake pretty quickly."

"In the movie, The Exorcist, what they did was..."

"Not now, Sean!" Father Alba snapped at the man. The priest's palpable fear was causing Sister Mary to have second thoughts about going into the chapel again. Her back really was hurting, probably from her fall, and she began imagining a long night spent relaxing in the emergency room eating Jello or ice cream, if they had any.

Father John gave his fellow priest a long odd look. "I think it might be best, under the circumstances, if I go first. Jim...you stay close, don't go wandering away. You never know right?" Jim only raised his eyebrows the slightest to show that he'd heard the priest.

Sean looked suddenly a little pale as if the mood of Father Alba had been contagious. "Hey shouldn't I have a weapon or...or a cross or something? Don't-cha think?"

"Your faith will be your shield," Father John spoke calmly, but this didn't mollify Sean who only shook his head, no.

"There's a large crucifix hanging on my wall, you can carry that," Father Alba said and the nun could now see that the beads of sweat on his head had reproduced to such an extent that they were forming tiny streams.

These ran down his face and disappeared into the black of his clothing.

Sean hurried to the office and came back bearing both a tremendous crucifix and a satisfied look. The size of the cross was impressive but it reminded Sister Mary that her hands were empty. The nun felt old and useless and perhaps worst, defenseless. She remembered the cross at the end of her rosary and was just grabbing it when Father John spoke.

"Sister, where in the church was the man?"

The cross seemed suddenly tiny. It was tarnished, slightly bent, and barely gleamed. It sat in her palm looking older and more useless than its owner. She didn't know what she had been expecting, but it seemed empty, devoid of...magic? Was that what she had expected? For it to glow with the power of...

"Sister...excuse me," Father John looked at her expectantly.

"I'm sorry, what?"

"Where did you leave the man?" Father John asked her gently and put his hand out to suggest that she would lead.

"The choir balcony," she said this and pretended she hadn't seen the hand gesture but instead made a great show of rearranging her rosary. Father John gave a smile at this and proceeded to walk into the darkened church, followed closely by Jim, Father Alba, and finally Sean.

Sister Mary couldn't move. She stood gripping her tiny cross, and terror at what lay in the church, caused her intestines to clench and retreat rapidly.

The others didn't know. They hadn't seen the blood and the casual manner in which the demon had wounded the poor man, or heard the voice. The voice came back to her and she remembered it had called her...

"Sister," Father Alba had materialized in the doorway. "It'll be ok. Remember you can't simultaneously have great faith and great fear. Trust in the lord." She wanted to laugh at him and condemn him for hypocrisy. His own fear he wore like a mask, completely covering his normal skin. Instead, she took a deep breath and stepped into the gloom of the church.

The other three men stood waiting just to the side of the door, with only Father John showing any signs of impatience. "Everything good?" He didn't wait for an answer. "Good...now Father Alba and I will do all the talking. None of you say a word, even if he addresses you. Keep quiet. Chances are this man is in need of serious psychological help...he may be dangerous, so we'll look out for each other and don't let him corner you."

He gave each a confident look and then proceeded to the light switches against the wall. The room was suddenly and brilliantly lit. The nun scanned the balcony but the man was not to be seen and relief flooded her until Jim said, "He's in the foyer."

The man could be seen standing in that unusual manner of his just beside the font of Holy water.

The four men, trailed by the nun, advanced toward him slowly and from a distance, she could see that something had changed in his appearance. His face was now covered in blood and as she walked forward, his blue eyes sparkled out of the dripping mess. The closer they got the more obvious it was that his head had been cut in numerous places around the hairline.

[50]

"The blood on the man's face...and the cuts, they weren't there before, it's another sign of..." the nun began, but Father John cut her off with an angry gesture.

The tan, raven-haired priest flashed a white smile at the bleeding man. He appeared confident and held his decanter in a casual manner, which was a direct contradiction to the way Jim held his. The big man grasped the decanter with reverence as well as great trepidation over the idea of spilling any of its contents. Father Alba stood sweating profusely holding his bible to his chest with both hands and Sean had his crucifix held out as if warding off a giant vampire.

"Hello, my name is Father John, what's your name?" the priest began confidently in an agreeable manner.

"You come to me in clothes for sleeping...do you wish me to bed you? Is that what you want?" the possessed man said this in that terrible voice and then laughed cruelly.

"It's late...but like I said I'm Fath..."

"I know you! You call yourself John Santos...Santos... Sanctus...Saint. This is humorous. Saint John, you are not!" The voice caused Sean to raise his crucifix even higher and for Jim to clutch at his own throat.

"You speak Latin, that's nice. Did you go to a Catholic school?" The priest was still amazingly calm.

"Alba! I know you speak this tongue. Stop cowering behind your saint. Tell me, do you pray to this saint? Do you get down on your knees before him? Do you worship him with your lips, Alba?" It laughed again and Sister Mary had to turn away at the sight of it. No part of the man laughed along with the demon inside of him. Only the voice and the eyes were touched by that evil laugh.

"I still would like to know who we're talking to," Father John said and for the first time, the nun noticed that his confidence had slipped quietly away.

The thing inside the man grunted and hawked up its inhuman language that she'd heard earlier and it gave her the chills.

Father Alba stepped forward. "Who are..."

"You know me, slinking coward. I am Ba'al Zubel and you burned the body of my witch. Now I have come for that which you pulled from its chest." The man's body drooped as the demon spoke and his voice was losing its power as if he was dying with the demon inside him.

Confused at the conversation the nun turned to look at Father Alba and was horrified at the sight of the man. His mask of fear had now enveloped his whole body, which shook uncontrollably so that he bible jittered about in front of his face. She saw he was taking little steps backwards and she started back as well.

"The Holy water...now, hurry!" he said not to Father John but to Jim, who reacted with a jerk and then started bravely forward. However, Father John beat him too it and put his free hand out and stopped him.

Father John looked uneasy at what had transpired, but said with confidence, "You say you're Ba'al and that you possess this man, yet you enter a Catholic church, where Holy water sits all about you..." He seemed unsure how to finish the sentence so he left the words hanging and taking a cautious step toward the man, flicked water at him with the silver sprinkler.

The water seemed to have no effect and the man gained strength in his voice, "You are full of falsehoods Saint John...I'll have you with me soon." The confidence in Father John's demeanor vanished with the words and he motioned urgently to Jim.

Jim took only a single large step forward and sent a great rain of Holy water onto the possessed man, who reacted in the proper manner. He tore at his exposed face with his bloody hands and took to grunting, "Uhn, uhn, uhn." After a moment of this, the man threw himself to the ground, rubbing the front of his body on the carpet, bleeding into it. For long moments, it writhed on the ground.

Jim asked, "Did I hurt it? Was that supposed to happen?"

Sister Mary's heart sank at the look the two priests shared...they didn't know.

"Yes it hurts, it hurts greatly...Ba'al Zubel wants to feel more." It staggered to its feet and going to the font, plunged its face, caked in layers of blood, straight into the water.

"No!" Father John yelled. He started forward, but Father Alba reacted with desperate speed and pulled him back.

"Don't touch him, whatever you do, don't touch him!" The two stepped back as the man squirmed for what was at least a minute under the water before he pulled himself out and threw himself back to the floor. He thrashed about for a long while and then unbelievably began to imitate intercourse with the floor, humping it in great undulating waves of its body.

Finally, the body jerked in spasms and Sister Mary felt her stomach roll over. She regretted the ice cream now as it worked its way up and she began to breathe heavily, until the moment passed.

Still face down on the carpet, the demon spoke in its strange language and paused for an answer.

"What...I don't..." Father Alba began.

The path! Bring it to me!" the demon said in English.

Father Alba, gripping his bible so that his fingers were white at their tips, stammered, "The path...I don't know..."

"The sword!"

"The sword." Father Alba stared at the blood stained carpet, his mind seemingly in another time.

The demon, lying face down, growled, "Oh yes, the sword. Remember the cold of it, how it hurt your hands? Remember the body of my witch, how it was frozen? You were Arthur and it was Excalibur. Yesssss...you should have burned it with the body, but you took it. Why? What made you work that blade back and forth in her frozen chest? It took a long time; back and forth, back and forth."

Father Alba was close to tears, his eyes were watery and bulging. They were snow-globes, glassy and wet, with swirling flecks of fear, dancing in the chaos of a storm. "How did you know?"

Sister Mary's nausea came back strongly with the image of the priest and the frozen body...and the sword. She knew she was going to vomit this time and she put her hand to her mouth and felt the sweat that had built up on her upper lip. She thought nothing would stop the vomit from coming, but then she saw Sean Shay take a step backwards.

He had gone alabaster in his fear and looked to be

about to sprint from the church. He was no Olympic runner, but despite the excess 200 pounds he carried, he was undoubtedly faster than the nun. It was this thought that had her ignoring the vomit, working its way up into the back of her mouth. She was the slowest one of the five of them and if it came to it, she'd never make it out of the church alive.

She looked at Sean and their eyes met. They came to a silent and unfortunate understanding. He would run and she would be left alone with *it*. Her heart began to palpitate painfully in her chest and she could feel each of the beats. They weren't rhythmic, but disjointed with beats missing at odd intervals and it was those missing beats that hurt.

In her distraction, she missed someone talking, but she certainly heard Father John ask his stupid question, "How do you know this man?" he asked Father Alba. She wanted to scream the answer at him but Father Alba beat her to it.

"It's not a man."

"I am Ba'al Zubel, Tyrant of the Void! The skin I wear is man...but on the inside, it is a game. Now give me the sword." It rolled over and stood in an awkward jerking motion. "Do not deny me, Alba! The penalty will be steep!"

"I won't do it...I won't give it to you." Alba seemed to holding onto the smallest scrap of courage.

The man smiled a bloody smile. "I will kill this thing..."

"Please don't!" Sister Mary Agatha cried out from behind the two priests. Her two hands gripped the small cross fiercely, the sweat from her palms making the rosary beads slippery.

"You seem worried for it, are you acquainted with it?" the man, or demon as she saw it, spoke over the top of the two priests at her. She took another step back and put the cross up to her face, protecting herself with it. She peeked foolishly around it, trying to see if she did indeed know the man, but he was a stranger to her. The demon smiled at the movement. "I will devour it, you know." With that, he put his hand to his mouth and fresh blood drained down his chin.

"Stop, stop...Father, give him the sword, please," she cried out.

Father Alba seemed unable to take his eyes from the blood, and he asked, "What do you want it for?"

"It is the path...it is the way," the demon said and looked again down at the carpet, his head back to being cocked over.

The priest became more resolved at this. "I won't give it to you. I know you. I have seen what you have done! You'll only use it to promulgate more of your evil."

The demon shrugged the man's shoulders. "Then I devour it. Another soul you have given to me...first the Gypsy, then the witch and now...an innocent."

Father John stepped over and whispered loudly, "We have to do the exorcism...it's our duty to try to save this man."

"There'll be no exorcism...you are fool Saint John. I will kill it. I will take it back with me." The demon stopped, waiting as if for a decision and Father John looked around for support, but when he glanced at Sister Mary Agatha, she was forced to turn away. Her chin began to quiver and she wished that she had never gone up those stairs to the steeple.

There was an odd guilt about that simple act, as if this was all her fault somehow. She looked over at Father Alba, wishing he'd give the thing what it wanted.

Despite his pasty, white skin, Father Alba seemed to rally his courage again and though his voice was pitched unnaturally high, it was also firm, "Then take him!"

"Father Alba, no!" Father John spoke angrily.

Ignoring his friend, the chubby priest ordered, "I said take him! We don't make deals with demons. We cast them out!" His voice grew stronger as he spoke, "In the name of Jesus Christ, I command that you leave this man in peace! Depart from him and go back to whatever hell you came from."

Sister Mary, her eyes riveted on Father Alba, felt hope expand slightly within her at his words. She turned to see what effect they would have on the demon.

It stood with the man's head still contorted down and to the side, blood dripping from his nose and chin. "You have no power over me, lackey."

Silence greeted this and with her courage fading like a sunset, she took another step back. Sean Shay saw this and upped the ante, stepping back *two* steps. There was now only the barest shred of sanity keeping her from running and she knew if Sean took only one more step, she would flee shrieking out of her mind.

He took two more.

"Stop!" Jim commanded in his great deep voice. He looked at his friend with the heavy eyes of a basilisk and the look froze Sean in place. Jim set the decanter of Holy water in the nearest pew, and said gruffly, "Father, I know this man's face. It was only when all the blood was washed away, that I saw it. I think he's the man the cops are looking for. He's got something to do with those kids that disappeared."

More silence as each of them stared intently at the man.

"Oh yes, I have the little ones, they are mine now."

"Oh, dear Lord, save those poor children," Sister Mary called out.

The demon laughed. "Don't bother wasting your time praying to your so-called God. He hides himself, afraid of the disappointment he would see in all your pathetic faces, if ever you would see him. No, if you want to save those children, pray to me! Get down on your knees, where you belong and worship me."

"Where are those children? Tell me!" demanded Father Alba in a hollow voice that was bereft of authority.

"Are you going to trade the lives of those children, for my path?"

The priest looked down seemingly unable to come to a decision.

"I will have my path, lackey! The children were to serve me in another manner, but I do like the idea of them slowly starving to death, with you being the cause. And there are so many other little ones, right? There are some in this orphanage that nobody wants, isn't that right? I want them. I will take them from you."

"No!" the nun shrieked at the demon and the simple act of defiance caused her courage to rekindle itself, if only in the very slightest manner.

"Then give me my path!"

"I don't have it," Father Alba said almost in a child's whine. "But...but I can get it, ok?"

Chapter 6

Talitha-Unrestrained

Talitha started toward the church, that cruel smile playing havoc with her normally beautiful features. The rock that she'd picked up, she put to her nose and sniffed at it idly.

"Talitha, please wait. The police might be in there." Will's morning was coming apart in great chunks. He felt a panicked desperation and he *knew* there was trouble and pain associated with going into the church. "Look, if you hurt one of them, they'll all be after you...hundreds of them."

"That sounds like fun."

"Talitha..."

She spun about, her face less than a foot from his chest. He felt like a giant compared to her yet he anxiously wanted to retreat a few steps. Her cruel smile widened at his discomfort and her teeth, looking hungry for violence, shone white in the October morning. However, it was her eyes that held him rooted to the asphalt. They weren't the soft, warm brown of his sister's. No, these were dead and icy, seemingly without a soul behind them.

The eyes, lifeless in a human sense, made the smile all the more wicked and Will felt his testicles scurry upwards in hiding. It had been a long time since he saw her eyes like this and without thinking, his left hand slipped down and went to his vulnerable groin. Not since the early days at the hospital, when the orderlies would find her in the mornings covered in blood, had her eyes been so devoid of humanity.

"I told you to shut it!" she said, with a touch of insane anger. "And now, I have to turn around with my back exposed to someone with a gun just to repeat myself?"

"I'm sorry...I'm sorry, it's just that..."

She interrupted him in a deadly quiet voice, "You will be sorry...later. You obviously need another lesson in manners. But first..." She trailed off, eyeing the church. Will could almost feel the blood lust emanating from her.

"I should tell you something, Tal. I should've told you this a long time ago, you're wanted by the police for murder and..."

Her immediate laughter was full bellied and loud, yet even through it, she kept her dead eyes full on his face as if watching for a sign. "Ha, ha, oh my! How we have the same parents is a mystery. The laws of this world don't pertain to me. I'm well beyond them. Not to mention, I'm insane, remember? They put me in an asylum for the insane. Crazy people can do anything they wish to. They're free...unrestrained by morals or laws, and your ridiculous society is too afraid to judge them for what they are."

Her laughter was as unnerving as her eyes.

Looking away from her, he asked, "Ok Talitha, how would you judge them?"

"The people who kill for fun, who can kill you as easy as shake your hand...they're truly evil. Every last man, woman, and child. Right down to their core, despite any proclamations of remorse they may make."

"Are you evil then?" he asked in a whisper. "The doctors seem to think you're suffering from schizophrenia."

"How can you even ask that? Of course I'm evil. Right now, I'm using you as a human shield, even though I'm the one with my back to the church."

He looked over her head at the building. "That's not possible."

"Sure it is. First, if it's the police, as you think, they won't shoot just in case they miss me and hit you. Second, with your wasted gift, if they do shoot you'll see it coming even before they pull the trigger. I'll just step aside and where do you think that bullet will go?" She poked him in the chest, drilling her fingernail into his shirt, smiling up at him as she did it. "Then I'll snatch you up and use your not-quite-dead body as cover. Shall I go on? Do you want to know true evil?"

He shook his head no, but she started speaking again regardless. "This is fun! Do you know sweet little Talitha is not the goody-two-shoes you think she is? That's right. I am her. She's the facade! The fiction I cover myself in, to get you to do what I want."

She kept up her dead-eyed smile and walked behind him, poking him painfully every once in a while. "I know if I looked like this every time you came over, you'd stop your little visits, and then where would I be? But big, gullible Will is always there to rescue his little sis. I use you. I let you get tortured every week so I can sleep in peace and quiet."

She paused, waiting for a response, but Will's brain was shutting itself down, and he couldn't find anything to say. She walked back in front of him, "You asked for this, right? You wanted to know. Don't worry, Will. The dreams can't last forever. I was only tortured and raped so many thousands of times."

They stood in the parking lot of the church and

nothing felt real to him. The crisp cool air, the smell of the burning leaves, the orange and gold forest, all of it felt like someone else was seeing it. Like it wasn't him standing there hating his sister. It was the surreal running over his reality, distorting it, bending it away from the touch of his mind. He almost didn't catch what she said next.

"And you should want the dreams to last, really. As long as I still need you, you'll be safe enough. But once they're done...you will pay!"

Her vehemence brought him around somewhat and he asked, "What did I ever do to you?"

"What did you do? You were the one who took me from the void! Have you forgotten?"

"I thought that was what you wanted." His brain was a bewildered beehive of noise that hummed along loudly, but without a sense of purpose.

He looked up at the church shaking his head slowly and realized he could hear the opening hymn to the mass. And now they were going to miss it and for some reason this bothered him nearly as much as Talitha's crazy rantings.

But they would've missed it anyways. There were men in the building looking out at the two of them and he could feel their impatience and their fear. People with that much fear could be dangerous; yet they were unlikely as dangerous as Talitha.

"Thought? You thought? You were never big with the thinking were you, Will? Once you step down into the void...that's where you belong, forever!"

Anger started to simmer beneath his confusion. "I don't get it. You aren't explaining anything with your put-downs. Why would you be mad that I came and got you?"

"Because Will, when I was there I had value. I was worth something. I was a commodity that was bought and sold... that is something you know. Even here, being valued is worth a lot. And! And!" she shouted this in his face. "I was becoming more...more than just Talitha. I grew stronger and stronger and it was I who brought pain. Now *thanks* to you, I'll have to begin again. The lowest of the low. I'll get back where I belong but it'll take time and plenty of pain—my pain!"

"But you don't have to go back. Free will exists even after death." He wanted to reach out and hold her, but as he put out his hands, she turned away.

"Do you think heaven will accept me? After everything I've done? Man, you are so naive. Do you know how many people I've killed? How many I've tortured into insanity?" His mouth was suddenly devoid of saliva and his tongue became thick and useless. He wanted to tell her to stop talking but he couldn't form the words and she went on, "Just escaping the asylum, I killed...hmmm, how many? Let's play a guessing game...how many people do you have to kill to escape from isolation in an asylum for the criminally insane?"

When they had come by the house looking for Talitha, the police had told them she had killed four people in her escape. He wondered now if there were more that they didn't know about.

Will had never asked her. He had always been afraid to know the truth. "Four, I think," the words came out of his dried out mouth, thick as if he could've chewed on them for a while.

"Oh, you knew. Well there goes my surprise...how bout I tell you what happened instead?" He shook his head, no, but that only made her flash her dead-eyed smile. "The orderlies, they would come out every night when the lights went down. Just like great horny roaches. They would take turns on me and I allowed it, not that I had a choice, but I even encouraged it. Despite how unimaginative and pathetic they were, with their dull repetitious back and forth, it passed the time. We both know that I've endured far worse, right Will?"

Her smile widened and the image of the creature with the great ripping horn came back to him, making his stomach undulate nauseously.

She walked away from him then, seemingly unconcerned about the men in the church and sat down in front of an aging Honda Accord. She still had her stone from earlier and she put it to her lips and rubbed it there gently.

"Men are such idiots when it comes to their dicks. I pretended to enjoy it, night after night. I waited them out patiently, knowing it was only a matter of time. You remember I was under full restraint around the clock? They were never supposed to bring the keys into the cell with them, but that time, one of them did. I heard them chink on the floor when he dropped his pants. All I had to do was bite down and they were mine."

His eyes blinked at this image of his sister and she laughed at him. "I didn't bite it off! Not then. I needed them to release me first. Ahhh...A guy will do almost anything you ask of him, if his junk is in peril. Well, I couldn't exactly ask him, what with his cock stuffed so far down my throat, but he got the point. His friend, the one banging away like he had a bus to catch, he...what's wrong, Will? Is the idea of your sister being gang raped upsetting you? You look all pale and green."

Will did feel like he was about to get sick, however Talitha just went on talking, "That's too bad. I was just going to tell you how once they unchained me, I bit that guy's dick off, right at the root. But I guess I shouldn't mention it, what with you being all sick looking. And you probably don't want to hear about the orgasm I had when I did it either."

His undulating stomach turned a summersault and he was sure he was going to vomit. He went to the nearest car, a rusted out Ford Mustang with balding tires, and leaned over its hood. The image of his sister, grinning, with a mouthful of blood and gore seemed to cling to his mind. It was glued to the inside of his skull, and the picture was as big and wide as a screen at a drive-in. She was being brutal with her honesty, hurting him with the truth of her evil.

"Why are you telling me these things?" he finally blurted out.

"Well, cuz it's fun, of course. Just like what I did to those guards...that was fun, too. You still look at me as if I'm your little sister, but I'm not her. That girl couldn't handle the void, but I could. And what's more, I thrived there, I grew stronger! This is why I won't be packing my bags for heaven any time soon."

A smug look came over her face. "You see, I like hurting people, I get off on it. In the void there's only one pleasure allowed and that's the pleasure in causing pain. I still remember the first time when I found that out, ahhh yes, that was good. It was Auraghnash, this Crae demon..."

"No, I don't want to know..." Will began weakly.

"He had this great reputation, and really it was an

honor that he traded for me, you know. The torments he'd lavish on his captives were so widely feared that I was in a perfect state of terror when I went into his chamber. He had this thing for glass, a fetish I guess you'd call it, and I found myself naked on this long cold pane."

Talitha savored the memory, enjoying it all the more when she saw Will's horror.

"It was mirrored glass and I could see my fear plainly, and he let me lay there for ages and I was just thinking he was drawing it out too long, when he started. Anticipation is half the fun you know. Your mind frequently conjures up worse images than the reality, but not this time. I figured he would cut me up or slice parts off, and sure that would hurt but it was becoming passé. You know, you've felt it."

Will had felt it in his dreams and she was unfortunately right.

She continued on, relishing the memory fondly, "There are many worse things than being cut on, and what Auraghnash did to me...was the worst. The glass pane fit me perfectly...in fact, it had been made especially for me. It was exactly my height and width and eventually the entire thing was in me.

"He slid the shards of it under my skin and into my joints and deep, deep into the marrow of my bones. The shards were long and fiendishly edged. They found the vulnerable parts of me. Parts I didn't know could even feel pain. But all that was nothing compared to what came next...he beat me with a large wooden bat so that the shards broke into thousands upon thousands of gritty, cutting particles that coursed their way throughout my entire body." She shivered slightly at the memory. "Every movement was fantastic in its pain. You have no idea."

But Will did. The memory of that particular dream came back to him and a wave of sweat instantly saturated his clothes and a sheen of it broke out on his forehead. His sick feeling doubled and he began to gag and she just smiled at his reaction.

"Do you want me to stop? Too bad! Let me just say what a genius idea that torture was. But in the end, he wasn't as good as his reputation suggested. In his excitement over having me, he went too far. You see you have to build up to these sorts of things slowly, or you'll constantly have to one up yourself. Don't get me wrong, that first time was pure hell. In fact, he ruined me for many of the lesser demons with their machines and flames...they became dull. For a while there, I thought I was starting to master the pain of the void, but then he traded for me again."

"Why? Why were you so valuable? What made you so special?" Will wanted to talk just to get his mind off his nausea.

"Because I was still alive. I still had real feelings and my pain was more...fulfilling. Anyway, he traded for me again, and I can tell you I pissed myself on the spot. No joke...splash! Just like that. I shivered and shook all the way to his dungeons and I cried a long time on that next pane of glass. My tears were sweet blemishes on that perfect surface and I'm sure Auraghnash creamed himself just watching the misery I was in. Again, he waited to start until I just about couldn't stand it and I wanted to beg him to get it over with. Eventually he began sliding the glass beneath the surface of my skin and, just as before, the pain was...how do you describe chewing on glass?"

She paused looking at him and he could only shake his head with his mouth hanging open. "Maybe I'll borrow some tricks from old Auraghnash and then you can tell me? What do you think?" Again, he could only silently shake his head, but the thought of it sent shivers down his spine.

She continued with her terrible recollection, "That second time was an absolute horror...but, it wasn't worse than the first. I feared it would be, like I said, but despite the monstrous cruelty of it, it wasn't. In fact, it had already slipped into a bit of a routine, so I knew what was coming next.

"This is really poor form. The victim can then start to count down the tortures and look forward to it ending. That's just stupid. Eventually he came to me and his dick was huge and sharply jagged with more imbedded glass, and I knew it would be just as it was before. Oh, the pain was dreadful, but I could see the moment coming when he would shoot his fire into me. The last time he had leaned in and this time was no different. That was the moment when I—finally— became my own person in the void. He had this long phallic beak of a nose, grey and putrefying, and when he leaned just a little too close, I sunk my teeth deep into it."

She gnashed her teeth and gave her head a vicious shake. "His blood was ancient, foul, and poisonous...oh my, it was nearly as bad as the tortures. It was viscous and rancid like semi-coagulated bile, but despite my almost uncontrollable gagging, I rejoiced. I had power! I was the one causing the pain! The demon screamed high and girlish and the sound was delicious, you have no idea how good I felt."

She smiled like an old ballplayer reliving his glory days and Will began to hate his sister, or at least this terrible version of her. Hate wasn't an emotion that he had often, so it was a surprise to him to feel the acid of it burning his insides.

Talitha didn't seem to mind his hard look. In fact she gave him a small smile, and continued after a moment, "Auraghnash beat me, even as I hung onto his nose like a rat terrier. I finally took off a huge junk of that stupid beak and that moronic demon demonstrated just how overrated he was. He picked me up and dashed me down among the few remaining chunks of glass. I died right there!"

She said this triumphantly and her eyes blazed away at Will, but he was a little lost and she saw it.

With a shake of her head, she explained, "No one dies forever in the void. You're reborn fully healed but there is a lag while you are traded or whatever. To be killed is the mark of an amateur."

"What happens if you don't die during the torture? You seemed happy that the demon killed you."

"Yes, you're catching on. The best tormentors leave their victims one cut, one slice, one stab away from death. That way you crawl away in the greatest misery, hiding yourself in the void, until..."

"Until what?" Will suddenly realized he had some sort of sickness that was indefinable, to ask that question.

"Until you want more," she said quietly and the triumphant voice had become a whisper.

"That doesn't make any sense...why would anyone want more of that?"

"The alternative is far worse," her voice had become so low that Will left the rusted hood of the Ford and went to her and looked down.

"There's no alternative that..."

"Yes there is," she interrupted. "Nothingness. The void itself. The total emptiness that's out there. How long can you sit in the dark without anyone or anything? Years? Centuries? Time has no meaning in the void and eventually your desire to see or feel...something, will overcome you and you'll crawl out of the blackness. You'll crawl, begging for the smallest contact."

She paused with a sad desperation on her face that suddenly turned icy. "That's why there'll be a great retribution. You see, I was becoming! After Auraghnash, I dedicated myself to inflicting pain. At first, I had to be subtle and conniving, dreaming up ways to get back at the demons that would hurt me. But soon even the lesser creatures avoided me. I had just mastered that slimy bastard, Juloo-anh-kjji when you came."

She shook her head and Will *saw* blood spray from it—a fine healthy red spray. It was a vision of the future. He looked up at the church expecting gunfire, but there was nothing. His hatred for her that had been burning a hole in his stomach, quite suddenly changed to concern. She'd be shot in the head—and it would be soon—but just when, he didn't know.

In his vision part of a white wall was visible behind her. For a moment, he couldn't picture the interior of the church, but then it came to him; dark brown for the chapel, but some of the office walls were painted white.

He glanced down at Talitha again. She was just

sitting there, looking just like his sister, but then she turned her dead eyes on him. They were eyes that were windows to an empty soul.

She didn't notice his look. "When you came into the void, I thought it was dad at first," Talitha said quietly. "He was always so heroic...and you were always such a pussy. With all that light around you, I honestly couldn't tell. Wow, what a fight that was..." she paused, looking again on a happy memory of death. "But then you stopped Ba'al Zubel, the tyrant and...and...you ruined me. I've become soft and slow and so, so weak! All the great pain I had caused! All the treachery...I played the game like a master..."

"But that was in hell!" Will broke in. "It's expected. No one would ever blame you for what happened there. And those men in the hospital...they were raping you, it was self-defense. You see yourself as this great evil thing, but there is good in you, despite your denials. I see it every Sunday morning."

"I don't deny there's good in me. You understand compartmentalization, correct? I have perfected that. In the void, I took your sister and I put her in box and hid her deep within me. I thought I was protecting her...myself I mean, but as time went on, she became a drag on me, a hindrance and I started to crush her little cage! The bigger I got, the smaller her cage became. Sometimes I would look down at her and wonder why I ever bothered keeping her about. But you never throw away something that might have future value, and she has come in handy with you Willy J! Every Sunday morning you're putty in her hands. She acts all sweet and innocent, knowing all the while that I'm torturing you! Do you like that sweet virginal look? Do you do her when I'm not around?"

Will's shoulders slumped. His concern for her had dried up like withered leaves and was being blown away by her constant diatribe. He felt like driving away—far away and never coming back.

"Ooh, look at your poor face!" Talitha cried in delight. "I never realized how much fun this would be. I should've told you this years ago."

"I think I'm done. I'm going home; try not to kill too many people." He walked back to the jeep, no longer worrying about the men in the church.

Still in the shade of the Honda, Talitha called out, "Did I go too far? That's the trick, right? Lead them up the edge, but don't let 'em step over."

"Sorry, but I'm stepping over." He climbed in and felt old. Far older than his twenty-five years.

"Then you don't want to know about how your sweet little Talitha, the *good one*...is a killer too?"

He was just shutting the door and it froze inches from closing. When he looked up, she was smiling at him. She began to hike up her flowered *Little House on the Prairie* dress and her tan thighs with their smooth muscles were already well in view.

He turned away. "That was you, not her."

She sing-songed, "*Yes it was*! Some of them at least...ask her about the bodies."

"No...I'm leaving."

She said nothing to this but still smiling she closed her blank dead eyes.

"I won't," he called to her as she opened her eyes and looked around.

"Hey what...aren't we late for church?" She checked the expensive watch on her left wrist. "What's going on? Why am I..." It was Talitha, his Talitha. She suddenly had a slight panicked look to her, and she began sniffing the air. "Will! Someone has a gun...in the church, I think."

She glanced down at her legs, which were exposed up to her pink panties and shock splashed across the troubled waters of her features. Yanking down her dress, she spun on one knee so that she could peer over the hood of the Honda.

"Did you know? Did she tell you...about the gun?" she asked.

The urge to leave his sister and never come back was a heavy weight in his chest. He stared at the steering wheel hating himself for his thoughts but also hating her more. "Sorry," he muttered to himself and put the jeep in reverse and that was when a breathless Talitha hopped in.

"Why are you stopping? We got to get out of here! Do we...uh, do you know who they are?" she asked with a wild frantic look in her eyes. He sat, wondering why he kept coming back to her every week and the feeling of apathy towards her grew stronger. "Will, come on! Move the jeep!"

"Why?"

"Why? She...I...I...we," Talitha spluttered and he could see the fear expanding in her eyes, like weeds growing and corrupting the fine rich lawn of her mind. "It's just ...we have to leave, before..."

"Before what? Before you kill them?"

She began to cry, then. Her tears were very real and they fell with abandon. She pleaded with him. "Yes, she will...I can sometimes hear echoes of her thoughts when I come back. She's being challenged, it's the gun, you see? That's why we have to get out of here."

Will saw the half second of his vision again, the gun and the blood, and he shook his head to clear it. There was a chance, a good chance that he could stop the vision from coming true, but he didn't know if he wanted to. He had a child to think about now and if Talitha was killing people when he wasn't around, perhaps it was for the best if this was the end.

He had tried.

The Lord knew he had tried to help his sister. He'd actually allowed himself to hope that she was slowly getting better. But it seems it was just a ruse.

"Get out of the car," he said.

"What? Will, you can't! Please don't do this. Don't leave me here all alone. She'll kill them...maybe all of them...the whole church, Will. You don't know what she's capable of."

"No it's you...I don't know what you're capable of."

"What? I would never kill those people."

"You've killed before, why not now?" he asked, his voice loaded with accusation.

She looked as if he had just slapped her. Her eyes were wide and the tears, which had never stopped, picked up their tempo. "I...am not going to talk about that. That was different...this is worse...please drive the car, please."

His insides turned to granite at her confession and he said quietly, but with conviction, "Not with you in the car."

"Take me with you please...please, please!" She wilted in front of him and the years melted away so that she appeared to be the little girl he had played with and shared everything with. But the granite wall of his heart dismissed that girl as well, fearing it to be another fake. She reached out to touch his arm and he shrank away from her.

"Don't touch me! I'm done, Talitha. I'm done with all of this. You've been using me—just so I would dream your messed up dreams for you!" His anger was a physical thing that she shrank back from.

"You're wrong. She's the one using you..."

"You're the same person!" he shouted into her face.

"We are and we aren't...it's complicated. But Will I... I..." she blinked rapidly, looked around the inside of the jeep, and gave a quick glance at her watch.

Talitha reached up and felt her tears. She gave him a snotty look and asked, "Did you have a good cry? Was it a touching brother-sister moment?"

Will's heart sank at the sight of Talitha's dead eyes. They were so black that the pupils were nearly lost. She wiped away the wet of her face and leaned back against the jeep's door.

"Talitha and I, we never talk," she said this as if they were gal pals having a chat about their first date. "So you're going to have to tell me everything. How did she kill them? What did she do with the bodies?"

"She didn't...wouldn't talk about it. You didn't give me enough time. Maybe if you brought her back."

"Sure that sounds like a swell fucking plan. You two will have a nice heart-to-heart while you drive who-knows where." She leaned towards him and Will slid back in his chair, but she only took the keys from the ignition. He knew she would throw the keys at him then and she did a second later. He blocked it with his forearm and it hurt, but his only other option was to lose an eye.

"Nice catch shit-for-brains. Now pick 'em up and know this, if you try to leave there'll be a lot more blood on your hands."

With that, she slid smoothly from the Jeep, the stone once more bouncing up and down in her hand. "Come on!" she barked at him.

Will bent down and retrieved the keys from the floorboard as panic started to flow outwards from his chest. She was in a mood for blood and he didn't know if he'd be able to even slow her down. He *knew* that there were at least two men to look out for in the church. He could picture their faces with his vision and neither looked like lightweights.

Walking to the church, Will asked, "Talitha, shouldn't we at least try to talk to them before..." Before she slaughters everyone? Was that going to happen?

"Maybe, we'll see. You don't understand me very well do you? I suppose it's not your fault being as dim as you are. I don't always kill for the fun of it. Sometimes there's a reason behind it." She giggled at this, but Will, sweating through his church-going jacket and tie didn't see anything funny in it.

At the front of the church, she gave him a slow venomous smile and he felt her hand on the back of his jacket. She gripped him in such a way that he knew she was in charge. After a tiny pause, she gave him a shove, keeping her hand on his back and he opened the doors to the church.

There was an odd moment of silence broken by the sound of an organ. It was a fine, old organ, that hadn't been played well once in the four years he and Talitha had been coming to the church. Their usual seats were just to the side of it, because Talitha like to feel the vibration of it along the pew as it was played. The church laid out before them was nearly full and the singing was loudly exuberant. The organist, Mrs. Fishbon, a sweet lady with sausages for fingers, was playing a congregation favorite.

Talitha held him silhouetted in the doorway. Feeling terribly vulnerable, he looked back at his sister. Her eyes were no longer dead, but were hard and alive with the chance to kill. They flitted about the room and she took in every detail of the congregation, until she seemed satisfied and directed him to the office door to their right.

The door sat open a few inches and Will, feeling even more like a human shield than ever, was pushed through it, but held just inside. The office seemed larger than it had from the outside, mainly due to the fact that it held little besides two large leather bound chairs. Will was surprised to see his priest from his days on Governor's Island, Father Alba, seated in one of them. Flanking him a few feet on either side, were two men— one of whom was a giant of man.

The giant, wearing faded blue jeans and an enormous Boston Celtic's hoodie, stood towering over the room just to the right of the empty leather chair. Will guessed his height to be about six feet eight inches, but his weight was beyond his ability to even make a stab at. He wasn't fat, but was thick and huge with muscle. His face, sporting scars and a crooked nose, suggested that he had seen his fair share of fighting.

The other man to Will's left had an air about him that fairly screamed *Cop*. He wore a tired-looking suit and at six feet, he wasn't small, but appeared so when compared to the giant.

In his periphery, he could tell Talitha was taking in the scene as well and after a moment, she pushed him further into the room and shut the door behind her. With a shove Talitha moved him forward and slightly to the right so that Will ended up a few feet from the giant. The man shifted his stance, spreading his legs to just over shoulder width apart and now looked ready for action. Will swallowed hard at the sight. Generally, he thought of himself as a big man, but next to this guy he felt like a little kid.

"Father Alba, it's so good to see you." Talitha stepped out from behind Will and beamed at the priest. It had only been five years since Will had last seen Alba, but the man had aged greatly. His thin hair had become thinner still, but it was his face looking ragged and on edge that made him look like it had been closer to twenty, rather than five years.

Father Alba, sweating and failing to appear calm, smiled back nervously. "It's good to see you as well. And you Will."

Will nodded at the man, he was so keyed up that he didn't trust himself to speak.

Talitha wasn't nervous in the least. "It may be good to see you...but not to smell you, whoa! I could smell your own personal brand of cowardly stench from the parking lot. Even with these goons you brought, you're practically pissing yourself." She tossed the stone absentmindedly up and down as she spoke.

"Talitha, this is important. Forget them..." Father Alba began.

"Are you telling me what to do? Do you think that

just because you're a priest, you can talk to me this way?" The cop stepped forward, looking hard at Talitha and she smiled at him. "Hello handsome," she said with a sexy purr.

The stone she had been carrying, she suddenly lobbed in a light under hand toss, high in the air to the man. It flew up lazily and floated as if it were feather light and that was when Will saw the attack coming. Unfortunately, his eyes were on the rock as Talitha had designed and as Will took a step forward, he suddenly found his legs kicked out from under him.

As Talitha had tossed the stone, she had dropped immediately into a spinning blur, her left leg out and extended, inches from the floor. She struck Will's lead leg with such force that it flew up and his body followed after. He was on in his back in a blink of an eye and he was able to watch as Talitha, smooth as a dancer, let the momentum of her spin carry her in a complete circle.

She rose like an ice skater in her turn, so that even as the cop foolishly reached to his right to catch the stone, she sprung at him. Her face held a startling look of happiness overlying her evil and she danced into the man lightly. Her right hand slipped under his jacket and her left, she held close to her body, but with the palm of it on the man's chest. They were nose to nose and her malicious joy was on full view as she gave him a light Eskimo kiss, before thrusting out with all the force in her left arm.

The man flew back with a stupid, startled look on his face, leaving his gun behind, looking gigantic in Talitha's right hand. His feet struck the side of one of the leather chairs and he somersaulted over it before hitting the far wall.

The giant reacted quickly, especially for a man of his size, but in this instance he was too slow. Talitha snapped her arm around at him pointing the gun into his face. He stopped in mid-stride and stared down at the girl, looking past the gun, which was flat black and impossibly large in her small hands.

The singing outside the room ended abruptly then, and there was a huge silence in which the springs of the inner workings of the gun could be heard distinctly. She was slowly drawing back the trigger as well as drawing out the last moments of the big man's life with sweet torturous ecstasy.

Chapter 7

Jim Meets Talitha

Jim Anderson was about six millimeters from death.

He had been warned about the girl, but the warning had seemed absurd at the time and he had ignored it. She was a murderer, she was insane, she could kill with her bare hands, and they were all afraid of her. Good for them. Let them cower, but he wasn't afraid and if she wanted a fight, he was her man.

He was hugely strong with tremendous shoulders and tree trunks for legs. However, he wasn't an Adonis and he battled against his waistline on a daily basis, but regardless of that, there were very few men that could take him in a fight. And the idea that a hundred-pound woman, no matter how insane, could stand toe to toe with him, was laughable.

He could see that she was fast...faster than he thought possible, but he was ok with that, he'd fought fast men before. She was strong as well. She had sent that annoying cop Milner, flying with no problem and that too didn't bother him. No, the only thing that bothered him was that he was going to die at the end of a gun.

It was a coward's way, especially when she had some sort of super powers. Now if he died fighting hand to hand, well that was that, but she wasn't going to give him the chance.

He gave her a snide look from around the gun. "I

thought you were supposed to be tough." This he said so calmly, you would've thought they were having a drink in a bar. The trigger continued its slow backwards motion a millimeter at a time. "I guess not," he intoned blandly and waited for the arrival of the bullet. It was going to be lights out before he knew what hit him.

Somehow, the girl held the trigger a hair from sending that bullet into Jim's face. "Are you questioning me?" Talitha asked.

With a slow smile, that he hoped would rile her enough to either pull the trigger or fight, he replied, "No, I'm questioning the reputation you have with the good Father here. He told me you were dangerous and powerful, but I see now that you're only a scared little girl hiding behind a gun. There're plenty of those running around all ready, who needs another?" Even though he was sure he had just sealed his own fate, the girl's brother relaxed visibly and laid back on the floor.

Talitha smiled in a strange exultant fashion, while her eyes came alive. "Interesting...you think you can actually take me."

Father Alba still seated and still sweating said, "Miss Jern, I'm sorry if we offended you in some way, but we're not here to hurt you or to challenge you. We actually came all this way to talk to your brother."

Talitha gave the priest a quick disgusted look. "I have to tell you, Alba, I'm not much interested in what you're here for, but I'm glad that you brought this one. I think I want to try him on and see if he's all talk."

The gun, despite its size, hadn't wavered an inch and Jim smiled around it at her. "Let's go out to the woods. I bet we can find a nice spot."

"No, James. Please, there're lives at stake here," the

priest implored.

"Yeah, don't be an ass, Jim Fella," Milner added as he got to his feet.

Jim's smile slipped into a hard look and his dislike was plain for all to see. He'd never liked Eric Milner. The cop had been in the orphanage as a kid and being older than Jim by four years had bullied him almost ceaselessly. When Jim reached the age of fourteen and was six feet in height, the two had fought a couple of times. He'd lost both fights, but he also stopped being picked on. Now, Milner was a cop and expected his ass to be kissed by everyone in sight.

Jim had secretly enjoyed what Talitha had done to him and seeing it replayed in his mind, caused the grimace to invert back into a smile. He said to Milner, "Just trying to speak the lady's language...something you obviously can't do."

"Ha, ha, ha," Talitha guffawed loudly and stepped back before lowering the gun. "I like him already. The priest called you James and the nitwit cop called you Jim Fella...what do you call yourself?" Her eyes gave him a long roving gaze and he felt like a prize bull at auction.

She seemed to hold onto his many flaws with her look and his confidence diminished rapidly. It may have been his hypersensitivity, but she took the greatest interest in his scars, his broken nose and most embarrassing, his cauliflower ears. The unsightly bumps and odd, ugly swelling of his ears was one of the side effects of years of wrestling. He always kept his hair long to cover them but he could tell by her look that they were exposed and he felt the first touch of a blush starting to warm his hideous ears.

Talitha had no flaws at all, not even the smallest pimple blemished her perfect tan skin. Her full lips glistened provocatively and her teeth, straight and white flashed out from behind them when she spoke. He realized he was staring and turning away, feeling the heat of his blush spread to his cheeks.

"Everyone at the orphanage pretty much calls me Jim and some of my old friends call me Jim Fella, but my name's James Anderson."

"Sure it is...what's your real name?" she asked him as she brought the gun to her nose and sniffed at it, in what looked to be a habitual manner.

"Uh, all I know is the Jim part. I never knew my parents...I was left at the orphanage."

"The orphanage? There's only one?" she asked still eyeing him in an unsettling way.

With the likelihood of a fight having disappeared, the last of his confidence went with it. Talking with pretty girls always made him feel even uglier than usual. "Uh, Saint Thomas' Home for Boys."

"In Boston, correct?" He nodded and she continued looking irritated, "I can tell by all the moronic accents...especially the cop's." Whatever was affecting her—insanity Jim supposed—came out in a withering look at Milner and he blanched at the sight of her face.

"Yes Miss Jern, we've come up from Boston." The priest looked like he was pulling himself together and sat composed in a luster of sweat, "We have a dangerous and delicate situation...you've heard about the recent spate of kidnappings in Boston, I suppose?"

"Oh yes, of course! And I'm glad you came all the way up, to hear my confession...it was me! I ate them, starting with their wee little toes." The girl then started to chatter her teeth up and down. She was no longer beautiful and looked on the verge of abandoning sanity altogether, smashing out the last smoldering ruin of it in the ashtray of her mind. Her brother gaped at her in horror, fully believing she had done just as she had said.

Father Alba had a queer, sick looking, half-smile draped over his face, "Miss Jern, there's someone else who claims to have taken the children." He was clearly afraid of contradicting the girl, "This man...is also possessed by the demon Ba'al Zubel!"

Talitha stopped her crazed chattering at the sound of the name and the tan of her face went white. "That's not possible," she whispered, shaking her head. Suddenly she laughed. "You had me going there for a moment. I assure you that it's not wise to be this great of a buffoon around me."

"And I can assure you that he's possessed." Father Alba looked put out not to have been immediately believed.

"First, it's not Ba'al, and second, a man can't be possessed at all. I thought as a priest you'd know this."

Jim was confused and the priest was right there with him. He held up the black book. "I don't want to be contradictory, however there are quite a few references in the bible concerning men being possessed."

"Yeah, but that book was written by men to be read by men. Women didn't count for much back then. You should trust me on this. I know a thing or two about demons."

Alba sort of half shrugged clearly fearing Talitha's response. "I think this one is genuine," he said. "The man knows thing he can't possibly know. He speaks in tongues, Latin, and some other horrible sounding language. I recorded it just in case I needed proof. He also bleeds at will, instantly in the form of the Stigmata. Do you know what that is?"

"Of course I do," she snapped at him irritably. "Let's hear these so called tongues, Priest and if its pig-Latin, I'm going to pull the cop's ears off and don't think for a moment I won't!"

Jim believed her and so did Milner. He backed away from her with a horrified look on his face until he hit the wall behind him. There he stood shooting his eyes back and forth from Jim and the girl's brother as if begging for help.

Father Alba dug out the Sony walkman he had borrowed from Sean Shay and without ceremony pressed the play button. The girl's reaction to the sound coming from the little machine was immediate as well as startling. Moving in a blur, she jumped full at the priest who squawked in fright and held up the walkman as if to shield himself. She snatched it from his hands and in one quick move dashed it to the floor. Without a word, she ground the thing beneath the heel of her black shoe.

When the plastic had been crushed into an unrecognizable state, she knelt, digging about in the remains of the machine, pulling at the thin tape of the cassette until moments later her hands were full of what looked like black spaghetti.

Now as she stood up, her brother had a strange look playing about his face. Sorrow and hatred seemed to battling for control of his features and he took a small step forward. His body tensed as if he was about to spring and Jim looked to see the cause.

It was the gun!

It lay as if forgotten next the girl's right foot and the man was obviously contemplating making a grab for it. Having seen the speed the girl possessed, Jim thought Will crazy for even thinking it.

Talitha seemed to have forgotten the gun in her distress. "Alba, you're such a moron! Don't record anything that man says, ever again. Ever!" she repeated in a shout. "And certainly never play something like that in a church."

"What language was it?" the priest asked wiping sweat from his eyes with the sleeve of his black shirt.

"It's a language that's used in the lower plains of the void. Very low," she added ominously. "Milner, give me that lighter in your shirt pocket."

Milner jumped at the sound of her voice, but hurried to obey. He reached into his pocket and looked surprised to find his own lighter there, even though that was where he always carried it. He started forward to hand it to Talitha, but quickly had second thoughts about getting too close and instead tossed it to her.

His shaking hands short armed the throw, so that Talitha had to take a long step forward to catch the lighter before it hit the ground.

Her brother proved no slouch in the speed category himself. Will made his move almost as if he had committed himself to going for the gun the second Milner had tossed the lighter. His timing was perfect and he and his sister seemed in complete sync as they both stepped forward with the same motion, she snatching the falling lighter, he grabbing the gun. She noticed the movement behind her a half second too late and even though she spun with amazing speed, Will had the gun up and pointed into her face.

"Don't try it!" he commanded. "I said, don't try it! I saw what you were planning to do...even you won't be quick enough." He held the gun with a steadiness that was impressive, but Talitha simply looked around it wearing a vicious smile.

"You're going to hand over that gun, Will, one way or the other," she said easily. Will just shook his head.

A sudden exhaustion overcame Jim and he went to sit down next to Father Alba, who gave him a light pat on the knee. The priest looked tired as well and it was no wonder.

The night had been long and completely without sleep. The possessed man had demanded that a room be set up for him in the cellar beneath the chapel. How he knew the rooms were there, was a mystery—pretty much like everything else about the man. The storage rooms were dark and fetid, especially the one he picked out. They were all along a single corridor and he chose the last, the one that routinely flooded and smelled of decay and mildew. He had asked for only three things, a mattress, a gallon of wine and to be locked into the room.

They were all too happy to give in to his demands, and Jim had felt a good deal of relief when he had locked the door behind the demon/man. The relief had been short lived however, because within minutes, screams of an inhuman nature came slipping around the doorframe. This caused a nervous Father John to order Sean and him to guard the man for the remainder of the night.

Now, Jim was blinking his gritty eyes, content to watch the brother and sister action play about before him. However, the girl had caught his movement out of the corner of her eyes and, ignoring her brother, she turned and looked at him with a small mysterious smile.

"So Jim Anderson, where'd you get that name? Did a nun give it to you as some sort of celibate joke?"

"Talitha!" her brother demanded.

She smiled at Jim as if to apologize for her brother's rudeness. "Just one second," she said and turning back to her brother, she pushed her forehead to the barrel of the gun. "Go ahead. What are you waiting for? Just tell me first, how are you going to rationalize this? Are you going to pretend that it's for my own good? Are you going to pretend that you'll be saving some stranger even though by killing me you'll doom the kids the priest is so worried about? How are you going to explain this to Lisa? Are you going to tell her the truth? That you killed me in cold blood?"

The brother swallowed audibly and there was great pain in the depths of his sky blue eyes. He pulled back on the trigger slowly, not out of maliciousness but due to the battle waging within him.

"Come on Will, be a man! Shoot me! We both know you're doing this to be rid of me. So you can sleep in on Sunday mornings! Come on you selfish bastard! Show me that you hate me."

Tears over flowed the damn of his eyes and he blinked hard and savagely, "You're right...I hate this part of you. You're the most vicious person...there's nothing here to love."

She gave him a smile that was almost endearing. "Now pull the trigger and I'll make sure to save a spot for you in the void. Come on! Paint that wall red and paint your soul black."

Father Alba got up from his chair in haste. "Will,

please don't. Murder is always wrong and besides we may need her. She speaks the demon's language. Will, put the gun down. The lives of five children are at stake here, please."

Talitha chided the priest, "No, that's a mistake Alba. I'm not the sweet girl you knew and lusted after. I'm very dangerous and Will knows it. He's always known it. I want you down in the void with me, Will...then it will be my turn."

The gun now wavered and Will's face screwed up in painful confusion. "If I don't shoot her now she'll eventually get the gun back and..." An odd spasm jerked his features around and he stepped away from the girl, lowering the gun.

She held out her hand for it. "I'll take it from you eventually, just as you said." When he still hesitated she added, "I'm getting bored here. Either give me the bullet or the gun, those children aren't getting any older." She giggled at her own sick humor and it deflated him. His shoulders drooped and he tossed the gun her way not caring whether she caught it.

Will turned from his sister and said to the priest tiredly, "What do you need me for? You say the demon claims to be Ba'al Zubel?"

"*He is a liar*," Talitha sing-songed the words and then brought the gun up to her lips touching it there gently. She turned her gaze on Jim and it seemed she mocked him with her eyes and the small smile again came to her lips as if she had some sort of special knowledge of him. He looked away deliberately but could still feel her eyes roving over him.

"Whether he's a liar or not, remains to be seen, but he did use that name and he did it with some authority."

Father Alba told her patiently, "The reason we're here...he asked for the uh, object I entrusted you with."

Will's eyes filled with alarm and as an involuntary action, they darted to his sister. He had to force them back on to the priest. "Did he say why?"

"No, but he was willing to trade the lives of the children for it."

Will seemed suddenly burdened with the news and his fatigue became more apparent. "I'm sorry, Father but I don't think I can give it up for this. When a demon offers to trade for something, you never agree to the deal. Talitha, this language of the lower planes, can someone learn it without being possessed?"

"Will, trust me, he's poss..." the priest began.

The girl interrupted, "I'll have to see the man first to know. Wait, Alba, did you actually make sure he is a man? Did you check his plumbing?" She walked up to priest, her face mostly hidden by the large gun that was constantly stroking her lips.

He seemed disconcerted by her proximity. "Uh, no...I told everyone to keep away from him and not to touch him."

Without asking, she pulled the Bible from the priest's hands. He had carried it about, non-stop since the night before when they had confronted the man.

Ignoring his look of surprise, she said, "That was wise...when you touch a demon inappropriately, he's bound to sue." Without warning, she tore out a good chunk of the bible and dropped it on the twisted chaos of the cassette tape. "Now since you aren't Jewish, you won't need the first few chapters in this book, right? It's full of trashy tales anyways and besides, all that dirty begetting gets me hot you know."

[91]

The priest's face turned into a frown at this, but when she bent and lit the paper on fire, he seemed to feel actual pain. "Are you done...with the rest?" He anxiously pointed at the remains of the bible in her hand.

"Sure," she flipped it at him nonchalantly. "Big Jim, you better pull that smoke alarm...what?"

He had never liked being called Big Jim and he hadn't realized it had shown on his face. "Most people call me, uh Jim."

"Well, I'm not most people, Jimbo. So reach up there and turn that smoke detector off before we have a panic on our...never mind, a panic will work too." She smiled innocently up at him, as he stretched out his long arm to the ceiling and took the battery out of the little white box, just as grey smoke began to curl up, heavily into the air.

"You're just no fun, Big Jim. So, you guys have beaten around my bush long enough, what does Mr. Zubel want? And don't lie! We're in a church and I'll be all too happy to administer God's punishment on you." She did seem happy at the prospect.

Will looked defeated still and shrugged his shoulders as if it wasn't a big deal, "He wants dad's sword...the one he stabbed the demon with."

Talitha's eyes went wide at the mention of it. "The sword," she said it quietly but with reverence.

For the first time since Jim had met her, she became alive in a normal sense. She no longer looked insanely evil. The skin of her face flushed with a healthy pretty pink and she smiled happily remembering something fondly.

"The sword...Oh my lord! I had forgotten, it was so

long ago. I think I was still young in the void when it came. It brought with it hope... at least I think it was hope. I'm not too sure what that's like anymore. But it also had that smell, dad's smell. Do you remember his smell?" She breathed in slowly through her nose as if she could still smell him.

"But the sword was fleeting and it didn't last. Isn't that funny? Everything else in the void is eternal...but not that sword. I remember I recognized it at once. The long silvery blade swept across the upper reaches of the void, making it seem like there was a sky and I knew it was dad's.

"Ha! The demons were at first afraid of it, all but Ba'al, and they hid themselves as best as they could and the tortured, free from their misery, for just that short time made a mad rush for it. But I...I don't remember what happened next. I woke in the dark and the sword was gone. However, there were parts of it falling everywhere, they were like shooting stars, and the void was in chaos. The tortured and the demons ran about like children, as if they were on holiday. It was even fun! I remember smiling till my face hurt." Her face now, was almost all smile, with light tears trickling down her cheeks as if rain fell from her eyes.

She looked about at the men towering around her, but saw none of them, she only saw the past.

"I'm not bragging, but I found the largest part of the sword. Some piss-ant thing had it and I killed him for it. I took it away and hid it in the void. A part of me knew it was wrong, but I did it anyways. I covered it in my darkness, so that it would be mine alone and when the last of the sword had long since disappeared, I still had mine. I gloated over it and I stayed near it all the time, but eventually it vanished. I woke once...and it was gone. It had been whole and perfect and alive and then...gone. But I guess that's the way it's supposed to be in the void...no light, no love, only nothing."

The room was quiet and she just stood staring at the floor, until Will asked her, "Why would a demon want that sword?"

Talitha spoke in a distant way, without looking up, "I don't know. I didn't even know it still existed." She shook her head to clear it of those fond memories and her eyes hardened. "Where's the sword, Will?"

"Near my home, but..."

"But nothing! It's time to see an old friend," she said this with malevolent glee.

"But..."

She raised the gun and the gesture shut Will up quick, which made her smile. "Good boy! Alba, take that cop and get the hell out of here. If I so much as smell him again, I'll hunt him down and cut off all his moving parts, got it?" She paused waiting and when he didn't answer, she turned the gun on its previous owner.

"Yes I got it, Miss Jern...I'll meet you in Boston then?" Father Alba asked hopefully.

"Probably," she murmured.

An hour later, Will drove his jeep at a speed that was worlds beyond reckless. In the front passenger seat, Jim gripped the console with near crushing force, and he feared if they took another turn like the last one, it would tear right off. He tried to concentrate on the passing scenery and relax, but it was impossible with the wind whipping through the bullet hole next to his right knee. The sound was an irritating high keen and it unnerved him so much, that he found himself staring at the noisy little hole, instead of at the pretty orange and gold trees zipping by.

Jim didn't scare easy, he hadn't even been afraid while in the presence of the demon plagued man—but that gunshot in the box like interior of the jeep, had nearly given him a heart attack. This was what Talitha called an attention grabber. As she would later tell them, she didn't like to have to repeat instructions, so she prefaced this one by shooting the gun as near to his leg as she could.

"The next one will go in his head, Will, if you don't pick up the pace," Talitha had said this with a happy grin at the reaction she had received from the gunshot. She then took to sniffing at the barrel of the gun in an interested fashion. Will didn't need to be told twice and he had pegged the gas pedal to the floor and unbelievably had left it there almost the entire time since.

Jim soon found out that Will had some sort of supernatural power to see the future. Twenty minutes after the gunshot he turned to his sister, "There's a cop up ahead; would you like me to slow down?"

Will's face held a look of disgust that had made Jim want to look back as well. Talitha was casually rubbing the fully loaded pistol between her thighs. Jim jerked his head away, embarrassed for her brother, who had turned a light shade of brick.

"Oh damn! Yeah, slow down. Just when I was *really* starting to enjoy the ride. Hey Jimbo? Want to smell the gunpowder on this thing?" She held the gun out to him and he could only shake his head, no, as he felt his own color rising. As a distraction, he looked out for the police cruiser, but there wasn't one in sight. Yet

Will kept the car tooling along at the speed limit, which suddenly felt unreasonably slow.

Two minutes later the cruiser came into view. Jim had to ask Will, "How'd you know it was there? Do you have a scanner hidden under the dashboard?"

"It's nothing...foresight, just a gift, it's nothing." He answered with embarrassment that Jim didn't understand. It sounded like more than nothing, and explained some of Will's quick reactions. Jim would've liked to be able to see the future. He thought it would be the coolest thing, but of course if it came with a complimentary insanely evil sister, he would probably pass on it.

He gave the passing scenery a little smirk, realizing he had just lied to himself. The only thing that he ever truly wanted was to be a part of a family. It had been denied to him, not once, but twice and with his ugly looks and freakish size, he wasn't likely going to get a third shot.

The first time had been when his natural mother had given him up. Maybe he'd been a big eater back then as well. Who knows the reason, but there he was in the middle of the night with nothing but his pajamas and a single name. As he always did when thinking about her, he tried to remember her face, nothing came; his memory of her had faded long ago.

His earliest recollection was still that first night at the orphanage when he'd been given the bottom bunk under Sean Shay. He had tried to hide his tears, but Sean had heard him sniffling and had talked to him while dangling upside down as only little boys would do. Their friendship had begun right there when Sean had told him that he'd cried as well on his first night.

Jim's second family had given him his second name.

The Anderson's, Nathan and June, had adopted him when he was in the third grade. They had visited the orphanage a number of times and they had liked his low-key style. The other boys had always hopped around the two of them like a swarm of crickets on cocaine. Since he had never considered himself worthy to be adopted, Jim hung back.

He hadn't been a cute child and he knew that was an import factor for most people. Not only that, everyone around him believed him to be a touch slow. Having never been to school before, he wasn't at all prepared for the second grade, but he was as big as the other second graders, so that's where he was placed.

Sister Mary Agatha, old even in his earliest recollections, had raised hell with the neighborhood school, but to no avail. The teachers didn't go out of their way to teach what they obviously considered a handicapped kid, but regardless he was passed along year after year.

Then the Anderson's had come along and took him from that life. For two glorious months he had been part of a real family. June seemed to care for him from the very start, lavishing affection on him at every opportunity as if he were really her child, but it had taken Nathan much longer to open his heart. However, on the day they had died, he had hugged Jim quite out of the blue.

"Did you have a good time visiting your new cousins?" Nathan had asked with a smile. He could still remember the smile on his dad's face to this day. It had been perfect. There was no lie behind it. He wasn't putting on a show in order to impress anyone with his generosity of spirit. It was just that he liked Jim...maybe even loved him and that was what made it perfect.

"Yes sir. It was lots of fun and they was real nice to me," he had answered and he remembered smiling also and thinking back, he hoped his smile was perfect as well.

"I thought at first, that it was very polite of you to call me sir, but...it's been a few months. I think it's time you started calling me dad. Do you think that's a good idea?"

"Yes sir...uh, Dad." It had sounded flat and awkward coming out of his mouth and the two of them looked at each other for a moment.

"That was weird wasn't it?" Nathan Anderson said as he came down to one knee. "Try this...Ok Daddy! See, make it peppy."

"Ok, Daddy I will," Jim didn't realize what he had just said and was about to be peppy like he been asked, when his father became his father. Nathan scooped Jim off his feet and hugged him fiercely to himself.

It was their first and last hug.

He could still recall that warm crushing feeling that was so wonderful. Nathan would be dead in fifteen minutes and June would die in the first light of the following morning, but they loved him. That couldn't be taken away, no matter what.

It was that desire to be a part of family that had been foremost in his consideration when he took the job at Saint Thomas. He figured the orphanage would be the closest thing to being in a family as he would ever get.

Jim looked over at Will, who gripped the steering

wheel with white knuckled hands, and felt a stirring of jealousy. A glance back at Talitha however, nearly killed it.

Her eyes knifed into his with an unsettling intensity. She smiled, "Ok Jimbo, where'd you get your last name? You never did tell me your, *oh so sad* life story at the orphanage." Her question following so closely on his thoughts, made him wonder if she had more powers than just the physical ones that she had displayed.

He thought: ARE YOU A MIND READER, as loudly as he could and waited.

Her response was not reassuring, "Come on Jimbo, out with it. I'm not a mind reader you know." It seemed like the just sort of thing she'd say if she was a mind reader.

"I was adopted and I took their last name. Kinda boring, I'm sure."

"Yeah very. Please tell me the 'Fella' part is a little more exciting." Her eyes were black as twin gun barrels and the thought made him look at the gun, which she had pointing at him from her crotch. An army of goose bumps broke out along his arms and arrayed themselves in proper formation.

He pulled his eyes up to her face. "I'm sorry, there's not much to that story either. There was just another guy in my class with the same name and I used to call people, fellow all the time, so I was called Jim Fella."

"No...you would have been called Big Jim. I take it the other guy was big as well?"

"Yeah he was," he answered, wondering why she was so interested in him.

"*Yeah he was*," she mimicked his slow deep voice.

He peeked back at her again; she sat looking out the window with her head pressed against the glass. She repeated herself again, "*Yeah he was*." Pivoting her head, keeping it on the glass, she asked, "He was black, right? And you were all too proper to call him Black Jim and you White Jim."

"Perhaps, I guess."

"*Perhaps, I guess*," she mimicked again. "Maybe I was wrong about you. I had the feeling that you were smarter than you looked. Of course, it could be the pressure. Does the gun bother you at all? I like to see how pressure affects people...look at me."

He turned back in his seat and the gun was pointing at his face; he had expected it. He looked past it and into her eyes. "What do you want?" he asked gruffly, irked that she was being such a pain.

"Here's the deal, White Jim. I'm going to test your intellect and if you get these answers wrong, I'll shoot you somewhere of my choosing." She smiled with joy over the new game she had invented. "Now I have to tell you that I brought you along simply to amuse me and you're doing a very poor job of it, so this may be your last chance."

She had been hoping for him to say something to this, but he only stared at her and she wrinkled her eyebrows at him, causing three little lines to appear between them.

"Playing it cool with a gun in your face...impressive. Plus 10 points! Now, question one, we'll start with an easy one...give me three numbers that when you add them, the total is 1011."

He wasn't going to play her stupid games and he just stared at her, looking into her eyes, which were not as lifeless as he had first thought. They were wet, bathed in the black waters of her insanity and everyone once in a while he could see a little question in them. The questioning look made her less of a killing machine and more of a person who had doubts.

She began pulling the trigger back slowly, again as he expected, and he said matter-of-factly, "Getting shot is a better way to go than dying in a car crash or getting eaten by a demon."

A girlish pout formed on her lips. "You're no fun! It's better if you're scared."

"Sorry. If you want to pass the time, we could play the license plate game."

"What? That's so childish!" With her lips pursed, she looked angrily out the window and proceeded to kick the back of his chair. He ignored it and it soon stopped. A minute later, she spoke in a grumpy voice, "A in Massachusetts."

She won the game easily, but it had the desired effect of passing the time without the fun of gunfire. The trip ended quite abruptly for Jim, who didn't know where they were going besides *Will's house*. They drove through the small but pretty city of Bangor and minutes later turned off of I 95. The area was wooded and hilly, looking like it should have been the setting for a postcard.

Soon after that they pulled up to a large white two-story house. It had a fine wraparound porch with a detached garage in the rear and as they got out of the car, a wonderful sweet smell drifted in from an apple orchard to the right of the house. The trees were pleasant to look upon, despite the wandering drunken fence that leaned against some of them to keep itself upright. The property had a splendid front lawn, that still held to its green and this ran down a small sloping hill to greet them.

Jim had never seen a home, more homelike in his life and he was sure that there'd be the smell of something baking when they entered. He was about to compliment Will, but the man looked more tense than he had yet seen him. His blue eyes darted about the windows of the house, never holding to one for more than a second. He walked in short jerky steps, leading the way to the kitchen door, which was a light yellow that matched the trim of the place.

When the door opened, Jim wasn't disappointed by the smell; Will's wife Lisa was definitely preparing something. He knew very little of her. Father Alba had filled him in on the pertinent details of Will's life on the drive up from Boston but he hadn't mentioned Lisa except in passing.

"Will, is that you? You're home early." A small slim lady with a great mane of blonde hair stepped into the kitchen from an adjoining room. She was pregnant, but not tremendously so and she wore a black maternity jumper with a long sleeved white shirt beneath it. His first thought upon seeing the outfit was, *penguin* but on Lisa, it was cute. She had a pretty face with narrow features that traversed from smiling to shock at the sight of Jim filling the kitchen door behind her husband.

He smiled back at her in a genuine fashion and because her look of shock wasn't tinged with disgust, he liked her already. She had just begun to reform the soft skin of her face into a smile, when Talitha stepped out from behind her brother.

At the sight of her, Lisa's face seemed to come

unwound from the inside out and her features sagged with her mouth coming open to stay. Her eyes, visibly green from across the room widened, not in shock as they had upon seeing him, but in dread.

"Hi sis!" Talitha exclaimed loudly with exaggerated insincerity. She advanced forward caressing the gun to her cheek. Lisa looked paralyzed at the sight of her sister-in-law and the only part of her that moved as Talitha advanced on her, were her eyes, which grew larger with each deliberately slow step.

Talitha seemed to be enjoying herself and practically screamed, "OH-MY-GOD! Look at you, all knocked up! And here I thought Willy J's willy wasn't working well." Talitha stopped abruptly and turning to Jim said, "Hey White Jim! Say that ten times fast...Willy J's willy wasn't working well."

He glared at her instead and her cruelty caused him to advance forward in anger but Will restrained him with just a hand. He must have *seen* something, Jim thought and stepped back.

Talitha just gave him a mocking smile before turning back to Lisa. "He can talk, I know he doesn't look like he could, but there are stranger things, right? Well?" Talitha flung out her arms, the big black pistol still in her right hand; she was obviously looking for a hug. After a moment, when Lisa didn't move, Talitha pulled her in close for a tight embrace. It was all one sided on Talitha's part and she held the embrace long enough to smell Lisa thoroughly.

"A girl...you're going to have a girl, but I'm guessing you already knew that, what with ol' Will's talent. Can I touch the baby?" Talitha actually paused for an answer. "You can tell me no, if you think that's wise. I have been called insane before you know...wait, that's right you do know. You visited me in the hospital...ONCE!"

Lisa's head was shaking back and forth slowly, but still no words came out of her mouth.

Talitha continued on, ignoring Lisa's imploring looks, "We used to be best friends, but you don't call, you don't write and now you won't let me touch your baby. That's upsetting...I don't think you really mean it, so I will ask you again: let me touch your baby."

Lisa's eyes were filled with tears and rimmed red with fear, she seemed mute, unable to form words. There was a long pause as she stared in terror at the gun pointed with purposeful indifference at her belly. Finally, a slight vibration of her head indicated that she had given her coerced permission.

"Relax Lisa, the baby won't feel a thing," Talitha said this as her hands reached out and caressed the volleyball sized tummy, the gun still in her right hand. Jim felt his heart start to hurt for Lisa as her great tears dripped down on the bulge of her belly. Again, he started forward to end the cruel game and again Will restrained him.

Talitha glanced back and her eyes seemed more inhuman than ever. "Look, Will, I'm holding two people. I have two lives in my hands... right in the palm of my hands. Will, honey, tell me where the sword is. Tell me right now or else. I won't ask again. Or...the...huh? The baby, uh...what?"

Jim watched the change happen right in front of him. He'd always considered people with multiple personality disorders to be frauds and he hadn't believed the priest when he had told him of Talitha's disorder. But he was a believer now. There was no faking what he saw, the girl was looking right at him with a nasty hard look that meant trouble and then suddenly, he saw life flood into her eyes. A multitude of emotions swept across this new Talitha's face and she blinked rapidly, staring about her.

Obviously, he was one of the first things she noticed and her startled expression was edged with that look Jim hated so much. He saw it before she was able to hide it away, it was a look reserved for burn victims and drooling retards: a look of disgust. Even with all her vile behavior of the last few hours, that look bothered him more than it should have.

Talitha then took in her brother, who was staring past her, not at Lisa but at the refrigerator and a dawning look of horror crept over his chiseled features. It made both Jim and Talitha look in that direction as well but there was nothing.

Finally, she turned all the way back around and saw Lisa's face streaming with tears. Fear and desperation warred for control of the blonde girl's features, so that she seemed to have developed a number of tics, as different muscles fought to align themselves in an acceptable order.

Talitha stepped back from her sister-in-law, "No!" she cried in desperation and brought her hand to her mouth to cover it. It was then she realized she was holding a gun and she eyed it with dreadful fascination. "No!" She practically screamed this at the gun and held it out away from her at arm's length. She looked back at the two men, her eyes were wild with fright, and tears filled them with a suddenness that wasn't possible.

"This can't be...Oh God, please no! I can't be here!"

Talitha's fear seemed even greater than Lisa's and her body began to shake uncontrollably, the gun in her out stretched hand waved and bounced about. She acted like it was a tiger she had by the tail. Something she couldn't let go of, but also a terrible thing she wanted as far away from her as possible. She looked past it at her brother and it seemed that she was holding it out for him to take it, but his face hardened with a marbled look of sadness and self-loathing.

This nearly brought Talitha to hysterics and she continued to hold the shaking gun out to him, she blubbered, "Please, Will...please. I can't be here. Take me away, take me back to the cabin! Please!" The last word, she shrieked but Will only stepped back, his own face a contortion of misery. Talitha deflated at her brother's odd reaction and stared open mouthed at the floor for a long moment before turning to look at a bewildered Lisa.

"I was going to kill you...you and the baby. It was there in my head...an echo...it's so strong. She hates you; she hates your baby...I gotta get out of here." She took a step to the door but then stopped with a dawning of understanding. "No, it's you that has to go! Will! Look at me! Take Lisa and go, now! The other Talitha can come back any second and...and she knows where you live."

Lisa saw that it was her friend who spoke and despite her great fear she smiled at Talitha and said, "I was always afraid of this day happening; the day when she would show up."

"I was afraid too, but now, with the baby...she hates your baby so much. And now I think she'll come after you. She'll hunt you down...but...but maybe there's something I can do." Talitha came to a decision. "Ok, ok...ok. I love you Lisa, you were my best friend. I'm sorry about this. Good bye."

In an odd silence, Will had been watching the two women and an internal struggle was clearly being waged throughout his body. Misery, sorrow, self-loathing, and fear had been revolving about the merry-go-round in his head and each came out in a distorted fashion on his face. Unmistakably something clicked when Talitha had said goodbye and he leapt toward her.

But stopped short as she stuck the gun to her own head.

She looked at him and her emotions were too many and too great to read in the short time before she said to her brother, "Love you." It was a quiet whisper and it barely registered on Jim's ears, before she pulled the trigger.

The noise of the gun in the kitchen was deafening. A fine red spray coated the refrigerator and the big man now saw that new alphabet magnets had been stuck there forming the words I LOVE DADDY. Now they were more than magnets, they were stencils in blood.

Chapter 8

The Suicide of Love

From the second Will had entered the kitchen, the vision of Talitha shooting herself began to replay itself in an endless loop.

He saw only the tip of the gun next to her head and then the fantail of blood spraying out. There was just a hint of a white wall behind her, it was his wall. His kitchen wall.

As Talitha, the evil one, spoke, he knew the vision was going to become a reality at any moment and he held the giant back with an outstretched arm. Here was his chance to get Talitha out of his life for good. He could now live like a normal person, without the weekly torture and the sleepless nights leading up to it. All he had to do was...nothing. It wouldn't be his fault and he knew...or he thought he knew, it would be for the best.

Not just for him, but for Lisa and the baby as well. His little girl would need a real father, not the empty shell that he felt himself to be. It would be good for Talitha also.

She had been killing.

It didn't come as a surprise that the bad Talitha was finding a way to secretly kill people, but the good one...that had been too much to take and he felt as if his world had been slipped out from beneath him when he heard it. Will had thought he was going through his living hell for her sake, so she could get better, but it turned out that she wasn't. He was wasting his time and his life, and he understood the only way to fix things was to do nothing.

As Talitha spoke to his crying wife, threatening her beautiful baby, he said to himself, "All I have to do is nothing." And when the real Talitha, the one he loved, came back and begged Will miserably to take her out of there, he thought, "All I have to do is nothing."

However, he wasn't a strong person. If he had been strong, he would've shot her at the church. No, he had been forever weak and his weakness was undermining what had to be done, which was of course, nothing. Unfortunately, his desire to be strong and stand his ground was a losing battle and he wanted to rush her and grab the gun from her hands and save her once again.

Talitha turned to him and told him she loved him and he believed her, and he saw now she was still the strong one. She knew what was right. She would kill herself and save the world a great deal of pain.

"Love you." Was all she said before he proved himself to be weak once again. In his vision, he had watched the blood shooting out of her head, but in real life he cringed and turned away. After the explosion struck his ears with a painful sharpness, he kept his eyes shut hard for a long time, terribly afraid of what he would see when he opened them.

A loud sniffle from his wife finally forced his eyes to open just a crack and the scene was frightful. Talitha lay across the floor at Lisa's feet with her once tan face staring up blankly at the ceiling. A pool of blood, like a red halo had formed about her head; it expanded outwards by degrees. There was more blood covering the refrigerator as well as the cute multi-colored magnets he had picked up for the baby...

Her hands shook as she removed each letter and dropped them in a glass bowl, which had one time held clear water. Now, the water was a dull reddish grey. Each letter had left an outline of itself in blood, so that the words, I LOVE DADDY, were stenciled on the white of the appliance. With the blood dripping down from the edges of the letters, the words looked like they belonged on the cover of a cheap horror novel...

The vision of Lisa cleaning up the mess smacked him in the face with its reality and he gasped. Tears, unchecked by care or consciousness ran down his face and he found himself reliving the gunshot.

"Will?" Lisa said with a voice that broke. She was a miserable looking thing and the green of her eyes stood out clearly from the red of the blood on her face. She had been standing just behind Talitha when the gun went off and somehow blood had sprayed her face so now she added gory red freckles to her natural ones.

He was supposed to go to her and comfort her...that's what people did in these situations. Will walked around the body and blood of his sister, feeling distinctly like a robot in a man suit. His emotions, so great only a moment ago, had left him completely and he felt hollow and the sound of the gun filled that void, it seemed to echo up and down the inside of his body.

She sobbed and he clutched her too his chest and knew there were important emotions that he should've been feeling but wasn't, and he worried that he was somehow broken.

Movement caught his eye and he saw the giant man that had come from the church with them, kneel at

Talitha's side. He reached out gently and Will wanted to tell him not to touch the body, but he couldn't remember the man's name. Talitha had called...White Jim? That didn't seem right.

Will hadn't spoken a single word to the giant in the three hours that he knew him and he suddenly realized how rude he had been. Now he wanted to say something to the man, who simply was staring down at Talitha, but absolutely nothing came to mind. His brain worked furiously, attempting to find anything to say, but it came up empty.

"Will?" Talitha had spoken, seemingly without moving her lips and he jumped at the sound.

"Will?" Now he realized it had been Lisa and he looked at her and again he was speechless. "Will? Hey look at me...what are we going to do?"

"Uh...uh..." That was the best he could do.

"Should we call an ambulance?" she asked looking down at the body. "Or do we let her die?" Lisa stepped back from the little pool of blood that was creeping aggressively toward her feet.

Will stepped back with her and said, "She's already dead...I think I could've stopped her...I know I could..."

Lisa interrupted, "I don't think she's dead."

The giant knelt down and felt Talitha's neck for a moment. "She has a pulse...it's very light."

"What? Not dead?" Will felt the floor spin beneath his feet. Not dead? That wasn't possible—not with all that blood and a hole through her head.

"What do we do? Do we let her die naturally? I...I can't kill her," Lisa was frantic while Will couldn't decide what he was feeling—he only knew that his feelings weren't right. This was his sister lying there.

Why wasn't he crying? Why wasn't he in hysterics? Was it because he was a man? Was it because he was broken? Had his weekly torture sessions damaged something inside him?

"Of course we can't kill her," the giant intoned solemnly. "Do either of you know anything about first aid?"

Lisa eyed the man as if seeing him for the first time. "You don't understand! She knows where we live! Who are you? Will, who is this man? Is he with Talitha?"

Will touched his head as if he would feel that broken part of himself. "No, he came up with Father Alba, and..."

"Father Alba! What's...what's going on? Is *it* back?" Her green eyes were magical emerald fires in her face and they seemed to burn their way out of the blood drying there. The giant stared into her eyes and his own narrowed in wonder at them.

"There's a man, he may be possessed by the demon," Will explained.

The giant rumbled, "He is possessed! And we have to do something about this girl before she dies."

Will bent down to his sister and felt her head as he spoke, "Ok, he's possessed, but it's not the same as before, Honey. He looks like a man...I mean he is a man, totally, there's no smoke about him and Father Alba says he's demanding the sword." Will found where the bullet had entered Talitha's head and was a little shocked to find that it had merely grazed the back of her head. "Lisa, please give some of those drying towels next to you."

He wiped away large clots of blood and could now

feel the wound better. His stomach did a barrel roll as he moved what he assumed to be a small part of her skull. The crease the bullet had made was about a half inch deep and ran nearly three inches across the back of her head. The blood seemed to be clotting with amazing swiftness but she had lost so much already that it wouldn't take much more for her to die.

"She might live...if we do something," he said and honestly didn't know what to think.

"Stop talking like that!" the giant said with some anger. "I don't get you two. There are more lives at risk here than just hers."

"Our lives are at risk as well, Mr..."

"Jim Anderson," he spoke with a touch of bashfulness.

"Well, Mr. Anderson, I have known Talitha for a long time and she's always been dangerous but now...she knows where we live! And the other one...the good Talitha, you heard her...I'll never be safe."

"She's been killing as well," Will mentioned sadly. "I don't know how many, but she hinted that it was a lot."

"So you see, Mr. Anderson, there are lives at stake one way or the other." Lisa looked to be falling apart as she said this and her tears, which had slowed down were now coming with more regularity.

"We don't kill her!" Jim said adamantly.

"Then tell me, Jim, what are we going to do?" asked Will angrily from across the body of his sister. "If you want her to live, then we need to take her to a hospital, where they will easily discover her identity and arrest her! How's that going to help those kids? Tell me! How many people will she kill in the hospital when

she escapes? People die around this girl all the time."
Will stared down at Talitha; she seemed so peaceful
and so much like her old self that his heart broke.

"I guess I don't know what we do then," the big
man admitted.

"What children are you talking about?" Lisa asked
holding onto her round belly.

"The possessed person, he may have kidnapped
five children...you know, the ones missing in Boston?
He may have them somewhere," Will explained.

The three of them stood in silence and Will could
see Lisa and Jim struggling with the same thoughts he
had been having. Will's heart felt like a stone, "If she
lives or dies, we're damned either way. I say we leave it
in God's hands. We bandage her up as best we can and
if she lives, she lives."

Jim had a look of disgust on his face, "You don't
sound much like a brother to me."

"I guess I'm not. I've wanted to kill her for years. I
used to think it was for her own good, but that was
partially a lie." The weekly visits were so terrible he
had known deep down he wouldn't be able to keep it up
much longer.

However, he knew the alternative for Talitha
would be a living nightmare. In the asylum, when
Talitha had to dream her own dreams, it had been
horrible. She'd spend day after day, fighting to stay
awake, fearing to close her eyes for even a second.
Eventually she'd sleep, and her screams would be
deafening and soul wrenching and she'd be a raging
animal afterwards, hateful and vicious.

His own dreams, terrible on Saturdays, were only
slightly better the rest of the week and insomnia was

becoming a constant companion. He could feel his life turning ragged at the edges and he would catch himself daydreaming of running away. Not just from Talitha, but Lisa as well. He feared he'd eventually suffer some sort of mental breakdown and didn't want her anywhere near him when he did.

Will looked at Lisa hugging her little belly and felt a tremendous guilt as he always did at the thought of running out on her. That guilt also extended to his sister and he said to Jim, "No, I'm not such a good brother, but what Talitha is doing to herself and to us...it may be for the best if she dies."

Lisa agreed, "I think you're right, Will. Let's put it in God's hands. Mr. Anderson, can you please pick her up and put her over here on the couch?" Lisa hurried to lay a blanket down on the couch. For Jim, the weight of the girl must have been nothing. She looked terribly small and vulnerable in the man's huge arms and when he'd placed her down he did so with a striking gentleness.

"Paper towels too please and there's an ace bandage in my gym bag," Will called to his wife as she rushed to their little first aid kit. He was just getting a better feel for the wound when she returned. "I thought she was really going to kill herself this time," he said.

"She was," Lisa said in a small voice. "This is my fault...I couldn't let her do it. She looked at me and it was her, Talitha. The girl who was my best friend...my only best friend. At the last moment I grabbed her arm."

Will put on a fake smile. "Maybe it was meant to be then." The smile felt plastic it was so artificial. Lisa had likely prolonged Talitha's agonies on earth and after her speech about hell, Will didn't think Talitha's agonies would ever end.

He dressed the wound as best as he could and then wrapped it with the ace bandage. It had stopped bleeding quicker than he had thought possible. Even for Talitha, it had seemed quick. She had an amazing ability to recover from injuries. During one of their many fights, his wedding ring had opened up her cheek. It had furrowed quite a gouge that had bled copiously, but the following morning it was as if she had never been touched.

After he worked on Talitha, he told his wife about the bizarre day he had, including the full story of the possessed man.

"And nobody knows why he wants it?" she asked.

Will shook his head. "No, unless this Talitha knows."

"Whatever a demon wants with the sword, it can't be good. I'm willing to bet it will end up costing the lives of more than just five children. I don't think you should give it up, Will." Her face was sad but resolute and he nodded in agreement. She turned to Jim, "I think you're going to have to tell Father Alba, we aren't going to give up the sword."

He sighed wearily. "I will...but tell me, is it true? Everything he said about the last demon, back in New York. Was there really some sort of witch?"

Will was too emotionally and physically spent to tell that sad story. He sat listening to Lisa tell it and hearing it again only made him more tired.

Lisa however was in full throttle in the depths of the story, adding color here and flavor there, until it sounded almost epic. Somehow, she left out the part where he had vomited right outside the house and there was no mention of him pissing himself. It didn't matter that it was only a few drops, he had still been that scared.

Watching her rambling on, with the giant hanging on her every word, made him sad for her. Lisa was basically friendless and had a need to talk and to listen like everyone else.

Bangor was an old city filled with old people and though they had tried, Will and Lisa had made no lasting friendships. When Will was away frequently, either on business or dealing with Talitha, and while he was gone Lisa was a veritable hermit and when he returned he would steel himself for the inevitable verbal avalanche.

Will was luckier with friendships; his business had him coming into Boston about once a month and he was close with many of the people he sold software to and could always count on having dinner with someone while in town.

His father and he owned a company that developed banking software. It was actually a triumvirate. William's job was to discover areas where new software was needed, or where updates on old programs could be used. He would give the ideas to Will who would then pitch them to Talitha, this usually occurred on Sunday mornings when she was in the best mood.

Talitha was a self-taught programmer, it was something she picked up with natural ease and she looked upon the challenges that Will would throw at her as if they were a great puzzle.

Will's position was the actual sale of the software. His ability to foreseen the future made his job closer to public relations than to sales. He would know even when dialing a phone number whether or not a sale was going to happen and if wasn't, he'd just hang up and go on to the next person on his list.

It was a very lucrative business and he could afford to buy Lisa the finest things. But life was funny that way; she didn't particularly care for high living and was content with building her family and her home. However, she did spend money flying out of the tiny airport in Bangor for visits, either with her brother, now living in Florida or with Will's parents in Arizona.

His parents weren't doing well; Will and Lisa would visit them at least three times a year. William was a shadow of his former self and Will had dreamed of his father's coming death many times. The death changed with every dream, but the pain never did, it only grew as his remaining days ticked away.

Early on, Will had warned his mom, who had only smiled sadly, already knowing the truth.

William had been steadily losing weight over the years, since his confrontation with the demon and now was hollowed-cheeked and rail thin. Scores of visits to a myriad of doctors ended last year when William discovered they had run out of new tests and were now just replaying his past favorites. Simply put, there was no medical explanation for what was happening to him, but his family knew the reason. He had sacrificed himself for all them, his death being only delayed.

He didn't seem to mind and despite overwhelming exhaustion, he was optimistic and happy at Will's every visit. Katie too was always happy to see them and was now practically giddy with the idea of becoming an aunt. She seemed to grow six inches with every visit and was now a long-legged beautiful freshman.

Outwardly, she seemed to be the only member of the family unaffected by the terrible night eight years prior, but Will knew better. Despite being tall, tan, and gorgeous, Katie seemed to have a deep-rooted hardness in her eyes, which could flare out if she became angry. Sometimes that hardness would be accompanied by a savage smile that reminded him of their father, back in the day.

Will smiled at the thought of his little sister and patted his wife's baby bulge gently. His own child would be blonde as well; he knew of course because he had dreamed her. When he was ever particularly down, it always helped to picture his coming child; she would be beautiful despite not having Lisa's fantastic green eyes. Hers would be a blue-green hazel that reminded him of images of earth seen from space.

Picturing his daughter's face elicited a long sigh that transitioned into a huge yawn. He felt what little energy he had depart with the yawn and knew he wouldn't be able to stay awake much longer. His eyes strayed to his sister, sleeping on the couch and a nasty thought struck him: if she were to wake up, which Talitha would it be?

Will dashed out to the garage and came back with the slimmest rope he could find. He carried Talitha upstairs to one of the guest bedrooms and tied her spread eagle to the four-poster bed there. Lisa hadn't protested this in the least and had left briefly, coming back with wind chimes that had once hung from their wraparound porch. These they secured to each of the ropes and when tested the chimes were muted but still sung loud enough to act as an alarm.

"Don't you think you're over doing it a bit?" Jim

asked as they all stood staring down at the trussed up girl. "She may be insane, but she's just a girl and a small one at that."

Lisa craned her head up at him and glowered. "Just a girl? I'm just a girl, but I can still slit your throat while you sleep."

Jim blinked in surprise at this. "Look, I didn't mean to anger you, but she's awfully small, is all I am saying. I don't think she'll be able to tear apart this bed."

Will spoke up, "She's very strong, Jim. I don't know if she can..." His brain suddenly lurched gently off the course of his conversation and he felt his hands go cold...

The water was icy cold and her hands and feet pained her greatly, she wished they would go numb already. A single rock jutted from the placid river; she slapped the shirt down hard upon it, Thwack!

The water was disturbed and rippling and she looked with satisfaction at the distorted images reflected up from the river. But it wouldn't do to let those waters calm too much and so she began scrubbing at the white shirt. She scrubbed. And scrubbed. It could always be whiter and it would eventually come clean if she just worked at it long enough.

Minutes later, a panicked feeling came over her, she had forgotten about the ripples and the water. Almost too late, she saw the surface lying down upon itself, becoming smooth and the images dancing upon its surface started to form into shapes that her mind could comprehend. Thwack! Just in time she had struck the washing stone with an exaggerated motion and the ripples were big ones, good ones...

[120]

"Hey...Will? You ok?" He heard Jim's voice coming to him and he blinked at the man giving him a long practiced embarrassed smile that was designed to show that he was just daydreaming...nothing more. Will looked around and saw that he was no longer by the calm river, but in a room with an insane person tied to a bed.

"He was just having a vision, he'll be ok," Lisa said with patience but also a touch of fear. "Was it important? Do you know if Talitha will be alright?"

He hadn't known before, but her asking the question triggered it and he did *know* now; Talitha would recover. A part of him, a part that he hated, felt keen disappointment at the knowledge.

"I'm good...I'm good. It was only a weird picture in my mind...nothing to do with this. But Talitha will get better...eventually."

Lisa looked anxious at the statement and Will knew she must've felt the same disappointment. "She will? Do you know how long it'll take? I'm just saying, I know you, Will. You're going to want to go to Boston and save the day, but you can't leave me with her."

"Don't worry. I would never leave you with her. In fact, if she does get better and needs a place to recover, I'll want you to clear out, maybe go look for a new place for us," he responded.

Lisa's face looked pained at the thought. She had put so much time into feathering her nest here in Bangor, that it would be a great hardship for her to leave it.

Will continued, "But you're wrong about me wanting to go to Boston...we aren't giving up the sword and it may be days before Talitha is well enough to go.

It just doesn't make sense for me to go."

Jim's face grew dark at this. "Without the sword, the girl may be our only chance at saving those children."

"I know, but I can't make her get better! For all we know, it could be a week before she even wakes up and those children can only go a couple of days without water. Besides, I'm sure the real exorcist will be there soon."

"They didn't call one," Jim said matter-of-factly. At the shocked look on their faces, he explained, "You don't understand the hierarchy of the church. Since there are children involved, the first thing they would've done was call the police."

Lisa was shocked. "You haven't called the police either? They could've searched the guy's house or apartment by now."

"The police know who he is already and they've been all over the man's place and got nothing. And I can tell you, they won't get anywhere questioning the demon! As for an exorcism, the man practically took a bath in Holy water and ignored Father Alba, when he commanded the demon to leave. A real exorcist won't come with magic powers, you know. Supposedly, it's a long drawn out process and can take many days. The kids will be dead well before then."

There was silence in the room and Talitha drew their eyes to her. They stood staring at her unconscious body and Will felt his chest thicken and start to ache. He'd have to go to Boston. His visions were likely the only way those children would be saved. He looked at his wife and saw in her eyes, that she knew it too.

"Go be the hero, Will. Go save the day! I knew this

would happen, but remember, you have a child too." Her eyes held accusations and angry fear.

"I don't want this, you of all people know I don't want any part of this," he said to her, avoiding looking into her eyes. Her look had hurt him.

"Maybe you don't, but you're like your dad was, heroic to a fault."

She was so wrong. The picture of his emaciated father, dying decades too soon came to him and Will knew he wasn't half the man his father was. Without his gift, his curse as he always thought of it, he would be nothing. He was no hero even with it.

His shoulders slumped as the heavy layers of exhaustion suddenly became too much. A glance at his watch showed that it was just past six pm.

"Sometimes I wish I were like him, but I'm not. I'm not what you think I am at all...right now I'm working on a dozen excuses to get out of going to Boston. I don't want those children to die; I just don't want to have to be the one that saves them. Does that sound heroic?"

She gave him a sad smile. "Are you going to Boston?"

"I have to."

"Then yeah, it does sound heroic." Another batch of tears skated effortlessly down the smoothness of her cheeks, "Go to bed. You look so tired...Jim and I will take turns watching over Talitha."

Jim nodded his large head and Will kissed his wife good night. He stumbled to his room, fighting to stay awake long enough to undress and without a single thought as to whether a girl with a head wound such as Talitha's could dream, he fell deeply asleep.

Just around 8 pm, Talitha's mind started kicking

out dream after horrendous dream.

Torture befell Will, turning the night into an endless agony, and it was just as dawn broke that Will dreamt of the stream. He was being tortured by a creature that was similar to a man, however, he had too many arms. These sprouted at odd angles from his body and the creature possessed a machine that seemed designed as he was. It had too many arms as well, but these ended not with hands but with barbed hooks.

The hooks were flatter than normal, and Will guessed their wicked purpose quickly upon seeing them, therefore it was no surprise, when the man-like creature slipped them under Will's skin. The machine came alive and began twisting his flesh. It was very painful, but worse was seeing his skin looking dreadfully like spaghetti entangled around a fork. The sight was horrendous and he vomited great heaping hot chunks. However, the man-like creature was mediocre in his artistry and Will choked on the vomit as it lodged in his throat and he died right there.

Death in hell is never permanent. Will found himself walking along a riverbank. Kicking a stone into the calm waters, he knelt down hurriedly to start his laundry, it was washing day.

Chapter 9

The Virgin's Sacrifice

At first, standing guard in the dark, dank corridor beneath the church had been terrifying. Sounds seemed to creep out of the darkness suggesting activity, sly activity from every hidden corner. It was especially true of the room at the end of the hall.

From that direction, not only was the slyness more pronounced, she could also hear screams and sometimes a knocking that would go on and on, until she was just out of her mind. But worse than the sounds was the silence. It was as if someone or something was listening for her and when it became too quiet she would feel a great desire to stay absolutely still and her eyes would be wide in the weak light.

Sister Mary Agatha's first shift had come at 8am just after Jim and Father Alba had gone off to get Eric Milner. That had been almost a day ago and during those long hours, she and Sean Shay had taken turns, three hours on, three hours off, sitting alone in the corridor. And now, after so long a time, the dark and the sly sounds no longer held the same heavy fear as before and it was becoming almost routine to hear the screams.

They had been worried at first that the children of the orphanage would hear the noise, but with the walls down here being so thick and the door so heavily built, the cries were imperceptible even when standing at the top of the stairs. Moreover, the screams weren't nearly as constant or as loud as they had been and the nun had the dreadful thought that the man was dying, being eaten alive from the inside out, by the demon. The notion shivered her and she glanced at glowing face of her watch, 3:26 am.

Time was different down in the corridor. It had only been three minutes since she last checked her watch, but it felt like ten. She was starting to have to fight the urge to look at it every few seconds and she wondered if this was how addicts felt.

Her wrist and the tiny contraption on it would frequently come up to eye level unbidden and she took to holding her hand over it, just to stop herself. But sometimes, out of the blue she'd see the watch right in front of her face and would realize she had let her mind wander and her wrist, left unattended, would feel the need to do its duty and show her that time was indeed moving at a snail's pace.

She blamed Jim Anderson.

Her mind fixated on him and after every check of her now hated watch, his smiling face would float out of the darkness and gloat at her. Father Alba had returned after dinner, disappointingly without the sword and perhaps worse, without either Jim or Eric Milner. He had told them that Jim would be coming soon, and along with the sword, he was unfortunately bringing some crazy girl back with him. However, he hadn't shown up and as the night progressed, the priest was getting terribly nervous for Jim, but she wasn't.

The nun couldn't picture any girl hurting a man his size and she thought it most likely that he was set up in some nice hotel and would be back later that morning. She pictured him sitting in one of those fancy Jacuzzi bathtubs and she imagined his great size overflowing the hot water, wasting it and she ground her teeth. Sister Mary had always wanted to try out one those tubs and she now pictured herself in it instead of Jim.

"Oh my!" she said quietly. It might have been all the coffee she'd been drinking to keep herself awake or the thought of the Jacuzzi, but either way, she felt a sudden great need to use the bathroom.

"Uhhh!" she was never quiet getting up out of the folding chair. Her size and her bad hip along with her age, made getting out of any chair quietly, an impossibility. But it was worse with the uncomfortable steel thing that dug into her spine and cut the circulation off from her legs.

Once up, she pressed her knuckles into her lower back and stretched, however the nagging pain there wasn't relieved. She hadn't really expected it to be. It would likely be with her for the next couple of days, she thought as she waddled, in a slightly more pronounced waddle due to her stiffness. Though she had to use the bathroom, she first went to the door at the far end of the hall to listen.

There were no sounds that her aging ears could detect; however there was plenty of smell. The demon had been down in that black pit of a room for just over a day and had not once asked to use the bathroom, but somehow the smell was worse than it should have been. It was the smell of a rotting corpse, not a body freshly killed but one that was wet with decomposition and its nasty aroma crept along the cracks of the heavy door and it made her wince.

But there wasn't a body in the room, there couldn't be.

When the demon had demanded this particular room, both Father John and Father Alba had accompanied the man in, while she had stood in the doorway. The room looked as it always had—dark. Even with the light bulb swinging on its chain overhead, the room was dim and the shadows were large and had a physical presence, but there were no bodies and the smell was only that of fetid mildew and deteriorating wood. However, in the late afternoon of the day before, the smell had blossomed fully formed, and had sent the nun scurrying for Father John and Sean Shay.

They had stood outside the door and the smell had walked among them and covered them with its richness and with its evil. They had called out to the possessed man but had only received screams in answer. They mutually decided, with an unspoken agreement, that it was in everyone's best interest not to open the door.

Since then, the stench hadn't abated at all and it was an effort for the nun to keep from gagging as she kept her head bent down next to the door. There seemed to be no sign of life from the other side, but she had a terrible feeling that the demon was just there, just on the other side, listening for her, even as she listened for it. Stepping back away, she moved with the greatest silence she could manage down the sixty-foot hall to the stairs.

She didn't like the idea of leaving her post with the feeling of the demon being so aware, but nature was pushing at the tired walls of her bladder and she had to go.

Coming abreast of the folding chair, the old lady paused to grab her coffee mug and gave a single look back, the door was barely visible and she got a slight case of the shivers.

"We need the police," she whispered. Without Eric Milner she was suddenly more than willing to overlook her past grievances with the police. She'd gone so far as to beg both priests to bring in more officers.

Sister Mary had been overruled.

The disquieting fear that thrummed through her body had made her nearly impervious to logic and the fact that they were harboring a known fugitive, was simply a technicality to her. She could understand not involving the entire police force, but she simply couldn't get past the insistence of the two priests, that no one else be told.

They could at least bring in some more priests or deacons...or even some more nuns, maybe younger nuns. Nuns whose knees didn't pop and make that awful crunching sound as they climbed the stairs.

"Hail Mary mother of God, pray for us sinners..." the words a dry habit, slipped out of her thin wrinkled lips almost on their own accord.

She was gone from the corridor for only seven minutes, but in that time she had mumbled her way through twelve prayers and it would've been more, however she paused frequently to take small sips of her coffee on her return trip.

Each of her shifts contained at least one bathroom break and as refreshing as it was to get out of the reeking corridor, having to go back in, made it not worth it. Her nose and her stomach had to get re-acquainted with the smell, which was bad, and she would have to get used to the anxious fear, which was worse, but it was the near complete dark that made her reluctant steps back down the stairs, a slow motion terror.

The one dim bulb in the center of the corridor only gave enough light to make the shadows larger, adding a tactile dimension to them, making them physical.

To get to her little chair Sister Mary had to walk past three open doors and it was a hated ritual of hers to look into the blackness of each room. Some sort of sinister presence hid within them and when she walked by her heart always sent her a warning of its age, as it thumped mightily in her chest. Had they been furnished with a light switch she would've lit each one by then, however the rooms held a single light bulb strung from the ceiling and she lacked the courage to brave the dark. What would her hands find as she weaved about, swinging her arms in order to locate the invisible chain? Her imagination kept her from making the attempt.

The chair, with its feeble yellowed bulb above it, was an island of safety for her and when she settled her weight onto it, she couldn't stop her wrist as it came up to her face, 3:38 am.

"Uhhg," she groaned aloud and then began, "Our Father who art in Heaven..." She'd go through her top forty at least once before getting up again.

The chair was just too uncomfortable and it was her habit to check the door at the end of the hall periodically if only to stretch her legs. This time she buzzed through her prayers quicker than usual...something was different about the corridor. Something she couldn't quite figure out and her fear ratcheted up with her every breath.

Far too soon she finished her set of prayers and sat there not wanting to move, not wanting to draw attention to herself. Time clicked slowly by...very slowly and her watch, against her will, appeared before her face, 3:47 am.

She almost groaned aloud again, but something inside stopped her. The demon was listening for her again but this time she had the feeling that she was being watched as well.

That was bad, however what was worse, was the small noise that came from the room down the hall back toward the stairs.

It couldn't be explained away. It had a live feel to it. Accompanying the sound was a presence, thick with malice—and from the depths of the pitch-black room, she knew something looked out at her. She tried to peer in, but the thing was in alliance with the darkness and hid within its inky bosom and her growing fear rattled her bones about beneath her skin.

The room and whatever it was it held, sat between her and the stairs and suddenly, quite unbelievably, she felt it might be safer to be in the room with the demon than out in the corridor alone. Holding her breath, she pushed herself up slowly, without her customary grunting, and walked backwards away from the chair. With growing anxiety Sister Mary dug for the key to the room, searching and re-searching her pockets and it was with fantastic relief that she found it.

Now she was torn between her fear of the demon and her fear of the dark, and being this close to the foul smelling door, it made her second guess wanting to go into the room. In fact, the smell of death was worse than it had been and she turned and sniffed at the door, her face contorted by revulsion. Quite suddenly, the single light in the tunnel went out behind her and she stood nearly alone in the jet black.

The bulb hadn't burned out, the chain had been purposely yanked, and she could still hear the light: chink...chink...chink of it slapping the side of the bulb.

Her heart seized up and her breathing ceased. The only part of her that felt alive, were her eyes and these grew to tremendous proportions as she strived to see into the darkness. The darkness was infinite however. It stretched away from her for miles and miles in every direction, yet at the same time, it was close. The darkness hugged her greedily to it, wrapping itself around her, making her a living part of it.

The nun was not the only thing living in the darkness...the folding chair moved with a little scraping sound against the floor. The sound shot through her body, bringing with it a rush of adrenaline that had her heart beating again and her lungs pumping. She spun madly to the door, uncaring of the danger on the other side of it and searched within the blackness for the doorknob. Again and again, her hands swept up and down the flat heavy wood, feeling the old and peeling paint, but not the knob.

Behind her the chair made a long, slow scraping sound, as if pushed by a hulking menace. In terror she whipped her head around, peering uselessly into the unending darkness—it held nothing but the sound of the chair scritching along and her breath, which was loud and harsh. The old lady turned back to the door and her hand struck the knob, she fumbled for it, lost it, but then touched it again. She held it tight, fearing it would move out of reach in the darkness and frantically tried to get the key into the slot.

The chair overturned behind her with a loud clatter,

but she didn't look this time, there was no point. "Oh God, please help me," she begged the nothingness in front of her and like a miracle the key slid into the hole and the knob turned. She felt the smallest moment of happiness and then the stench struck her full force. Wavering, she almost didn't go into the room. The smell had a physical presence, an acid that burned her nose and made her gag.

However, it wasn't the smell that had her in a panic of indecision about stepping across the threshold; she was struck with a sudden incredible fear of falling. When she'd opened the door, the view in front of her was exactly as the one behind her. It was as if she had opened an invisible door to a black world and even though the small part of her that could still reason told her the floor of the room was as flat as the hallway, the rest of her mind rebelled. It felt as though the floor ended just in front of her and that she stood upon the edge of a tremendous chasm of black.

"Sisssster?" the voice of the possessed man called out softly from behind or at least she thought it was behind her. In the darkness, directions had lost all meaning and she suddenly didn't know if she was facing the corridor or the room. But it didn't matter, the voice was full of malicious intent and after only the slightest pause, she took a cautious half-step forward, still clinging to the invisible knob of the door. When her foot landed upon cement, she quickly took two more shuffling steps and was in the room. She hauled the door shut behind her and threw her weight against it, scrambling again to find the key hole.

In a second, the door was locked.

Now she waited—gasping and panting—fully

expecting the demon to launch itself at the door. In her mind it had grown to outrageous proportions, filling the darkness and she prayed in her speeding, mumbling fashion for the door to hold against the weight of the thing. Seconds ticked by and her mouth filled with the nasty dead smell of the room; it was putrid and she wanted to spit but a thought occurred to her. If the demon was out there...maybe the man was here.

"Uh...sir? Mr...Ba'al?" At the moment, she didn't know if that was the man's name or the demon's. "Are you in here? Could you turn on the light?" There was no sound in the room, but then a knocking came at the door and she leapt in startled, frightened surprise. Harder she pushed up against the door and how it was possible, she didn't know, but her fear grew stronger and her panting kept getting quicker and shallower. The knock came again and she jumped just as before and clung to the doorknob with all her might.

"Go away," she cried out in a high scared voice.

"Let me in...I left something in there."

She caught herself foolishly looking around at the blackness. "Ba'al, there's nothing in here," she replied with a touch more strength.

"Yes there is. My snack is in there," it said.

Her brain whirled over the last thirty or so hours and she realized they had brought him nothing to eat. It was she that he was after.

"No Ba'al, we had a deal! The sword for the children. That was the deal," she pleaded.

"I have a new deal..."

She didn't want to hear the new deal...she knew *she* was part of the deal. A pain began to spread in her chest, making it hard to breath. "No, Ba'al please no.

We have a deal already; the sword will be here soon. Ok? Please stay out there."

"Stay out? Your walls can't hold me, if I don't want them to...feel."

Both of her hands still rested on the doorknob and despite the fact that it had just been locked it began to turn beneath her fingers. She tried to grip it tighter but her sweat made it so she could barely hold it at all and the knob continued all the way and then, though her full weight was hard up against it, the door opened just a crack.

She screamed into the black, "No please no, Ba'al we have a deal, ok?" Sister Mary's panic was near complete and she almost went running off into the darkness, chasm be damned, but suddenly the knob turned to the left and the door shut.

"I was supposed to have my path by now...that deal is gone, but I have a new one. Except you have to want it. You have to beg me for it." The possessed man's voice, though muffled was now more man than demon and she could understand it just a bit better.

"No, I want the old deal...it's very fair I think."

"Don't you want to even hear the new deal?"

"No. No I don't. I want the old deal!" The new deal would hurt, she knew it. Her fear was horrendous; she was losing control of her muscles and she shook from head to toe in the darkness. Her hands repeatedly slipped off the knob and she had to wipe them on her habit every second or so to keep any sort of grip. Her mind began to go over a litany of tortures she'd heard about, but then the demon spoke again, interrupting her.

"I will do you a favor and tell you anyways..."

"No!" she screamed.

"Here's the deal..."

"NO!"

"I want to kill tonight...before the sun comes up," he said. "Now, I think you are worth six of those boys up there..."

"Nooooo!" She was in misery and the word she screamed was a long terrified wail.

"You haven't even heard my proposal yet." He seemed a little pouty over this. "Now don't be too quick to answer...do I kill you or six of your boys?"

Sister Mary Agatha felt like she was just about to float away into the black. Numbness spread out through her entire body and in the darkness, it seemed as though she were evaporating. She wondered vaguely if she were about to faint and even as she thought it, she did.

A half-second later, she hit the floor hard, smacking the side of her head and face on the cement. It snapped her back to her terrifying reality and she weakly scrambled to the door, only to find a wall where the door had been.

"Sissster?" The word came from her right. She crawled toward the sound, and her questing fingers touched the door. She pulled herself up using the knob as a grip and stood there trying not to fall back over, speechless.

"Sissster?" He was a little more impatient this time. "That's ok...I understand. You can't find it within you, to tell me to go kill six little boys. Just remain silent and I will take it we have a deal."

"I...I...I," she couldn't form the words, she couldn't form any words.

"I what? You or the boys...if I don't get a firm decision, I will make it seven."

"No...I..." her mouth hung open and the putrid stench was no longer a factor, only her fear was important. It was everything and even though she loved her boys she couldn't bring herself to say the words that might let them live.

"Seven it is then...good! That's what I hoped you would say..."

"No," she whispered it in the weakest manner.

"I'll be back in the morning...I think I will start with the little red headed one. Who wants a red headed kid anyways, right?"

"No, not Jeremy! Please no." His precious face appeared in living color in her mind and she realized then that she was crying. She touched her face and habit, they were soaked and she wondered how long her tears had been falling.

"Not Jeremy?" the demon asked, considering. "Then you pick the seven."

"I can't"

"Then open the door and invite me in." He said it quietly and she knew that he was evil beyond any man that had ever been.

She turned the knob with numb hands and a part of her hoped that she would faint again. The door opened only a little way, perhaps a foot and then it stopped, held there by the possessed man just beyond. Sister Mary gave a little gasp and the breath that she drew in from the corridor was amazingly fresh compared to the poisonous rot of the room she was in.

"Before you agree," he began softly and she jumped back, his voice was far closer than she expected. "Are you sure you really want to do this? It's only seven boys and we both know, nobody really wants these children anyways, right Sister?"

"Don't hurt them...I'll do anything, just don't hurt them."

"That's it? You aren't going to fight me or scream?" he asked with bogus amazement. She knew screaming would be a waste of time. When the demon had first walked into his room, the one he had chosen, he had screamed bloody murder, but it had been impossible to hear, even just above in the church. At the time she had been thankful.

"No I won't scream...just...you can't hurt the boys...that's the deal." She felt the tiniest amount of courage seep into her wretched miserable soul, but he took it away again in the next second.

"But I want you to scream. Don't you know what I'm going to do to you?" He was very reasonable sounding and that made his evil all the worse. She figured that he was not driven by insanity, but by a lust for pain and she knew it would be terrible.

"I think so," she mumbled the lie. She didn't really know what he would do but only knew that it would hurt. Thinking about it made her aware of her body again...she couldn't stop her old muscles from shaking and her legs were threatening to buckle beneath her.

"You don't know, Sister. Tell me you are virgin, please." He paused breathing heavily, waiting for her response but her own breath stuck in her throat. She was a virgin. Even as a youngster, she had been homely and instead of fighting her genes, she had decided to save herself for God.

"I can't hear you Sister...before you die, am I going to be your first?"

Her legs did indeed buckle beneath her and she

held to the knob with the last of her strength. There was a spinning sensation but with the blackness there was nothing to spin and she could only pant like a dog and the only other sound was a tiny, lipp...lipp...lipp, as her tears struck the floor.

"I told you, you didn't know...but I think you got me all wrong. I'm not going to rape you. I mean you're old and fat and ugly. Why would I want to rape you? I would rather kill those children, so if you don't want that, you're going to have to convince me to fuck you. But I don't see how you will, short of begging. Come on ya old saggy slut, beg me, or am I going to make it eight?"

The number eight came to her from a mile away and it brought her back again from the precipice of fainting. "No not eight...you can't." But he could. There was no way she could stop him. "Ok...ok. Please come...um do the uh..." She didn't know how to beg for it.

"I don't think your heart is into it...don't worry you tried." The door started to shut from the other side.

"No, please...I want you...uhh badly um, please make love to me?"

"Not! Good! Enough!" he roared the words at her. In terror she stepped back into the room and lost her hold on the door. She panicked at this and swung her arms about wildly, only the room seemed to have expanded greatly because she didn't come in contact with anything. Up and down began to lose meaning and she half-fell, half-sat hard upon the floor and sobbed there, blubbering loudly in the endless dark.

"This is my fault," the demon said and his voice seemed far away. "You're new at this...I like that...it gets me hard. Now I've always wanted to do a nun, so I'm going to help you. Say this: Oh yeah fuck me hard!"

Her mind rebelled against it and she had trouble saying anything with her crying so heavily, but she finally whimpered, "O-yeah...fuck me...hard."

"Now say, oh baby, that's right do me good." He was closer, somewhere in the room.

Sister Mary Agatha curled into a ball and said to the floor, the only part of the world with any substance, "Oh-baby-that's right-do me good...Hail Mary mother of God..." Pain suddenly exploded in her back.

"No praying...except for when you say: *Oh God! Oh God!*" He laughed maliciously and then he loomed over. She could feel him hot above her. "Now take off your clothes you little slut," he whispered with excitement in his voice.

"Ohhh nooo," she cried in quiet misery but took off her clothes all the same until she lay naked upon them, her body shivering with the cold and the terror.

Now there was only a painful silence, and it seemed that the demon had moved away. For a second hope flared that he had left her—that it had all been a cruel joke but then the door to room closed with a finality that sent a shiver down her soul and when he suddenly touched her in the darkness, she screamed. The darkness swallowed her many screams and no ears would ever hear them.

Chapter 10

Talitha Meets Jim

"Lisa."

It was a whisper in his dreams.

"Lisa."

Jim cracked an eye and saw that the girl was awake. He blinked rapidly, feeling the grit and the exhaustion. For some reason Talitha refused to look at him and she went silent with the slightest apprehension on her face as he stirred. He scowled slightly at her, not liking to be ignored, but she ignored that too.

Their silence drew out and he eyed her closely. She wasn't much to look at, despite the fact that she had slept more than anyone in the house, if indeed a coma was actually sleep. Her dress, the same one that she had worn to church the previous day was stained with hard dried blood. Her hair was tangled and stiff, again with blood and he didn't envy her trying to get it all out.

The girls hands, still tied to the bed posts were a repulsive purple and Jim suffered a slight pang of guilt at the sight, but since the restraints were a necessity he tried to look past them. Her face held relatively little of the red/brown smears and she looked healthy and well rested despite the gunshot wound to the back of her head.

She was the only one in the house who could make any claim to being well rested. The night had been easily the worst night Jim could remember and he rubbed hard at his eyes trying to clear the sleep from them. When he looked back at the girl, she still wasn't looking at him though at least had turned to face him slightly.

What a peach, he thought testily and before he could stop himself, he yawned in a great opened mouth gape, forgetting to cover his mouth until he was nearly done. She ignored that as well, staring off at the wall to his right. He figured he was seeing the *good* Talitha, since this one had a different, almost vacant look to her eyes, while the *bad* Talitha had always eyed him with such unsettling perception. The other one had been quite the talker as well; this good one, just sat their mutely.

The silence stretched from seconds to minutes, until the usually taciturn man felt an odd need to say something. It was odd in that he was uncomfortable instigating any type of conversation, especially with a pretty girl. They were generally insensitive, if not outright cruel. However, even the average person could be difficult for him to talk to since he had found out a long time ago that his opinions were basically not wanted.

Jim appeared to be a big stupid oaf and almost no one beside Father Alba ever looked past his exterior. This was true even in school where he was passed along every year with no expectations placed on him whatsoever, except to play football. College was no different. He got into Syracuse on a football scholarship, and the moment he blew out his knee it was understood that he should give up the remains of his scholarship and move on. Even though he still had a right to it, he left school; he wasn't going to stay where he wasn't wanted.

He made an exception that morning—Talitha clearly didn't want him around. When nearly fifteen minutes had passed, Jim couldn't take the silence anymore.

"Are those ropes too tight? They look painful."

She said nothing to this; she simply continued to stare at the wall; however her lips pursed the smallest amount and Jim realized how stupid his question sounded. Embarrassment reddened his ears and he looked down feeling like an idiot.

Talitha must have seen his discomfort. "They're properly tight...you don't want them any looser." Her head inclined toward him. "You were at the church weren't you? I could smell the Irish Spring on you; my brother uses that brand of soap as well."

"Yeah, I was there." He hoped his discomfort didn't show. He'd been told that she suffered from schizophrenia and it was strange to have to re-introduce himself to her. "My name is, uh, Jim Anderson and..." He trailed off wondering if he was he going to have to repeat the entire conversation he'd shared with her other self.

She paused only the slightest before saying, "You probably already know this, my name is Talitha Jern. It's nice to meet you Jim. I noticed there was the slightest hesitation when you said your last name...is that your real last name?"

Her brother seemingly had a magic power to see the future and Talitha's other self had read his thought with such accuracy he wondered if she was indeed a mind reader. Perhaps this Talitha would be more truthful.

"Can you tell what I'm thinking or something?" He

felt stupid for asking, but she smiled sweetly in that slightly unfocused way.

"No, I'm just perceptive. What is your real last name?"

He told her that he didn't have one and then he told her a great many things about himself that he had rarely, if ever, told anyone. For him it was a bizarre conversation, in that it flowed easily and naturally from topic to topic, as if they were best friends. This was a first for Jim and he figured it was due to the girl's *perception*. Though she claimed it wasn't, it sure seemed like mind reading to him and for the first time in his life, he opened up to a woman.

There seemed no logical reason to hold back since she could tell a lie from a mile away. Moreover, unlike many people and her evil twin in particular, she didn't stare at his ugly features and this diminished his self-consciousness considerably.

When he glanced at his watch he was amazed that an hour had passed during their talk. "Wow, we've talked for just over an hour...or should I say, I've talked for an hour." She had steered the conversation away from herself at every opportunity, which he hadn't even noticed until now. "Lisa tells me you program computers or some such, do you like doing that?"

"Yes I do...I like your voice," she said with a distant smile. "It's so deep, that I can feel it on my skin when you talk. It's like the foghorn on an island I used to live on."

"BEEE-OOOHH!" He mimicked a foghorn, his voice coming out in the deepest bass. "The kids at the orphanage like it when I do that."

"An orphanage...that's nice of you. Tell me, is it

only a place for unwanted children? Or are there, uh, adults there?"

"Oh yeah, there are three nuns on staff, and then there's Sean and I, we're counselors for the kids." Jim said, suddenly proud of his work.

"Oh...I see. Tell me about the orphanage. The sound of your voice makes it seem like home."

"It sure is, but first you need to talk about you. There was a question about computers that you dodged...is it really boring, I ask because it looks boring."

"I don't want to talk about myself," she replied with a half frown. She continued her practice of not looking him in the eyes, but was staring at his stomach so much that he involuntarily looked down to see if he had spilled some food. There was nothing there.

Jim sucked in his stomach a little. "I had heard that talking about things was supposed to be good for you."

Her frown deepened. "There's nothing about me that I want to talk about. Let's talk about something else or let's not talk at all."

He smiled inwardly; her little threat had stung him more than he would've thought possible. "Sure, we can talk about something else," he agreed amiably. "Programming computers can't be anything but boring anyways."

"Don't make assumptions, Jim. It can lead to trouble," she said this with a small smile and it lightened Jim's heart to see it.

"You don't make assumptions...ever?" he asked cocking his head to catch her eye. But just then, she looked down at her bedding and gave a little shake of her head.

"I won't say never," she answered. "But I try only to judge things for what they are, in the context, in which they were meant to be interpreted."

"Me too," he said, suddenly self-conscious for the first time during their conversation. She was clearly far smarter than he was. "But even though I try...I still do it, uh make assumptions that is."

"Well that's good, Jim. It's good that you can admit to it. It's not often you find someone who's so willing to admit to a character flaw."

"Do I say thank you to that?" he spoke with a smirk and she smiled as well. "Do you have any character flaws that you'd confess to?"

He had meant for it to be just a light joke, but her face froze in mid-smile and then as she turned away it went into a blank looking stare. "You've seen me already, Jim. You know my flaws."

He couldn't believe how ridiculously insensitive he'd just been and his mind flailed around searching for something to say that would show what he had truly meant.

"I...I only meant this side of you...uh, I kinda assumed that since your other self is so, uh bad, that you," he pointed at her for emphasis, but she ignored him completely. "The good you, would be all good...you know what I mean?"

"What did I say about assuming? Jim? Can you do me a little favor? Can you please look at my head? It feels big...almost like a pumpkin." Her smile froze on her face, and her eyes held a trace of nervousness.

Talitha tilted her head away and he leaned forward in his chair, inspecting the bandaged wound. There didn't appear to be any swelling that he could see from around the bandages. It was hard to see through her hair, which was thick and matted with blood. He wondered briefly, how they were going to bathe her and an image of him washing her popped into his mind and he hung onto the image a touch too long.

"Is it ok, Jim?"

He jumped a little. "Oh yeah, uh, no swelling. You look ok back here...well actually it looks gross." He started sweeping away the dried blood from her pillow, but more of it rained down from her head and he stopped.

"I hope you don't find me rude but I'm just going to face this way for a bit, it was becoming uncomfortable facing that direction for so long," she said and Jim couldn't image how anything was going to relieve her discomfort short of cutting her loose.

"Sure, that's no big deal, here." Picking up his chair, he walked it over to the other side of the bed, and plunked it down quietly. He didn't want to wake Lisa or Will; their night had been even worse than his own. When he'd sat back down, he said evenly, "Now you know, you dodged another question. Does your good side have any flaws?"

The girl sat quiet for a moment. "Did Lisa tell you what she was going to name the baby?"

Jim laughed quietly. "You won't answer, will you?"

"No."

"Then you're practically forcing me to make assumptions."

"You have free will, Jim. Use it." She was cool to him but at least she was still talking, which he took to be a good sign.

"How about this? Since you won't talk about you,

how bout you tell me...what about you, is not true, but everyone thinks is true? That's not talking about you. It's talking about what others think of you."

"Tricky, tricky, but it won't work. I don't know anyone that doesn't already know all about me. Except you of course and we already discovered your silly assumption." She gave him a faint smile, which he returned broadly.

"Ok, how bout before? Before all this happened to you?" He was happily surprised that she was obviously thinking about his question.

"Some people thought that I could dance, when I never could." She said it quietly, as if it was a secret shame that he shouldn't share with anyone.

"That's funny. When I was a kid, I thought all girls had beautiful penmanship and that they could all naturally sing and dance well."

The indistinct smile on her face firmed up at this. "My handwriting is pretty good, but I can't sing or dance."

"That doesn't seem too bad. Did it bother you? You know people thinking a good thing about you?"

She saddened and her eyes dropped to the bed. "No, it was just that I was disappointed with myself. I thought I was going to be a natural dancer...like my mom, but it never happened. And despite secretly practicing, I was terrible."

"I'd bet I'm worse than you, but who knows?" He'd never danced before. Not a single time. He looked down with a tired melancholy, glad for the moment that she didn't like to look at him. He didn't want her reading his face just then, but when he looked up she was staring not at him, but through him it seemed.

"Why wouldn't you know?" she asked. "A person has to know if he can dance or not. Are you saying you've never been in a dance contest?"

"Nope. Never been in one, but you're changing the subject again. We were talking about your dancing." In truth, he wanted the subject changed badly.

She shrugged as best as she was able with her hands outstretched, tied to the posts. "What is there more to say? I can't dance. You know...part of my problem was they kept changing the dances. I would learn the *Hustle* only to find out everyone was on to a completely new dance. They were like month long dance fads and I couldn't keep up. Do they still do that?"

Jim didn't follow dancing at all. "I don't think so...there was this song a few years back, *Thriller* by Michael Jackson and there was some sort of dance that went with it."

"Michael Jackson? The boy from the Jackson 5?" she asked. She looked up at him for the answer, their eyes met briefly, and his heart felt suddenly bigger in his chest.

"Uh...no, I mean yeah. He does his own songs now. I saw *Thriller* at this bar once, I didn't get what the big deal was."

"You saw it? Were you at a discotheque?" She smiled prettily at his loud guffawing. "What is it?"

"No, it was on video. You're like a time capsule. By the way, disco is dead...long gone," he said. She kept smiling at him and he had trouble looking at her. He wouldn't have thought it possible but he realized that he liked Talitha and he was afraid that she would see it in his eyes.

"I for one am glad it's gone," she replied. "I was definitely not a fan...chamber music is more my style."

He felt like a moron but said, "I don't know what that is...I-I've never heard of it."

"You have heard of classical music of course. Chamber music is actually like that but on a smaller scale, thus the term chamber suggesting it can be played in a small room," she answered and looked a little bashful doing it. "It's no wonder I can't disco-dance right?"

He chuckled. "Disco-dance...it's been such a long time since I heard that phrase. But you can dance to chamber. I went to the ballet once with some kids from the orphanage and it was all chamber." His voice had risen from its normal base into a baritone and he realized he'd just got excited. Despite the girl's reluctance to look at him, he composed his face into a stony block of neutralism.

That he loved the ballet was not something he was going to tell Talitha. She'd laugh at him and he knew that it would be painful coming from her, especially now.

That one time at the ballet, with him stuffed into his best suit, sweating the fact that the seams were threatening to let go at the slightest cough, had been all it took for him to fall in love with it. But it was a secret love and an unfulfilled one.

The slight lithe bodies of the woman and the strong but agile bodies of the men had enraptured him. There movements, so fluid yet still so exact, had him mesmerized and dreaming, wishing that he could look that way, dance that way. It was all so fantastic to him, yet he'd never gone back and never would. It was just another place where he wasn't wanted. And not just by the unfortunate people seated behind him, whose view consisted solely of his massive shoulders, it was everyone.

He'd been openly gaped at, and laughed at, and whispered about. It might have been all in his head, but the eyes darting away from him, followed by mocking laughter cut him to the bone. He knew how he looked next to all the fine people in their expensive clothes— like an ogre, and they stared and stared.

The suit he wore was his only one and it had been let out so much, there was nothing left to let out. He had gone to the restroom and was startled by his own appearance, not just by the cheap suit, but also by his face, which was an unhealthy red. His shirt had taken him ten minutes to button at the collar and choked him terribly, but he didn't feel he could undo the button. There were men in tuxedos and ladies in beautiful gowns and his clothes looked already like a beggar's compared to them. Ducking his head in shame, he had returned to his seat, knowing he would never go back to the ballet and he hadn't.

Talitha was frowning slightly, staring at his mouth, which he realized was hanging open. He shut it with a snap and her smile returned abruptly, she said, "Ballet? I'm the worst at ballet. You have to be graceful and smooth...I'm not a klutz or anything, I'm just not ballet material." Jim pictured the memory of her dropping down into a spin, sweeping her brother's legs out from beneath him and then flowing back up, only to leap forward.

"Your other self is pretty agile, maybe you are too. Have you tried to uh, dance since, uh...since?"

"No, dancing isn't on my mind much. I just read my books and write code. You asked if programming is boring. It is, but in a good way. I can focus on it and it keeps me from thinking of...stuff." Her face was growing cloudy and despondent.

He saw that going down the road of discussing computers was a dead end, so he shifted back to dancing, "Uh, your mom was a dancer? What kind?"

Talitha smiled her finest smile yet and Jim couldn't help but smile too. He liked it when she was happy, it lit up her face and made her eyes come alive. But for some reason those sparkling eyes never would look into his for very long. It was as if she wouldn't or couldn't stand to look at his eyes for more than a second. It was a little depressing for him, but it was also more than any other woman had given him in a long time.

"My, mom? She was a ballerina, supposedly the finest ballerina in all of Omaha. Maybe in all of Nebraska since there is not that much outside of Omaha."

"That sounds nice. Is the ballet big in Nebraska?" he asked.

Her smile had drifted off of him, but when he spoke, it shifted back and he looked to catch her eyes, but she stared past him perhaps thinking of Nebraska. He felt the keen edge of foolish disappointment when she refused to look at him and he tried to reign in his feelings, which had been growing with every second he spoke with her.

"No, Nebraska is not the place for a dancer. When my mom she saved up enough money she moved to New York."

"Is that where she met your dad?" he asked with

genuine interest.

"No she didn't meet my dad there...she starved there. You see the finest dancer in all of the great state of Nebraska, makes you number ten thousand in New York." She sighed as if it were her dreams that had faded away under the lights of Broadway.

"So what did she do?"

"I don't know. Worked I suppose, but she left New York for a spot in a small time dance company in Connecticut and that's where she met my dad. They fell in love and she gave up any chance at her dream to be with him."

He shook his head, wondering what it must be like to give up your dreams. His own dream was as simple as it was unlikely to attain, he wanted to be normal. He wanted not to be this giant freak of a man. "Wow, gave up her dreams just like that."

"Yes, love makes you do the craziest things." Her voice came out from deep within her and it was a hollow whisper, devoid of any strength. Her smile had become a thin line on her clouded face and her eyes suddenly brimmed with tears.

Jim knew what she had done to the last man that had loved her. Lisa had told him the story during the long agonizing hours they'd spent together the night before and now he sat there speechless. Not knowing what to say, he kept his eyes down so as not to embarrass her and they became mired in another long silence.

"Have you ever been in love?" she asked quietly.

He swallowed hard, wishing she'd asked about anything else. His history of relationships was short and cold. He'd never loved anyone and no one had ever loved him, and even though he had been in a few relationships, they hadn't gone anywhere. The only type of girls he seemed capable of attracting were very large women and with each it became obvious they were with him strictly because the alternative was to be alone.

On these rare occasions, he'd tried to be a good boyfriend, but eventually their baggage and selfish desires would drive him away. He knew it would be different if they'd ever liked him for who he was, but he always felt like a servant catering to their needs, without his needs even being noticed. And unlike them, he preferred to be alone.

"No...never been in love." There was bitterness in his own voice and he kept his eyes averted from Talitha.

"Oh, I'm sorry. But sometimes that may be for the best," she added trying to make the fact that he was unloved an ok thing. It grated on him and he became slightly angry that a beautiful, intelligent girl would presume to tell him, that it was all right not to be loved.

"You're wrong...it's not for the best." The conversation was an acute embarrassment for him and coupled with the lack of sleep over the past two nights his irritation grew.

She seemed slightly upset to be told she was wrong and said with growing ire, "You don't know...the alternative could be..."

He cut her off, "In this case you're wrong, Talitha. It's always better to have loved and lost than..."

"Shut up." Talitha said this dangerously quiet and her eyes flashed with black anger. "That saying is crap! I wish you could trade..." With her jaw working back and forth in rage, she stopped in midsentence, making

Jim wonder if he was seeing the other Talitha now.

He didn't care which Talitha he was talking to and his resentment over her blindness to his feeling came out in his voice. "Ha! You wish you could trade places with me? I know what happened to you...and it's the worst thing I can imagine, but, you are loved..."

"I killed the only boy who ever loved me," she broke in icily and with menace. "I didn't *lose* him. I tore his throat out. Now please tell me again, how it's better that I *lost* this love?"

Her words were a knife in the continuum of his soul, but she hadn't said anything he didn't already know. "I still believe it."

"Then you are as stupid as you look."

"And you're blind to what you have! I was told that you were smart but I'm not seeing it. Can you tell me what unconditional love feels like? I can give you the definition, but I've never felt it before, have you?" She refused to answer but only stared off stewing in her anger so he went on, "How many people love you? Damn it, I can't believe you can't see this! Lisa? Your brother? Your mom, your dad? Your little sister...uh, Katie? Brian?"

"Brian's dead...or have you forgotten?"

He ignored her. "At least six people! And at least three of them were willing to give their own lives for you. And two of those were willing to be tortured for you. That is so huge."

Her anger disappeared in her tears that formed large in her eyes. "But, I am...was the one doing the torturing."

"Yeah, but they still loved you. Brian, to the day he died, still loved you. Lisa told me he doted on you every second of every day. I can't believe you're going to pretend you would want what I have, or should I say, don't have? Do you know how many people have loved me unconditionally?"

Her tears became great pools in the dams of her eyes, yet they didn't spill over but grew and she said, "There had to be someone."

"No, I don't think so. My parents threw me away like yesterdays garbage and the closest I ever came was my adoptive parents. They liked me, I hope they loved me, but I only knew them for two months before they died, so I don't know."

"What about a girlfriend? Do...you have one?" The dam finally broke at this and her eyes poured forth their pent up misery. The tears became two small rivers racing each other down her face.

The sight of it emptied Jim of the last of his anger and his heart broke for her. He tried to put a smile in his voice, "What do *you* think? Look at this ugly mug!" She didn't turn her head toward him and he said still lightly, "Am I that repulsive you can't look at me?"

"No, it's not that...I'm just blind." She was so calm in her delivery that he at first didn't catch what she had said.

"You are...what?" he asked in disbelief.

"Blind. The bullet damaged the back lobe of my brain, the occipital lobe. It's where the visual processing center is located in the mammalian brain." She paused as if for a comment but Jim was too stunned by what she was saying and even more, by how she was saying it. She went on still in the calmest manner, "Injury to that portion of the Cerebral Cortex usually results in some vision loss, mine just happens to be total vision loss."

Her mannerisms of the past hour or so came back to him slowly and he felt enormously stupid for not having seen it. "I'm sorry Talitha...this is terrible."

"I'm not sorry at all, Jim. I hope it's permanent."

"What? Why?"

She didn't answer because it was so obvious, her other self would be far less of a threat this way. Instead, she gave a little shrug. "Back to our conversation, which by the way, I was enjoying immensely...I'm sorry I shouted at you." Her tears had stopped at her clinical description of the cause of her blindness, but her face was still damp with them and she looked like a sweet kid after a fall from a bike.

"That's ok...uh, I'm sorry too. Our situations are so..."

He had run out of words and there was a silence again until she said, "I don't think you're ugly by the way."

"You only saw me for a moment," he laughed feeling a funny joy at her words, thankful that she was being so nice.

"Generally, a moment is all I need. As I said, you aren't ugly, though I wouldn't put you in the handsome category either. It's just that you are so startlingly big. When...hold on, there's someone moving about, it's Lisa." An odd anxious expression came over her. "Jim, how do I look, honestly?"

She was a bit of a wreck with light smears of red-brown on her face while her hair was thick and hard looking with the dried blood and it went in all directions. "You've been prettier. There's a little blood on your face and your hair's in need of help."

He went to her and tried to smooth down her hair, he was only slightly successful. Her face was a mask of worry. "Can you get the blood off my face? Is it a lot?"

"It's not a lot, but I don't have a rag or anything," he said.

"Could you just...get it off?" she asked and he knew what she wanted. He stuck his thumb in his mouth and wiped at the blood and did a fairly good job, she grinned at him as he did it. The childlike innocence in her blind eyes made him suck in his breath and it was all he could do, not to bend down and kiss her.

He came to his senses and got off the bed before he could do anything stupid and asked, "Can you hear them? How do you know it's her, maybe it's Will?"

"I feel the vibrations of her steps upon the floor; it comes up through the bedposts and down ropes. I know it's her because she's much lighter." She gave a little laugh and said, "You on the other hand, are like an elephant! I could feel your steps even in my dreams..."

Her laugh froze on her lips for just a moment and then her eyes went wild and tears erupted from them, rolling once again down her cheeks. She began to shake her head back and forth. "No...no...please no! Please, Jim you have to tell me that Will was awake last night. Please!" He couldn't tell if she was begging him for the truth or for him to lie to her.

Chapter 11

A Glimpse into the Void

For Jim the night had been long and loud and horrible, so much so that even thinking about it caused him to feel his chest tighten. However, for Lisa it was as if she was sharing the torturous pain of her husband. Will's screams elicited screams of agony from her and his tears were double only by hers. She'd done everything possible to wake him up, including dousing him with water and when that hadn't worked, they had tried to wake Talitha, but had failed at that as well.

Hour after hour, they stood by his bedside, while he went on screaming in such misery that it hurt Jim even now to think about it. Every once in a while, interspersed with his screams, Will had begged in a high girlish voice. Sometimes he'd begged the torturer to stop, and sometimes he had begged for death. However, the cruel thing to whom he pleaded ignored him and the torture went on and on throughout the entire night.

Lisa was a complete ruin. When just before daylight Will had unexpectedly stopped his cries, she'd sat there weeping with hitching sobs until Jim had gone and hugged her small body to his great one. When Lisa had explained that Will went through this on a weekly basis for his sister, Jim had been staggered and his foolish words: "*You're not much of a brother*," came back to haunt him. Tremendous shame over his stupid ignorance swept him, and he wondered how he could ever face the man again.

That worry was now doubled since he couldn't even look in Talitha's blind face to say, "Yeah, he was asleep. It was, uh..." It was impossible for him to describe.

"No, I can't do this anymore. Jim, help me please. Kill me...I need to die." Her pain at the misery she was causing was written across her face in tears. "Do it now before she comes in! You can say I died in my sleep, Ok? Strangle me...don't worry, it doesn't even hurt much...I've been strangled before, it'll be a mercy."

"No!" he said, and the single word spoken with his deep voice carried all the authority he could muster and it stopped her begging. She sat leaking from the eyes, her chest hitching with each breath.

A minute later, she said, "I'm sorry, Lisa. I didn't mean for it to happen."

"Well it did," Lisa's voice was icy as if from the depths of a blizzard and when she stepped into the room, her cold anger was a presence. "Tell me last night was a bad night. Tell me they're not all like that."

"I don't know," Talitha replied in a small voice. "I'm always asleep. I don't know what happens."

"This is done Talitha. Last night was *the* last night!" Lisa was growing in her anger, while Talitha had become tiny in comparison.

"Yes, of course. I'm so sorry."

"Stop it! You're not sorry. You're hurting him...maybe even killing him." Lisa's anger started to dip below the red-eyed veneer of her exhaustion and she walked over the bed. The bound girl looked deeply remorseful and she tried to hide her wretched face from her sister-in-law, by hanging her head as low as the ropes would allow.

"You're right. I tried to stop him, at first, but he kept coming back. But...but I'll move to...I don't know, somewhere," Talitha murmured through the hair that dangled in front of her face.

"You won't have to move. We're the ones that'll have to move, now that you know where we live, and trust me it'll be far away."

The words stung Talitha; tears, and snot ran down her face, Jim couldn't help it and wiped them away as if she were his child. She shook her head. "No, stop it. Leave me alone. I need to be left alone. Please do move Lisa. I won't look for you. I promise."

Lisa's stony face cracked slightly and a touch of emotion shown through, but it seemed that she shook it off. "You better not. The next time I see you, I plan to shoot to kill. I have to protect my family."

Talitha suddenly looked hopeful. "Kill me now! It's the only way you know you'll be safe."

Lisa stepped back at this and her face showed open shock at the plainly stated request. "I can't do that. Not in cold blood and besides, you might be needed. There's a...a thing going on, but I'll wait for your brother to get up before I say anything else."

The hope fled Talitha's face and she tried to hide behind her hair again. "He's already awake."

There was a heavy pause as Jim and Lisa turned to face the doorway and even though Jim had expected Will to look poor after his ordeal, the man was almost unrecognizable.

His passing summer tan had faded into alabaster and the dark circles under his eyes, that Jim had first noticed at the church were now an unhealthy blue black. Sporadically, the right side of face would come alive with a spastic twitch that would start near his mouth. The muscles jumping beneath his skin would jerk in a staccato up to his eye, causing a rapid involuntary blinking.

Will halted in the doorway as if surprised to find everyone in the room and he eyed them after a nervous guilty fashion. Lisa went to him slowly, obviously as alarmed at his appearance as Jim; Will flinched back from her and looked on the verge of bolting from the room.

"It's ok, honey," she said sweetly, and gradually took him in an embrace, hugging him about the chest. His response shifted from fright to relief and his face started to regain some of its natural color. When Will closed his eyes, a long silence ensued that Jim was afraid to disrupt, and he only watched as Will's facial tic started a leisurely parade across his face.

A moment later, he opened his eyes and seemed to notice Jim for the first time and the big man remembered his guilt. "Uh, good morning, Will," Jim said in his friendliest manner, forming a crooked smile to go along with his bent nose.

Will rubbed at the muscles of his face, looked at Jim and said, "Hello...um, uh." It was clear that he was still trying to come to grips with reality after his dreadful night.

"Jim Anderson, dear." His wife interjected quietly, giving Jim an embarrassed look.

"Jim, right. I remember, I'm sorry, I just had kinda a bad night." At this, his tic did a small racetrack, the muscles chasing themselves hurriedly and Jim could only nod, feeling his crooked smile go plastic, hardening in place at the sight of it.

Lisa gave her husband, who towered over her, a small ineffective push. "Let's get you back to bed. You need to get some sleep, it'll be alright, Talitha is awake now."

"Which Talitha is this?" he asked.

Jim answered from his seat next to her bed, "The good one." His new feelings for her made him want to defend her at every opportunity and he fought the urge to reach out and touch her leg.

"Oh good...what's wrong with your eyes?" He asked her, looking sharply into her face. The concentration brought about a noticeable improvement in Will, his face became reanimated and the bleached look of skin, colored slightly.

Talitha, realizing her head had come up when her brother had entered the room, quickly ducked it back down. "It's nothing, Will...don't worry about me. Why don't you go back to bed? I promise to stay awake. Jim will make sure I do."

Will's face continued to regain a semblance of life but his look of concentration shifted suddenly to one of surprise. "Can you see me?"

"No...but it's nothing," Talitha responded with a large fake smile. "Why don't you go back to bed? I can tell by your voice that you...didn't sleep well."

Lisa came up to the bedside wearing a puzzled look. "You can't see at all?" For emphasis, she waved her hands in front of Talitha face.

"No, but I can feel you waving your hand; it stirs the air."

Will looked aghast. "What are you going...Oh my God, look at your hands! They're purple. We have to loosen those ropes."

He started forward and both women shouted, "No!" in unison. Lisa, shaking her head vigorously, said to Will, "We can't, it's too dangerous." Talitha nodded in agreement.

"But her hands! That color can't be good for them...can't they rot and fall off without proper circulation?" Will looked at his own hands as he said this, acting as if he were seeing them for the first time. His tic was going crazy, drawing Jim's eyes to it, but Will didn't seem to notice it and only continued to stare at his hands.

"What is it, honey? Is it a vision?" Lisa asked with a heart full of worry showing on her face; her hands holding the baby within her protectively.

"No. It's my hands they look so big." Will said, and finally started to rub at the muscles of his face. "It was one of my dreams, it was weird...I was..."

Will stopped speaking and Jim was heartily glad for that. He didn't want to know what would cause a grown man to scream as he had. Lisa also looked ashen face at the prospect. She touched her husband and said, "You can dream normal dreams now. Please go back to bed...you don't look good."

"I can't," he said.

"Yes you can. It'll be alright this time."

"No it's not that, it's those children. I need to do something for them and I've got to do something about Talitha...your poor hands. They can't stay like that, doesn't that hurt?"

"Pain is not only subjective, but relative as well," she said calmly and then each of her hands gave a little twitch that was unpleasant to see. "As for my blindness...sadly it won't be permanent."

Will, ignoring the small tugs from his wife, went to the bedposts and inspected Talitha's hands. "Relative or not, we have to reposition these ropes. Jim, come here and take hold of her arm, just in case."

Jim did as he was asked, settling his bulk on the bed, which sagged significantly under him. As her brother undid the ropes, Jim looked down at Talitha, glad to see she was looking up at him pleasantly and even though she couldn't see it, he flashed his gap-toothed smile at her.

Will eyed Talitha's hand closely, worrying over it. "Jeez, it's so cold. Jim, massage her arm at the bicep and the shoulder." Jim had only just begun, when Talitha drew in a sharp breath.

"It's ok Jim, it's not you. It's just that the return of the blood flow can be invigorating," she said.

He went back to massaging her arm. "Invigorating? You mean it hurts, right?" She gave him a small shrug and he continued, "Are your hands going to be ok?"

"They'll be just fine. It feels better already, go ahead and put the rope back on."

Will who was staring at Talitha's hands, said, "In my dream your hands were all pruney..."

Her arm twitched beneath Jim's hands as she interrupted her brother, "Don't talk about the dreams, please."

"This wasn't one of those dreams...this was almost like a normal dream. You were at this river and you just plopped down and started doing laundry..."

Talitha interrupted him again. "Did you look in the river?" she cried in terrible anguish, her blind eyes wide in panic. Just looking at her made goose bumps rise silently on Jim's arms.

Will seemed taken back by her reaction. "No. I was afraid to. That was the only reason why I knew it wasn't a normal dream...that fear of looking into the water. What was down there? It felt terrible."

"It was nothing," she lied unconvincingly and hid herself with her hair again. Her arm muscle had tightened considerably in his hands and Jim gripped her harder in response, but she didn't seem to notice.

Lisa, who had been watching all this silently, now gave her husband a look that obviously meant he was supposed to demand an answer from his sister, but he was already ahead of her.

"No!" Will said harshly. "That's not going to cut it. We've been dancing around the truth, about you and these dreams...and the other you, the evil you, for too long. Now tell me, what was in that water?"

Talitha's face looked as if her fortress, the one that guarded the remains of her soul had been breached. "Nothing. I'm not lying to you. I stood in that water and touched it many times."

Will buried his face in both hands, sighing heavily. "Talitha, I know you won't lie to me, but you also won't tell me everything. We both know there was something there. Something terrible that you didn't want to see, what was it?"

"It was...I don't...I," she stammered breathless with fear and her arm under Jim's hands kept trying to gesticulate as if it could speak for her. Torn between a perverse curiosity and a desire to protect her from her own memories, Jim could do nothing but look into her blank empty eyes with pity.

"It isn't important. I was just...the river was..." she

went on incomprehensively and then pushed her face into Jim's chest and spoke into the soft flannel of his shirt. "There was nothing in the river, Will. It was the surface...there are images or pictures of stuff that I had been forced to do, horrible things. The river will show you your guilt. It's terrible, but it's better than being tortured and if you keep working hard, you can keep the water moving too much to see the images well."

Jim felt his shirt turning damp—Talitha was crying. Her breath hitched in her chest as she spoke: "I found the place by accident, the other Talitha, she had forced me to go to the pits at Rek, in her place...and I had to go. She was too powerful at that point and I couldn't stop her. But, I decided to try something new. Something I had been practicing in secret: meditation. You know to calm the mind since...since that is all you are in the void."

"Did it work?" Jim couldn't help himself and interrupted her.

She nodded into his shirt. "Yes it did. I suddenly found myself outside...not just outside the pit, but out in the open. There were trees and rocks and dirt. And the river. It was very calm and I could see the hills around me reflected on its surface. I wandered down to it and saw a woman there. She was older than I was, maybe forty and she was plump with black hair and had a hint of a black moustache. She was doing laundry in an old-fashioned manner. Hitting her clothes against the rocks and rubbing at them with a large block of soap." She paused staring into Jim's chest, remembering.

He was about to ask if she was frightened of the woman at all, when she started speaking again. "I don't know why, but it bothered me to see her working like that. She was at it with a focused rhythm and a concentration that I was afraid to disturb. Therefore, not wishing to bother her, I walked away, up into the hills, but as the saying goes, *All roads lead to Rome*, I kept finding myself coming up on the river. This started to aggravate me, which began to erode my concentration and I feared that I would return to the pits if I couldn't remain focused."

"Therefore, I went down to the river, finding my hands holding a basket of clothes and my own bar of soap. Even though there was nothing special about her I was unable to take my eyes off the woman and even as my toes touched the cold water, she drew my eye. I was near to her and gave her a friendly smile and she smiled back in a neighborly fashion. In all my time in the void this had never happened.

"I called out to her, 'Hello,' and standing up, she smiled at me easily and said hello back, however she glanced down into the river near me and when she looked back up, her face had congealed into an evil look. I was shocked at this and she turned from me in contempt. I was about to ask her what was wrong, when a sight in the river, just in front of *her* caught my attention. The water had been calming after she had stood and now it was as flat as a movie screen and the lady was reflected there.

"The reflection was her from another time and it showed what she had done. She killed her family, one by one in a slow cruel way." Talitha's voice broke; she blinked back tears and then gave a small rueful laugh. "I had seen so much depravity in the void, but this was real. This was something she did here...on earth and that made it all worse somehow."

"The lady must have seen that my look of disgust now matched her own and she pulled her eyes from me and with painful hesitation, she looked down and saw what she had done. She started screaming at the image and I felt like screaming as well but I didn't. Instead I ran from her. But as before, I kept coming back to the woman who still screamed and screamed...it was so disturbing that my concentration slipped and I was back in the pits at Rek."

"Did you ever try to go to the river again?" Lisa asked.

"Yes...every time I could."

"Did you ever look into the water yourself?" There was a hint of accusation to Lisa's question that caused Talitha to pale visibly.

Her mouthed worked silently for a moment as she tried to spit out words but she finally spoke in a quiet whisper. "Yes...I couldn't help it. I didn't want to look in the water but my eyes...it was like a magnet."

"What did you see?" Lisa asked with that same tone to her voice.

"Just stuff...like sins I committed, that sort of thing."

"Talitha! It was more than that or you wouldn't have been so nervous about looking into the water." Lisa's face was gravely serious and her eyes had become hard emeralds, lacking any pity.

"I think we should let her be." Jim said with a quiet menace. He didn't like how Lisa was badgering Talitha. "Her sins are between her and God."

"Mr. Anderson," Lisa began in a cold voice. "The Talitha I knew, back when we were younger, did not have any sins worthy of hell. These must have been sins she was going to do in the future and I think it behooves us to know if she's going to commit any of them soon."

Her logic was sound despite the fact that Jim didn't know what she meant by behooves. He glanced down and asked Talitha, "Did you see your future sins...did you see what you did to Brian?"

Groaning as if in pain, she shook her head, tears splashing down her face. "No, it wasn't the future, it was the past. Things that I did in the void. Things that I was forced to do...to others." Her blank eyes flicked briefly to her brother and then back down. Tears fell on Jim's arm and they were warm and full of the agony of life. He couldn't help himself and he reached out and wiped her face clear with his most gentle touch.

"Oh," Lisa seemed to deflate, her worried look exchanged for an ashamed one.

Will rubbed at his twitch again, making the skin of his face red. "How can anything you do in the void be considered a sin? Wait...don't answer that. I really don't want to know about any of it. I'm just glad that I had that river dream instead of the other ones...I don't know how much longer I can take those. Let's retie her hand, Jim."

A question nagged at Jim. "Am I missing something? You were in hell for only a day, how could you have had time to sin, let alone go through...all of that." He had been confused on this for a while, but had been too embarrassed to bring it up; worried he was the only one not understanding.

"Time flows differently in the void. Either that or one's perception is skewed, but they both amount to the same thing...I was there far longer than just a day," Talitha said.

"I need some coffee," Lisa announced tiredly and without asking if anyone else wanted any, she turned and walked out of the room, her slim shoulders slumping.

Jim cinched the rope down tight on Talitha's left arm and the two men then went to work on the right, loosening the ropes and massaging the muscles. Jim looked down into Talitha's face and somehow sensing this, she arched her eyebrows.

"What is it, Jim?"

"What is what?"

"You want to ask a question of me," she stated confidently.

"Yeah, I guess I do. You said the other...uh, Talitha sent you into the pits. Wasn't that just you? I don't want to call you crazy or anything like that but..."

She moved her head in the direction of her brother and there was a sheepish cast to her features as if she were now embarrassed. "I created the other Talitha. I know what the doctors say, but she is not a psychosis or a disorder; she is a separate individual from me. When I was in the void...it was horrible, terrible and I had to do something, so I took a part of me. The hardest part of my being and I created her. It was a mistake that I couldn't take back. Of any sin that I have ever committed, that was the worst. I made someone whose sole purpose was to feel the pain that I should have been feeling. To be tortured in my place."

"How is that even possible? Creating a whole separate person?" Will asked, his hands massaging hers tenderly.

"I don't know. I didn't even ask to see if was possible. I just did it, but I wish I hadn't. She hated the pain, but seemed to revel in it as well and she grew stronger. Somehow, she took the hate and the misery and used it or adapted it to her own ends and that was when she found out she had power over me. Then it was my turn once again to face the torture. However, I hadn't been entirely idle while she had been growing stronger."

"I saw what she was becoming and I worried that the day would come, when she would be too powerful to control. I began meditating," she paused smiling and shaking her head. "Before. Before all of this, I had always considered meditation to be pure...I hate to say it, but pure crap."

Her cheeks turned a slight pink and her brother smiled sadly at this, but said in an exaggerated tone, "Talitha!" He gave her hand a light slap.

"I know I shouldn't be so vulgar, but that was how I felt. Either way it worked and I discovered the river. I would go to it and I would clean my clothes like the others, trying not to look into the water and wait."

"What would you wait for? Why didn't you just stay there?" Jim asked.

"For my body to be killed...my body in the void that is. The demons would eventually tire of abusing a body that wouldn't respond and they would kill it."

Lisa came in then bearing a tray of mugs and a pot of coffee; she proceeded to hand out the mugs, including one for Talitha.

"Should I be thirsty? What time is it?" she asked.

Will yawned largely and took a gulp from his mug before answering, "Almost nine, we got to get going."

"You're taking her, right?" Lisa asked slightly alarmed. She eyed Talitha nervously as she put the coffee to the bound girl's lips. Talitha pulled her head back.

"You have to take me. Wherever you're going, I have to go too! I can't stay here. You mentioned that there were children in trouble?"

Will grimaced before answering, "I'm sorry Tal, but...you may be more trouble than you're worth. The Talitha is too unpredictable. Would you consider going back to the hospital?"

Talitha lowered her head, her hair falling again in front of her face and said in a voice that broke slightly, "Yes, please put me back in there."

"It's just that you know where we live now," Will sad. "And you threatened Lisa, and...and you've been killing, not just her, but you too."

Lisa jumped, spilling coffee. "What? You've killed people too? Oh my God! Why would you do that?" Talitha refused to answer and kept her head down, unwilling to look her sister-in-law in the eye.

"Answer me!" Lisa shouted her demand.

"It's not what you think. It wasn't me exactly," Talitha said as her head wagged from side to side. "It was the other Talitha. I would wake up and there would be...people. She'd leave me people...as a sick joke. They would be dying in the worst way, in tremendous pain and I...I would have to kill them. I had no choice! She's an expert at slow death; she can make it last days."

Talitha paused a moment and when she began speaking again it was with a flat voice as if emotion was beyond her, "The first time, I couldn't bring myself to do it and the person lingered, howling in misery for hours, begging me to kill him. We were out in the woods; I had no idea where and I ran away from him, telling myself I was looking for help, but I was only running from the sound of his voice. You could hear him for miles, but we were alone in the woods. Just him and me and his screams..." She trailed off staring down at her stained flowered dress.

Lisa appeared aghast at first and then apologetic. "That's horrible," she said to Talitha. "She made you kill these people? Couldn't you have called an ambulance?"

"There was never any hope for them. Besides, she disfigured them so much they sometimes weren't recognizable as human. No one would want to live like that."

Jim's heart broke for the girl. There was an actual pain in his chest, just behind his breastbone. "I think we understand, Talitha. It's obvious you had no choice. Will, I think she should come with us. I think she should be given this chance to make up for what she's done."

"Atonement? It may be too late for me." Talitha declared, still without emotion.

Lisa shook her head. "I don't know. The way she...the other one looked at me and at my baby!" She shivered slightly as she said this.

"She hates you, Lisa. Almost as much as she hates me," Talitha said.

Lisa slapped her thigh in frustration. "I didn't do anything to her...I've tried to be as supportive as I could."

"She's jealous. Look at you. Look at what you have. It's everything a girl ever asks for...a handsome, loving husband. A beautiful baby girl on the way. Plenty of money. A great big house with lots of land.

That's why she's jealous, but the reason why she hates you, is that it could have been you tied up in this bed, with the dead boyfriend and all the pain and the killing and the..." Talitha went quiet.

"That's not my fault." Lisa said quietly, looking at Jim and Will, her eyes hoping that they would agree with her.

"Of course it isn't. It was a coin toss and you won," Talitha agreed but with resentment seeping out into the words. "Of all the girls on the island, we were the only ones who hadn't...done it. It was down to you and me, and she hates you because...well, because you just got luckier."

Will spoke up, "But that's not true. There were plenty of other girls on the island, who were virgins. It could have been any of them."

"No. It doesn't work that way," Talitha replied. "I don't know everything about the rituals and incantations that can open a gate onto the void, but when a virgin girl is called for, her virginity in of itself is not enough, otherwise you could use a five year old. There's more to it than just virginity, there is virtue as well." She paused, but the others only stared at her with interest.

"You see there's no virtue in being a virgin, only because you're so ugly that no one will sleep with you. Nor is it virtuous to be a virgin simply because fear stops you. Fear of becoming pregnant. Fear of what your friends will think, fear of your parents, fear of the act itself. No. No, there is no virtue in fear, none what so ever."

"However, when a girls recognizes her virginity as the wonderful gift that it is, and holds onto it, waiting for the perfect man and the perfect time, to give herself freely in the act of love, that is virtue." She smiled sadly toward Lisa. "Out of all the girls on the island we were the only ones that fit that description. We were the only true virgins."

Lisa's mouth hung open and her staring eyes were large green orbs. She looked as if she had been slapped. "But...I still didn't do anything to her. She shouldn't hate me."

"You didn't have to do anything to her. It's just that you have everything." Talitha paused sniffling. "I wish I were you." The two girls faced each other and Lisa's fear and anger seemed to dissolve into sadness for her friend.

"I'm sorry," Lisa said, her voice straining with emotion.

"Don't be. You shouldn't be sorry for doing the right thing." Talitha sat silent for some time, looking lost but eventually said, "We were talking of sending me to a hospital, but is there something that I can help with first? You mentioned children."

"Yeah, maybe you can give us some insight," Will answered and then with Jim's help commenced to tell the story of the demon at St Thomas. Talitha sat stone quiet, taking small sips of coffee from Lisa at short intervals. She remained nearly expressionless, except for her lips that tightened increasingly as the story progressed. It was only when Will mentioned the sword that her look changed slightly to wonder.

The look was not lost on Will, who paused and smiled at his sister. "Your evil twin had that same look on her face when she heard about the sword."

Jim nodded. "It's true and it almost made her look, uh...happy." He had nearly said pretty and the thought of saying it out-loud had made his throat tighten. She smiled up at him in her vague way and his throat tightened even more; he swallowed loudly.

Talitha cocked an ear at the sound and her smile became almost impish as if she could tell what Jim was feeling. Talitha turned, tossing her hair at him and said to Will, "Did I ever tell you what happened when the sword came? I was deep, locked away inside Talitha. She was already stronger than I was and when I wasn't useful to her, she would keep me in the cellar of her soul. But the light from the blade, shone right through her and it was as if she became glass and I could see out. Somehow I just stepped out of her, like I was wearing her and she seemed to evaporate.

"The void was in complete chaos around me. It was crazy. I remember, everyone was running about, screaming, yelling, and jostling me as I stood there. The creatures were all making a run for the sword, thinking that they could escape and for a second, I was caught up too and I ran along with the rest of them. But then I smelled...Dad. I could smell him on the sword high above us and I stopped in the midst of the rushing souls, confused.

"I was trampled and crushed beneath them, until they had all passed me by and at first my heart broke, because I knew I would never leave the void and I would never see him again.

"I sat down and cried for ages alone, but then I felt Ba'al coming. He was a storm that raged toward the sword. He was in a great eagerness, wanting to come into the world and he was so fierce! Nothing could stop him, not even dad, and all of his courage.

"I knew dad would try to stand against Ba'al, but he

could never win, opposed by such a monster, so I screamed for him to run. The void has known screams for eternity, but mine was not a scream of pain or fear, it was filled with my feelings for him. It amazed me. I was stunned by the life I still had in me. The scream was tremendously loud and seemed to shake the foundations of the void and I watched as the sword took the sound within it, vibrating slowly at first, but then rapidly and then bang! It exploded.

"I fell back as the shock wave hit me and that was when she returned, Talitha that is. She shut me up tight and I had no way of knowing what had happened to dad." Talitha paused, her face troubled and clouding over, so Jim put his hand out and patted her leg. However, he withdrew it embarrassed as she looked toward him.

"Sorry, I uh didn't mean to, uh," he stammered feeling his face flush.

"It's ok...it's nice of you," Talitha said and Jim was shocked to see her face go pink as well. "Uh...where was I? Oh yes, dad's soul. I was trapped within her until she found dad's soul and she..."

"What? Dad's soul?" Will was flabbergasted. "The other Talitha told us that she'd found a part of the sword, not his soul."

"She is a practiced and accomplished liar, Will. A prevaricator without any scruples. Never believe her about anything that you can't prove yourself."

Jim remembered the conversation clearly. "Maybe she didn't know it was a soul. She seemed to really believe it was only part of the sword."

Talitha shook her head. "That's even worse, Jim. She has lied so much, she has convinced herself! Trust me when I say there was no mistaking it for a sword."

"So, dad's soul was in the void. You know, he has never mentioned it." Will said.

"That's because there's an awaking period for souls newly dead. Moreover, dad wasn't there very long as far as I could tell. He likely didn't even know."

Will wore a rueful smile on his face. "All these years, I thought I had saved him, when it was really you. How did you get him out of the void?"

"Talitha had enmeshed him in a web of blackness. I pulled him free and he just floated away," she said dreamily, her head rising as if she were seeing the soul drift away even then.

Lisa looked at the two men, confusion making her forehead come together in three little lines between her eyes. "He just floated away? Didn't anyone try to stop him?"

"No, the void is infinite and only a demon very close to us would have even noticed him, and what's more, the void is voluntary in a manner of speaking."

"Wait...wait...wait! The void is voluntary?" Will asked, wearing a hybrid look of disbelief and anger. "You could have left at any time?"

Talitha shrugged. "Not at first, but later, yes...but where was I supposed to go?"

"To heaven... or anywhere but the void!" Will cried in exasperation.

"Heaven!" The word was acid on her tongue. Her blind eyes flared with anger, but then she drooped suddenly, hanging her head again, so she faced out through the wild thicket of her bloodied hair. "You're right, Will. I should've gone to heaven; that would have been smart of me."

"Again you act like you don't deserve heaven," Will said.

Talitha kept her head down. "You don't understand. You can't understand." She stopped talking and it seemed to Jim she wasn't going to elaborate.

"Perhaps she should take a look at the sword," Jim suggested in order to change the subject.

"It's in the attic, I'll go get it," Lisa half ran from the room. Will, Jim, and Talitha sat on the bed in a brooding silence that seemed very long, until Lisa came back.

"Here it is." She gingerly held a green bath towel out away from her body, her eyes a little too wide and a little too wild, seemingly on the verge of chucking the towel and running. "I always get the heebee-jeebeeies when I'm to this thing," she added, feeling the need to explain herself.

"You have it? I can't smell it at all!" Talitha drew in air deeply through her nose.

"It's wrapped in a towel...try now." Lisa carefully unfolded the towel as if she were unwrapping a cobra. In the thick green material lay a broken sword, barely over a foot and a half long. It looked as if it had been struck by lightning or pulled from a fire; the blade was blackened and jagged. The lower part of the sword was in slightly better shape and Jim could see a light stylized etching along the outer guard and it still had little gold braid around the handle.

"I still can't smell it. Can you bring it a little closer," Talitha asked, her face deep in concentration. Lisa brought it just under her nose.

Talitha's blind eyes went wide and she spoke in sudden alarm, "Don't touch me with it! Get it away from me!"

Lisa pulled it back quickly and rewrapped it. "What's wrong with it? Why's it always so cold?" she asked as she placed the towel on a dresser in the room.

Talitha took a moment to calm her breath, which had accelerated into a pant in the short time the sword had been near her. "Make sure nobody touches that sword with their bare hands! This is worse than I thought. From your descriptions of it, I had considered it likely that the sword represented a weakened area in the boundary that separates this world from the void. However, now I think the reason for the swords intense cold, as well as its lack of smell is that there may actually be an opening to the void somewhere along it or in it. If there is an opening, my guess would be that it's microscopic in size. Have either of you inspected the sword?"

Lisa and Will paused a moment to shake their heads at each other. "No not really...I mean we've looked at it but I wouldn't say we have inspected it," Lisa said.

"Please don't. Keep it wrapped up and put in a box, lead lined if you can find one."

"Sure," Will eyed the sword, his pupils large with fear.

"Father Alba touched the sword, when he took it out of the frozen witch," Jim said, eyeing the green towel with apprehension. "He said that it hurt, like his life was being pulled from his body through his hands."

"Frozen witch?" Lisa asked giving her husband a sharp look.

"Yeah, I didn't tell you that part of the story, it was too gross. After we stabbed," he paused and sighed. "I mean, after I stabbed Mrs. Harris, and sent the demon back into the void, you were awake, Talitha but nearly catatonic and dad was looking so grey that we decided to get you two back to the hospital. By the time, Father Alba, Brian and I returned to the house, Mrs. Harris' body had frozen solid."

Again, he paused and just shook his head as his eyes looked back to that time. Finally, he spoke again, "We put her in the back seat of our station wagon, along with poor Adrina and that was the last I saw of them. Father Alba went somewhere up state and burned the bodies. It was a great shock when he turned up a few years ago with that broken sword."

Frozen corpses gave Jim the creeps and he decided to change the subject. "What did you think the sword would smell like? Do they smell a certain way?" Jim asked, again hoping he didn't sound like a moron.

"The average person would likely only smell the agents used to clean the sword, but even metals have distinct ligands, which are basically the odor molecule of a substance. Everything radiates ligands, and with my hyperosmia...I mean my increased sense of smell, I should have been able to smell the sword easily. Since I can't, it is my conjecture that there is an actual physical opening into the void, which is acting as a vacuum of sorts, drawing in the smell."

"Oh," Jim said feeling like a moron. "The demon called it a path; do you think this opening can get bigger?"

Talitha shook her head and attempted a shoulder shrug. "I don't know, but since it's been used as a path of sorts twice already, the answer goes from possibly to probably."

Lisa asked, "What do we do with it?"

Talitha shook her head. "Don't try to destroy it, melt it, or break it in any way. If you do, you will likely draw attention to the weakened area, and that's the best case scenario, in the worst, you may make the opening larger."

"Then what are our choices?" Lisa voice was becoming shrill and she started to pace the room.

Will stood and went to his wife, hugging her. "It'll be alright. We've had that thing with us for five years and nothing has happened...it's not going to suddenly start shooting out demons." He looked at Talitha, who nodded her head in agreement. "See? For now, the only rational plan is to hide the sword."

"I suggest that you put me in an institution, Will. That way you can know that you're reasonably safe..."

He interrupted, "No. First off, you escaped once before and you will again. I won't feel safe at all unless I can keep an eye on you myself. Second, there's no way we're giving over the sword now that we know there's a hole into the void on it. I think we should take you to Boston and see if there's some way you can help us to get those kids back."

Lisa was practically in tears. "Will! It won't be safe. I need you. The baby needs you."

"I'm sorry, but the fact is, that unless we kill Talitha right now, we'll never be safe." Will eyed his wife solemnly and there was a long silence before he continued, "I can't do it. I can't kill her in cold blood. But if you can...I won't stop you."

Lisa shook her head. "I can't either."

"Then I take her to Boston. I feel it's the only way I can protect you from her and this other demon."

"I don't want to go," Talitha said unexpectedly. "Unless you and Jim promise to kill me if I...the other me gets out of hand."

"I promise," Will stated flatly.

Jim figured lying was not as bad a sin as killing, "I promise," he said, knowing he could never hurt her.

Chapter 12

Beneath the Church

They were cruising at 26,000 feet when the other, not so nice, Talitha returned. The sudden chimes, ringing with musical insistence drifted through Will's dreams and he came instantly awake.

"What? What the hell? Hey...uh, hey, Will!" Talitha began thrashing. In response the chimes tied to her ropes began a merry frenzied jingling. Jim was closest and took two large steps, bent over in the tiny cabin of the plane.

Placing a hand on her shoulder, he spoke in an urgent hushed voice, "Quiet down!"

"Who is that? Jim...White Jim?" she asked as she sniffed at the air.

"Yeah it's me. Now stop yanking on those ropes or I'll be forced to cinch them tight enough to keep you from moving at all." He growled this low in her ear, despite the loudness of the interior of the plane's cabin.

"Why can't I see anything? What's going on? Where are we going?" she asked in rapid succession, her head straining around and her eyes wide.

Will checked his watch, 10:38 am. He rubbed some sleep from his eyes and slipped up the tiny isle, climbing into the leather chair just behind hers. "Talitha, it's Will..."

"No shit! I can hear just fine, moron. I just can't see! What the hell happened?" She was loud—Will took a quick peek up toward the cockpit. A single heavy curtain shrouded it and he could only hope the pilot had his head gear on.

"You need to quiet down," he ordered sharply. "You're blind because...you shot yourself in the head."

"I what?" Talitha asked incredulously, her head wagging back and forth, making her freshly cleaned brown hair sigh gently as if in the wind. "How'd she do it? I mean, I should have seen it coming." She was speaking to herself and thankfully in a quieter tone.

The plane took a sudden lurch, the lightness of it putting them at the mercy of any turbulence. Will was used to it, having flown on this very plane a dozen times in the last year alone, but it was clear that Jim wasn't. His eyes went wide with the buffeting and his face paled noticeably.

"You ok?" he asked the big man.

"Yeah," Jim said breathily almost breathing the word out. "I'm just a little air sick."

"Damn it! She shot me." Talitha cried out. Her indignation was a little amusing to Will. "You know what I'm going to do once..."

"Yeah, yeah, yeah," Will spoke over her. "We've heard it all before Tal. So do everyone a favor and shut up." His tic bounced again on his face and he worried at it, hoping it would go away soon. Seeing it jiggle in the mirror before they left for the airport was a nasty shock and he kept his hand to his cheek whenever he could.

Turning about as far the ropes would allow in her chair, Talitha gave him an angry look. "Aren't you the cranky one? You're not the one who was shot, Will!" She pouted for a few moments and then her pert little nose started taking in air purposely. "You haven't fed me, have you? How long have I been...away?"

"I don't know, fifteen hours there abouts." Will suddenly felt guilty about not having given his sister anything to eat. "I'm sure we could come up with a snack or something. Are you thirsty?"

"Some big brother you are...ok, let me see if I got the situation down right? Talitha shoots me in the head and you're too much of a pussy to finish the job?" She paused waiting to see if he would answer, but there was nothing to say and she continued, "We're at about 27,000 feet, on a south by south west course, in a plane built for...what twelve people?"

"Ten passengers, one pilot."

"Sure, ten then...but there are only the three of us and a single pilot. So having had me shot, you now are flying me to Boston, for me to help you deal with some putz who's pretending to be possessed. And I'm going to do this, why?"

Again, he didn't have an answer. He gave Jim a look that said, *what do I say to that*? However, Jim was greening like springtime and Will turned back to his sister not wanting to embarrass him. "Out of the goodness of your heart?" Will suggested.

"Yeah that's a good one. So where was I...oh yeah...I don't smell the sword or Lisa, so I can assume that she's at home packing like mad. And the only real surprise in all of this, and it's a shocker, is that big White Jim is carrying the same gun that shot me in the head. How'd I do?"

Jim's eyes went wide at this and Will put his finger to his lips. "You did pretty well." She was actually spot on.

The blind girl turned back toward him. "Pretty good? Is that all I rate? I can tell you more if you want.

You had another night of fun and games, didn't you? I can tell by your voice, that you've been screaming like a girl. Little miss goody two shoes had you tortured good and proper."

Will was glad that she couldn't see the muscles twitching in his face. "That was my fault, not hers. I probably should've gone to a motel."

"And let your little sister get tortured? That's pretty selfish, and hardly very Christian of you."

Jim spoke up suddenly and surprisingly on his behalf, "I think he goes above and beyond what any other Christian would do."

She rolled her unseeing eyes. "Yes, Will is quite the saint. But what about you Jimmy? You're packing a heater. What's that about?"

He looked gravely serious and gravely nauseous. "Uh, that's for you...uh, just in case you get out of hand."

With what seemed like genuine surprise she exclaimed, "Wow! What did I miss? I thought we had a little something going on between us... a little spark. Are you mad about me playing around with Lisa? That was all in fun."

"You were going to kill her! And don't bother lying, the other Talitha told us," Will said.

"Ok, I was upset...jealous really, but I'm over it. I promise I won't hurt her."

"After she saved your life, you better not," Jim drawled slowly, almost as if warning her. His face went white as the plane dropped precipitously and even Will felt his stomach in his throat.

Talitha didn't seem to notice. "Lisa saved my life?" She sat in silence for a while and her look was unreadable. She turned to Will conversationally, "Tell me, did Talitha explain how she was able to surface like she did?"

Will's eyes narrowed in suspicion. "No and I wouldn't tell you if she had."

"That's ok. It would be cheating if you had told me. We like to play this game, a mind game, you might say." The plane gave another lurch and a glance out the window showed Will that they were flying through restless dark clouds. She went on seemingly in a chatty mood, "I think it might've been a mistake not to bring the sword. I mean it's obviously important to the demon and we could've used it as a bargaining chip."

"You care now about the missing children?" Will didn't think that was possible and he wore an openly skeptical look that was lost on the blind girl.

"I won't lie to you, Will," she lied blatantly. "I'm more interested in the demon and what he wants the sword for, but if I happen to rescue some children, well good for me."

"So you don't know what the sword does?" Jim asked dubiously from his seat across from her.

"Oh, I have lots of guesses, but I don't know anything for sure."

Will climbed from his seat behind her and moved to the one just in front and knelt upon it, looking over the headrest at her, "Your other self thought it might be used as some sort of gateway."

She said nothing to this and only the slight rise in her eyebrows lent any indication that she had even heard him. Will became irritated and his voice got louder as he spoke, "Well? I asked a question: can it be used as a gate?"

"Perhaps...I don't know. I haven't seen it, remember?" Her response was icy.

"I remember and don't think for a moment that I regret it," Will answered. He looked out of the window but there was nothing to see but an ocean of grey all about them. It was depressing after the sunshine of autumn Maine. After a minute of staring into the chaos of the clouds, he looked at his sister's face. It was like she hadn't been shot just the day before. She was smooth and seemed refreshed, where as he felt empty and sick.

Talitha knew he was looking at her and smiled disarmingly. "Will, let's forget about the sword for now. It's the demon; we should be putting our minds to."

"So you believe there really is a demon now?" Will asked, again looking hard into her face, searching for indications of deception. However, the plane bucked hard, as it began a sloppy decent, deeper into the storm and he grabbed on to the headrest for support, his eyes flicking to the window.

"What did the other Talitha say? I hate to admit it, but she's the smarter of the two of us," she said this with a sigh, but Will didn't believe her for a second.

"She wasn't sure, she...dang it!" he cried in alarm. The plane felt like it had dropped a hundred feet straight down and for a moment he was weightless. His stomach had jumped to his throat and he held the seat in front of him, gripping with white knuckled hands.

"Dang it? Will, you got to learn to curse like a man." She turned her dainty features toward Jim. "Hey Jimbo...Big Jim? You can curse, I'm betting. Why don't you give my nancy-boy brother some tips on how to act like a man?"

"No thank you," Jim growled.

"Sure thing...but...but something has happened, right? Your voices are holding something back from me." She became excited and eagerly asked, "You have found some of the boys dead, right? Were they mutilated? Spoiled in a kinky way, perhaps?"

Will grimaced at her.

The hungry look on her face was unmistakably evil and exhaling heavily, he turned to see Jim staring out of the window at the grey nothingness. The big man put one of his large hands to his face and Will thought it likely he wasn't wiping the sleep away this time.

"No, that's not it. The demon somehow got out of his room and killed a nun," Will whispered to Talitha and the glee in her face became annoyance at being wrong.

Right after Will had chartered the flight into Boston, Jim had called the church to let Father Alba know the situation concerning Talitha and the sword. His face had come crashing down, scaring Will into thinking that the possessed man had somehow escaped. He wished he had.

"Did the man get away?" Talitha asked sharply as the plane smoothed out.

"He could have. But he just dumped the poor lady's body out into the corridor and somehow locked himself back in the room."

"Hmm," she faced toward the window. It was just then that they found a sunlit valley in middle of the looming clouds. It lit up the cabin of the small plane for a precious few seconds, but the moment passed and the gloom of the storm surrounded them once again.

"You know, I've always thought nuns to be so

pathetic." Talitha began after the light departed. "They don't get the respect or the power of a priest, nor are they allowed a family, like a deacon. What's more, they're all clearly hiding from life..."

"Talitha," Will murmured.

"...afraid of the choices the rest of society has to make. Who to love, where to live, how many children they should..."

"Talitha! The nun was a friend of Jim's. Show some respect or shut up," Will snapped irately.

She stopped talking, and faced towards Will, her head slowly nodding as if in understanding, but her eyes narrowed and a mocking smile played along her lips.

"You're really feeling it, aren't you? Your two bitches conspire to blind me and now you think I'm at your mercy. You think I'm your dog now? Sit Talitha. Shut up Talitha. Roll over and let me fuck you Talitha! I got news for you, I won't always be blind, so it's you who'd better show some respect."

"Wrong," Will replied with savage anger in his voice. "I'm tired of your crap and if you get out of line, even for a moment, Jim here is going to put another bullet in you."

Talitha face broke into a wicked smile. "Sure...right! You're willing to commit murder, Big Jim? Are you really willing to spend the rest of your life in jail?"

Still looking out of the window, Jim said, "I'm not afraid of prison."

"Yeah? What about hell? If you aren't, you are a bigger fool than you appear to be and that would be quite the fool. Here on earth you're a big guy...I bet nobody messes with Big Jim. But, down there...you'd be nothing. An ant, a maggot." She smiled a nasty delicious smile and her blind eyes came to life at the prospect of Jim in the void. "This is all moot anyways. Jim would never pull the trigger. Not to hurt sweet little Talitha."

"That doesn't mean I won't pull it on you," Jim murmured to the window.

"Right. I see the way you look at me...or I guess I should say, I saw the way you looked at me. Not to mention the way you smell. Do you know what pheromones are?"

Will did and he snuck a peek at Jim, who was reddening up the back of his neck as he stared out the window. The big man snarled, "I know what they are, but they..."

Talitha spoke over him, "Then you know they're perceived on a subconscious level...with most people. But I'm all too aware what your *musk* is saying to me."

Jim glanced back at Will in worried embarrassment, the color rising in his cheeks. Talitha seemed aware of the look and paused for affect before going on.

"You got a randy scent coming off of you in waves! Jim, you must really have the hots for her. Tell me *Big* Jim, is she the first girl to smile at you, to give you the time of day? Did she even get a look at that ugly face of yours? Or was she already blind and you thought: here's my chance!"

"It wasn't like that," Jim declared the pink of his cheeks now becoming an angry red.

"Sure it wasn't; no really, I believe you. After all, you're quite a catch." Her sarcasm was a knife to Jim, and glowering, he turned back to the window as the airport came into view below them.

She continued, "Now don't pout. Will, how's he going to kill me if he can't stand up to a little fun? Jim? I know I'll be there for the honeymoon, but will I be invited to the wedding as well? Are you going to be wearing white? I know she won't be."

"He'll be able to pull the trigger, if it comes to it. And if he can't, I will. Now please lay off the man." Will turned and sat down in his chair as the plane began a light bucking.

"Shouldn't he know about his bride to be? Sorry to be the one to tell you, but she ain't no virgin. Yeah, gang raped at sixteen in an insane asylum...pretty sad if you think about it.

A sharp breath by Jim alerted her and she put on a facade of sympathy. "You didn't know about the nightly rapes?" She asked in a tone that dripped sweet venomous honey. "Already secrets between you two...I don't see this lasting too long. But, since you attracted Talitha with your *stunning* looks, I bet you have other girls lined up around the block."

Will felt drained by his sister, exhausted. "Can you please just leave him alone?"

"Sure thing," she said with a satisfied smile and relaxed back in her chair.

Will sighed heavily, and purposely didn't look in Jim's direction but instead watched Boston from his window as the plane's angle of descent became more pronounced. He never cared for Boston at this time of year; it was a dull city, perpetually grey and wet.

Now, adjacent runways came into view on either side of the plane and it would only be moments before they touched down. "Talitha, listen to me. Make all the snide comments you want...go right ahead as long as you're quiet about it. If you draw too much attention to us, you'll just alert the police and we both know what that means."

She rolled her eyes but remained quiet.

Will continued, "We're heading to the church and you're going to talk to this demon. If you try to run or if you try to hurt anyone, we will shoot you."

"When you speak to me like that I just might not be in the mood to talk."

"Then we take you to the police right away and let them deal with you," he explained calmly. The plane gave a jerk as its wheels tasted the airstrip and it bounced a moment before they got a proper grip on the paved surface.

"Yeah, but maybe I'll tell them how you harbored a known fugitive...you know what? I think that's a felony!" Her mouth came open in simulated surprise.

He hadn't considered that, but the answer came to him quickly and now it was his turn to smile in a nasty manner. "I'll turn you over to that cop you threw around at the church...what's his name?"

"Milner," Jim said in between deep breaths. The rough weather and choppy landing had given impetus to his nausea; he was clearly concentrating on not throwing up.

Talitha's face turned sour and Will couldn't help smile at it, saying, "Yep, I'm sure Milner will do a thorough job in his investigations. However, I bet he'll be even more thorough interrogating you."

"Alright, fine!" Talia's anger boiled over. "I was just having some fun. Either way, I already told you that I *wanted* to talk to the demon. You know, figure out what he's here for—look for clues that sort of thing."

"Sure Tal, that's fine. As long as you know we're serious." Will went about cutting her loose, stowing the ropes and wind chimes in his bag.

A few minutes later: "St Thomas off Warren and Moreland, please," Jim said as he eased himself into the front seat of the cab. Will guessed his weight at over three hundred pounds and the cab settled perceptibly in his direction. The cabbie, small and swarthy had a smile on his mouth, but his eyes were full of worry and he glanced frequently at the giant sitting next to him as if he were fearful that Jim would eat him.

"How can you stand the smell of this city, Jim?" Wrinkles of disgust lined Talitha's face. "It's a mixture of decaying buildings, rotting garbage and old sewage."

Will gave the air a tentative sniff, but it smelled like rain to him. They were driving into Roxbury, an area of Boston that he'd never traveled in before. It was an older neighborhood, one that was near its death in the slow phoenix like cycle that all cities go through. The houses were a 1950s vintage, small, and crammed close together. The yards, generally covered in either weeds or trash were so tiny, Will didn't see the point to them.

Most of houses, like the yards, were uncared for, slowly crumbling around their occupants like igloos in a rain. Porches sagged, shutters tilted, and ancient shingles were worn nearly to the roof by the dull grey showers that drenched Boston year after year. It was a depressing sight, but not a smelly one at least as far Will could tell.

"Uhg! You two don't smell that? Does this city have gravity fed sewers?" she asked Jim.

"I dunno," he said with a shrug of his wide shoulders.

"Of course you don't," the words were coated in oily contempt. The girl faced out the window, blindly staring out at the rain, sampling the air every few seconds.

"It could be worse, Talitha. Over by the Bay, on the south side, it smells like fish year round. And there's this oil plant...talk about smelly!"

"Oil plant?" she asked with a sad look and a shake of her head. "Try petroleum processing facility. They don't make oil there, Jim."

He said nothing, but his jaw clenched in anger and he scowled out the front window. The cabbie eyed him with a growing fear, and he shifted slightly further to his left. For a few minutes, the cab was silent save for the rhythmic movement of the windshield wipers keeping a lonely beat.

"I'm sorry, Jim," Talitha blurted unexpectedly. "I suppose it's not your fault that you didn't have a dad and mom around to correct you like I did."

Jim sat stock-still and silent.

"Jim, I said I'm sorry and I meant it. Aren't you supposed to forgive me or something?" Jim only sighed in weariness when Talitha went on, "Jesus would've forgiven me."

"Yeah well, I'm not Jesus. Why do you want me to forgive you anyways? You're only going to say something in five minutes that will piss me off again."

"Fine, be that way...Will? Where are we? I smell old industry mixed in with the housing."

Will wiped away the condensation from his window and peered out at the dismal view. "Yep, that's what I see."

"We're almost there," Jim grunted.

"Then I guess a nice hotel is out of the question," Talitha responded and then for some reason, she stuck out her tongue, and blew a raspberry at the window.

Will had just been hating her for the way she had treated Jim when she did it. That little thing. Blowing a raspberry like a kid, made his heart remember her with fondness and his shoulders slumped; he was too weary to hate just then.

"I'm picturing broken windows and trash and graffiti," she said dully.

She was correct and he turned in his seat to get a better look at her, worried that her eyesight might be returning, but her eyes were vacant orbs.

"Unfortunately, it's just like you're picturing it," Will responded, wondering why anyone would choose to live there.

"Hey!" Talitha said suddenly. "Cabbie slow down...Will is the graffiti old around here?"

Will looked at her first, wondering why she would want to know, before peeking through the rain at what looked like an old tire plant. "Cabbie, don't slow down. It looks old, I guess. Jim, is that old or what?

"Yeah, I think so. Graffiti always gets tired looking after a few weeks. Why do you want to know?" His question was one Will wanted answered as well.

"Just thinking about the socio-economic stratus of this city and how the decay..."

Talitha went on for some time, but Will tuned her out. She was speaking for her own benefit, just to hear how smart she was. A moment later, the cab turned onto a street where the buildings were in better shape, but Will saw a freshly sprayed indecipherable word. He was just about to point out the new graffiti to Talitha, when Jim spoke.

"There's the church...on the left." Jim took a deep breath and ran his hands through his thick brown hair. A look back at Will showed how nervous the big man suddenly appeared.

Will glanced out to see a good-sized, red brick church with numerous stained glass windows. Attached to the rear of it and forming a rough T, were two more brick buildings, both of which had lights burning away visible in the gloom of the midday storm. The church on the other hand was dark and unwelcoming.

At the sight, Will felt the first ripple of fear undulate through him. He paid the cabbie and helped Talitha out, her footing only slightly unsteady after the cab ride. They went under the eaves of the church and Will pulled on the front door, expecting to enter, but the doors were locked.

There was a pause as Jim and Will looked at each other, uncertain. Terrible images of what could be going on in the dark corridor beneath the church threatened to run amok in Will's mind, but he forced them away and rapped hard on the doors.

A minute passed with no sound emanating from the church, Jim, with his fist twice the size of Will's, pounded loudly. The sound could be heard echoing throughout the building, giving it a deserted feel. Another glance between the two men and now Will's fear became manifest and he looked away hoping the big man wouldn't be able to see it growing in his eyes.

A peek toward Talitha helped. She was quite casually stretching her legs like a ballerina. "You can stop your oafish banging, there's someone coming."

Seconds later, Will could hear footsteps advancing toward the door and then a priest, medium height with black hair and handsome Latin features peeked out. His eyes were wild and darted about until he took in Jim's great frame to the side of the door.

"Jim, thank God! What took you so long?" the priest asked with irritation coloring his voice.

"Complications," was all Jim said.

"I suppose they do happen...you must be Will Jern." Will's hand was shaken by the priest, warmly in the manner of a politician, but damp in the manner of a man in great fear. He then looked with trepidation at Talitha, not offering his hand.

"And you are Miss Jern? I am Father John Santos. Thank you for making the trip."

Clearly, she could sense his hesitation and she mischievously held out her hand. His warm smile turned crooked on his face and robot like, he took her hand at arm's length.

"It's very nice to meet you, Father." Her voice came out deep, husky and sexy. With firm, unrelenting gentle pressure, she pulled him close to her so that they were practically nose-to-nose.

Will's muscles tensed preparing to rush her, but she only breathed the priest in. A long slow inhalation with her eyes shut and a contented smile on her lips, as if she were enjoying his scent.

She breathed out slowly, "Good."

Once she released his hand, he hurriedly wiped it on his black clothes, the uniform of the priesthood,

"What do you mean, good?" he asked.

"Mainly I mean there're no cops in there. Things would've been a little touchy if there were."

"There's the reputation of the church to consider, you see. However, since you *failed* to bring the sword..." The word failed, came out as an accusation, directed at Jim. "I'm afraid we'll be forced to bring the police into this, if your negotiations, Miss Jern aren't successful."

"You are already afraid. You stink of fear. You should be embarrassed by it. Are you?" She advanced on the priest as she spoke and he stepped back into the protection of the church.

"Actually I am."

"Are you afraid because what he did to..." she stopped in mid-sentence, because Jim did something Will thought wasn't too smart.

Putting his hand on her shoulder, Jim held her roughly in place. "That's enough playing around, Talitha." His voice was deep and held father-figure authority.

Her muscles bunched and for the slightest moment, Will thought she was going to strike the big man, but instead she pouted, "Sure...sure, no fun for poor Talitha. Maybe we can have some fun later." She was suddenly cheery and wrapped her arm around his huge one, as if ready to take a stroll. She smiled up at him prettily and he went stiff.

Will intervened, "No, sorry Tal, you're with me." He came between them, purposefully ignoring a tiny look of disappointment in Jim's eyes and took his sister's arm in his. He led her into the church's foyer and glanced about.

There was a large red-brown stain on the floor just to the side of the Baptismal font. At the sight, his fear, ignored by him with the stress of his sister, now began throbbing like a toothache, sitting in his chest like a stone. It put out little feelers, spider like arms that crept down his veins and into his hands and these began to shake at the sight of the stain. The stain was very large. When Talitha began sniffing at it, dog like, he became repulsed and pulled her away.

"Where to, Father?" he asked, putting his back to the stain, his mind however, was still on it.

"Just down here," Father John lead the way into the church, taking a quick right in the main room, he went to a set of double doors that led to a long hallway.

Will stopped just inside the hallway. A vision of what he was about to face came to him then.

At the end of the hallway was a door, behind which were stairs that led down into a darkened corridor, a corridor that seemed almost a tunnel. There was only a single bulb midway down it and standing stooped over beneath it, clutching themselves in fear were two men. They sweated freely and they both had a mad look about them. A sudden noise and Will was sure they would flee in terror.

His visions were beyond his control and he looked past the men despite a tremendous desire not to. The corridor was black at the end and he could barely make out the lines of a thick heavy door. Death lay beyond that door. But whose death, and when and how, these were unanswered. He only had a certain knowledge that someone would be dead soon.

He saw into the room, then. It was lit also by a single bulb and what it threw its feeble light on caused his mind to rebel and thankfully, mercifully at that point the vision ended.

Talitha knew from long experience what was going on and stood still waiting for Will to come out from his vision. When he did, she asked, "What's down there?"

At first he couldn't answer, the room had been covered in blood and now it was all his mind could see.

Chapter 13

Entering the Demon's Chapel

"You saw something, Will. I know you did, now tell me what." There was concern in her voice and that only made the horror that filled him worse.

"I don't know...maybe a real demon. I didn't see it. I just felt, something; something bad. And there was blood...lots of it. Maybe from the nun, but I don't think it was, at least not all of it." His mind wanted a replay of his vision and he shook his head with a frown.

Talitha bit her lip and grew silent and thoughtful. Jim, who had been ahead of them, was now most of the way down the hall. He turned with a look of worry on his homely features.

"Is there something going on?" His voice was loud in the empty building and it made Will cringe.

Hurrying forward with his sister, Will waited until he was closer before whispering, "I just had a bad feeling."

Jim eyed him with a queer expression and Will found that he couldn't look the man in the face. His fear was an embarrassment to him and he kept his eyes down. They started walking again, toward the door that Will knew would lead to the dark staircase.

Sweat stung his eyes and he tried to blink it away, to no avail. He made to wipe his face with his sleeve but as he watched his hand, shaking, come up, he stopped and brought it down quickly before anyone else could see it. His other hand, pressed around Talitha's arm shook as well and he wondered why she wasn't making a snide comment about it.

Looking down at her, he saw why; she was deep in concentration, her brow was furrowed and her right arm, thrown out, touched the wall as they walked. She seemed to be talking to herself or perhaps counting.

After a moment, she sniffed the air and it was then that Will caught a whiff of something sour and unpleasant.

The stench worsened as the three of them caught up with Father John, who stood waiting at the door at the end of the hall and when the priest opened it, Will fairly gagged. The aroma was like nothing he'd ever smelled before; it was a vile evil stench and his stomach rolled over.

Jim seemed strangely angry instead of afraid. "What's that smell?" he demanded of the priest.

"We don't know. It started yesterday afternoon and it just keeps getting worse," Father John's tan was paling before the smell and pasty white didn't suit his handsome face.

"That's not Sister Mary?" Jim asked, his anger slipping away into confusion.

"No, we moved her body into my office. The smell is something else." Will wasn't the only one sweating now; the priest wiped his forehead with the sleeve of his black tunic and started down the stairs.

Talitha didn't seem to mind the odor and sniffed repeatedly like a bloodhound on a trail, her blind eyes still narrowed in her concentration.

"Describe the room in front of us," she commanded her brother, her tone holding authority over him.

"It's not a room, it's the landing of some stairs

leading down," Will said as he stepped in.

She breathed out loudly with annoyance. "Keep talking, any lights? Any windows?"

"Only one light, about four feet above your head and there won't be any more until we are down in the corridor below us. There aren't any windows, anything else?"

"Hey, how'd you know there aren't any more lights?" Father John's voice held more than a hint of suspicion. "Have you been down here before?"

Jim spoke up, using his normal voice, which again seemed unnecessarily and startlingly loud, after the whispers of the others, "He can see the future, Father. Or at least parts of it."

The priest eyed Will with an odd mixture of disbelief and reverence. "Really, Father Alba didn't mention…"

Talitha spoke over him, rude but uncaring, "Will, you say there's one light down there, what about in the room where the demon is?"

Father John answered first, clearly annoyed, "There's only a single one, but…"

She interrupted again, "Describe the fixture it's attached to."

The priest gave Will an exasperated look before answering, "It hangs from the ceiling on a chain and I don't know the wattage, in case you're wondering."

"I'm not wondering," she said sharply. "Come on, let's go down."

Will took her by the arm and steered her down the stairs. When they reached the bottom, just as in his vision, he saw the soft plump form of Father Alba standing, midway down the corridor under the light of the single bulb and with him was a large fat man, who sported a sheen of nervous sweat on his forehead, visible even at that distance.

They hurried down toward the two men, Will holding on to Talitha's arm, clutching it really, as if she were there to protect him. While she, just as before, trailed her hand along the damp concrete walls. Jim lumbered after, seemingly taking up the entire corridor behind them.

"Will...Will, how was your flight in?" Father Alba greeted them, trying to come across in a conversational tone, however his voice was high and reedy. He wore the gold and white vestments that were usually worn at the Easter mass, right down to the stole.

Will felt an urge to laugh at the ludicrous question, but smothered it. "It was fine." It had been an odd attempt at conversation and having failed, nobody looked to try again. A sudden quiet enveloped the six of them, as they stood close in to each other, huddling in the cone of pale light cast by the single bulb.

To Will, everything outside the light held dangerous and evil possibilities, especially the door at the end of the corridor. It held a dreadful fascination for him. Death lay beyond that door. He didn't know whose it would be, but at least one of the six of them, would be dead soon, and this included himself.

With each surreptitious glance down the hall, Will felt his heart thud in his chest just a bit harder and he tried not to look that way, but his only other option was to look into the faces of the people around him. He couldn't help but wonder who it would be, how it would happen and when.

His eyes settled on the fat man, who he hadn't been

introduced to and he felt an unpleasant shock when his mind let slip, *I hope it's him*. The appalling thought reverberated through him and he quickly looked away, embarrassed that he could think such a thing about a man he'd never met.

It was then that Talitha asked, "Who's the mouth breather?" Obviously referring to the man, Will had just wished would die in his place. Father Alba introduced him, "My apologies…my apologies, this is Sean Shay. He's a counselor here at our orphanage." Sean stuck out his large hand to Will, who sheepishly took it. He was only barely able to look into Sean's face, worried that his eyes would betray his improper thoughts.

However it was a painful realization that came along with the handshake: Sean Shay would not die that day, or the next or anytime in the foreseeable future. The muscles of Will's face began to jump again. His mind however was locked on to the fact that his odds of dying had just jumped up considerably and when he began rubbing his face, it was completely subconscious.

"What's the matter, Will?" Talitha asked from next to him, breaking in on his morbid calculations; somehow she always knew when he was troubled.

I hope it's that priest.

As before, the immoral thought just jumped into his mind. He put both hands to his face and groaned aloud, trying not to picture Father John, hoping not picture anyone.

"Will?" Jim asked. "You ok?"

"Yep...it's nothing...everything will be ok." He took two large breaths praying to God that he wouldn't wish death on anyone else.

"Is it a vision or the smell?" Jim's own face was

pale and he was sweating as well. Jim took up almost the entire breadth of the corridor behind them and Will felt sudden claustrophobia. His chest began to constrict and he tried to look unobtrusively past Jim at the stairs further down, but he couldn't, not with everyone now staring at him.

"It's nothing...like I said." He was unconvincing even to himself.

"Yeah right, Will. You've always been the worst liar ever," Talitha said "You saw something...and judging by your pathetic attempts at lying, I'm guessing someone is going to die?" Mouths gaped at him and he kept his face down, afraid to look anyone in the eye. He was afraid he would see their death...or worse, afraid he wouldn't.

"It's true, but I don't know whose, or when." There was silence now in the corridor as each person considered the possibility that their own death was near at hand. "Remember that the future isn't set...if I can change it so that nobody dies, I will, ok?" Will added, but he felt no reassurance at his own words.

None of them were mollified in the least and fear was seen on all of their faces. Only Talitha seemed incapable of the dread of dying and she broke the moment of stunned silence that had come with Will's pronouncement of impending doom.

She smirked, with casual indifference to anyone's feelings. "*Que sera sera*, or maybe not with you around, Will. So if you're done seeing all of *their* deaths, Will, I need you to tell me about the room."

"The room?" Will pictured the room and his stomach rolled over again and he had to fight down his lunch. "It's a big room, maybe thirty feet long and there are shelves lining the walls with boxes on them. In the middle, there's crate, a wood box. It sit's under the light and just behind it on the floor is a mattress..." his voice trailed into a whisper and then into nothing. Lying on the mattress had been a body, or most of a body. He coughed. The vision and the stink making him queasy.

Talitha, small and frail looking compared to the men around her, took charge. "Good. Now listen up. If you want to get those children back you'll do what I say, *exactly* what I say. Any interference will jeopardize their lives and worse, piss me off."

"I think we understand. Consid..." Father John began but she cut right across him.

"And no unnecessary yapping! Do what I tell you and keep your mouths shut. The only voice I want to hear is Will's. When we enter, Will, I want you to give me a quick rundown of the room, act like you are speaking into a tape recorder, be clinical; the subject is lying on the mattress five feet in front of me...that sort of thing. If he moves at all, do it again, unless he is talking and moving, then I'll be able to hone in on his voice. Clear?"

Will nodded and she went on, "Another thing, all of you, do not under any circumstances let on that I'm blind. Demonstrating weakness in front of a demon can be deadly. Lastly, don't mention this death that Will has foreseen, it may trigger a desire to kill and once started, demons like to go on killing sprees."

Jim, easily the most relaxed of the group besides Talitha, asked, "What do you plan on doing in there?"

"You brought me here to talk to the man, right? I think I'll start with that. Alba, since the demon knows you, I want you to stay right behind me. Father yapper,

I want you to move to my right as we enter and keep the mouth breather with you. Will and Big White Jim stay to my left. Does everyone understand where they're supposed to be?"

Will nodded along with the rest of them and glanced over at Jim's relatively calm visage and felt a slight feeling of relief come over him at the prospect that Jim would be near him.

However, the feeling was short lived.

Talitha began to bark orders again, but Will only really heard the first one, "Will I want you to go first…" after that his mind tuned her out and the moment of relief he had felt, died a quick death, scared into its grave by the simple words.

He looked down the dark corridor and the door seemed larger than it had, and what lay beyond it even greater, taking up his whole world. The fear that had lain behind his breastbone had been growing slowly and was now a boulder of ice, making breathing difficult. His breath was a tiny thing that seemed to go only to the back of his mouth and then was spat back out again. He caught sight of Talitha and her lips were moving and his mind came back in time to hear the tail end of her sentence, "…waiting for?" She seemed perturbed.

Will's mouth came open wider. He didn't know if she was talking to him, and he honestly didn't know if he should say something or not, but luckily Father Alba came to his rescue.

"I think we should say a prayer." His voice was a rough little whisper.

"Uhhg," Talitha rolled her eyes. "I think we shouldn't. God ain't down here, Father.

"Then perhaps it would be best if we invited him.

Now everyone...Our Father, who art in heaven..." The priest said the prayer hugging his large bible to his chest and Will fumbled and mumbled along. He was having trouble concentrating, because he couldn't help but thinking that one of the priests would be a better choice to go first. Well maybe not Father John, who stood crookedly; his fear made him look ill, distorting the lines of his body, making him appear as if he had been broken and put back together ineptly.

But he did have a large cross hung about his neck, just as Father Alba did. Will had nothing, not even the gun and he considered asking Jim for it, but then the prayer was over. It had gone by far too fast.

When the prayer ended, Talitha's sarcasm came out, "Great! Thanks Father, we're all safe now." She gave a shake to her blind head and sighed.

Everyone now looked at him expectantly and Will gritted his teeth and made to turn around, but his legs were adroitly reluctant. It took a conscious act to move forward, and robot like, he walked slowly into the stinking gloom.

"Uh...oh Lord, eh...eh...eh!" His throat began an involuntary retching. The stench grew more over powering with each step and Will fought to keep from throwing up. The smell was otherworldly, it was a hellish mixture of feces and rotting flesh. He had to pause a few feet from the door and wipe away the sweat that was going from beads to rivulets on his brow.

"Eh...eh...eh!" The fight to keep his gorge down went on, but with the greatest effort, he finally began to breathe easier. However, the urge remained lurking just under his Adam's apple, looking for any excuse to come back.

He was not alone in his misery, the others wore matching masks of pale green nausea. All but Talitha, who stood near the back of the group and said impatiently, "Come on, Will! Get moving."

The door was feet from him, just visible in the velvet blackness. His chances were 1 in 5 of dying if he walked through that door. He couldn't move.

"Go on," Sean Shay groaned from just behind him in a voice that grated on Will's sensibilities. He wanted to turn and punch him in his fat face. Sean had nothing to fear and Will's unnamed jealousy riled him, but also catalyzed him into stepping further into the dark stench.

"Sorry...sorry," Will said without meaning it and he dragged his feet forward and reached out with a slow hand and took a grip of the cold doorknob. With a deep breath of the foul air, he screwed up his face and turned it.

It didn't budge.

The door was locked! The thought was a triumph within him and a wave of stupid relief went through his body as if the locked door meant he could turn around now and go home.

"The d-d-door is l-l-locked," he said embarrassed at his stutter.

"Here you go," Sean Shay held out an old brass key and Will looked at him angrily. The fat man looked like a large pudding sweating in the sun. He jiggled around the edges and Will hated him. Sean had nothing to fear, but Will forgot that he didn't know it yet and his anger at the man's useless fear was bitter.

He refused the key and stood aside to let Sean at the door to open it. However, Sean just stood there, his fat wiggling under his arm as his hand shook. Neither moved for seconds, until Sean won the cowardly battle simply by pressing the key into Will's reluctant hand.

Will's hatred for the man spiked, but disappeared altogether forgotten, as he turned to the door. The smell and what lay beyond it consumed him. His own hands shook so much that it took both of them to guide the key into the lock and this time the knob turned easily.

The smell was terrific.

The urge to vomit came back greater than before and he breathed in great gasps to keep from hurling up his breakfast, but someone behind him threw up. It was loud and noisome and the sound of it splattering on the concrete was too much for Will. He doubled over and hurled up a great mess.

Strength left him and he fell to his knees still vomiting, holding up his left arm pathetically, to ward off any attack from the demon. But none came and seconds went by and still he retched and heaved, bringing up nothing but loud unpleasant burps. Finally, he stopped and knelt there sweating and feverish, looking back he saw Talitha alone still stood.

The men around her, were on all fours or knelt in varying stages of sickness and the mess on the floor beneath them was enough for Will's stomach to threaten him again and he turned away looking into the room. What he saw there was worse; his stomach's issues went forgotten as his mind struggled to come to terms with the sight.

A single light bulb on a chain hung from the ceiling, even as he envisioned it. It was old and dim, but still shed enough light for him to see the grizzly details his premonition had missed. He hadn't seen that the walls were covered in uncouth satanic symbols, drawn undoubtedly in blood; they were now a dark black with reddish-brown edging. From the shelving that ran along the walls, long strips of flesh or meat hung, and beneath each, puddles of dark fluid collected. Upon the mattress, which was stained with enough blood to have turned it black, a body reclined, its skin had been peeled away, and the bones of it stuck out unnaturally as if someone had rummaged through the corpse in search of something.

Finally and worst of all, a man like a king on a bloody throne sat on the crate in the very center of the room. If ever there was a king of blood, this was it. He seemed covered in it from head to toe, layered, with fresh red blood glistening over the blackened dried mess below it.

The only part of the man not covered, were his eyes. These shone out of the ruin of his face, burning with insane joyful malevolence at the sight of the men vomiting in the corridor. They were blue and strikingly so compared to the red black of his skin.

Those blue eyes now locked on Will's and with a private smile that sent flakes of dried blood raining from the corners of his mouth, he showed Will something.

It was a bone, heavy with meat and wet with blood. He held it up for Will's enjoyment before biting into, tearing at the meat and chewing with gusto.

Will's eyes bugged and his legs began to tremble as the strength to stand drained away. Will tried to run from the sight, but succeeded only into knocking into Sean Shay, who also stared, eyes bulging. Will looked for a way around the fat man, but he took up the entire doorway.

The king on his throne of blood spoke then and the sound of his voice sent ice running through Will's veins, "Come in Will Jern."

Chapter 14

The Demon's Disciple

"Don't leave Will Jern, you only just got here." The man's voice was ripping up his own vocal cords and Will felt the empathetic need to swallow, but the sight of him chewing the meat wouldn't allow it and Will could only grimace as if in pain.

"How…how do you know my name?" he asked, tearing his eyes from the man and looking instead at the cement floor where a constellation of dried blood drops, were sprayed about haphazardly.

"Ba'al has a long memory for those that would defy him."

Will's mind shot back eight years, to that brief moment when he had stood upon the gleaming path denying Ba'al. But the memory must have been of another person. The man on the bridge had been strong, standing upright in defiance, while here in the room Will was weak and clutched at the blood-strewn walls to keep from falling over. The man on the bridge had looked death in the face without wavering and his hands were steady, while Will's shook uncontrollably and he couldn't bear to even look up.

"Who is…is that?" Will pointed to the mattress behind the man.

"That is a very special friend. I don't know his name if that's what you're asking, not that it matters." Ba'al looked down fondly at the ravaged remains of the corpse and calmly tossed his bone into it.

Will jumped as he did so.

A hand, heavy and fat had come down on his shoulder. "Go," Sean nudged him in the back and Will lacked the strength to resist him and was pushed further into the room. He still couldn't look directly at the man possessed by Ba'al, but he watched him with his peripheral vision until he heard the horrible voice speaking to Jim and only then could Will look at the gore-covered man.

"Jim Anderson, welcome back, you were missed. At least the tasty, tasty nun missed you." Jim's face was equal parts fear, anger, nausea, and shock. It looked as if the muscles of his face couldn't decide on which emotion to accompany and thus they twitched in an odd, somewhat random order, as he walked to stand next to Will.

Will could sympathize, his own twitch had progressed to the point that his right eye was nearly useless, opening and closing with such rapidity that he was forced to squeeze it shut. His face now looked like it had frozen in the middle of an exaggerated wink.

"Who is that hiding behind you Sean? Well, it's the saint. Saint John and look, Father Alba dressed for the Easter Bunny." From the side Will could see the villain grin at each in turn, but none could stand to look at the demon for more than a second, before turning their eyes away in fear.

All that is, except for Talitha. She stood beaming in the general direction of Ba'al, and she seemed altogether unfazed by the horror that surrounded her.

The voice slipped into a harsh lechery, "Now here is a treat, Talitha Jern, still so beautiful."

She ignored him and inclined her head toward her

left. "Will, if you please?" For a moment, he stared at her clueless to what she wanted and it sent her eyebrows sliding together in annoyance.

"Oh yeah…uh, the subject is sitting cross-legged on…" He described the scene leaving nothing out of his description of the man or the room. Talitha's face, other than a look of deepening concentration remained solidly placid, but Will, who knew his sister, both aspects of her, could see there was a ripple of trepidation creasing the edges of her calm façade.

Finally, when he was done, Talitha spoke to the blood covered man, "This room, with its symbols and blood and gore…are you thinking this will frighten me?"

"I know what frightens you, and it's not a room. Teeth have always frightened you and of course glass as well… Auraghnash," he paused staring closely at Talitha, who remained absolutely still, perhaps too still. "Auraghnash sends his love."

Her jaw tightened visibly, but she rallied, "Ba'al is now the messenger of Auraghnash? Things have changed in the void since I've been gone, and for the better."

"Amusing. Still I don't recall you laughing when we were together in the pits at Rek."

Talitha paled, which sent a shock of fear through Will's heart. He had thought her afraid of nothing and the knowledge that she could be afraid, even in the smallest way of this man, made his own fear double. He was not alone in this, the priests glanced into each other's faces with eyes that had grown huge, and Sean Shay was slowly edging into Father John as if for protection.

Talitha, whose tan had now completely faded, spoke angrily but without looking full into the man's face, "I know you're a fraud. I know it. Somehow you are."

Ba'al turned his ice blue eyes on Will then. Will tried to look away, but Ba'al had him, holding him with the ferocious intensity of his gaze and Will could do nothing but step back into the wall, as Ba'al spoke with a mouth that trickled blood from the corners.

"When she first came into the void, I was there waiting on her and I took her down into Rek." He smiled at the memory and for a moment his eyes were off Will, who quickly looked away, down again at the floor. When Ba'al started again, Will could feel the words coming at him, but he dared not look back up.

"Oh, her screams were so *lively*. They had such strength! I can recall each of them, however my favorite was your first. Do you remember? You tried to be strong and defiant! Tell your friends what made you scream."

It was a command, but Talitha refused it, shaking her head. This only made Ba'al grin. "You aren't embarrassed are you? We were betrothed that night and…"

"You are not Ba'al!" She quivered in fury, her hands clenched.

"Then how did I know that? How do I know that your brother pissed his pants the night he took you from me?"

Will's eyes went wide and shot to the man's face in shocked surprise. What Ba'al had said was true, but Will had told no one, not even Lisa.

Ba'al had paused but now went on, "And Father

Alba, how do I know the fact, that you cried like a baby and couldn't stop vomiting when you burned the body of my beloved witch? Or how do I know that Saint John the Hypocrite isn't so saintly after all?"

Father John's mouth became unhinged and fell open, which only made Ba'al laugh his grating cruel laugh. It sounded like, hreah, hreah, hreah. "You like that dark meat, don't you? What was Mrs. Johnson doing on her knees last week? Worshipping you or servicing you?"

Father John with his mouth still open and his eyes bugging shook his head in amateurish denial. He looked as though he were about to say something, but Talitha spoke then in a monotone voice.

"You're a fraud, I know it."

"Can you not look past this skin I wear? I expected more from you. And!" he thundered the word at her. "And I expect my path. Father Alba, tell me you brought more than this damaged girl."

The word seemed to wake Talitha up and she held up her hand to Father Alba, snapping her fingers sharply. "Damaged?" she asked, challenging Ba'al.

"Do you prefer malformed? You're not quite human, not quite demon, something pathetically in between, but I can fix that you know. I have that power."

"What power?" Talitha shrunk with the whispered words, while Ba'al grew. He smiled his awful smile and looked more than ever like a king holding sway over a bloody court.

"Ihgse xythm ey jsuit..." The demon spoke in his hell language and the hair rose on the nape of Will's neck. He realized that coming here had been a horrible idea and he glanced at the door, wondering if he could get past his sister. The look showed that Father Alba was having second thoughts as well; he had retreated into the corridor and was barely visible.

"I don't have it," Talitha said looking down and backing up slightly.

The demon glowered, his anger palpable, and Talitha took a second step back, and it was then that Will *knew* another one of them would die. The knowledge came like a shot out of the blue and following it was a wave of adrenaline coursing throughout his whole being, making his skin feel alive, tingling.

In the next second, however it went dead, numb.

There would be a third death. The knowledge simply popped into his head and there was no taking it back.

Will didn't bother hoping he would live. That he could avoid dying seemed highly unlikely and he sank into a warm haze of apathy, watching the demon's anger grow to frightening proportions as it began yelling at Talitha in his hell language.

However the yelling seemed to have an odd effect on Talitha, she no longer looked as though in the least fearful, instead a fire of hate burned behind her eyes.

Ba'al must have seen this as well and he quite abruptly changed tactics, becoming conciliatory, "You don't have the sword, but you can get it, right? Ba'al can be very generous when the mood strikes him."

From Will's point of view Ba'al should have remained angry, because Talitha now became mocking, "No, you are miserly and cruel and a liar. And not a very good liar either. You were never planning on giving back any of those boys you took, were you?"

"You do know me well, Talitha. Those children are mine to do with as I please. Why should I give them up?"

She shrugged as if she couldn't think of a reason, "I don't know. I wouldn't give them up." She gave a little wave of her hand dismissing the topic of the missing children. "In what way would you be so generous, Ba'al? The sword is worth far more than a handful of children...what are you offering?"

"I know what you crave above all else." His eyes glittered with secret knowledge. "You want a name. I can name you."

She drew in a sharp little breath, her eyes growing large at the prospect and for what felt like a significant portion of eternity, the two of them faced each other in heavy silence.

Will knew nothing of what they were talking about, but the fact that his sister was even considering trading the sword, burned through his apathy.

"What does he mean, name you?" Will asked, his voice shrill now that he had found emotion again.

They both ignored him and after exchanging a worried look with Father Alba, who had poked his head back in the door, Will said with more conviction, "Talitha! Tell me about this naming business."

Still they ignored him and minutes passed in heavy silence before the possessed man spoke, breaking the spell, "It's good that you're considering this."

Talitha let a smile slip across her face, a mysterious one and where a few minutes before she had backed up, now she advanced on Ba'al. "What would you name me?"

"Hesda Arad Olad'fa," the man said this in the rasping tearing language of his and Talitha cocked an eyebrow at it.

"Keeper of the Bridge of Blood…very cool." She moved even closer and stood just in front of him as he sat high on his tall crate, her shoulders even with his knees.

"Yes it is, very cool. What do you think?"

Talitha put both of her hands on the man's thighs and ran them up his legs before answering, "I have a better name, one that is more fitting, Ba'al Fie-ere…Denier of Ba'al."

The man's blood dripping smile transformed in an instant to look of hate and this was followed a split second later by a comical look of pained surprise. Talitha had shot her hand out striking the man square in the gut and even before all the air had shot out of him, she grabbed him and threw him bodily to the floor.

She wasted not a second before pouncing on him, but shocked them all when instead of attacking the man, she tore at his clothes, searching.

"Uh, Talitha?" Will asked hesitantly.

She ignored him and after a moment, she stepped back away from the man, her eyes roving blindly around in worry. To Will she looked as if she had just realized she had miscalculated, badly. The man, in the mean time, had found his breath and despite his labored breathing, he was making his way to his feet, his face wreathed in a frightful anger.

Talitha sensed it somehow and took a step back, running into the blood-stained crate. This sparked a new idea and turning, she heaved hard on the lid of it, straining for a few seconds before it came open, the wood screaming, or so it seemed.

This was the source of the horrid smell. What came from it then was far worse than anything they had yet experienced and it dropped Will to his knees retching and gagging. The others were in the same plight except for Sean Shay who had passed out all together, falling over as though he had been pole-axed.

Talitha in the mean time had somehow ignored the smell and was half-in and half-out of the crate rummaging through it, blindly fishing about the contents before pulling her upper body out. In her hands she held a small sheaf of yellowing paper.

"No!" the possessed man roared sending a chill wash over Will, but Talitha was now fearless of the demon and swatted him backhand across the face, a casual smack for her, but the man reeled from it.

Unbelievably she sniffed at the paper and Will begged her, "Please shut that…the crate. Shut it." This she did, displaying an act of humanity that was unlike her. The smell diminished immediately and a moment later Will was able to rise, sweating and coughing.

Relaxed now, Talitha strolled over holding out the papers. "Can you read any of this?"

Will took the papers; they were scrawled with odd letters and a maze of diagrams. Turning them over in his hands a few times he said, "Mostly no. It's in a language I've never seen, but there are some notes on the edging in English. It says something about diagram placement, but it's got yellow brown stains…maybe coffee and I can't read it very well in this light. Do you know what this is?"

Ignoring the question, she turned back to Ba'al. "Coffee? You'd drink coffee around this?" She seemed outraged at the idea and after taking the papers from Will's hand, she advanced on the man, turning her head slowly in different directions. "So, what will Ba'al do to you when he gets a hold of your soul?" she asked conversationally.

"Do not mar those papers! I am a servant of Ba'al and it's your soul you should be worried about." Will watched and heard but there was no comprehension on his part.

"Trust me, I do worry about my soul." Talitha raised an eyebrow and tore the sheets in half.

It was as if a light switch had been thrown within Will—something had changed. Something about the room and the man and thankfully even the smell, seemed less than it was, dampened or even diminished. The blood and the body and the symbols were still all about them, but now they lacked the power of fear that had saturated the room.

Even Sean Shay must have noted it, because he immediately started groaning and then struggled to stand.

"No..." the possessed man said, his voice now tired and strained as well as suddenly human. He wilted before Talitha and that was no wonder. She seemed to have grown and there was an exultant smile on her beautifully evil face.

"Yes!" she cried jubilant, holding the torn sheet up over her head in triumph beaming around the room as if expecting the men to applaud her, however Will's mind, like a tree bending under too much snow felt near the breaking point, and he was lost as to what was going on.

"Talitha…" he started, but she held up her hand.

"Hold that thought," she tilted her head slightly, pivoted on her left foot and with a speed Will didn't think possible, she tilted her body and kicked the man in the face with a snapping round house. He dropped in an instant and lay moaning, clutching the side of his face, while Talitha stood, demonstrating an amazing balance with her right foot still in the air.

She moved in reverse, with purposeful slow motion, bringing her leg back down with the grace of a dancer. "Wow, I feel good. Did you see that kick, Will? Unerring!"

"Yeah, that was great, Tal, but why? Why'd you do that? We may never get those kids back now."

"Kids? I hope I'm there when your brain finally turns on," she said this sweetly and Will felt his face get hot. "He just told us that he never planned to give those kids back. Weren't you paying attention?"

"Yeah, but…" He left off, not knowing what to say. She was right of course, the man had said that, but just then Will didn't know if that was Ba'al talking or a man.

"I can tell that you're confused as usual, but that's ok, I'm used to it." She spoke to Will as if he were a five year old and his face burned hotter with anger and embarrassment, but she couldn't see it and went on calmly, "You want those kids back and I can help you with that, however, it's not going to be pretty. So why don't you take your little friends out of here and go make some tea?"

Father Alba, who stood just inside the room asked, "What are you planning on doing, Miss Jern?"

"Torture of course. We tried it your way talking, blah, blah, blah. Now we'll do things my way."

"No, Miss Jern, we…" the priest began, but she cut right across him.

"I'm so tired of you talking to me in such an insolent manner, Alba." Her voice was low and fairly dripped with venom. "And another thing. No more of this Miss Jern crap, I am now Ba'al Fie-ere."

The man, Will still thought of as Ba'al Zubel, had just struggled to his feet, and started to say something, but Talitha alerted by the sound of his movement punched him dead center in his chest. He went down again, his breath came and went, a tiny squeaking sound, high and weak, and to Will alarming.

They all stared at the man in shock and when a minute went by and the squeaking hadn't progressed, Will asked, "Should we do something about him?"

"He'll be fine. You know, I killed a man a few months back with a punch to the solar plexus, wham! Dead center." She shook her head sadly. "What a waste, he went so fast. But you won't have to worry your pretty little head, Will. I learned my lesson; this one won't die so easily. I'll make sure it will take a long, long time."

Her smile made him cold.

"See, he's moving, I told you he'd be fine." Talitha turned her vicious smile back to the man. His breathing had progressed past the squeak and into a wheeze, which was helping his complexion. He had been a fearful purple beneath the dried blood and now, Will could see that he had turned a high pink.

Grabbing his hair, Talitha helped him to his feet by it, before slapping hard across the face. It was like the sound of a cracking whip, but with volume and the man collapsed again at the feet of Father Alba.

The sound triggered something in Will. It was like déjà vu, but he knew it was a vision. He saw blackness suddenly lit, followed by a crash. The death, the first one was creeping closer. His chest constricted painfully and he checked his watch 11:58. It would be soon.

"Miss Jern," Father Alba stared at the man groaning at his feet, "You can't..."

Talitha leapt over the possessed man, just as pretty as a deer clearing a fence and landed a foot to Father Alba right. She slipped in close to the startled priest, pivoted around him, and within a second had him by his throat.

"Hey! Uhhhng!" The priest's eyes bulged as she applied a healthy squeeze.

"Talitha, no!" This was shouted in chorus by Will, Jim, and Father John and they each stepped nearer to her.

"Stop!" her voice, startlingly loud, stopped the men. "I can tear out his throat in an instant. Ask Will if you don't believe me."

No one asked, but all eyes went to him and he nodded rapidly.

"Talitha, please..." Will began, pleadingly.

"Ba'al Fie-ere! My name is Ba'al Fie-ere!" she yelled, her face a furious mask that came and went in a second only to be replaced with a sudden blazing triumphant smile. "I have named myself! As is only proper."

"I'm sorry...Ba'al Fie-ere," Will had trouble spitting out the name. "Father Alba is about to pass out. Could you please...uh?"

"Uh, what? Not kill my hostage? I guess so, for now. Hey look at that." Talitha's head turned slightly back and forth at the blood covered man who crawled toward her in something of a delirium. She backed out of the room still holding the priest by his heavy jowls.

"Good doggy," she wore an unpleasant smile for the man. "Look at that, Will. If only you were so well trained, I would consider keeping you around, when my dreams are done."

"What are you doing...Ba'al Fie-ere?" Will had nearly forgotten to add her new name and she had glanced up with a new menace in her eye.

"I'm doing you a favor."

"What favor? I don't understand."

"What else is new, Will? When do you ever understand, shit?" Clearly aggravated she stomped on the man as he crawled up to her. "Let me spell it out for you: I'm going to hurt this little bastard! I'm going to make him scream and beg for death. I'm going to make him really bleed! And he's going to learn, he can't fuck with me!" She screamed this more at the man than at Will.

However, she calmed suddenly, the manic air about her turning sweet. "I'm going to do this for you, Will...dear brother. I know being the good guy can be so constricting, so limiting, so damn boring! You can't hurt him like you really, really want to. Deep down, I know you want to. You want to hurt him bad for what he's done, you want to punish him for what he did to that nun. Doing it in her ass, making her..."

Jim's face had grown red with a tremendous rage and Will worried that he would rush her, not to hurt her but to kill the man. He stepped in front of Jim. "Talitha...I mean Ba'al Fie-ere, please stop. Ok, I understand, I guess, but...but what do you need the priest for?"

"I had planned on taking him as a hostage the moment I heard his cowardly voice. I knew you wouldn't let me cut up this pathetic fraud without having proper collateral. He sure did have me going there though..." She looked down at the man, hatred marring her features. Grabbing the priest by his thinning hair with one hand, she pulled him down. Kneeling, she turned the possessed man over and dug through his pockets.

She held up something small and thin that glittered, "Looky! A razor blade, for sudden unexplained bleeding and..." She dug about again and brought out a key, shiny and new. *"He somehow got out of his room and killed a nun,"* she mimicked her brother's voice making him sound idiotic. "He faked the whole thing, so he could get his hands on the sword." She pulled the priest up and stood gazing down, quiet, and contemplative. "But how did you even know about that?"

"Ok, I get it...but you have Ba'al, you could just..." Will began.

"He's not Ba'al Zubel, you idiot! He's not a demon! He's not possessed either, and never was, damn it!" She shouted at Will, shaking the priest easily as if he were a kite rattling in the wind—there was a wild fire of insanity raging behind her eyes

"Yes, yes, of course. I'm sorry." Will's hands were out uselessly attempting to placate the blind woman. "You're right, he's only a man."

"His name is Luke, I think," intoned Jim in his deep voice.

Will went on, "He's just a man, I get it, but, you

have the key and the other is still in the door. You don't need Father Alba, you could lock us all in here. That way you could do…whatever to the man and we won't even try to stop you."

She nodded thoughtfully. "That does sound reasonable, but you've driven me beyond reason, Will."

The sound of an audible and deadly click came from Will's right. Jim stood, holding the gun that had traveled to Maine and back. It was small in his great hands, however in the dim light it was jet black and filled with an uncaring deadly malice.

The sound was not lost on Talitha's keen hearing and she slid easily behind the priest. "So, Big Jim has finally grown a pair?"

"He won't shoot, Talitha," Will said, but was contradicted a moment later.

"Yes I will," Jim told her. "I want answers. What the hell just happened? Were we under a spell?"

"Actually it was an incantation…"

"Is there any damned difference?" he snarled at her, and she only smiled slyly. "Forget that...forget it," he said talking mostly to himself. And then to her, he demanded, "Let the priest go, or else."

"Or else what? You'll shoot?" She gave him a little giggle. "Come on cowboy, take your best shot." She ducked left and right, playfully behind Father Alba, whose wide eyes stayed fixed on the weaving gun in Jim's hands.

Will wanted to protest. He wanted to step in between Talitha and the gun, but he realized that this could be one of the three deaths he had foreseen. He paused at the idea, hating himself as he calculated the odds of living if Father Alba were to die just now. He would go from a three in six chance down to a two in five chance and if he could...

"I can't," Jim murmured.

The sound of the gun clattering on the cement near Will sent his appalling calculations out the window. With a perverse longing, he stared down at the gun, which conversely represented life to him. If he were to possess it, he could decide who lived and who died, who would be afraid and who wouldn't. The thought triggered Will to take a sly glimpse at the men nearby and with relief, he noted they were all taken up with Talitha and no one eyed the gun, but him.

"That wasn't very smart, Jim," Talitha said and in Will's periphery he saw that she had moved to her right, out from behind the priest. Will's eyes flicked over to her, and he saw that she now had one foot on the back of Luke's neck and was grinding her heal down onto it.

The man struggled weakly.

Will didn't care. His eyes darted furtively back down to the gun and he wondered why he didn't just pick it up. After all, Talitha wouldn't know. She was blind. But there seemed to be an inertia within him that was greater than his yearning for the gun. He fought the feeling, knowing there was no reason for him not to command it and bending down, he reached out his hand...

There was a flash in the pitch black, it was brilliant, and it lit up a silhouette of a man just in front of him. Following it was the roar of the gun. It echoed all around him, and in him as well, shaking his inner being. He felt a wave of nausea wash over him, but that feeling was secondary, he needed to know the time, desperately. He pulled back the sleeve of his coat with a hand that sweated against the grip of the black gun and the familiar orange glow of his watch showed 12:19.

He came back to the present with a snap and found himself in the horrible fetid room and he gasped loudly, but the sound went unnoticed. His hand still reached out for the black gun—the one he'd use to kill and seeing this, Will's fingers curled inwardly with an involuntary motion. He pulled his hand back to his chest and glanced around, this time without any devious notions, but with worry that everyone had seen his vision as well and knew what he was going to do. However, they were all still in the exact positions they had been in, as if Will had froze time to see his vision.

With a start, he tore frantically at his sleeve and the friendly orange glow showed the time, 12:01 pm. Eighteen minutes.

"I've dropped the gun, that's what you wanted," Jim said loudly as if Talitha were deaf as well as blind, making Will jump. "Now, please let Father Alba go."

Eighteen minutes, Will would kill in eighteen minutes. He had killed before, twice. This would be his third murder.

"The future is not set," Will didn't know if he had said the words aloud or if he had just thought them, but nobody seemed to notice, nor did they notice him backing away from the gun, eyeing it as he would a dangerous animal.

"But I'm not done having my fun, he's still so squishy and lively," Talitha grabbed the priest's fat stomach and gave it a playful shake. "And besides, he's still moving."

"Don't kill him," Jim pleaded. Will looked at him and saw the tears, the real, factual tears on Jim's face.

They had sprung up out of nowhere.

To Will, it had all the relevance of seeing an apple sitting on a counter. Will's mind was in another world, seeing himself as a killer, again! Knowing that if his soul wasn't forfeit already, it would be as soon as he pulled that trigger. And the fact that Jim was upset mattered nothing to him.

"Kill him?" Talitha asked. "Killing is childish, sophomoric. I'm past that, I've evolved you might say. I'm into pain." Talitha's eyes were now filled with a fevered mania and in their own way, it was worse than the cold evil that had been Ba'al's. Will saw this, but couldn't find it within him to care about that either.

That is until he heard his name sliding from his sister's mouth like warm spit. "Does that make you feel better, *Will*? That your priest will live? Disfigured, maimed, hopefully insane, but alive? All because of you."

Will's mouth came open and he stared at her stupidly, the conversation that had gone on around him, slowly bubbled up from the molasses of his mind. "My fault?"

Father Alba shook his head, the fat of his jowls swinging back and forth. "Don't blame yourself, Will."

"No, do blame yourself. I warned you, remember?" Talitha wasn't going to be denied. "I told you to speak to me with proper respect but you wouldn't listen. You had to go and be an asshole. So now, whatever happens to the priest will be on your head, I hope you can live with yourself."

"I'm sorry, I wasn't feeling well. I dreamed your dreams and they make me…edgy."

She glared at him, harshly. "If that had been the

only thing you'd ever done to me, I might have forgiven you."

His mind cast aside thoughts of his upcoming murder and blundered about trying to recall what he had done to Talitha. "Taking you out of the void? I was trying to help."

"What about this?" She gestured at herself, from head to toe. "This is all your fault. Everything for the last eight years has been your fault! If you hadn't been out trying to dip your wick into Lisa, this wouldn't have happened. Dad left me to find you, remember? He left me alone with a demon! You were supposed to be home."

A great bonfire of guilt turned him cold inside. "I'm sorry."

Her pretty face turned nasty, feral. "I don't care about sorry. I care about payback. Come trade places with the priest. Remember the demon Juuba' al-ex? Remember the teeth? Let that be you, instead of him."

Goosebumps flared at the memory of the dream and Will took another step back away from her. The priest's eyes, huge and brown were on him. They held a desperate fear. A brave man would have traded places with the priest without hesitation; his father would have. But Will had gone through too much and he knew too much. He knew about the pain.

He hesitated a second before answering. The vision of Juuba' al-ex and the teeth, the endless teeth coming out of the black made him hesitate. And when he heard his own screams echoing in his mind, his pause stretched out.

His mouth came open, but no sound issued from it and the taste of the horror in the room settled on his tongue but it was nothing compared to the dreadful memory and it went unnoticed.

Talitha shook her head; the tremendous contempt in her smile staked his heart. "I thought so. Coward!"

"No...wait," He fished about in an empty mind for something to say, but before he could, she twisted the bitter stake into him, splintering it.

"Don't you have any of your father in you?"

"I'll trade places with Father Alba," Jim's words finished what Talitha had started and Will felt himself shrink at them. He became nothing.

"No. I want only Will," she said.

"Ok," the word was inaudible to all but Talitha, who smiled with cruel intentions. Will took a deep breath and tried again, "Ok, I'll switch...if you want me to."

"It's too late, coward," she sneered at him.

At that moment he hated her with unnatural passion, but the hatred that he felt toward himself was nearly as great and the feeling of being small went from figurative to literal; his shoulders slumped and his back stooped.

"Talitha, I want you to know, that I forgive you for what you have done and...unnnghh!" Father Alba went instantly red with the force of her squeeze and slowly, he turned a purple color in her hand.

"I didn't ask for your forgiveness and I don't want it," she said quietly.

"Talitha!" Jim growled a warning, which brought about a smile from her. Jim's eyes flashed at it and he barked, "Talitha, damn it! Let go of him."

Surprisingly she did, "Damn it? So manly, so forceful, I like it. Hey, Will. Try adding that to your

vocabulary. It might make you feel like a man."
Releasing her grip on the priest, she took the white stole from about his shoulders and with amazing strength, tore it in half lengthways.

Twisting one section, she tied one end of it around the neck of Father Alba, making a combination noose and leash.

"Ba'al Fie-ere, what are you doing?" Will asked, using her adopted name. It didn't matter that Jim still called her Talitha; Will knew that if he tried it, someone would get hurt.

"I'm tying up my prisoners, duh." She was sitting full upon Luke's back, working the second half of the twisted stole into a knot.

Father Alba, who had been gasping for breath, said, "I forgive you regardless…"

Talitha gave her end of the makeshift rope a sharp tug, tightening the noose suddenly. "Maybe you should wait until I am done with you before you forgive me. I promise to leave your tongue intact, so that…" She paused and swung her head around. "Jim! I hear you, now step back."

Jim had taken two quiet steps toward the door. "No. You call Father Alba a hostage, but you talk of torturing him, why shouldn't we just rush you right now? It won't be any worse for the priest."

"I'll tell you why. First, you're too slow and I'm not just talking about your lack of brains either. You'll never make it. I'll have his throat out in a heartbeat." She paused and gave a tug on Luke's leash bringing him to his feet. Ignoring his gasping, she slammed him face first into the wall, pinning him there. "Second, this isn't my fault and after what's been done to me. I'm in a very eye for an eye mood. Hey, Father? Isn't that in the bible somewhere?"

Somewhere in the last eight years, Father Alba had discovered a reserve of courage within him. He said in strong voice, "Jesus instructs us to love our enemies."

She snorted, "Yeah he was always bit fruity. But you ducked the question. Does your bible say something about an eye for an eye? The reason I ask...look at me. Remember what happened to Father Menning?"

The priest craned his neck around to look at her, his eyes bulged in fear. "Please...no."

"Oh yeah! Father Menning clawed his own eyes out, driven insane by Ba'al Zubel.," She paused, her own eyes were wide with excitement. "I don't have any of those fancy mind tricks yet, so I am going to have to take your eyes out by hand."

"What did you say?" Jim asked, with equal parts outrage and disbelief.

She ignored the big man and spoke to the white-faced priest, "Look at what Will did to me, he took my sight, soooo, an eye for an eye just like your bible says."

"Jesus would actually instruct you to turn the other cheek," the priest said in a quavering voice, his desperation sapping the strength from it.

She turned smug, "So you say, but you won't follow that command, so why should I?"

"I will," Father Alba declared quietly.

"Father," She said with a little smirk. "When I take your left eye, it won't be clean like in those Kung Fu movies; it won't just pop out. It's going to burst and I'm going to have to dig around in the socket to get all of it." She paused for the thought to sink in and Father Alba let out an obliging moan of fear. Upon hearing it, she smiled broadly and went on, "So, in accord with Jesus' teachings, you're going to then turn your head, to let me at the right one as well?"

The horrifying room with its blood-strewn walls was silent. Will shook his head back and forth, pleading desperately with wide eyes, but Father Alba refused to look in his direction and was long in answering, but finally said, "Yes I will."

Chapter 15

The First Death

Will *knew* she would attempt to lock them in, perhaps even before she did, but she was faster, closer and though blind, she moved with an astounding nimbleness and the door slammed shut in Will's face as he threw himself forward. The boom of the heavy door against the jam had a finality to it that threatened to overturn the now delicate workings of his mind and as he stood leaning his forehead against the door he could feel the vibrations coursing through it.

They triggered a thought that pulsated throughout his body: Three would die. He looked around at the men with him. The others had not moved and they had all stood as if helpless spectators, as Talitha entombed them with a mutilated corpse and the unimaginable stink. They looked not only helpless, but useless as well.

A scowl creased his features before he turned back to the door and pounded on it with his fists. Ignoring her new name, he shouted at the top of his lungs, "Talitha! Don't do this! Don't do this! I'm warning you. You can't come back from this!"

Will paused to listen, however there was nothing but the slight shaking of the door and the thought came to him again: Three would die. It came with more urgency and Will checked his watch, 12:06.

He felt fatigued by the sight and sagged against the door, however it was sticky with a black viscous goo and letting out a low groan, he pulled away from it, revolted to his core.

"What do we do?" Sean Shay asked as if he were a little boy, unable to think for himself. This earned him another scowl from Will, but it was also a catalyst for Jim. Striding over to the door, he gripped the knob and yanked and heaved at it, straining, becoming roused with the effort.

He was not just a tall man, but hugely strong and muscular and the sinews of his arms swelled as he pulled with all of his considerable might. But to no avail. The door held firm without the slightest shimmy and he paused to take a few big breaths.

Will only saw one way out. "Forget the knob. Tear down the door!" he barked the order to Jim and stood back out of the way. It was well that he did too, because the giant unleashed an amazing fury on the door blocking his way.

Time and again, he threw his entire weight, bodily against it, irregardless of any pain. It was an awesome sight but even he tired after a minute and at the first pause, Will order Sean at it. Sean charged it without complaint and he too was something to see, however he tired far more rapidly and still the door had not budged.

Will sent Jim to relieve Sean, who was panting like a mule and checked his watch, 12:09. Ten minutes. He would kill again in ten minutes. His eyes went back to the gun, no longer coveting it, but repulsed by it. Yet for reasons unknown to him, he went over to it and picked it up and hefted it in his hand, liking the weight.

He stared down at it, absorbed by the reality of death it symbolized. Time ticked away.
Thud…thud…thud! The noise was rhythmic and it was

a second before Will realized it was occurring outside of himself. Jim was kicking at the door, his great leg pistoning out, angry sweat dripping from his face. Thud...thud...thud!

"Use the gun, Will." Father John stood beside him, his face no longer handsome, but aged by fear and creased by worry.

Will's first thought, *It's not time yet*, made him check his watch in the exact same manner as he would at 12:19. With the gun in his right hand, he pulled back his sleeve with his pointer finger...his trigger finger and the orange glow told him it was still 12:09.

He gave the priest a puzzled look, not at what the priest had said but at the fact that it was still 12:09. Time, it seemed, was an ally of death and was holding itself back to ensure Will kept his appointed fate.

"Shoot the lock," Father John prompted.

"Huh?" It took a moment for Will to realize, the gun might have another use. "No, you do it." Will pushed the gun into the priest's hands and stepped back nodding encouragement and pointing at the door for emphasis.

"Ok, I guess. Stand aside you two!" Father John was small and thin, conversely the gun looked all the more powerful, and when he pulled the trigger, the sound of it in the room was shocking.

Jim went to try the door but stopped a few feet away, it was plain, the priest had missed. There was a hole a foot above the lock.

"Get closer," Jim suggested to the priest, who obviously didn't like the idea and only took two baby steps nearer. Will covered his ears this time.

Blam! Blam! Blam! On his fifth shot, he hit the

lock dead on. Jim wasted no time and attacked it again, yanking and pulling with all of his might, but still it wouldn't budge. He turned back to Will perplexed.

Will was baffled as well, always in the movies this sort of thing had worked. He studied the lock for a second. "Get closer…no right here. And shoot at an angle."

Since he kept turning his head at the last moment, it took three more shots before Father John hit the lock a second time.

"Hold on!" Jim roared and again strained at the knob, and now there was obvious movement. He went back and forth and moments later the lock gave and the door flew open. The air of the corridor, fouled by the vomit of five men was cool and wonderfully fresh compared to the terror of the room.

The men dashed for the stairs. The feeling of relief at getting out of the horrendous room was indescribable. Will found himself grinning as he jogged along and he wasn't alone in this. Puffing next to him, his many chins bouncing up and down was Sean Shay and he sported a huge grin as well.

Will scowled at him.

He couldn't help it. He hated the man. He couldn't help that either. Will tried not to think about him and when they reached the stairs, Sean quickly fell back breathing loudly.

Mid-way up the stairs, Will caught up with Jim and as they reached the top, they tore down the hall together, but when they entered the chapel itself, he stopped.

"I don't see the trail!" Jim said, anxiety coloring his voice. He swung his huge ugly head back and forth staring down at the carpet. "There were blood drops all the way up here and now they're gone."

With the lights off in the main room, the carpet was very dark and there was going to be no chance to see blood on it. Will dropped to his knees, his hands out running his fingers delicately over the carpet.

"Here's a drop, they went this way." Will was up and racing for the front doors. As he entered the foyer, which had more windows and thus was better lit, he could see the blood plainly.

"More blood," he called out excitedly. "With Luke bleeding like this we should be able to track them easily!" He saw blood on the handles to the double doors and shot through them, eager to catch up to his sister, who couldn't have gotten very far, not with two hostages.

The rain was coming down as heavy as before and Will ran into it but stopped only a few feet from the front doors. There was no longer a blood trail. The rain flowed over him, washing away the last of his enthusiasm.

"Damn it!" Jim raged against the storm and then went to his hands and knees searching the running water.

"Stop," Father John put his hand on the giant's shoulder. "The trail's gone, but it doesn't matter, look." He pointed to a nearly empty parking lot. "Father Alba's car is missing, it was right there. They could be anywhere."

Jim stared long at the parking lot, his face congealing miserably, but then he became animated by sudden anger. "You!" he thundered at Will. "You can see the future!" It came out as an accusation and he advanced on an alarmed Will. "Where are they?" he demanded, grabbing Will and shaking him.

"I don't know."

He towered over Will and his rage made him look even bigger. "You do know; now tell me where they are!" Jim had his fist raised to strike and for a second Will wanted to be punched. A punch from a man that big would certainly knock him out, and he'd lose any chance he would have to kill…whoever it was.

"I'm sorry Jim, but it doesn't work that way. The visions come to me, I can't make them happen." Even as he said it, Will realized that may not be true; after all he had never tried and with good reason.

"Are you sure?" Father John looked at him with brown eyes that were sharp and flinty with accusation. "Father Alba told me just last night that the old lady…from before could see into the future if she wanted."

"Yeah, did he tell you that people died when she did?" Will was suddenly worried that they would ask this of him and he became defensive and angry in his own right.

"People are going to die anyways!" Jim cried and gripped him by the shoulders. Will had strong broad shoulders, but they suddenly felt frail and easily broken in Jim's tremendous hands. The man gave Will a healthy shake and continued. "I think blinding Father Alba will be just the start if we don't get there to stop her."

"And she's going to torture that demon-guy," Sean Shay said from the warmth of the church.

"He deserves it!" Will spat out angrily at him.

"You're right, Will. He does deserve it," Jim agreed

reasonably. "My worry is what information she'll get from him. He knows things he shouldn't, even Talitha thought so. He might know how to use the sword."

The rain thrummed loud all about them, but the four men were silent. Will checked his watch, 12:12. Seven minutes left.

There had been seven people in the room when he had his final two premonitions and three of them would die soon, one very soon, but would any of these deaths be his fault? Would looking into the future cause them to happen?

Yes.

Unfortunately, that answer was easy. After all, he could just sit down in the rain and let the time run down until his watch read 12:20. There would be no flash of light, no roar of the gun and no blood on his hands.

Or perhaps there would be more blood. How many would die if he did nothing at all? Father Alba and Luke to start with, but if he didn't stop Talitha now, there could be hundreds. Maybe even thousands. His heart told him many thousands.

"Ok I'll do it...I'm not sure if this will work, but I'm willing to try," Will said.

Jim pulled his hands off of Will as if he had a disease that was catchy. "What should we do?"

"Nothing," Will spoke quietly, a nervousness had begun thrilling through him and he wrapped his arms around himself, for warmth as well as to keep his hands from shaking.

He thought that looking into the future would be more difficult than it turned out to be. He simply reached within the core of his mind and the vision sprang to life before him.

"It's very dark…they're going down stairs slowly, warily… they're nearby, right down the street, Haikes Rubber and Tire. I can read the sign! They're deep down in the place, underground in a sub level maybe? I'm not sure…there's a body!" Seeing it hurt Will's head, a sharp stabbing pain that went through the middle of his brain.

"Is it Father Alba's?" Jim asked in alarm.

"No…it's…a boy. Oh no!" The body was that of one of the missing boys. Will didn't how he knew that, but he did. The boy was tied, kneeling down over a box and in a second, Will saw all that he was going to see. He pulled himself out of the vision and with horror he wandered out into the rain.

He stared up into it, letting the water run into his eyes, but it didn't help, the boy was still there in his mind, he had been dead for days. His skin was a sick black color and parts of it were bloated and filled with toxic gasses. In other areas on the boy's body, the skin had split in great fissures, and these were now home to maggots roiling over each other by the thousands.

"Oh, God, no!" Will shook his head hard. Swinging it back and forth, making himself dizzy, but it didn't help and when he opened his eyes, the boy was there, just in front of him—kneeling over the box, his pants down around his knees.

Will rubbed hard at his face, the twitch jumping madly around his right eye, obscuring reality, but leaving the vision of the boy still perfectly clear. He had been sodomized in a horrendous fashion. The flesh back there was an open maggot filled gaping hole.

"No!" Will screamed at the top of his lungs.

The vision of the boy's rotting body wouldn't stop,

everywhere he looked, it was there revealing more of it terrible surprises. He could now smell its sweet sickening stench and then he heard the pathetic soul wrenching cries of the boy begging for his life and then begging to die.

"No!" Will screeched again even louder. Nothing was stopping the vision, now. It came regardless of what he tried to do and Will strayed over the edge of insanity and played in its shallower waters. He struck himself with tremendous viciousness across the face and then again and again until Jim finally came up and pinned his arms to his sides in a great bear hug.

His head throbbed, however the blows had been worth it, he no longer saw the body. But it was there as a memory and the sadness of it made him cry a deep soul-wrenching cry. He sobbed into Jim's chest feeling like a child in the arms of his father.

"Ok, you did really good, Will." Jim's voice was a soothing rumble and it felt good on his aching head to hear it. "Really good, thank you…Father get your car quick…good job, Will. Good job."

Within in a minute Will had calmed somewhat and heard the approaching car, an old boxy Volvo with Father John behind the wheel. Jim released him from the bear hug and Will staggered a little but then found his legs and climbed in. There was an uncomfortable silence in the car and Will was convinced that everyone was secretly questioning his sanity, and he didn't blame them, on the contrary, he joined them.

There felt to be a great crack running through his mind, one big enough to hold a body, not the body of a little boy, but that of a grown man. Somebody would have to fill that crack and he knew that if he walked away now without finding Talitha, the crack would grow larger and larger until it was big enough to swallow him whole.

Adrina, the gypsy from whom he had inadvertently received his talent, had considered looking into the future purposefully as something unnatural, and death was the punishment for attempting it, but Will looked on death now as a form of payment. He saw and now he owed. He had been steered across a river no living man should be allowed to travel and had seen the other side. And now, the ferryman was demanding payment; a life.

"Fuck that!" Will muttered angrily. He wasn't paying anything and if he could help it, no one would.

"What's that?" Father John asked without taking his eyes from the road that was flying under them at fantastic speeds.

"We can still save Father Alba, hurry," Will demanded, and thought: the future is not set.

"No! He's good, Will. He's doing fine," Jim said in a voice that was much higher than usual.

Will felt a moment of irritation until he recognized that they were already hurrying, possibly far more than was smart. The priest had turned out of the parking lot and was now pushing the Volvo to its limit, and with the heavy rain and the great speed, Will felt mild alarm. The two men in the back seat were well past alarm and held on to the interior like a couple of tomcats on the way to the vet.

It made Will smile, but it lasted less than a second and then his face went back to the tired grave look he had worn most of the day. A part of him, larger than he would ever care to admit, welcomed a crash, especially a fatal one. The last two days had taken a psychic toll on him and the idea he was rushing to murder someone or to see that boy's body, killed any fear of a car crash, it fizzled inside him leaving only apathy and a single hope.

The future is not set.

He remembered the flash of light in the darkness. "Hey, Father? Do me a favor and keep hold of the gun."

The priest's eyes came off the road just long enough to glance at Will, look down at the seat next to him, and then back up again. "What?"

Will looked down. The gun, like a hard black snake, lay next to him on the seat, practically touching him. It was offering its grip to Will as if it knew where it rightfully belonged and the barrel pointed at the priest. Seeing it that way bothered him and as casually as he could Will spun the gun.

When he did so, it was with a disquieting feeling of playing Russian roulette, and the deadly end of the gun didn't make a full circle and caught on the seat belt, facing Will. He looked down that dark barrel and a wave of shivers washed down his back, but he ignored a sane desire to point it away from himself and instead checked his watch, just in time to see it click over from 12:15 to 12:16. Three minutes left.

"I want you to…" He couldn't finish, the priest hit the brakes hard, and everyone leaned well forward, the gun skipping off the seat. Will bent down to retrieve it, experiencing a moment of nausea as Father John turned the car sharply to the left. The gun felt alive, it eagerly bounced up and settled into his hand, comfortably, becoming an extension of himself.

The feeling was welcoming as well as repulsive as if he liked it too much. Will jammed the gun in between the back cushion and the long bench of the seat, just as the Volvo roared into the parking lot of Haikes Rubber and Tire Company.

"To the left!" Jim yelled from the back seat. "I'll take Sean and go through the employees' entrance, you two go through the front doors and move down and to the middle. Will, do you know what level they're going to be on?"

*The boy knelt over the box with his pants down...*Will shook his head savagely, forcing himself not to think about the vision. "No, just somewhere very deep."

"We'll do our best...right there," Jim's long arm came between Will and the priest pointing to the obvious. A loading dock and a series of boarded up doors were in front of them and the Volvo screeched up to it.

The two men started to squeeze their huge bodies out of the chunky car and Will felt a flutter of panic seeing Jim go.

He called out to them, "Remember, she's very dangerous. Try to trap her if you can and don't engage her if at all possible. Use your bulk and smother her, until we get there."

Jim gave him a last look, a queer one filled with mixed emotions that he couldn't read. "You gonna be ok, Will?"

"Yeah...yeah, I'll be fine, now get going." Will didn't know if he would be fine or not.

"Ok, good luck, Father," Jim said to the priest.

Oddly the priest kept his eyes fixed on the steering wheel. "You too, Jim."

The two men turned and jogged to the dock and

Father John, not giving them a second look, hauled the car about and gunned it around the building. His eyes flicked to Will twice and it made Will slightly self-conscious. He wondered what he looked like. Crazy he supposed; he certainly felt that he was still trailing his coattails just over the edge of crazy.

"It was only a couple of times…three times actually," Father John spoke, slowing the car to clear an overturned dumpster. The parking lot that surrounded the building was nearly empty, barren of cars, but strewn with trash. Glass lay everywhere, papers, mostly newspaper hugged the fencing, old chairs and desks, broken and unusable lay in random piles and tall green rivers of weeds jutted up through the pavement in long lines.

"Three times?" Will was confused and wondered when he had missed the conversation Father John was referring to. The church was only a few hundred yards away and the trip couldn't have lasted more than a minute.

"Mrs. Jackson," the priest whispered it secretively to Will and it went nearly unheard over the sound of the car. He grabbed the door as the Volvo took a sharp turn; the front of the building was now in sight.

"Mrs. Jackson? I…I don't know her." Will was clueless to what the man was talking about and gave him a shrug hoping he wasn't being offensive with his look of bewilderment.

Father John grimaced and took a deep breath. "The demon mentioned her…and… he wasn't lying."

Understanding hit Will like a club, as did the weight of the man's guilt and for some reason, he found he couldn't look at Father John. He kept his face forward, eyes on the looming entrance.

The priest continued, "I didn't mean for it to happen. It's just… she was in a vulnerable place. Her husband is not a good person you see. And I tried to comfort her…it was only a couple of times and I tried to end it, but she was so needy, I thought she would fall apart if I broke it off."

The car pulled up, stopping hard next to an old Plymouth station wagon. Will went to get out, but Father John held him back. "You believe me right?" The man seemed desperate for Will to understand, but he didn't.

"Why are you telling me this?"

The priest's eyes slid off him and went back to the steering wheel, "Because, I need forgiveness."

A look of shock flashed across Will's features. "I'm…I'm not the one you should be asking forgiveness from. This is between you and the Jacksons."

"You're right, but you are near to God. He has touched you." The priest reached over and grabbed Will's hand almost reverently, however with a look of fear as well. "I'm afraid…I've been afraid of the demon and now I'm afraid of your sister. I just think. I just think that it would be best to confess my sins now, while there's still time."

We don't have time for this, Will thought in anger. However, the man's look of sad desperation quelled his temper. He looked into the priest's brown eyes. "God sees into your heart, if you are truly sorry, then," he paused feeling blasphemous, "Then you are forgiven."

Father John smiled in relief. "I am sorry. Thank you so very much."

Will smiled as well, but felt sleazy as if he had

perpetrated a fraud and slid out of the car in one fluid motion. He glanced back in and Father John was still there, looking at him in a way Will didn't like. The look was of adoration and Will tried to ignore it, checking his watch purposefully, 12:17. Two minutes to go.

"Grab the gun, Father, but whatever you do, don't give me it, ok?"

The priest didn't seem to hear. He pulled himself from the car and stood holding the gun, smiling. He looked to have regained some of his youth and handsomeness and there was a lightness to him. "It feels so good to get that off my chest. Thanks again, Will."

"It was nothing...*remember* don't give me the gun. It's very important. But now we got to go." Will started for the door trying not to see that the look of adoration had not left the priest's face.

The priest held him back again. "I'll go first, I have the gun after all."

The front door of the building was at one time glass but now was constructed of graffiti scrawled plywood boards, one of which had been yanked off and lay on the cement a few yards away. Father John stepped through the opening and disappeared into the blackness beyond.

"Be careful, there's glass all over the place in here," he said from inside and it was almost as if the building itself had issued the warning. It caused a moment of hesitation on Will's part, but then he ducked in through the makeshift door.

The first thing that struck him, was the powerful stale smell of old urine, it burned his nostrils as he breathed it in, causing his face to contort. The odor reminded him of the bums he had seen about Boston and the room, once obviously a receptionist's foyer was now a trashed out mess and likely a home to one of the bums.

The empty and aging beer cans and the partially broken liquor bottles littering the floor suggested this as well and there was even a disgusting shredded sleeping bag in one of the corners. Father John walked over to it, his feet treading over the glass making it crunch in a nasty way that had Will vaguely recalling a dream.

That was the only good thing about his sister's horrible dreams, they faded from his memory just as normal ones did, however this one was fresher and with a jolt, Will realized the sound was similar to the crunching of his bones when that demon had chewed off his fingers. He couldn't remember if he had dreamed that last night or the night before, but it didn't really matter to his stomach, which felt suddenly queasy.

Father John had moved away from the sleeping bag and pulled on the main doors, he whispered, "These are locked, try that one." He pointed to a door on far left of the room, nearer to Will.

"Sure." Will's own feet continued to make the crunching sound as went to the door. He tried not to think about his dream, but then the image of a boy tied to a box came to him. His queasy stomach turned a loop and that was far more difficult to ignore.

He concentrated on the door instead.

Covered in many layers of spray paint, it was unexceptional, save for an odd little peephole located at chest height. Bending down, he looked into it but the room beyond seemed black as jet. He gave the door a try, it was blocked from the other side and budged only a few inches.

As he started to turn back to the priest to tell him that they would have to find a different way in, he saw a little placard. It too was covered over in paint and was completely unreadable, but when he ran his fingers over it, he felt the word, *Stairs*.

"Over here," he called over to the priest and then bent his shoulder to the door and shoved hard. It began moving with difficulty, but when Father John also added his weight, it moved far enough to allow them to enter.

Will went first.

The door opened onto a wide cement landing with stairs going off in both directions. Just as the peephole had suggested the stair well was blacker than night, with the only light coming in from the gloomy reception area. Will reached out and felt what was blocking the door; a great jumbled mass of office furniture had been piled as high as his shoulder.

"Look out," Father John cautioned from the narrow space in the doorway. With no other choice, Will took a few steps up the stairs and the little priest slipped in. "What is all this? Oh, furniture." He felt the mound. "I think we can get around, over here."

"Where's over here? I can't see you," Will said, starting toward the pile only to misjudge it, he barked his shin and the pain shot through the bone exquisitely. He wished he had thought to bring a flashlight and used the next best thing.

He pulled back the sleeve of his coat and the orange glow of his watch seemed very bright, much brighter than usual, 12:19.

Relief and excitement filled his chest; he had

somehow averted the first death. His initial thought was that his forced vision had cancelled something out, but he didn't know for sure. He wondered about the next two deaths, but when he tried to recall the feeling that they had given him, he saw the boy tied over the box instead.

Will had to shake his head hard to clear the vision, which wobbled him slightly and the darkness moved oddly around him, making him think of the ocean at night.

"Are you coming?" Father John asked nervously from the other side of the pile. Will bent to the task and found it relatively easy. The orange glow from his watch was no help at all, but feeling his way wasn't as hard as he thought it would be, and in a few seconds, he had cleared the pile.

Father John had moved down a few steps to wait for him. "I doubt your sister took two hostages this way."

Will could hear the man's voice retreating down the stairs and he hurried to catch up, only to run into him in the dark.

"Sorry about that."

"You are forgiven, Will," the priest said jokingly and went down.

Light flashed.

It was a bright white, a bolt of lightning, a strobe light...hot and fast and there was Father John in silhouette. The roar of a gun, more like an explosion, echoed hugely bouncing off the walls of the cement stair well. The noise ran through Will's skin and penetrated deep into his being, deep into his soul.

He hadn't averted the first death after all.

Father John collapsed onto him, knocking Will back onto the stairs. The priest's hands were out stretched and by a quirk of fate, the man's right hand found Will's and the gun, invisible in the blackness, slipped into his own, as if it belonged there.

Bafflement flooded through him and his mind struggled to realize what had just happened. He was past the time! He had to be. Reaching across the lifeless body of the priest, Will pulled back the sleeve of his coat with his trigger finger, 12:19… a second later, 12:20.

The vision matched reality, exactly.

He realized then that the gun was cold against his skin, it hadn't been fired, and that meant only one thing. He wasn't alone in the stairwell.

Chapter 16

Beneath the Factory

Will was not alone. That thought sent a chill through him and he reacted without thinking, bringing the gun across his body, he fired three quick shots down the stairwell. Will paused listening, his eyes wide in the absolute blackness, clutching Father John's body closer to him, making him a human shield.

The shots had sent a knife-like pain stabbing through both ears, but he was still able to hear the sound of metal moving on the stairs. His breathing, quick shallow breaths, stopped cold at the sound. However, his mind quickly reclassified the sound not only as friendly, but merry as well.

One of the brass cartridge casings ejected from his gun, danced and skipped about, making its way down the stairs. It seemed to go all the way to the bottom, taking its sweet jubilant time and Will listened, all the while holding his breath.

Once it stopped it, Will let out the pent up air, slow and quiet. He sat there straining to hear the least movement, but none came and after a few minutes he felt his arm growing heavy. It had remained outstretched, pointing the gun, but now he laid it on top of Father John's chest and it was then, he felt the blood. The priest's chest was drenched with it.

He pulled his hands back and a second later he heard his first sound since the dancing bullet casing; it was far off, down below in one of the sub levels, a scream of intense pain wailed up out of the blackness. Will pictured his sister tearing out Father Alba's eyes—it got him moving.

With the gun held out at arm's length, ready to blaze away at the slightest noise, he slid out from beneath the body Father Santos. Keeping to the wall, he took a step down and felt something under his foot. Reaching down he found a heavy length of cord running across the stair. He followed it until it came to what felt to be an eyebolt drilled into the wall.

Remembering the peephole in the door at the top of the stairs, he realized that Father John must have set off some sort of trip-wire trap. For a second a touch of relief flared within him, but then the feeling died in the dark as sweat broke out down his back.

There could be any number and type of traps hidden in the darkened stairwell—steel-toothed bear traps, heavy bladed pendulums, thin-wired garrotes...

Will nearly froze in place. His only solace was the knowledge that Talitha hadn't set the traps. If she had he would've turned around right there knowing the futility of trying to make his way in the dark. This was the handiwork of...Luke. The name Jim had mentioned took a moment to squirrel out of his memory. It had to fight its way past his fear and the lurking vision of the dead boy.

The vision wanted to come back and Will hissed out, "Stop it!"

He had no time for visions—two more would die.

Moving in a slow shuffle and keeping away from the center of the stairs, Will followed the cord down and at the first landing, he accidently kicked something wooden. Feeling it, his fears were confirmed. It was a chair and on it pointed up the stairs was a rifle. String ran from the trigger and threaded through another eyebolt drilled into the wall behind it.

In the complete blackness there was no way anyone could've avoided the trap and it was happenstance only that saved Will. Yet would it save him a second time? Were there more traps ahead? He shivered in the dark and cautiously stepped around the gun.

Now his fear grew. What was out there? What new death did the dark hold? His shivering picked up in pace as his imagination ran wild and at the edge of the landing his shuffling steps stopped cold. He felt like he was standing in front of a great yawning abyss and he pictured a new trap. Perhaps there were no stairs in front of him, or maybe just one or two and then…nothing but a long fall.

Until his right shoulder and the side of his head hit the wall, he didn't know he was dizzy. In the dark there was no up or down and he let out a little yelp when he collided with the wall. But now that he had a hold of it, he could feel his head swimming and the wall felt like it was tilting back and forth.

He put his hands out and laid his cheek upon its invisible surface, breathing loudly. As long as his left hand roved up and down the side of the wall he felt better, it gave him context and placed him in the world and not…in the void. Will rarely dreamed of the void itself, but when he did, it was like this; at once eternal and infinite but also close, as if he were deep underground trapped in a lightless, airless casket.

Another scream came out of the darkness, a long horrible wail that went up and down in the scale of misery. He pictured Father Alba again and realized with a start the priest was probably now in this sightless world as well. Not as a frightened timid visitor like Will who was nothing but a guest in the dangerous world of the blind, Father Alba was a permanent resident.

"The future's not set," Will murmured, lying to himself and to the blackness.

The words didn't echo as he thought they should and the darkness squeezed more closely around him, but only for a moment. Desperation gave him impetus to reach out with both hands and he felt the wall on one side and the railing on the other. He slid his foot out feeling the stair below him cautiously, but he didn't step down.

Instead, looking to bypass the obvious, he mounted the railing and like an overgrown boy, he slid down. After a few seconds, he could feel his too large butt cheek slide off the railing and he landed, crouching as low as possible, but there was no gunfire. Giving up on the railing, he slid down the stairs on his belly, trying to feel in front of him with one hand while the other acted as a brake.

He gained the next landing, which turned out to be the first sub floor and again there was a pile of furniture in front of the door. It didn't stop him. Will knew he had to go lower but he felt a burning need to see light and began pushing the pile aside frantically. Once the door had the slightest amount of room, he pulled it open and slipped through.

After the absolute darkness of the stair well, the factory was surprisingly and reassuringly bright and he stood breathing the light in with great heavy gasps. He saw that the building had been constructed along the lines of a long rectangular atrium with the interior of it open from the skylights high above, all the way down to the lowest basement, two floors below him. The derelict factory was in a shambles and from where Will stood, he could see over turned workstations, broken desks, and light fixtures dangling by thin wires.

Rusting machines, looking asleep but still dangerous, sat haphazardly about and pipes of all sizes wove in and around them on their way to who knows where.

Will went to the railing overlooking the atrium and peered down into the lower levels, hoping to catch sight of Talitha. However, the light from above seemed to lack the power to penetrate the depressing gloom below him and everything down there appeared vague and shadowy.

Just as he turned away from the rail he heard another cry, different from the others, in that it was muffled and less urgent. Will dashed back to the rail, but still there was nothing to be seen and he began to feel a frantic desperation to get down to the lower levels, however that feeling butted directly against his dread of the possibility of traps in the blackened stairwell.

Across from him, he spied an elevator and had taken a few steps toward it before his brain kicked into gear. There was no way it would be operational and if it were…he pictured it plummeting down.

This left him with the unappealing choice of climbing down the pipes that ran up the sides of the atrium. Seeing a small set that looked as if they could hold his weight, he jogged over and was pleasantly surprised to find a ladder nestled in them and after giving it a cautious shake, he stuck the gun deep into the waistband of his jeans and swung his legs over the rail.

He made his decent as quietly as possible, pausing every few rungs to listen and to wipe the sweat from his palms. With each successive rung down, the gloom settled on and around him more firmly, but that was only part of the reason that he began to feel a terrible anxiety. There was something else. Something that he knew lurked down in the depths of the factory.

The bodies of dead children.

Decomposing horrible bodies. The stench was outlandish, second only to the smell that had radiated from the crate beneath the church, but for Will this was worse. The smell went hand in hand with the vision of the boy tied to the box and the image of it kept blossoming up, ghastly and hideous.

Will's hands began to sweat freely, and he now added a fear of falling to his anxiety, but since he also felt terribly exposed out in the open like that, he quickened his pace, and was down a few seconds later, the gun yanked from his jeans and pointing outwards.

Down there the smell intensified and his stomach threatened to explode. He fought the urge to dry heave with every ounce of concentration he could muster and his breathing came in hard gasps. If he went down to his knees gagging, Talitha could be on him before he knew it and he'd be death number two for the day.

Somehow that thought calmed his breathing and his stomach relaxed as well, giving him a chance to focus on the rooms around him. Unlike the areas above, the basement was far from open; there were more walls and doors for one thing. But it was the dark and the smell coating him with indecent filth that lent the level an oppressive constrictiveness.

The basement seemed to form a grid. Long pipe-filled hallways intersected each other like avenues in a city and Will was at a loss for which way to go. On a whim, he started toward the front of the building, but hadn't gone far when he heard a fast stomping or perhaps a drumming of someone's feet against a wood board.

Turning, he advanced quickly in the direction of the sound, his arms out stiffly, his hands gripping the gun hard. The thumping ceased and Will slowed down, moving with caution, but not enough caution. His foot came down on a piece of glass making an audible crunching sound and he froze in place. But then the thumping came again with more urgency, it came from a room maybe twenty feet from him.

Despite the near overwhelming dread that ran through his bowels, he also felt silly when he jumped into the room with the gun outstretched, like a cop from a bad TV show. What the room held for him made that silly feeling depart along with all the feeling in his hands and feet.

This was the room from his vision.

But it was far worse in person. The gruesome details were fresher, alive with the richness of the aroma of death. In a cleared space in the center of the room, the boy knelt over what eternally would be his box. This Will had seen, but there were other things, he hadn't.

For instance, he now saw that the box was made from wood and that it was blackened where the boy's blood had run down it. The ropes binding him there looked to have been knotted by an experienced sailor, one with cruel intentions and they cut deep into the remains of his flesh. The gaping maggot filled remains of the boy's anus writhed with the undulations of the horrible creatures, but there was something else he hadn't seen before, something inside the boy...Will gagged and turned away.

What Will saw, he absorbed in a blink of an eye, but even that was too much for him and he felt shocked to depths of his soul and his mind reeled.

The rest of the room was lit by the indirect gloom from the hallway behind him and he now saw that the boy knelt in the middle of a symbol painted in blood, it was a five pointed star with two circles running along the outside of it. Strange lettering spelled words within the circle; they were of no earthly language. He *knew* it was a hell language.

More symbols, black blood again, adorned the walls even as they had in the room beneath the church, and just as he had seen in the pits at Rek, where the great demon dwelled. The memory of those dungeons came and went, leaving him stunned and sick. He had seen this room before, not just in a vision, but in his dreams as well.

For Will, everything about the room was an illusion of hell.

His mind revolted and threatened to shut down completely at the sight. He turned back to the door wanting to leave, picturing himself out in the rain, but it was then a small movement caught his eye, Luke lay upon the ground, trussed up in the torn remains of Father Alba's stole. He was wriggling like mad, trying to escape and had butted up against the cinder blocks that made up the walls, his feet scraped at the cement of the floor and for a second he reminded Will of an inch worm.

Will was slow to realize that there was nothing wood nearby that Luke could have been kicking. The sound had to have been made by someone else.

From his right came a blur of motion followed by an amazing shrieking pain. His arms had been outstretched, holding the gun away from his body, and Talitha, lurking just behind the open door, had leapt out with a flashing front kick that struck him above the elbow. Two inches lower down and his elbow would have swung both ways. As it was his arm from the point of the blow down went instantly numb.

Helplessly, he watched as the gun tumbled from his deadened fingers, landing just in front of Talitha. She was so close to it that he feared she would get to it first, but she wasn't after the gun. Even as he bent down to retrieve it, she leaned her body to the left, and her right leg swung in a hard fast arc, a roundhouse kick that would've taken his head off if he hadn't seen it coming.

Even though he knew where it would land, it wasn't as helpful as one would think. She was too fast to avoid the blow completely and it struck him just on the top of his forehead, snapping his neck back and sending him reeling into the wall behind him—it was the only thing that kept him upright.

His head swam momentarily and he had to spread his hands on the wall to keep from sagging to the ground. Death surely awaited him if he ever went down. Talitha danced to her right, inches from the gun, swinging her head back and forth. Will suddenly realized that she could see, perhaps not well but enough.

He took an intentionally loud step to his right, trying to draw her away from the gun and nearly lost his testicles in the process. She heard the movement and sent a second roundhouse, this time high up at his face, but he saw it coming and ducked away, however that had been a feint and just as her right foot landed, she flashed in toward him with another snap kick. She held it back till the last moment giving herself a choice of targets and ruining any chance Will would have to stop it with his foresight.

He relied instead on his knowledge of his sister; she would go for the *balls*. They weren't the easy target most women assumed them to be and Will was able to turn just enough to take the blow on his thigh instead. That also hurt.

"Almost," she said. Smiling and flush with the action, she was pretty in the dim light. Will didn't say anything, the muscles in the top of his leg had knotted instantly by the blow, and he rubbed at them in furious silence.

"I'm honestly surprised that you got here as quick as you did," she said, moving to keep him close. "You spoiled my fun with the priest you know. You made me cut it short with all of your ruckus. So, who were you shooting at? A pigeon scare you?"

He nearly answered and the memory of Father John's lifeless body laying over him almost made him miss the snapshot of the future. A deft sidekick aimed square at his midsection. Anyone else would've had their ribs stove in, but Will dodged adroitly, still moving to his right.

"You're getting pretty quick," she complimented.

"But you didn't answer my question. I can smell the blood from that yapping priest on you; was it a ricochet, or did you just get tired of him running his mouth?"

He thought again of the lifeless body of Father John and with a pang of regret, he realized he had just left him there without saying a prayer or even arranging the body. He'd been too wrapped up in his fear of traps.

With a sigh, he answered, "A trap got him." The door was just behind him and as Talitha made another feint, he stepped back through it.

She advanced on him, but paused in the doorway, her face screwed up in puzzlement. "How did the bullet miss you...oh my God. You filthy coward! You let that little priest go in front of you."

Talitha was right in a manner of speaking, but Will had been more afraid of killing than in being killed— still the acid of her accusation burned him.

Will kept backing into the hallway and she followed, looking expectant. "Are you giving me the silent treatment? If so, you got the wrong gal, it wasn't my gun, I just left..."

He saw it coming.

In mid sentence she let fly with a heavy left hook and he stepped back again—the speeding fist literally whistling by his face. He saw the next fist coming and the two that followed, but they flew so fast, one after the other that seeing the future became practically useless. After the fourth swing missed, he saw the fifth coming and knew he was out of position to dodge it and too slow to stop it.

It came at him hard and fast—the fist seemed to grow to huge proportions, he tried to step back, to lessen the effect it would have, but his foot caught on a pipe running across the floor and he fell over it. Talitha's fist just clipped him on the jaw and he went sprawling head over heels.

He landed hard on a thick clay pipe, hitting in the center of his back, knocking the wind from him. She advanced to finish him off, but her inability to see slowed her down. She wore a puzzled expression and swung her arms about in front of her, obviously not seeing him in the dim light of the surrounding pipes.

Taking advantage of her predicament, Will scurried like a rat under the larger pipes thinking to flank her and make a run for the gun, but she heard him and dodged to the side, somehow cornering him. Looking back, he saw a maze of piping that he couldn't climb over or under.

Now his only chance for the gun was a desperate dash past her. He feinted to the left and then leapt high over the pipes on the ground, it was a quick move for him, but she was so fast. Talitha caught a hold of his coat in mid-air and reeled him in with it.

Panic seized him.

It was the combination of her total maliciousness and the fact that his coat had become too constraining. This had never happened to him before, but he had been feeling an undercurrent of claustrophobia since entering the room beneath the church and now when the coat stretched taught around him, the sudden constriction caused him to explode in a bizarre panic.

He didn't struggle so much against her, than against his coat. Will tore at the zipper, while his shoulders jerked and twisted violently—and then he was free. He stumbled backwards and then ran blindly down the hall still very close to panicking.

Though he raced as fast as he could, she kept pace, dogging his footsteps, her feet softly landing on the cement of the hallway. It was as if she were out for a jog; she even had a small but very nasty smile on her lips as she loped along with indecent ease.

With the knowledge that she could outrun him, he dashed into the first room that he came to, slamming the door behind him. With the door shut, the room was black like the stairwell had been and he had to scramble around for the lock blindly.

His hands wove up and down until he realized with dread: there was no lock. Talitha threw herself against the door and Will dug his feet in, pushing back as hard as he could but it in vain and he slowly slid inwards.

"Aw man!" she grumbled unexpectedly from just on the other side of the door. "Right when it was play time. Will, it looks like we're going to have to get this over with quicker than I wanted. I just heard someone knocking into things upstairs, probably that big oaf, Jim."

She gave another hard shove and now the door was open a good foot and a half. He shoved back hard, hoping that help was on the way, but Talitha had only been toying with him before and now she pushed back with greater strength. Again, he slid inward and as he did the room became lit by the dim light of the hallway and the slow lighting revealed a new horror.

A boy tied to a box.

It was a different boy, this one had been here much longer, and the blackened flesh, what was left of it, hung from its bones that peeked out from the remains of the child cadaver. It was covered with a constantly shifting black haze of flies that buzzed loudly. That alone was too much for Will and he turned away with a moan coming from the back of his throat.

It was then that he saw Father Alba.

Near a long wooden table, the man was stretched out on the floor, his arms flung wide, unmoving. His face was a Halloween mask of horror. Where his eyes should have been there were two gaping holes seemingly large enough for Will to put his fists into. The priest looked to be crying—not with tears, but with blood and gore, which dripped thickly from the wounds.

The sight of it caused something to snap in Will. His fear of his sister forever vanished in that instant and in its place he felt a cold hatred, the malice of which sent a surge of power through his limbs. He felt that he could've held the door shut against her if he wished, but he no longer looked to hide.

He rolled away from the door, and came to his feet facing her. Talitha, surprised at Will's action didn't charge into the room; she was cunning and suspected others to be as well. Instead, she stood turning her head at odd angles to catch a glimpse of him.

"Whatcha doing, Will? Finally grown a pair, have you?"

"Yeah, I'm done running."

Her head swiveled in his direction, orienting on the sound of his voice and with a smile she stepped full into the room. "You've been a bad boy, Will. Ruining my fun, letting me get shot, all because..."

He intruded on her soliloquy which he knew from experience would be long and self-serving, "Cut the crap!"

"That's not nice," she pouted prettily in a girlish

manner, something that might have touched his heart before, perhaps easing his anger, but now Will's heart was an icy stone in his chest.

"I don't care about being nice. All I care about is hurting you." He meant it.

"Whoa! Big talk. Have your balls finally dropped? Are you finally going to start acting like a man, after being such a disappointment to dad?"

"Enough Talk! Come on!" Will yelled angrily as his body geared up for the fight, adrenaline pumping into his system—he felt strong.

"Just one thing. Do you think you can beat me because I'm blind?"

That was a largest part of it, but there was no reason to admit it. "All these years, I've been holding back. That's done with."

She seemed shocked, "Are you planning on killing me?"

"Yes," his voice spoke the truth and the word came out hard.

Talitha gave him a giggle. "Where's the love? I'd never kill you. Lisa and your little baby girl, yes, but not you. I'm thinking quadriplegic; you know to keep you from running away. So you can keep doing me that little favor you do, dreaming my dreams."

"That's not happening." Her words were a goad, burning him up, turning him mean, he liked it.

"Because I can't see very well? Dear brother…you keep forgetting that I'm smarter than you, much smarter." Her teeth were a dazzling white and like the Cheshire cat, they were the last thing he saw as she shut the door, drowning his world in utter blackness.

He was now as blind as she was.

Chapter 17

To the Death

The plunge into sudden blackness froze Will in place, but for only an instant—then he *knew* he was about to be struck, yet it was only a vague warning. In the absolute darkness, his *vision* was practically useless and her first blow sank deep into his stomach, knocking the wind from him in a great, "Oof!"

His only advantage was knowing his sister; with Jim on the way she'd attack without mercy or pause and he threw himself backwards feeling the air just in front of his face roil in disturbance as a kick or a punch swished through it. He landed on his back, yet didn't remain there for more than half a second—rolling to his left he came up against something hard that stopped his momentum and in a flash changed course rolling back to the right.

The odd sounds coming from just below Talitha caused her to misjudge her next strike and there was a loud crack next his head. He wasted no time thinking or caring what she'd just hit and instead rolled faster, log like, trying to get clear of her. A second later, his face hit something hard and tacky.

It was the box the boy was tied to.

A great disease filled buzz erupted all about him as an untold number of flies took flight. The air seemed filled with them and one struck his lower lip, he had to suppress a sudden need to vomit, he scrambled up and away, only to *know* he was about to be hit again by

Talitha. He didn't know from what direction, he just knew his face was about to feel tremendous pain and he dodged left, hoping to avoid the invisible attack. However, he guessed wrong on the direction and a clumsy, club like punch struck him on the side of the neck.

It jarred him and sent him spinning away from the box and further into the nothingness of the dark and he realized then, he was completely lost. Will had no idea where the door was, or where Father Alba lay, or even where the boy knelt, but worst of all he had no idea where his sister was.

The darkness was all-encompassing and to him she was everywhere and nowhere. While he huffed and puffed still working to regain his breath from the first blow, she was absolutely silent. He could feel her though. Talitha was out there orienting on his labored breathing, trying to judge his exact position. Will lunged blindly to his left, arms outstretched in a spastic attempt to snare her like a fish in a net, but he came up empty and he paused, listening.

To the right he heard her giggled and it turned his hatred to rage, which sent him flying in that direction, but he grabbed only empty black air. He stopped once more and listened, a foolish mistake.

Again, he *knew* a strike was coming, and again he guessed wrong where it was coming from. Pain exploded in the large muscle of his thigh—she had landed a heavy kick and the muscle seized up immediately. He tried to jump back as before, but she knew his moves now and jumped with him, striking out in a series of blazing fast punches, hitting him on his face and neck and stomach. Her accuracy for a blind girl in the dark was astounding.

Pain seemed to erupt spontaneously all over his body but it was over in seconds and he didn't know he was falling until he hit something heavy on the way to the floor. It was the table he had seen earlier and acting on instinct, he tried to crawl under it, only he moved tortoise like, slowly dragging himself forward and it was nothing for Talitha to find him. And like a tortoise, she flipped him over, exposing his vulnerable area.

He felt her land on his chest, straddling him and he lashed out with a punch that hit something soft and yielding. It had been weak, terribly impotent and had no effect on her at all. Talitha began to punish him then. Punches rained down on him out of the black sky, hitting him everywhere, making him grunt with the force of the blows, but she was holding back, wanting his to remain conscious, wanting him to feel the pain.

She got her wish, but only to a point, then his arms sagged down and he no longer attempted to protect himself. The punches landing now felt distant as if they were happening to someone else. Talitha must have realized he was near to blacking out and she was up off of him then.

For a few seconds he couldn't tell if he was awake or in a deep sleep and just laid there uncaring where his sister had gone to. Suddenly small hands gripped him and he felt himself lifted off the floor. Talitha had him high over her head, and her strength was astonishing, she brought him down fast, slamming him onto the wood table. It collapsed under him, practically disintegrating and he went through it to the floor.

It didn't hurt at all, but the movement up and then slamming back down had brought him around from his near stupor. His head cleared somewhat and he felt her grip his feet and pull him from the mess of the destroyed table. Struggling against her, his hand found purchase on a chunk of wood, the leg of the table, he thought.

Turning slightly he meant to attack her with it, but she was invisible in the darkness. Near or far, he had no idea and he hesitated with the make shift club pulled back waiting to strike. He knew he would have one shot but now indecision was even taking that from him.

"How you feeling? How's the back? Can you still feel your…?" she began.

Just as she had done, he oriented on her voice and he swung the table leg hard at it. There was a thud and the leg jarred uncomfortably in his hands, sending splinters into his palms, but these went ignored. He swung a second time and again hit something however, it was moving and there was less force transferred to his hands.

From a sitting position, his next blow whistled through the air, hitting nothing and he then scrambled up, swinging the leg back and forth, but still not finding a target. He knew where the table was and guessed a direction in which the door stood. Swinging the table leg in short vicious arcs, he went in that direction and felt the leg hit something unexpectedly.

It grunted.

Talitha! He attacked with more strength, but she seemed to evaporate and his club swung in vain. A moment later, he struck the wall. The club flew from his hands, which had gone instantly numb with the force of the blow.

There was no point even trying to find the club in

the black. Instead, he weaved his hands over the wall, searching with a frantic speed for the door and in seconds, his questing hands found the frame and he had the door open in a snap.

The light, which had been dim before, dazzled him and he spun about. Talitha was there. Squatting in an odd position a few feet away and Will saw that at least one of his swings had done some damage, her head was bleeding profusely down the right side and the shoulder of her dress was already soaked.

She glared up at him, evil and hating, seeming to be little more than the small demon she so desperately wanted to be and the sight of her put a fire under his hatred. The club lay closer to him and he dashed forward and grabbed it, but she barely moved, only swinging to the side to face him again.

Her squatting position made him wary, fearful of the fact that she could lash out like a coiled snake and with this in mind, he juked one way and then danced back the other and swung the club. Her vision had improved; he guessed by the way she blocked the blow from the club with an out stretched arm. It was a solid blow to her left forearm, but she did little more than grit her teeth. He repeated the maneuver and with the same results only this time she grunted from pain and anger.

Her squatting seemed strange and limiting and he took full advantage of it, he next dashed halfway around her before striking, she spun in a tight circle and again blocked with the same arm, her left, but there would be no more blocks coming from it. It dangled useless now, very likely broken. He kept up the attack swinging hard for her face and now she could only throw herself back onto the floor to avoid the blow and

Will now saw why she hadn't done more.

One of his strikes in the dark had been lucky, her right knee looked turned around and swollen. There was a pause as his eyes took in the sight of her mangled knee and she put up her right hand, and pleaded, "Ok! You win. Don't hurt me."

At that moment, his hatred was at its greatest and it was easy to ignore her words, he took the table leg as if it were a baseball bat in both hands and gripped it tight preparing to finish her quickly, however pain shot from his left hand. Looking down at it, a jolt of shock went through him.

Two fingers on that hand stuck out sideways looking grotesque; they had been dislocated defending himself in the dark. The sight of it made his stomach queasy and he paused for a moment, unable to take his eyes from the deformity.

"I said you win, Will." Her words were still pleading, sounding desperate and now her evil glare was gone. She was his sister again hurt and bleeding, or so she would have him believe, however he could see the cruelty lurking beneath. It was something she could no longer hide and it made his hatred that much easier to bring out.

He focused on that hatred and glared down at her, needing to be furious to do what he had to do—this was going to end here and now.

"What? Are you still giving me the silent treatment?" She paused concentrating. "Oh, I understand now. You want to kill me, is that it? I can't believe it. You would kill your own sister?"

"You're not my sister," he said, contempt forming the words, making them hard. "You're Ba'al Fie-ere, remember?"

Unbelievably she smiled and lay back tucking her good right hand under her head. She seemed to be relaxing, enjoying the moment. "I am Ba'al Fie-ere. Thanks Will. It's so good to hear you saying my name."

"Bitch! How's that for a name?" Without waiting for an answer, he jumped at her, swinging the table leg at her face. Though injured she was strong and quick and spun about kicking at his knee, intending to maim him just as she was, however, he saw it coming and dodged it.

Still relaxing, she laughed softly, "Sorry Will. It's going to be harder than you thought to bludgeon me to death, but I like the idea and not only that, I like the enthusiasm you have."

Her eyes lit up suddenly. "Picture this: You, waking up in a cold sweat and you try to wipe it off frantically, because in your mind the sweat is blood. And this goes on night after night. You no longer dream my terrible dreams once a week, but every single night! Every night you kill your sweet innocent sister, breaking her bones, deforming her pretty little face, but somehow she lives longer, far longer that you could believe. And it takes swing after swing before she stops moving and even longer, until she stops crying and still you hammer away, because you are afraid! You keep going because she just might get up and take her revenge!"

Talitha paused and sighed in obscene happiness at the image she had conjured. Will stood aghast and then he became angry, but it was an impotent anger, because he feared that part of what she'd said would be true.

She slapped the cement with impatience. "Ok, Will

start swinging! Hurt me slowly." She waited for only a second before going on, "Let's go! Don't worry, I promise to make it good…I'll scream at every blow…I'll cry real tears, I swear. I'll even beg you to stop, here watch."

Talitha's face lost her evil happiness and Will stared amazed and outraged, as she suddenly looked lost and afraid, in pain. "Will! Stop please, I didn't mean it," the words shrieked out of her as if he had really been hurting her. "No, don't, it hurts! Stop please! Stop…stop." She blubbered quietly, tears running down her face and the performance was so realistic that his arm, the one holding the table leg, slowly lowered.

She might've saved herself right there, but she began to giggle like a little girl, "I wish I could see your face better. Heck, I wish I could see mine. Did I look like Talitha, did I capture her essence?" Her questions seemed sincere, but they were lost on her brother, who attacked her in a fit of rage.

"Will, no it's me Talitha," she screamed in terrific fright as Will swung the club at her leg. He missed and she pushed herself further back, "She's gone! The other Talitha has gone! It's me." She wailed, but he attacked again striking her calf. "Please stop, it's me." Her face was screwed up in pain and fright, something Will found nearly impossible to ignore and he stepped back for a second.

The moment he did, Talitha's smile returned. "Good, that was good. I like the way you don't try to rush things, remember slow pain is good pain."

"Damn it!" he roared with empty defiance.

"I told you it wouldn't be easy." She smiled wickedly. "You have to really want it."

"Yeah, but shooting you won't be hard at all," Will said with a touch of wickedness of his own.

"Damn it," it was her turn to curse. "I was hoping you had forgotten the pistol. Well let's see if you have enough rage left in you, because I gotta say you sound kinda tired."

Tired wasn't the word he would've used, he felt well past exhausted and his head was beginning to throb with what he figured would be a headache to beat all headaches. "I may be tired, but I hate you, and that will be enough."

"But do you hate the real Talitha, your sister. I was just faking back there, but if you use the gun, it'll be on her." He paused not knowing what to say and the delay brought back the evil smile. "There's only one way to find out if you hate *me* enough to kill *her*."

Talitha came back then.

Will had seen it happen enough to know it wasn't a fake this time. The provocative smile drained away slowly into puzzlement, however that look lasted less than a second until the electricity of shock lit up her face.

"Will?" It was a whisper. Her eyes shot wide and rolled about in their sockets, but her head was still, unmoving. Her nose however went into overdrive, sniffing quietly, breathing in the horror of the room.

"Will?" This was a little louder.

The fire of Will's hatred was dying slowly in him and he knew if he waited any longer, it would be gone, and he wouldn't be able do what his prudence knew to be the right thing. He took a step toward her and she jumped back afraid of the sudden movement.

"Will, is that you?"

"Yes, stop moving," he growled this through gritted teeth.

"Ok...I can see a little, shapes and shadows...Is Father Alba going to be ok? I can smell his blood and I can smell...lots of blood. Did I do all this? Did I kill all these people?"

He stood behind her trying to work up the hatred again. "You killed Father Alba and in a way...Father John as well."

"Father John?" she asked, whispering the words. "I don't know who he is, where..."

He didn't let her finish, but reached down and grabbed her good arm and began pulling her with savagery, dragging her across the floor.

"What're you doing? What's going on?" Confusion, pain, and fear made up the alarm in her voice. Will kept his face toward the door, afraid to look down and see his sister, knowing his heart would break if he did, knowing the other Talitha would win.

"Will?" she pleaded again when he didn't answer.

"I have to kill you," he said as he hauled her back to the room where some poor boy knelt bound to his eternal box.

Talitha went limp, resigned to her upcoming death. "Ok...I understand...I'm so sorry..."

Feeling each of her words loosen the bolts, holding his anger in place, he asked in a choked voice, "Please don't talk. Just be quiet."

He gained the room and pulled her inside. The gun lay near the decaying body, which he refused to look at, but saw all the same. He couldn't help it. It was the movements of the maggots, they were horrible but hypnotic and his eyes remained on them even as he reached down, fumbling for the gun.

It was a blessing to turn away from the child and with a large shaky breath, he went back to the grim task he had to perform. Talitha hadn't moved, except to sit up, and she stared vacantly at the floor, tears small and noiseless trickled from her eyes and found their way to her chin, leaping off in an attempt to escape the inevitable.

Will, knowing he couldn't shoot her in the face, went around behind her. This was better. Here, the blood of her wounds was visible and there were no familiar sad brown eyes staring up at him, holding him back.

"I'm sorry Talitha," he thumbed the hammer and aimed at the back of her head, but then turned his face away unable to watch.

"Will!" A deep voice rumbled from the doorway, "What're you doing?"

Will kept his face turned away from both of them. "It has to be done!"

"Go away, Jim, please. Don't look at this," Talitha's voice was shrill with embarrassment.

But Jim didn't leave, he advanced on Will, his face set in determination. Will swung the gun in his direction, but Jim ignored it and then ignored Will as well, calmly going to one knee, he put his great arms around Talitha.

Both Will and Talitha were stunned into a moment of silence by this, but Will found his voice, it was a child's petulant whine, "Get away from her, I mean it."

"No, if you kill her, then you kill me," Jim said and his voice was an adult's, it held gravity and significance.

The gun lowered, dropped would be closer to the truth, and Will stood impotent with it dangling against his leg. There was no way he could shoot Jim. In addition, the fire of his hatred burned away leaving behind bitter ash and all that was left in him was a sense of duty; he had a responsibility to protect others from his sister.

The boys she had come to Boston to help were all dead, as was her purpose here. Talitha realized this as well and pushed Jim away with her good arm, saying, "Thank you, Jim. That was sweet, so wonderful of you...but I'm a lost cause. Go back to your orphanage and back to your children, they need you."

Jim leaned away trying to peer into her small pretty face and she held him there with a stiff arm, "Ok, Will. Do it...kill me quick." She meant it.

Will brought the gun up, fully intending to shoot his sister, but when he turned his head away, not wanting to see the blood he would cause, he saw something. Or more closer to the truth he didn't see something. Where Luke had once lain trussed in the knotted stole, there was now only an empty patch of cement.

Chapter 18

The Pewter Cross

When Jim saw the horror of Father Alba's face, he seriously questioned his vow not to hurt Talitha. And when he saw the blood, drying on her hands, the blood that stained her with guilt, the vow went out the window completely.

But then he saw something else, a girl, small and vulnerable and in truth innocent, and he gave up his pretense of anger and moved in to hug her and to protect her and if he had to, die with her.

When she held him back stiffly, he only paused a second, before he moved her arm out of the way and hugged her tight, his face against hers and she didn't fight him but instead began to cry. Her tears were warm and soft, tickling him as they traced the border where their skin met. They were also, in a sad way that broke his heart, wonderful.

He knew her tears were partially because of him, perhaps mostly so. In their long talks, he had the sense that she'd been desperately lonely and he had shown her by his hug that he cared for her. He felt her hug him back hard, clinging, and afraid to give this up, the one true moment of affection she had experienced in years.

Jim waited for the shot to ring out with a strange feeling of contentment. He realized he could die this way and be happy. But no shot came.

"What?" Will asked perplexed.

Jim glanced up at the oddness in the man's voice

and saw Will staring at an empty spot on the floor, as if looking for answers from the mute cement. Jim's contentment died right there and not because of a bullet. It was then that he noticed the hideous smell and saw the atrocity tied to the wood box in the center of the room.

"Luke...he was right there," Will muttered and sudden fear overwhelmed the perplexity on his face. He snapped the gun up and swiveled it around the room, searching the dim corners. "Jim, did you see Luke at all when you came in here?"

"No. It was just you and Talitha and...that," he added grimacing at the sight.

"Damn it! Where's Sean? Is he still alive?" Will asked urgently.

"Sean is with Father Alba, but where's Father John?" Even as Jim asked the question, he felt he already knew the answer.

When Sean and he had been trying to find a way into the building, they'd heard the gunshot. It came low and distant, a muffled noise but still unmistakable for what it was. The back entrance to the factory had proved impossible to get through and they were in the process of trying to break into a second story window when the sound of the gun, and the others that followed had nearly sent Sean and him into a panic.

They threw subtlety aside and tore the frame of the window out by hand, uncaring of the noise. They were frantic to get inside, but both men were so large that each took turns getting stuck going through the small opening and it was minutes before they could get in. They were slowed even more when they tried to race into the stairwell.

It was blocked with furniture just as Will's had been and the two men had to charge repeatedly at the door to get it wide enough to allow Sean to fit through the opening. This slowed them down, but it also saved Jim's life. The great force they sent into the door had knocked a chair loose from the pile of furniture and this had bounced down the stairs, hopping miraculously over the trip cord and into the gun, disturbing the trap that had been set for them.

When Jim, panting and sweating, came upon it minutes later, his intestines turned to water. Even in the unrelenting dark, there was no mistaking the gun and the purpose of the string and the pulleys. Jim's frenzied desire to find Luke and help Father Alba vanished almost completely and the two men were nearly paralyzed into inaction by the fear of another trap.

They had moved snail-like down the stairs and then with painful slowness had gone from room to room in the basement. Even when they heard the unmistakable sounds of fighting, they couldn't force themselves along any faster.

That Will had won the fight with his sister wasn't immediately obvious. His face was a terrific wreck and he stood bleeding gently, the red drops a quiet rhythmic lip...lip...lip, on the floor. Will didn't answer the question, but Jim could tell that Father John was dead by the man's expression.

"Was it one of the traps," he asked Will as gently as he could.

Will nodded vaguely, however he contradicted the movement, saying in a hollow voice, "No. I killed him...my cowardice killed him." He gave his head a short violent shake, spraying Jim with blood, and went to the door. "Sean! Luke is loose somewhere in the building! Come on down here." His voice was rough as sand paper.

"We should go to him," Jim said getting up. "He's with Father Alba, he can't leave him alone." He then bent and with ease, lifted Talitha up into his arms. She grunted in pain and it was then that he noticed her less obvious injuries, her left arm hung limp and sported spectacular vibrant purple bruising, her right knee, exposed by his lifting was swollen to twice the size of the left. She was in bad shape, but her brother was worse.

However, he didn't seem to notice. Not even the flap of skin hanging over his left eye, it bled like rain onto the shoulder of his shirt, which at one time had been tan, but now was a red brown. Will looked down his now bent and bleeding nose at Jim.

"Father Alba can wait, we need to find Luke."

"No. Father Alba needs to get to a hospital, right away," Jim answered.

Will blinked, confused. "What? Wait...is he still alive? How?"

"I don't know, but he is. Come on." Jim led the way carrying Talitha, who looked shell-shocked by everything that had gone on around her.

In seconds, they were in the room with the priest and the other horrible child corpse. Sean Shay knelt behind Father Alba, cradling his head on his fat thighs. "His eyes...are gone. They're just gone." His tremendous belly jiggled with his rapid breathing and the priests head bounce along keeping time.

Will knelt down and peered into the gaping holes. He reached out both hands to touch the wounds, only to stop slightly confused, and he stared for just a second at the two dislocated fingers on his left hand. The pinky and ring fingers were bent back and to the side. The sight of it bothered Jim, but when the man calmly yanked the fingers back into position, with grizzly popping sounds, Jim eyes fairly bugged out of their sockets and he felt his stomach roll queasily.

Will massaged his fingers absently for a moment, before again reaching out for the priest.

"How do I look?" Father Alba asked unexpectedly.

Everyone jumped, startled. Without eyes, Jim couldn't tell that the man had been awake and just assumed him to be unconscious.

"Oh hey, Father...you look, well..." Will trailed off into silence, inspecting the wounds closer. Jim could see that the left eye looked the worse of the two; there the eyelid and eyebrow had been torn off completely. On the right side at least, the skin still hung there like an old curtain.

"Sean, prop him up higher, we don't want the blood to drain back," Will commanded and then to the priest said, "It's not so good, Father. Your eyes are gone and the skin is going to take some work to look...more normal. I'm sorry, I should..."

The priest interrupted, "It's not your fault, Will. But please tell me you didn't kill your sister."

Jim felt Talitha begin to cry again and he watched as she used her good arm to pull her broken one to her chest and tuck the blood stained fingers into a pocket of her dress, she then hid her right hand as well.

Will's eyes flicked toward his sister before he answered, "No I didn't, but I wanted to...I want to." His voice was matter of fact, cold and seemingly heartless and it pained Jim to hear it.

"Your reaction is normal...human even, but Jesus wants us to be more than that. I forgave your sister, even after she blinded me, Will."

Talitha had begun shaking against Jim's chest and she spoke up in anger, "I don't deserve forgiveness...I deserve to die."

"Remember, Talitha..." the priest began, but was interrupted again.

"Enough! I don't have time for this crap," Will cried angrily and pulled himself up. "I don't have time for your crap, Talitha or yours...uh Father Alba." Will realized too late, that pointing at the man was now useless.

"Will..." Jim was cut off as well.

"Or yours," Will turned angrily to Jim. "We have that God damned freak Luke running around. We have to get Father Alba to a hospital. We have to somehow keep from getting arrested, seeing as we harbored two mass murderers...and we have to do something with...something about..."

"Father John?" Talitha suggested meekly.

"Yeah, Father John. We can't leave him here." Will looked down in concentration and blood trickled into his eyes. He wiped it away, pushing the flap of skin back up onto his forehead absently, as if it was hair that had blown out of place by the wind. "First things first, we get Father Alba to a hospital. Sean help me carry the Father. Jim carry my sister."

He spoke in such a way that nobody second-guessed him. They traversed the building slowly, fearful of every shadow, but the factory was as silent as a tomb. Talitha was able to sniff out two more traps that stood in their way, one a gun trap similar to the ones found in the stairwells and one that they guessed was a pressure sensitive bomb. They gave it a wide berth.

The five of them paused at the body of Father John, while Father Alba gave a short prayer and then they were in the pouring rain a minute later. Luke had made a clean get away—only the old station wagon of Father Alba's sat in the parking lot and they hurried the priest into it.

"He's gone, God damn it!" Will swore when they got into the car.

"That's enough," Father Alba scolded him and then said gently. "Luke is gone and I doubt he's coming back, so you have time to move Father John's body."

"Excuse me Father, but Luke may not be so far out of reach as you might think. Will, here can see the future, maybe we can find out where he's..." Jim began, before Will broke in.

"Are you kidding? I'm done with this. Father John is dead because of me," Will said outraged.

"Will, stop blaming yourself." Jim replied, "Father John is dead because of a...I got confused, was Luke possessed or not?" he asked Talitha and everyone except Father Alba looked at her.

"Who was possessed?" Talitha stared about in puzzlement.

Jim paused for a moment, before deciding to ignore her question, since the explanation would take some time. "Father John was killed by a madman, not by you, Will."

"Either way, I'm not doing it, I won't look. He's the police's problem now," Will responded and stared out the fog-covered window.

"I'll help if I can," Talitha volunteered. "We can go by his job or house and sniff around, maybe we can find some...clues." She blushed oddly, but for what reason Jim didn't know. However, Will seemed to, and looked at his sister a long time; as he did the edges of his anger wilted.

"I guess I'm willing to go with Nancy Drew here, and look around his place," he said and she blushed harder; it was endearing to Jim.

"Will," Father Alba spoke weakly, "I don't feel well...I keep passing out, not that you could tell." He chuckled faintly. "Take this." He struggled to take the heavy pewter cross from his neck and Will helped to take it off of him. "Wear it. Remember God is always with you. Do what you can to stop Luke, please."

The request seemed to cause Will pain, he grimaced. "I will...everything but looking into the future...Father?" There was no answer from the priest and alarm shot into Will's face. "Sean, take him to the emergency room. Make something up...tell them you found him this way outside the church and..."

"Talitha," the blind priest said quietly and they all jumped, startled again.

"Y-yes, Father," she stammered.

"I have forgiven you, now you must forgive yourself. Don't take any sins with you if..." he trailed off and without eyes, his horrific expression didn't change and they were clueless whether he was awake or not.

Seconds passed in silence and then Will barked an order, "Everyone out of the car. Sean go, don't dawdle."

Talitha and Will pulled themselves slowly and painfully from the car, while Jim was just as slow due to his size. In moments they stood in the pouring rain watching the car disappearing into the deluge.

"What do we do now?" Jim had to yell due to the noise of the storm.

It turned out there was much to be done.

They started by going from room to room in an attempt to erase any sign that any of them had ever set foot in the old factory, but they hadn't got far before Jim mentioned in passing about the weird diagrams and symbols painted on the floors around the bodies of the five children.

The three other corpses, they found with ease, using Talitha's sense of smell and the positions and drawing had been identical. A spasm of anxiety rippled across her features, as Jim dutifully described in detail the symbols and drawings. She then demanded a play by play of all their dealings with Luke as well as the other Talitha.

"What's all this for?" Will asked

"I'm not sure, I almost wish the other Talitha were here, she would know."

"Don't say that, it's not funny. Just give me your best guess." Will's mood hadn't improved. He was obviously now feeling the pain of the fight and he frequently rubbed his head gingerly and let out little groans. This was the opposite of his sister, who healed so fast, that she was already limping about unassisted.

"Best guess, it's most likely some way for this Luke person to communicate with creatures in the void."

"Really?" Will walked around the circle studying the markings. "Don't you think a Ouija board would be simpler? I told you that Henny Harris used one, right?"

"You did," she assured him. "However, a Ouija

board might be simpler to use, but that may mean it gives a simple message as well. Have you ever seen one? You can get answers to yes or no questions easy enough, but anything more complicated has to be spelled out."

Will nodded, staring down at the symbol without seeing it. "You may be right. Luke knew very personal information, things you'd never find out by asking yes or no questions."

Silence followed this and Jim, who couldn't stop staring at the decomposing corpse of a child who would never throw another baseball or open another Christmas present, said, "Why would he do this to little boys?"

"Do you mean defile them?" Talitha asked.

"Huh?" Defile wasn't in his relatively small vocabulary. "What do you mean?"

"Judging by the smell and their positions...it's obvious these boys were raped." Wearing a look of disgust, she turned and hobbled for the door.

"But why boys at all? You had spoken about virgin girls, not boys," Will said, stopping her at the door. "I want you to stay with us, don't wander about alone." It came out gruffly.

"I'm sorry, but being in the same room with...him, is depressing." She had a haunted look in her eyes, perhaps of a memory she wished she could forget. She sighed wearily. "Boys or girls, does it matter? It's all sad."

"I agree," Will said, "But it may matter to Luke. He went from snatching boys and doing...all this stuff, to then faking a possession and demanding the sword."

Jim felt puzzled at the conversation. "Was he faking it with that spell thing? It seemed so realistic."

"Oh I'm sure he was faking it. When the other Talitha ripped up those papers, it was like a switch was thrown and I could see the guy as he truly was. The other Talitha sure thought so, even from the very beginning, she said boys couldn't be possessed," Will remembered.

"I am tempted to believe the other Talitha," Talitha said. "Women are built structurally to carry another living being inside them. Perhaps this isn't strictly physical, perhaps there is a spiritual component as well."

Will nodded understanding. "That makes sense, but why boys for this? Was he just a whacked out pederast, or was this some sort of messed up ritual?"

Jim, feeling stupid asked, "What's a pederast?"

Will answered, "A gay guy who likes to you know, sleep with young boys."

"That's sick!" Jim was appalled and also slightly nauseous. He walked over to a heavy pipe and sat down. "But...but this Luke asshole, he also uh, defiled Sister Mary."

"Wasn't she old? I mean really old?" Will asked and when Jim nodded, Will went and sat down next to him. "Gross," he exclaimed and Jim nodded again.

Talitha stood turning her head this way and that. "I think we can throw out the pederast theory. My guess he used the boys as energy to power whatever spells or incantations he was using. The old lady? Probably just trying to increase his mystique, make everyone more afraid of him. That or he's just gross."

Will shrugged. "Seems logical. Talitha, what are you doing?"

She had been turning her head about oddly. "My

eyesight is coming back. It's like being able to see for the first time, it's interesting."

"Oh," Will sounded disappointed. "How soon till you can see normal again?"

She gave a little shrug. "An hour, maybe two."

Will and Jim shared a look and a worry for the future, the bigger man turned back to Talitha. "So where does any of this leave us?"

"He has an apartment, we should go there," she answered. "If we don't find anything, then I don't know what to do. After all, this is his secret lair. It's unlikely that he has a secret-secret lair, with hidden passages and laboratories filled with bubbling test tubes." The image made Jim smile, and she seemed to sense it and smiled back.

"There could be some clues somewhere in here?" Jim waved his arm indicating the entire factory.

"I'm sorry but his scent is everywhere. If he had a secret diary or more incantations, they could be anywhere, which is one of the reasons why, we have to burn this whole place down."

Chapter 19

The Crush

From the steeple, looking through the canted stained glass windows, Jim saw the black smoke rising from the remains of the Haikes Rubber and Tire Co. And this was despite the rain that came down in steady sheets.

Talitha, freshly showered and looking young and beautiful, watched with him. They shared the same small window, which afforded the best view of a whole lot of nothing: some trees, the tops of buildings, a little smoke, and a lot of rain. But for Jim, the best view was the slender curve of her neck; an artist had created it and he could stare at it forever.

"I'm worried about the rain dousing the fire too soon," she said with a sigh.

He sighed as well, but wasn't worried about the rain at all. Even though the factory had been closed for years, there was enough flammable material to cause quite a bonfire.

"I don't think you need to worry too much, the flames were plenty high."

"No offense Jim, but bigger isn't always better," she replied turning from their window and looking up at him, craning her neck far back to do so. "It's the temperature that's most important. Have you ever read *Fahrenheit 451*?"

Jim could vaguely recall a book of that title that he hadn't bothered reading in tenth grade English—a class he'd passed regardless. "No, we must've read a different book."

"The title of the book is supposedly the temperature at which paper burns. If you ask any high-school student who has read the book, what temperature does paper burn? They will all tell you 451 degrees," she said this with a knowing smile.

"Is the title of the book wrong?" he asked, thinking it must be.

"Yes and no. It's funny, the author Ray Bradbury, didn't ask a scientist what the right temperature would be, he asked a fireman." Talitha smiled at this, Jim did as well, even though it sounded reasonable to him. "It just so happens that this particular fireman was very knowledgeable and gave him a pretty good answer."

"How could it be pretty good? Either he was right or he wasn't."

"Well that brings me to my worry about the rain," she answered. "451 degrees will auto ignite a certain weight of dry, untreated cellulose based paper, under proper conditions."

Jim's slow stare made her retry.

"What I mean to say is there are lots of variables the fireman didn't take into consideration before answering and some of these same variables are worrying me if Luke hid spells in the factory. For instance, there needs to be a proper amount of oxygen for the paper to burn, if they're in a sealed pipe, discoloration may be all we get. But I'm most worried about the paper."

"You just might be over thinking this. Isn't paper just paper?" Jim asked.

"No. Cellulose based paper, paper coming from

wood pulp, can be of varying weights—what you would call thickness. The thicker the paper, the higher the temperature needed to start and sustain a fire. But there are other types of paper, and an incantation especially an old one, might just be written on vellum."

"Is that a special kind of tree?"

She smiled at him, but it wasn't a hurtful smile. It was a cryptic smile. "No, vellum is actually a writing surface created from the skin of mammals. Usually calf skin or sheep, but it could be almost any mammal, including human."

"Gross...that's just so gross." Jim shook his head at the idea. "But knowing this sick freak, I wouldn't put it past him." He looked again at the smoke, it was still thick and heavy, even after three hours. He sighed again and this time it was she that followed suit.

"How's Father Alba?" she asked nonchalantly. They had been up in the steeple for twenty minutes and she had clearly wanted to ask him about his phone call to the hospital the entire time.

He had talked to Father Wheal, a priest from a neighboring parish who'd been kind enough to sit in with Father Alba. Jim told Talitha what he'd been told, "He's going to live, but there's no chance for the eyes, and there will be lot's of scarring."

"It's what I expected," she replied without emotion, but that facade crumbled quickly, and her face broke, close to tears. "What are we going to do?"

He took a peek at her before answering, but it turned from a peek into a stare. He couldn't help it. In truth he didn't know if he could help it or not; he didn't try, he just stared.

Her features seemed at once delicate but strong, the

two near opposites meshing to form a noble beauty. But sometimes her features would swing over to the extremes, one moment she might be delicate and sweet; childlike and in need of protection. And the next, the opposite, regal to the point of queenly, haughty, superior and sometimes dangerous.

She was beautiful, but in a way that was unlike any other woman he'd ever known. And he stared. He stared until she turned her large brown doe eyes up to him and then he looked away quickly, pretending to admire the dismal rain covered city.

"What are we going to do? I was going to ask you the same question," he said. It was the truth at least.

"For once, I'm all out of answers."

"Why do I doubt that?" he replied and they matched smile for smile. "Tell me, what would the other Talitha do if she were here?"

She slumped. "Kill someone, I guess."

"No really...well apart from that I mean." There had been too much truth in her statement to try to gloss over it.

The girl sighed again, hugely. "She'd go to his apartment, search it, terrorize his neighbors, torture his friends, and kill their dogs. She's very thorough you know." Putting her back to the window, she worked her left arm back and forth with little twinges of pain showing on her face.

"Getting better?" he asked.

"Yes, unfortunately yes." She looked down at her arm and glared at it for a second. "Have I been fed or watered lately? Did the other Talitha eat anything?"

"Are you hungry? I can make you something," he swallowed hard, wishing he hadn't just said that. His cooking skills were notoriously poor, outside of reheating frozen goods.

"I don't actually get hungry, but I still need to eat. However, I don't like the idea of eating food from an orphanage." She smiled her shy smile, one of his favorites. "It feels too much like stealing."

"Are you picturing all our boys in grubby clothes, eating small bowls of porridge, three meals a day?" he asked.

She laughed heartily. "Yes! I've never been to an orphanage; my only frame of reference is Dickens and Little Orphan Annie."

"You're not the only one. Every time we buy oatmeal at the grocery store, we get dirty looks."

This caused her to laugh again, the second time in just a few moments, it made him feel good inside to make her happy, even for a little bit.

"You know what I'm in the mood for?" she asked with a big sigh. "Ever since I heard I was getting to come with you guys to the city, I've craved pizza."

Jim's stomach rumbled loudly at the thought, but before he could be embarrassed, she reached out and patted his slightly bulging midsection.

"Excuse me, sorry," he said faking embarrassment; he was secretly thrilled by the way she had casually touched him. It wasn't that it was sexual in any way, because it wasn't. It was just that she wasn't repulsed by him, which may seem like a simple thing, but to Jim it was huge. "I always crave pizza. There's a very good neighborhood place that delivers, do you want some?"

Her eyes lit up. "Yes please!" They were a match made in heaven or so he thought.

"Onions, mushrooms, green pepper, sausage,

pepperoni, and black olives...oh and spinach if they have any," she said.

So much for the perfect match, his would be strictly meat. "Do you want beer? You can't have pizza without beer."

She suddenly looked back into the rain. "I'm sorry, but I'm not as hungry as I thought. But you can get some for yourself and Will."

Leave it to him to screw up a good thing. "Talitha...I don't need any beer. I'm not an alcoholic or anything."

This brought out a long weary breath from her. "It's not that...I'm just being stupid."

"I honestly don't think that's possible," he said, feeling like he'd somehow walked off the edge of a lovely green lawn only to find himself knee deep in a swamp and now he feared to move in any direction.

He put his hands on her shoulders and gently turned her around. She looked up at him with her most delicate of looks, as if she were as insubstantial as a snowflake that would melt if he were to turn angry.

"I'm sorry. Whatever I did to spoil your mood, I'm sorry." He gave her his friendliest smile even though it was gap toothed and turned his ugly face into a mess of long laugh-lines; it was all he had to work with.

His stomach didn't help the situation. Having heard the word pizza so many times, it was getting impatient and rumbled a loud demand for it.

It brought her around. "Sounds like it's two against one, I guess we're having pizza." He was about to ask if she was sure, but she beat him to it, "Yes, I'm sure. Now go call before I change my mind."

"I'll be right back," he was gone in a jiffy,

squeezing his broad shoulders sideways down the narrow stairs of the steeple, heading for the second floor of the management building. There were closer phones in the offices, but just the sight of the office doors nearly killed his hunger and he proceeded to the common room instead.

Walking in, he was quite surprised at the scene. A man Jim had seen, but had never been introduced to, was sewing up the big flap of skin hanging from the top of Will's forehead. This had gone ignored all afternoon.

Jim guessed the man to be a doctor by the precise weaving pattern his hands created as he sutured up the large cut. The needle was curved and tiny, and the thread was not the usual thick black string, but an almost invisible filament.

He leaned in close and saw that Will had already been stitched up in two other areas and the handiwork was impressive. "I'm going to use the phone, if that's ok?" he asked the doctor.

"Sure thing Jim, just don't knock the table," the doctor said, and Jim gave him a closer look at the sound of his own name, but still he was sure they hadn't met.

"I'm getting some pizza, do you two want any?" The doctor didn't look up from his work, but grunted out a no.

"I would. Pepperoni if you don't mind and if Talitha is getting any, get her a whole pie, or she'll eat most of yours. When she gets going, she can be pig," Will said from beneath the dexterous fingers of the doctor.

Jim ordered three pizzas, one for each of them and they arrived shortly after the doctor had finished taping Will's fingers together. A buddy splint, he called it.

They ate in the steeple, something Jim had never done before, but the rest of the church haunted him with memories. At first they were quiet as they ate, concentrating on the food, but the conversation picked up, at least for Jim and Talitha. Will was sullen and barely said anything.

When Jim finished eating, leaving nothing for the squirrels, he checked the time, which set off a small chain reaction. First Will then Talitha checked their watches as well, 6:11 pm.

"More milk?" Jim offered Talitha after she chugged the last of hers. He couldn't help smiling at the faint milk moustache she wore afterwards, it was endearing. She didn't seem to think so and wiped it away on the back of the sleeve of her borrowed habit.

"No thank you," she said a touch coolly, as if he had only offered her the milk so she could sport a new moustache. "Any idea when he'll call?" she asked adjusting for the hundredth time, the overly large black dress that she wore.

"No, in fact he might not call at all. He's still a little mad at you," Will said around a bite of pizza. He was eating very slowly on account of his swollen lips and missing molar on the lower left side of his mouth. With the blood cleaned away from his face, the newly sutured lacerations didn't look so bad, however the bruising and swelling was terrible. Especially obvious was the freshly set broken nose and the two black eyes.

For the moment, Jim was the better looking of the two men. He checked his watch again, 6:12, and felt an undercurrent of the awareness of time, which had started innocently enough when he had been waiting on his pizza. For him, time always seemed to flow in slow motion when a pizza was supposedly on the way, however the feeling remained even when the food arrived. It wasn't nearly as obvious, but when he wasn't actively talking or thinking, he felt anxious about the time.

Right now, they were waiting on a call from Eric Milner, hoping to get the address and key to Luke's apartment. There were a couple of other things they needed the cop's help with as well, the bodies of Sister Mary Agatha and Father John had to be explained and buried. There was also the issue of the body on the mattress in the charnel pit of a room beneath the church and the thing in the box, which no one but the other Talitha had even seen yet.

"He'll call," Jim said with confidence. "He'll make us sweat it out first, but he'll do it." Milner would do it for Sister Mary, not for Jim. She'd been a mother to Milner, something Jim had been endlessly jealous of as a kid.

Will frowned at the statement and then touched his face gently as if the small movement had been painful. "I don't think I can sit around waiting, I'm going to call him again."

This he did, leaving Jim and Talitha staring at each other, waiting for the sound of his footsteps to recede. While he was in their presence it felt like they were being chaperoned and they both struggled to keep from smiling or laughing.

Finally, the sound of a door far off at the end of the chapel could be heard and Jim said, "He's a little too nervous. Do you think he's had another vision?"

She turned slightly in the direction of the window and Jim was able to see her profile perfectly. "I don't know. Sometimes he hangs onto an old vision, worrying over it until it happens and then...what are you staring at?" she asked touching her face self-consciously.

He'd been staring at her small nose. He generally found the human nose, like the penis, funny looking and oddly designed by God, but her nose was perfect, small and slim, exactly proportioned to accent her high cheekbones and to set off her large brown eyes.

She had a beautiful nose. His resembled a medium sized potato.

"Oh...nothing," he turned away putting his hand over his face, hiding the potato. He hadn't realized he'd been staring or more accurately, he knew he was staring, but hadn't realized that he wasn't being discreet about it.

He couldn't help stare at her, she was an addiction. A happy one that he lost himself in voluntarily, or so he figured, self-reflection wasn't his strong suit. He just knew that his emotions were askew. The sadness and grief that he should've been feeling were wispy and weak, ghost like—they were there within his heart, but they lacked urgency. Anger too should've been burning him up inside and when he thought on it, he could feel the fire of it grow, but it would puff out of existence when he looked on Talitha.

These emotions, the ones he thought of as correct for the situation; sadness, anger, hatred, grief, were eclipsed or blotted out altogether by his one fiction.

He loved her.

It was stupid. Very stupid and normally he would've laughed it off and done his best to keep away from her, not wanting to bother her with his oafish presence. He knew that he wasn't in her league in any way. Not just in looks, but intelligence and personality, accomplishments and potential. He was a huge nothing and knew he would remain so, while she had everything and would only become more.

However, this wasn't a normal situation and Jim knew it was the nagging feeling of running out of time that had him embellishing his fiction instead of ignoring it. He knew consciously that what he felt for her was likely only puppy love or a crush; it wasn't real. Yet, the affect she had on him was very real.

At the sight of her, his chest would swell from within and every time she touched him with her long thin fingers, he'd feel them warm and soft, even after she removed her hand, as if his skin was trying to keep the memory of her touch for itself.

His eyes were always on her, wandering over her flesh, drinking it in, feeling the exquisite smoothness of her, but not in sexual way, no, his eyes were on her like an artist's. An artist who has seen a beauty so dazzling that it was beyond his ability to capture. An artist afraid to make even the first stroke of his brush, knowing even that little thing would never compare.

And what would an artist do in such a situation but stare longingly in vain, wishing his talent was equal to her magnificence.

That was Jim Anderson.

He would feed his crush with her loveliness, but like the artist, would never make the first stroke, knowing with doomed certainty that it would go awry and end his fantasy.

Still if he were to draw her, it would be her neck that he'd begin with. Presently she had her head tilted to the side and he took in her long slender neck as it rose to greet her jaw, the line of which was strong and could only be described as aristocratic.

Her eyes flicked to him, purposely to catch him staring and he turned quick to look out of the window.

"It's ok. You are allowed to look at me," she grinned as she said it.

His cheeks suddenly felt hot and red. "Sorry...I didn't mean to stare. It's just you have a nice smile is all."

"Really? How about now?" She made a face at him, pulling back the corners of her mouth, sticking out her tongue and crossing her eyes. It was wonderfully carefree and childlike, the sweetness of it made him love her even more.

"I like that smile most of all." And he did too. Her silly smile had been for him alone and in his lonely and loveless world, it was unique.

"If you liked that then you are beyond my help." She remained smiling at him, her normal pretty smile, white teeth against her tan. "It feels weird to smile...with everything going on."

"I know. I feel the same way. It's strange, like I'm being wrong somehow," he responded.

"For me, I know part of it is the fact that Father Alba forgave me. He really meant it, at least for now. But I still feel lighter inside," she nodded happily at the memory, while Jim felt his own smile slip. The priest's face with its gaping holes was a sight that would haunt him for a long time.

"What do you mean for now? He's forgiven you, that can't change."

Her smile remained, but became edgy with

bitterness. "He was in a state of shock. Wait until he's walking into walls. Or wait until he's trapped in his apartment, afraid to go out without someone there to guide him. Or wait until his depression boarders on suicide; he'll be cursing my name for certain."

"Oh," Jim's face dropped as he imagined a blind Father Alba sitting in a dark apartment, alone. He wouldn't let that happen. "I'll take care of him, Talitha. I'll make sure that he's not alone."

"I know you will. You're a good man," she said patting his arm. The feel of her hand caused a little shiver of excitement that he squelched, but only with difficulty.

"Uh, what about you? What do you plan on doing when this is all over with?" His question was lame, but her hand had felt hot on his skin and it was taking up a large part of his mind and not a little of his body as well.

Her incredulous look dismayed him however. "Me? I guess go back my cabin." She said this nonchalantly, but untruthfully.

Jim was screwing up his fantasy. The last thing he wanted to do was to make her sad. "Whatever you do don't become a poker player. You're a terrible liar, maybe the worst I've ever seen. If you ever went to Vegas, you'd lose everything and be broke in a week."

Her smile came back, an honest one. "Sorry I lied. I was just enjoying our conversation and I didn't want to ruin it."

Concern and fear for her safety exploded in his heart. "Do you know something? Did Will tell you something?"

"No, but he is a bad liar as well. I can see it in his

eyes and hear it in his voice...he thinks one of us will die." She said this quietly but a second later, incongruously, Talitha stuck a huge toothy smile on her face. "That's why I'm going to be extra peppy! If I have only a little longer left, I want to be happy. Happiness is not allowed where I'm going, so I better get all I can, while I'm here. What about you? Will you join me in celebrating our impending doom?"

She held out her hand, and he was slow to take it. The idea that his death could be hours away, occupied a potion of his mind, but Talitha still held sway over the majority of it and he reached out his great paw and swallowed her tiny one in his.

Her touch was like magic and his fears and worries vanished. He held her hand for over a minute without looking at her. He wanted to remember this touch for always, but finally he looked up and said, "I will, for better or worse."

Chapter 20

Will Doesn't Like E.T.

Luke's apartment turned out to be a complete bust.

Eric Milner had called just before seven, giving Will the address to the place, which turned out to be only a few minutes away by car. Jim didn't own a car, something he was embarrassed to admit and they were forced to use Father Alba's, which still bore the stains of his blood.

Talitha refused to get in until Jim cleaned up as much of the mess as he could and even then, her new peppy smile, bogus and strained, clashed with the misery in her eyes. It made for a quiet ride and even the rain, falling in little more than a light mist felt subdued. But thankfully the place was close and Jim was quick to hop out and open the door for Talitha, something that earned him a genuine smile.

He smiled back at her and then at her brother, but Will only scowled at the ground making his way to the door. They found the key where Milner said it would be, under the mat and as Will fumbled with it, Jim caught a nasty smell coming from the apartment.

"What is it with this guy and stinkiness?" He was putting on a show of cheeriness and Talitha after a little sigh, added to it.

"I know. You would think he just got elected mayor of stinktown."

Will gave them a questioning look, one that was hard to read in the dark. "Can you two keep quiet? This is technically illegal you know," he admonished them. They were serious for a second until he turned his back on them bending to the lock and then Jim shared a look with the girl.

"Sorry Mom, we'll be good," Talitha said quietly with a mischievousness in her voice.

Will popped back up, fear and anger in his eyes and he looked hard at his sister. "Talitha?"

"Yes?" she replied. "Oh, you think I'm the other Talitha! No it's me," she patted her chest which did nothing to convince him.

"This is the good Talitha, don't worry," Jim reassured him.

"How do you know, she very tricky." Will grabbed his sister roughly by the arms pinning them to her sides.

"Will please," Jim put his hand on the man's shoulder in a friendly manner. "I know, because she'd have called me ugly and stupid ten times by now."

Oddly, Jim felt a little insulted when Will agreed with him. "You're right, she would've. But what's with you two? You're both acting...a little drunk, and there's a serial killer out there."

"Sorry Will," Jim mumbled, feeling like a kid again after being rebuked by a nun.

"I'm sorry as well...we know our situation," Talitha said, still with her arms pinned. "We know death could strike at any time, it's just we want our time left to be as happy as possible."

With the explanation, he seemed to sag and his anger melted away. "Oh. I'm sorry...for jumping down your throats. I'm just stressed, there's so much going on to worry about." He pursed his swollen lips and blew out heavily. "Lisa. She isn't happy about me staying and she doesn't even know about all of this," he waved his hand in front of his mangled and bruised face. "Who knows, if I die, maybe she'll never have to know." He gave them a grin, but with the dim light and heavy bruising, his face looked demonic.

"How about you join us and put on a happy face?" Talitha asked her brother, just as the key finally found its way into the lock. The door swung open revealing a room in complete shambles and a fearful smell billowed out of it. It was similar, but not as strong as the one from beneath the church.

Will coughed at the odor and looked back at his sister, his face now looking even more wretched; with green showing beneath the bruises. "Sure sounds great...I'm gonna throw up!" He didn't, but it was a near thing. He walked about for a bit in the parking lot, breathing heavily for few minutes before trying again to enter the place.

Jim was similarly affected, but he remained stoic trying to impress Talitha who only wrinkled her nose at the smell. "At least we don't have to worry about putting things back where we found them."

Her attempt at lifting their spirits failed miserably and they spent the next two hours sifting through the remains of Luke's belongings. There wasn't much left or hadn't been much to begin with, but either way they found nothing that would hint at where he was now. Dejected they made their way back to the car, where Talitha began a conversation with her brother by raising an eyebrow.

Will caught the look and with an angry sigh, glared out the front window for a moment, but then said, "I can't."

"Actually you can," Talitha responded.

"Ok, I won't." Will gripped the steering wheel hard enough to turn his knuckles white.

"Will, it's our only hope."

"What's our only hope?" Jim asked confused and getting upset at being left out of the conversation.

Will gave him a sharp, slightly irritated look, but spoke again to his sister, "People will die if I do."

Talitha still ignoring Jim, said, "People will die if you don't, probably more people."

"Who's going to die?" Jim asked, real anger slipping into the deep growl of his voice.

Will kept his eyes on his sister. "You may die."

"I'm ok with that," she responded evenly and it was clear she meant it, despite in Jim's opinion, having the most to lose. Jim hoped he'd be as tough as her, if it came down to sacrificing himself.

"Jim could die," Will added, refusing to budge his eyes back to where Jim sat.

"What? Hold on..." Jim felt flustered. Talitha finally looked back at him and gave him a large wonderfully fake smile, which in no way touched the worry in her eyes.

"I'm trying to convince my brother to look into the future," she explained.

Jim's mind replayed the conversation and he nodded with understanding. "Do you know which one of us is going to die?" This he asked and then took a large deep breath, preparing himself for the inevitable answer. He figured it would be him. After all, the brother and sister both had amazing powers, both were intelligent, and both had survived worse. While he pictured himself as a very large target that only a legally blind person could possibly miss.

"I...I..." Will couldn't seem to go on and the rain, which had picked up slightly, kept a steady beat. It added tension to Jim until he thought he was about to explode all over the inside of the car.

"I don't know, what I know," Will replied and the answer was hardly satisfactory to Jim, who felt his insides caving. Will obviously couldn't bring himself to tell Jim about his upcoming death.

"Why don't you just tell us what you saw?" Talitha asked, her lips pulled in, so much so they were hidden completely.

"It wasn't a vision exactly...I sometimes just know things."

"And what sort of things do you know?" She sounded like a perturbed mother coaxing a child. She'd said she would be ok with dying, but there was nervousness to her. Talitha was trying to appear outwardly calm, only Jim had been staring at her all day and saw small telltale signs. Her jaw clenching, the movement of the muscles now visible beneath the skin; her fingers worrying over an errant piece of thread, sticking out of the car's seat; her head nodding almost imperceptibly while she waited for Will to answer.

Now, Will looked back at Jim, but it was a quick guilty look. "I know that two of us will die...soon."

There was sudden white static, a roaring of blood in his ears, but Jim could still hear his own voice ask as if from far away. "Two? Which two of us?"

"I don't know...there were seven of us in that room and that's when I *knew* three of us would die. Father John was the first but I don't know who will be next, however I do know," Will paused and shook his head with a sad smile, "That Sean Shay, isn't going to die. I don't know why, but he lives."

A pang of jealousy startled Jim with its fierceness, but then Talitha, for no obvious reason held his hand, rubbing his fingers gently and at that moment, he wouldn't trade places with Sean for anything. He was going to miss him however.

Will wasn't the only one who *knew* things. The touch of Talitha's hand, still caressing his fingers made Jim realize that his crush on her, his puppy love, his fiction, was a lie. He did love her, completely. It didn't matter to him that she didn't love him back, he loved her unconditionally and perhaps stupidly, but love was love. It couldn't be helped.

There were two other things that he knew with absolute certainty. First, was that he loved her enough that he'd die for her and second, that he would kill for her as well.

"I'm going to make sure that damned Luke is one of the two of us that dies," he said harshly making tremendous fists of his great hands.

Will gave him a look that was both sweet and sad. "If it were that easy, I would've looked into the future already. There's no saying we'll win out in the end. Two of us could die and the other might live out his life as a quadriplegic or as a vegetable in a coma. You see why I'm not jumping at this great chance? It's my fault Father Alba is in the hospital and that Father John is dead—what did we get out of that?"

Talitha riled at this. "First off, Luke is the reason Father John is dead and I'm the reason Father Alba is blind, not you. Secondly, we stopped Luke from doing whatever he was up to and I am sure that was a very good thing and third we stopped...me, the other me! From gaining access to Luke and that as well, is a good thing. I know I'd rather face..." she looked a little confused. "I mean if I were you, I would rather face Luke than me...darn it! I mean the other me."

Will wasn't backing down at her reasoning. "Who's to say we won't have to face both of you. I mean... not the both of you, but you and Luke. Do you know what I mean?" This he was asking of Jim, who was in fact, still playing catch up.

"Can we call the evil Talitha, E.T. for short?" Jim asked. "It might make things simpler."

"Sure, good idea, Jim," Will agreed with a nod. Jim felt an embarrassing amount of pleasure over this small bit of praise.

Will continued, "Like I was saying, we might have to face Luke and E.T. at the same time. She has a tendency to show up, just when she can hurt us the most. Can you control her at all?" he asked Talitha.

"No, E.T. can come and go as she pleases and she seems to know when I'm particularly stressed."

Will looked at Jim. "I'm sorry, but I don't like E.T."

"Who would? I'm sure Luke doesn't," Talitha said.

Jim smiled at her. "No, he's talking about the nick name. E.T. was a good guy; it just seems weird to say."

"What? The E stands for evil, remember? You were right here! You made it up for goodness sakes." Her perplexity caused the two men to come close to laughing, but there was also an edge of annoyance with her perplexity and they both held it in.

"We're talking about the movie, you know E.T.?" Jim waggled a finger at her. "E.T. phone home," he said in his smallest voice. Her face was priceless. Confusion ran amok there, plucking at muscles in a seemingly random order. It was clear she had no idea what he was talking about.

"It was a movie that came out when you were in the hospital. It was cute, we should rent it when this is all done," Will explained.

"Rent? What do you mean the whole theater?" Talitha was sadly lost and she was in her vulnerable state that Jim found adorable.

"No. You can now rent movies and play them on a VHS..." Will started, but a light popped into Talitha's eyes and she interrupted him.

"A video home system, I read about them before... you know before. They were big in Japan. I take it they're sold here on the mass market?"

"Yeah, we got one in '82. You'll like it. You can catch up on all of the movies that you've missed." Will said, but there was sadness in his voice as if he knew she wouldn't ever see one.

Now the car was quiet, except for the ever-present rain. Talitha stared out into it with a lost expression and Jim stared at her. He thought about the last eight years and everything that she had missed hidden away in her cabin, or trapped in an insane asylum, it didn't seem fair.

She suddenly put on a smile, "I'm being mopey, when I'm supposed to be happy. Sorry about that, where were we? Naming the evil me...how about Evil T?"

Will made a sour face. "You've never heard of Rap music have you?"

Before Talitha could answer, Jim stepped in, "Evil T will work just fine. We were talking about finding Luke and maybe people dying. I'm wondering if Luke is really all that dangerous now. Maybe going after the sword was his one big shot."

"No, I'm sorry, Jim," Talitha said. "He's after something big. Maybe he's trying to bring Ba'al into this world, I don't know, but I don't think he's going to stop until he gets what he is after." She turned to her brother. "Lisa should take the sword and leave, someplace far away."

"She is. She'll be packed and gone by eight tomorrow morning." Will's face drained of color. "I told her not to tell me where she's going, but now I don't know how I'll find her when this is all done."

Talitha took her brother's hands in her own. "Don't worry about that, you'll find her, I know it. But the danger to Lisa is another reason, you need to look."

"For once your logic is flawed. If I look and I die, who'll protect Lisa from you and Luke; she'll be in even more danger then."

Another silence followed this, but Jim was fidgety and he broke it. "I vote we take the fight to the enemy. Running and hiding? I'm not very good at either." His huge frame taking up nearly the entire back seat attested to this.

"I'm with Jim," Talitha agreed. "That makes it two against one in favor of looking."

"I can't," Will moaned and Jim was shocked to see tears coming down the man's battered face. Talitha was alarmed at the suddenness as well and touched her brother's hands again.

"It'll be ok. Jim and I will be right here with you."

Bitter mocking laughter rang out, loud and shrill from Will. "Right! What are you going to do when the visions get stuck in my head and I go insane? I...I can't do it. Ok? You don't know how it was. I could feel the maggots..." His body shuddered horribly and his tears were nonstop.

Jim recalled how the man had gone mad in seconds, right before his eyes, screaming, crying, and then hitting himself with such viciousness. Jim began to have second thoughts.

"I know that it was bad last time, Jim told me, but it may not be this time. Luke has only been gone, what eight or nine hours? He's probably in hiding tonight," Talitha added as she bit at her lower lip.

Will's tears lessened and then stopped altogether, but he didn't look up. With shame coating his words, he whispered, "I can't. I'm sorry."

"I understand, Will. It sounded horrible," her tone was all sympathy. "But what would Lisa want you to do?"

Will barked a short laugh. "That's easy; she wants me to come home right now."

"Then why aren't you going."

The rain filled the long uncomfortable silence, but at last Will spoke softly in the tone of a condemned man, "I'll look in the morning...maybe. Sometimes I will have a vision when I dream at night. If tonight I don't have one...then I'll look."

"I think that's all we could ask of you." Talitha kissed her brother lightly on the cheek.

"Yeah, I agree," Jim said and then yawned a great cavernous bear like yawn. Talitha looked shocked but followed it with an amused smile, Will however seemed suddenly nervous.

"Jim, I know you're tired, but...you can't go to sleep. You have to stay awake and keep Talitha up."

"Will, I'll be ok. I've slept two nights in a row, that hasn't happened since before," Talitha reassured her brother.

Will ignored his sister and pleaded to the big man, "Jim, please promise me that you'll stay awake."

"I will, don't worry."

"We'll keep each other awake," Talitha said with a touch of Jim's hand that sent a shiver right up his back.

Chapter 21

Love and the Illusion of Love

The Volvo's windows had long since fogged over and Jim was beginning to get cold despite the coat that he wore. Talitha, who had on just the ankle length black habit seemed very comfortable and smiled at him when he zipped his coat up tight.

"So where do we go?" she asked. "Are there rooms at the orphanage?"

There were at two least vacancies tonight, but they had been the priest's rooms and Jim wasn't keen on the idea of spending the night in one of them. "Naw, at least none that we should use, but I know a motel nearby. Actually, it's not so close, all the motels around here are gross, roaches and stains and such. But I had a friend who stayed at this one place that was ok."

"Wherever you pick will be fine with us, but I need to make a stop first," Will murmured in a small voice.

The stop surprised Jim.

Jim drove and at the first liquor store that he saw Will demanded, quite urgently, to be let out. Moments later, he came out swigging from a brown bag. With his battered face and torn up clothes, Will looked like nothing more than one of the bums or hood-rats that populated the neighborhood alleys in that part of the city.

Both Talitha and Jim plastered happy smiles over what had been shared looks of alarm only a second earlier and Talitha asked her brother, "Do you expect it to be that bad?"

Will's thousand-yard stare matched the way he shook his head in a slow distant manner, and taking another pull from the bottle, he justified, "I just want to be able to sleep. That's all." After this, he was moody and sulked quietly, slumped in the back seat, not saying anything during the short trip, but only taking frequent sips from his bottle.

When they arrived at the motel, Jim secured two side-by-side adjoining rooms and tried his best not to let his excitement mount too much. However, when he opened the car door for her, Talitha beamed at him, sending his pulse hammering through his veins.

"Wow, such a gentlemen," she said as he took her by the hand. He didn't trust himself to say anything, his tongue felt huge, dry, and unruly, so he only dipped his head, feeling warmth spread out through his chilled body.

Unfortunately, his happy feelings were doused by Will. He stopped in front of his door and instead of opening it, he simply stared at it drinking. A minute passed and still he hadn't budged or even spoke.

"We'll be right here, if you need anything," Talitha spoke brightly. Will seemed to remember they were there and gave her a half smile. He then unlocked and opened his door, yet still didn't enter. Another minute passed and now Will had finished a third of the bottle.

Jim remembered the previous night and the horrible screams. "You know, he should just look into the future and save himself from this." The two of them hadn't entered their room either, it didn't seem right to leave him out there in the calming rain all alone.

"I know, but he'll blame himself for everything that

follows," she whispered back.

"That's stupid, the..." He was being too loud and she shushed him with pursed lips.

Will glanced over to them, his face glistening with sweat and the last of the rain and he only just realized they hadn't gone into their rooms. "Oh, good night...sweet dreams," he swayed slightly in the doorway.

"Good night, Will," Talitha said with quiet fake cheerfulness. Will took a final deep breath as if preparing for a long icy plunge and stepped into his room, shutting the door behind him.

With that, Talitha and Jim entered their own room, one that seemed to be the model for all motel rooms ever built. Two lamps, two chairs, one writing desk, one TV and a large bed with a standard issue floral comforter, and this last, not only dominated the room, it dominated Jim's mind as well. As he looked about, his eyes lingered longest on it and it spoke to him suggesting interesting and unlikely possibilities.

Talitha, however ignored the bed completely. Not even having a purse to fling down upon it, the bed represented no more than an obstacle and she hurried around it to the door separating the two rooms. Jim followed a trifle reluctantly and pressed his left ear to the door, facing Talitha.

From the room next door, Jim could hear only a smattering of muffled sounds and he figured what he was hearing was Will drinking himself into a stupor. He made an honest attempt at caring what was going on in there, after all, he did consider Will a friend, but after the first sniff of Talitha's hair, he knew Will would have to get drunk without him eavesdropping.

She faced him, with her right ear to the door and due to the narrowness of it and his great size, he was right on top of her. She smelled of idealized flowers. Were ever a meadow to smell as she did, he would never leave it. He stood above her, breathing her in, making her a part of him, and he would've stayed there all night, but the smell triggered another reaction.

He became alarmed at the swiftness of his body's response to her scent and the warmth of her closeness. Jim turned bodily towards the door and studied the fake wood grain with deep concentration, hoping to take his mind off of Talitha and the fact that his pants were starting to push outward painfully in the crotch.

However, in seconds he realized that wasn't going to work and he turned, putting his right ear to the door.

"Uh, this is my good ear," he mumbled as if he were eighty years old. Now he tried his best to listen to Will's drinking, but there was nothing coming from the other room that would distract his mind and he kept slipping into the memory of the bath Lisa had given Talitha that morning.

Lisa had been very discreet, covering Talitha with a towel, but it clung to her curves in a way that had been tremendously erotic. The hints of her tan skin, glistening and soap covered had been more arousing than if she had been totally naked. Thankfully, Jim had a large arm full of towels to cover his erection, but he had no such luck just then.

"Move your butt," she whispered leaning into him, "You're taking up the whole door." Feeling her against him was too much. He was becoming harder; bending at an odd angle and a glance down made him realize he would have to shift his apparatus quick.

Without explanation, he walked quickly to the writing desk and sitting down he attempted to slide himself under it, but he was too big in more ways than one.

"You ok?" Talitha asked, her ear coming off the door as she turned to him.

"It's nothing," he spoke this quickly and glancing over, he saw that she was concerned for him. She took a step in his direction and he became filled with a stupid embarrassed panic. He struggled out of coat and balling it up, he crammed it onto his lap, "Just...just hot that's all."

"Is it hot? Temperature is so relative, that I can't tell sometimes," she sat on the bed, feeling the comforter, running her hands over it gently, absently. "I hope he goes to sleep soon, or I should say, passes out soon. Drinking that much, that fast can't be good for you."

"He's young still," Jim replied curtly, trying to keep his mind off Talitha and his erection, however when he got his mind off of one, it would jump directly to the other and he went back and forth between the two, a ping-pong of perversion.

"I suppose so," her worry lines creasing her forehead, eased only slightly. "It could be the least of his problems." She kicked off her plain black shoes and laid back on the bed, the long dress riding up innocently, erotically.

"Yeah," his eyes went to her calves, which were coltish and slim, but well muscled, and appeared soft and smooth, hairless. He felt his pants were about to rip open at the sight of such a simple thing and this amazed him. He looked up the lines of her legs, past the flat of her belly and saw her looking at him in a perplexed manner.

Jim felt his face go pink and he tried to think past her body, to what she had been saying. "Yeah...the dreams, he's got to worry about those. I'm just glad it's not me. When you...the other you, told me about his seeing the future, my first thought was *lucky bastard*, but after last night...I'm happier not knowing what's to come." This topic was effectively killing his erection; he felt it diminishing by the second.

"I have to agree, *Que sera, sera*, right?"

He kept his face neutral. "Right." The other Talitha had said the same thing and he was still equally clueless as to what she meant. He felt so stupid compared to her and this drained away the last of his erection.

She had her eyes on him, studying him, it made him feel uncomfortable. "Jim, do you know what that phrase means?"

"No, not really."

"And you think you're stupid because you don't." This wasn't a question, but a statement.

Now his ears were really burning, in shame, but also with a little anger. There didn't seem to be any reason for her to be pointing out his faults, they were glaringly obvious. "Yes, among other reasons."

"Jim, you are mistaking knowledge for intelligence," she said this, sad for him. Or perhaps it was pity he saw in her eyes. Either way he felt like he was waking from a wonderful dream, and it was slipping away from him as if it never was.

"That's pretty stupid, too huh?"

"No, it's not stupid, it's a mistake, a common one made by most people. There's a difference between knowledge and intelligence, let me show you. Tell the name of a play in football, make it a good one."

If he were smart he would know what she was trying to get at, but he didn't have a clue. "Ok, a flea flicker."

She grinned happily at the words. He couldn't help himself, and got lost in that smile and he watched as her lips parted and her teeth rose and fell and her tongue, small and pink, slipped about. "That's an easy one. A flea flicker is when the ball is given to the smallest boy and he is thrown into the goal area."

She was being cute and he liked it. "No, not even close."

"So, does that make me stupid, since I don't know something I've never heard before?"

"No, but..."

"But nothing! Intelligence is not gauged by the amount of trivial knowledge one acquires." She came to the side of the bed nearest to him.

"Yeah, but it does make you look smarter."

"I suppose it does and I like that. I like to appear smart. I also like to read and study, but that's me. Not everyone likes that sort of thing, what do you like to do?"

He had to think about that. "I like to help my boys. Play with them; teach them things they won't learn in school. Show them how to be a proper man, a good person."

Her face went deeply sad and it was no longer a sad look for him, but for herself. "You like to build your soul, while I like to build my brain...in the end, who's the smarter of the two of us?" she asked.

He had never looked at his life like that and it made

him feel better about himself. However, she appeared worse, not in his eyes but in her own and her smile was gone.

To cheer her up, he gave her a big gap toothed grin. "You're still smarter, I'm sure."

She looked at the grin with a touch of weariness and then forced herself to match it. "Yep, I'm the smartest. I just wish...I wish I could have a do-over. Start my life over again." She became glum, but for only a moment. And then she perked up with great insincerity—clearly remembering their pact to be happy. "What did you want to be when you grew up?"

"Are you serious?" he asked with sudden embarrassment.

"Sure, why not? We have all night."

He chuckled, feeling absurd. "Ok, I wanted to be a soldier at first. We used to play war all the time, me, Sean Shay, Timmy Heddles."

"War? Sounds like tons of fun," she said, being playfully sarcastic.

"Hey don't knock it! It was fun, better than those goofy tea parties...please tell me you didn't throw tea parties."

She beamed, the genuine article. "For a few years, I admit that I threw daily tea parties."

"So what kind of tea set did you have? Barbie?"

"I didn't have Barbie and I didn't want a Barbie tea set, my tea set was real," she said importantly. "Wipe that smirk off your face...the boys in my neighborhood didn't find my tea parties goofy."

He exchanged his smirk with a look of frank surprise. "Really? Boys would play tea? I've never heard of such a thing; I'm being honest."

"Well, my mom would let me serve lemonade and real cookies."

Jim laughed hard at that. "Oh yeah, I would've come a running too. The girls where I grew up, made mud pies and served tap water, if you were lucky and puddle water if you weren't. And there was always..."

He trailed off when he noticed her eyes had gone to the adjoining door, he could tell she was listening to her brother. "What is it?" he asked.

Her face snapped back to his and she said, "Nothing."

"Nothing? Are we keeping secrets, now? So early in our relationship?" He meant it to come out as a joke, but it sounded flirtatious instead and she gave him a look of surprise. However, her eyebrows slowly went back down as concern pushed its way onto her face.

"Huh? Secrets? No...I mean yes." She looked pained for a moment. "It's Will. Sometimes when he's been drinking, he becomes morose. I didn't mean to be secretive. I just didn't want to embarrass him."

"Morose? You mean sad? Why would that be embarrassing?" Jim asked.

"He gets weepy sometimes when he drinks. But it's not his fault," she seemed desperate to defend her brother. "He's had it so tough...and he keeps coming back."

"Look, you don't have to defend him for me," Jim said, gently taking her small hands in his. "Last night and today, I've seen what he goes through and I gotta tell you, I would weep to. In fact, since we're being so honest, I've cried more today than all the last twenty years combined."

"It's been a tough day," she agreed. Jim blinked and

fought the urge to rub his eyes. He didn't ever want to let go of her hands, but she looked at him with a small concern. "I'm sorry you can't go to sleep, you look tired."

"Tired? Me? Heck no, I could talk to you all night."

"Really?" She seemed simultaneously hopeful and thankful, and something passed between them. For a moment, their eyes locked and Jim felt the impossible to be just within his grasp.

"Really," he said tenderly, but it was then that they both realized they were still holding hands and a coolness slipped over Talitha.

"One second." She pulled her hands from his and crept to the door to listen for her brother.

Jim's face fell and his soul sighed, a lonesome wind in a barren desert. Going to the door had been a polite excuse on her part to let go of his hands—she could hear all she wanted from the bed. And even though he felt a keen pain from within him, he wasn't angry with her. He had expected this. He was a great hideous ogre of a man and she was drop dead gorgeous. Had this been a movie, they would be together in the end, but this was real life and he knew he'd die alone.

So he put his now familiar practiced fake smile on to cover his embarrassment, "Is he doing anything else?" He had wanted the question to sound natural, as if he hadn't noticed that she was repulsed by him, but it came out overly cheery instead.

Her eyes closed for a second as if she had felt a hidden pain in his words. "No...only that he has quieted down. I think he might be asleep soon." She wandered away from the door nonchalantly and now went to the curtained window and peeked out. Their view was a parking lot and the back of another building.

She stared at it a long time.

"Good, I hope his dreams are productive." He said it, but secretly hoped they wouldn't be. If they were anything like his dreams from the day before, the night would be a horror.

There was a silence now between them and it was uncomfortable. Jim tried to think of something to talk about, but everything that came to mind either was related to the terrible events of the last day or concerned her and his growing feelings. Neither a suitable conversation at the moment. But thankfully, Talitha ended the silence.

She squared her shoulders and drawing in a deep breath, she looked him in the face, and asked, "So what else did you want to be when you grew up?"

"Huh?" The question was unexpected. He had figured by her quick preparations that he was going to get a, *I think we should just be friends* talk.

"You said earlier, that you wanted to be a soldier, at first. What did you want to be next?" she asked.

He let out a laugh that was partially relief; he hated the *let's just be friends* talk. "I...this is going to sound silly, but I wanted to be Spider Man."

She laughed loudly too. "You know that Spider Man is a fictitious character and not an occupation, right?"

"Are you trying to ruin the dreams of my six-year-old inner child?"

"Oh no, of course not." She sobered up, becoming professional, "What I meant to say, is that the position of Spider Man has been filled. However, if you fill out the spidey-application, we will notify you if an opening becomes available."

"That's better," he grinned through the words. The tension of a minute before was gone and their relationship, their one sided relationship was as it was before. She would be his friend and he would love her, and Jim was fine with that.

"Did you have Spider Man under-roos?" she asked teasingly.

"Oh man, I wish! The orphanage was way too poor and we only got cast offs and hand-me-downs."

"Used underwear? Yeesh!" she said and he laughed at the cute face she made. "So why Spider Man? Wasn't he a small guy? Wasn't his secret identity...puny Parker?"

"Peter Parker and yes he was small, but back then so was I. I had no clue that I would turn out so big." He leaned back in the chair and it creaked loudly under his mass. "I felt small next to the big boys and I wanted to be like Spidey, small but superfast and strong." His memory of those years was patchy like a puzzle missing half the pieces, but there was still enough for him to smile at his goofy six-year-old self.

She gave him an appraising eye. "Look at you now. I would make a better Spider Man."

"What? No way. You probably don't know the first thing about Spider Man." This may have been the silliest conversation of his entire adult life, but he didn't care.

"Sure I do, I knew his alter-ego didn't I? And I know he can shoot webs and climb walls." She wore a smug self-satisfied look.

"His name is Spider Man! For a genius, you're not impressing me with shooting webs and climbing walls.

How did he get his powers?" If she knew that, he would definitely be impressed.

However, she didn't know and squirreling up her face she replied, "Magic?"

"That settles it. I'm Spider Man. Oh and did you hear that? It's Spider MAN, not Spider-woman."

"This is a new era my friend, woman's lib and all that. I'm faster and stronger than you, I'm Spider Man." She no longer was smiling, but had a challenge brewing in her eyes.

"I'm stronger." Jim insisted. He loved a challenge, especially one where strength was involved. "You want to arm wrestle?" He asked half-jokingly. He knew she was strong, but there was no way she was anywhere near as strong as he was.

"Come on tough guy," she beckoned him with her hands. He shrugged and turned the desk around and put his chair on the other side, settling in across from her.

"If I win, I'm Spider Man," he said and though he tried to keep a straight face, he broke and smiled. She had to bite her cheeks and suck in her lips, but she didn't smile, except for her eyes, which beamed like that of a child's.

"Ok, but if you lose then I'm Spiderman and you're Wonder Woman. Your boobs are bigger than mine after all." She pulled the black dress tight across her chest and looked down. He looked as well. Her breasts were high and firm, and though normally lost in the shapeless black dress, they were now quite visible beneath the tight material.

He looked up quickly when she did and tried not to think about the sudden stirring in his loins and said, "I don't have boobs. I have pecs." He gave her a quick show, flexing his massive muscles and she imitated him adding a little, "Grrr!" She was being adorable and cute and silly and sweet all at once. It was wonderful.

"Show me what you got big boy." She got herself into position, but Jim had to scoot his chair far back in order to bring his hand down low enough to hold hers without lifting it up. It was a terrible position to arm wrestle from, but Jim didn't think it would matter; he'd never in his life lost at arm wrestling.

Jim looked into her brown eyes. "On the count of three, one, two, three!" They both began, not using their full strength, but ratcheted it up quickly, until their faces were red and straining. Talitha's power amazed Jim. It was like trying to push back against the half-buried root of a tree. He was forced to put every ounce of strength of his great arm into the challenge before she started to bend against him and it was another minute before he could finally pin her hand down.

Taking a deep breath, he asked, "Tell me you didn't let me win!"

Rubbing her wrist, she shook her head. "No, that was all you. I actually can't believe it; I didn't think you would win, especially with that angle you were at. I could use my whole shoulder and most of my back and all you had was part of your arm." She looked impressed and Jim felt a foolish warm glow. "You know, the other...Evil T, she isn't afraid of you at all. She's afraid of Will, but not you. She should be though."

"I didn't think she was afraid of anything."

"Well, she's not afraid really, but she knows Will plans on killing her the next time he sees her. I felt it distinctly the last time we switched places. I can hear her thoughts, her last thoughts, before we change places."

"And you don't think she's afraid of me? She thinks she can take me in a fight? That's crazy," he smirked in disbelief.

"I don't know about it being crazy," she said it slowly, smiling another challenge. "I know for a fact that she's pretty quick and you would've to catch her first, something I don't think you can do."

"I bet it'll be easier than you'd think, all I'd have to do is this." He stretched his long arm across the desk to grab her, but in a blur she kicked herself backwards. A happy smile lit up her face, as she and the chair fell straight back.

Jim leapt up alarmed that she would crack her skull on the floor of the room, but she rolled with the chair as it hit, turning a tight summersault, pausing midway through the motion to push herself into a tall handstand.

She held it for only a second, however it was enough time for Jim to see the full length of her long slender legs, as the black dress slid down them. Just as he caught sight of the gentle curve of her small round buttocks and the tantalizing whiteness of her cotton panties, she went into a back walk over, ending up facing him three feet from the desk, the smile having never left her face.

Jim stood spell bound, his mouth hanging open by the simple gymnastic maneuver, but Talitha giggled at him and then casually kicked the desk, hard, sending it sliding into Jim's thighs and he fell back into his chair.

"Ok, this is serious now," he said, hauling his weight up. He took the desk, upended it, and stuck it against the door leading to the parking lot. He shoved the chair aside as well.

Reek, reek, reek.

Talitha, like a five year old, was jumping on the bed, smiling, looking insane with glee. Jim cautiously moved toward her expecting her to jump away at any moment, but even so, he was too slow. Reaching out to snatch her, she emitted a loud girlish shriek and ducked under his arm, rolling across the floor in a tight ball, before popping up and jumping onto the low dresser.

"What are you doing? You're gonna break something," Jim said.

"Are you calling me fat?" She was still smiling and playful; Jim's heart felt huge, full of her. He jumped at her again, but again she was too quick. She became a giggling electric butterfly. Weightless, alighting upon the bed or dresser or chair, only to flit away without reason or purpose, in random directions. A half dozen times he could have caught her, but he was having too much fun.

Finally, she purposely allowed herself to be caught, practically leaping into his arms, but once there, she went spastic, wiggling and kicking, all the while keeping up an endless giggle. This forced him to drop her onto the bed where he smothered her with his bulk. He knew how his size and weight could induce temporary claustrophobia and he quickly rolled off of her. He lay beside her panting slightly, however she, despite the fact that she had ran about like mad, wasn't winded in the least.

But now the game was over.

Talitha was irresistible. Her thick brown hair splayed out around her head, shimmering, catching the light in such a way that Jim couldn't help himself and he touched it. He ran his fingers through her hair, running its length. It was amazingly soft and he was about to comment on it, when he saw her lips part.

They were full and alluring, and the temptation to kiss her was nearly uncontrollable, but now he became the fearful artist once again, afraid to make that first stroke, seeing failure past every action. But then she licked her lips.

This one small compelling movement sent a surge through him and casting aside his fears, he bent down gently and brushed his lips against hers, not engaging in a full kiss yet, just touching his lips to hers.

This was perfect.

And natural. So natural that her body reacted even if her mind still hesitated, her lips parted invitingly, hungry for affection.

And then they kissed as new lovers do. Exploring the beginnings with tentative almost fearful excitement. The kiss was glorious and alive, and Jim felt it run through his body as if her tongue traced a conduit directly to his penis, causing it to leap and throb.

The kiss blazed huge, but somewhere his artist's stroke went awry and Jim suddenly felt Talitha stiffen coldly beside him and her lips withdrew from his and she turned her head away, only just so.

Surprise kept him silent, but he had the sense to lean back away from her so she wouldn't feel trapped and to his dismay, she promptly slid from the bed and stood with her back to him.

"I'm sorry, that was..." He felt the need to call what just happened a mistake, but it felt too right. But he said it anyways, "That was a mistake, it won't happen again."

"What?" Talitha asked quietly as if she hadn't been listening. She turned and he caught sight of a single tear coming down her cheek.

"I'm sorry that I messed this up," he said.

She looked around the room, which appeared to have been struck by a hurricane and after taking a deep breath she replied, "Turn off the lights."

It was a command, spoken in a voice low and husky, and it sent Jim's heart hammering in his chest. And when the room went dark, the thudding of it seemed to magnify, but it got worse, becoming a trip hammer, when in the dim light he saw her slowly unbuttoning the black dress.

He noticed how white her teeth were in the dim room when she said, "There's no need for you to apologize. I was wrong. I was thinking of Brian, when I should have been thinking of you." She strode toward him, the long black dress now completely open and the sight was undeniable. He couldn't have torn his eyes from her even if he wanted to and the sudden throbbing of his penis became pleasantly painful as it tried to fight its way out of his jeans.

He wanted to say something, but she wouldn't let him. She pulled his face down to hers and they kissed in earnest and she was no longer tentative, but hungry. As they kissed, she undid his pants, releasing him and then stroking him. While he gently slid the black dress off her shoulders, it whispered down the length of her body, gathering in puddle at her feet.

Jim pulled away from the kiss, meaning to take his shirt off, but he paused at the sight of her wonderful tan body. He felt a moment's hesitation, knowing this couldn't be real. He was hallucinating, or in a dream, or in heaven.

She was too perfect, all of her, there wasn't a scar or a blemish to mar her smooth skin. His eyes travelled the length of her body taking every inch of her in and he knew he could stare at her forever, but she wasn't in a pausing or hesitating mood.

Quickly, she helped him out of his clothes, before leading him down to the bed. There they kissed and explored each other's bodies with their hands and he found that she was not going to need much foreplay. She was wet, deliciously so, and moaned loudly at his touch.

He moaned at her touch as well, but it was a moan of pain, she was not experienced and it quickly began to hurt. She was very strong and he had to take his hands from her body to stop her.

"Just excited," she said with a smile that spoke of ravenous sexuality. "Here, this will make it feel better." She pulled him on top of her and he slid in like he had been greased.

He was not a virgin, but no girl he'd ever had could come even close to this. She was hot wet silk and had spectacular muscles that rolled, undulating up and down him, but there was something else that drove him wild and nearly had him exploding in minutes, it was her desire.

Her need.

Nothing is more provocative to a man, than a girl who desires him, who wants him as badly as he does her and Talitha was animalistic in her passion. Her moaning became intense and the undulating muscles rippled in a frenzy and squeezed him to the point where there was no going back and now he groaned as well, deep in his throat.

"No," she said, "Don't...not yet." However, there was a momentum building in him and try as he might he couldn't hold it back. But Talitha could. She slid her hands between his legs and pinched him viciously hard on his inner thigh.

The pain was similar to, but far worse than a wasp's sting. Jim never knew that such a thing could hurt so badly and his body jerked back from it and his great building lust was gone, just like that. He was still rock hard though and Talitha began grinding herself against him, coaxing him.

For a second he was angry with her, but her eyes pleaded with him to keep going and her hands pulled at him, to enter her again, "Please," she whispered. With that one word, his anger was a distant memory in a second and when a minute passed, he was glad that she had pinched him.

She began to moan and thrash uncontrollably and her muscles, spasming and squeezing his penis reached a fevered pitch. And even with the spot where she had pinched him, throbbing painfully, he was close to coming before her, but he was somehow able to hold back.

Suddenly she stopped moaning and her body relaxed beneath him, "That was good, that was good," she smiled up at the ceiling, "You should be proud of yourself." She lay there for a second and he thrust again into her, his need still with him.

"Hold on." She wrapped her legs around him, tucking one up under his right arm. "There you go," she said and she began squeezing him as he thrust deeper and deeper into her. He was only a moment away and she could tell; she wore a predatory smile, a wicked one that were he thinking straight, would have baffled him.

"I told you I would be there for the honeymoon," she whispered into his ear and sent one last fantastic ripple up the length of his penis. He pulled his head up in time to see the smile vanish from her face and now there was only puzzlement, which turned in a flash to revulsion. Right then, even as he began exploding into her, he realized he had been with the wrong Talitha

"No! No! Stop!" she suddenly started screaming from beneath him.

His Talitha was back, but his body was practically paralyzed by the intensity of his orgasm, waves of pleasure turned his muscles to jello and as she thrashed and struggled to free herself, it only made the feeling more forceful. They were a tangle of arms and legs and sheets, but finally, he got her leg from off his shoulder, which allowed some space to come between the two of them, and Talitha took advantage of that space.

The last thing he saw was her fist flying up at his face.

Chapter 22

12 Shots and a Dream

Will fell asleep with the murmur of voices coming in from the room next door and began dreaming almost immediately. This was his way every night, drunk or not, and if he were ever to wake up in the middle of the night, he could remember every last detail of the dream. At least until he dreamed again.

He never talked about his dreams, not even with Lisa, and not because of their horrifying or vivid nature—not all of his dreams were scary, but they were all vivid. He never spoke of them because he absolutely hated to hear anyone else's dreams and couldn't imagine anyone enthralled over his. As a rule, dreams are only interesting to the person who dreamt it; to everyone else they are senseless, fragmented, meaningless, and above all dull.

His first dream was a fine example. If Will ever had to mention it, he would say, "It was about how I tried to fix my lawnmower, but I ended up cutting my hand and had to see a doctor." That dream last 56 minutes, from 10:08 to 11:04, and in it, among many other things, he sailed a boat in search of a doctor, traveled to Washington DC by plane, met the president while he was eating lunch, but in the end, never did fix his lawn mower, or his hand.

Senseless, fragmented, meaningless and above all dull.

Of course, his main purpose tonight was to dream

in the opposite fashion. His dream needed to make sense, it needed to be whole, and it needed it to have meaning. He could only hope it was dull, but he wasn't counting on it.

In fact, he was afraid it would be far from dull and he drank that night because of that fear. He had only looked into the future on purpose once and it had been horrible beyond the telling. Now he was trying to use his dreams for the same purpose, it made his insides quiver.

There was a chance that this wouldn't work, that he'd dream all night about lawn mowers and rabbits and lunch dates with the president, but once again, he wasn't counting on it. Despite almost his entire being, demanding to dream nothing but trivialities, there was a small part of him that couldn't be denied and insisted on seeing what lay ahead.

Like a single grain of sand in his lunch, or a splinter in his palm, this tiny part of him, his sense of duty, would be noticed whether he liked it or not and it would order his subconscious about.

And this occurred at 11:21.

One minute he was arranging orchids with Lisa, staring at her, seeing her belly now huge, and the next he felt an ice-cold wind sweep over him. It brought with it a familiar feel, as if he had dreamed this once before. Perplexed, thinking he was supposed to be dreaming of the future and not the past, he turned from his wife and saw the source of the cold.

He was now in an office building and in front of him was a bank of heavy steel doors, one of which stood open—he went to it, and discovered it to be an elevator. The buttons for the floors were strangely arranged with G for the ground floor at the top and the numbers counting down instead of up.

Will figured he would find what he was looking for, somewhere in the building, but didn't know for sure where, so he decided to start at the top and work his way down. He hit the lowest button, 36 and oddly, the elevator went down instead of up.

At the 18th floor, the elevator came to a halt and a man in what looked like a space suit stepped in. Will shrunk back afraid, but the man ignored him and punched 22 and four floors later, he stepped out into a dimly lit corridor and it was then that Will noticed the man's boots were huge and heavy, causing him to walk slowly in an exaggerated fashion.

Will decided to follow the man and he trailed him at a distance, agonizing over the slow pace, and long dull minutes slipped away as the man passed door after door, all of which were constructed of heavy steel. Finally, he found the door he was looking for and after pushing buttons on a numbered pad next to it, entered.

Once in, the room was a complete disappointment to Will. It held two caskets that were made of steel and glass and there was a monitor attached to each, similar to what one would find in a hospital. One of these showed what looked to be a very slow, but regular heartbeat, the other was a flat line.

"Damn!" came the muffled voice of the man as he bent over one of the caskets.

Will leaned over his shoulder peering in and saw a blonde girl of about fifteen, who looked to have frozen to death. Her lips were blue and her skin frostbit in places, was a very pale white. Will then went to the other casket, which housed a live woman of about thirty, her hair was black and her skin tan. She seemed asleep and in perfect health.

Will left.

So far the dream was meaningless as well as dull. He made his way back down the hallway checking doors as he went, they all opened under his touch, and they were all identical to the room he'd already been in, except they held live women.

Getting in the elevator, he hit 36 again and didn't plan on getting out until he reached the bottom. When he did, he wished he were wearing one of the space suits. The cold was indescribable and even though he knew he was dreaming, he was afraid of freezing to death, but there was another fear down there as well. The cold, once again, had a familiar feel and his mind kept picturing Ba'al Zubel.

Looking around he saw a long row of lockers and inside, happily, were space suits and he soon donned one feeling immediate relief from the cold. Will saw also that the lockers held oxygen tanks like a scuba diver would use and he quickly attached it to a hose at his side and slung it over his shoulder by a strap.

He was now ready, but for what? Heading away from the locker, he followed arrows on the walls until he came to an intersection where hallways met. To the right was a door that he would never walk through in his waking life.

There were danger signs of every sort written in a dozen languages: cautions not to proceed, cautions about proper gear, cautions about authorized personal and so on. He went anyways. Everything about the place so far had fairly screamed: secret military base, but he was wrong.

The door was pressurized, as was the one after that and the third. Each led to a small chamber, where the door behind would shut before the door to the front would open. Finally, he knew he would see what all the fuss was about. The last door, covered with more of the same cautions was all that stood between him and the cause of his dream and the unforgiving cold.

But he couldn't bring himself to open it.

"It's a dream, it's a dream, it's a dream," he chanted repeatedly but he still didn't move. Ba'al Zubel was on the other side. Will *knew* it and he didn't see any reason to go on. He knew the future now, Ba'al would be somewhere in a great underground building, what more did he need to know?

Obviously, his subconscious and his stupid sense of duty wanted more and the door in front of him began to open all by itself. The air in the room was sucked out first and he felt himself pulled to the door, almost as if her were falling sideways. Too late he read one of the caution signs about attaching a tether line to his harness.

He slipped out of the door, thankful for the weight of his boots; they gave him enough time for him to cling to a tether line by hand. The room was a gigantic steel cylinder, lit by hundreds of huge spotlights and there was a tremendous vacuum in the room, sucking him upwards and on instinct, he pulled himself up the tether and wrapped it around his arm. It was then that he felt the true presence of Ba'al.

The power of the demon made him go numb and he suddenly didn't care about the tether, or the dream. Millions of bees worked busily, buzzing throughout his mind and for how long he clung to the rope before his brain began working its way through the noise, he didn't know. But finally, feeling slow and stupid, he was able to comprehend what was around him.

Looking up he saw a tremendous column of black and dark grey smoke, many stories high. It whipped about furiously as if it were boiling when in fact, Will knew that it was cold. Colder than anything possible in nature. He felt the cold now, even through his suit, it pulled at him, making his joint stiff and his eyes water.

The smoking maelstrom was huge, over a hundred feet tall. And now he began to see the faces under the outer stratum of smoke. Layers upon layers of them. They cried and screamed in silent agony and Will suddenly felt like he was going to throw up in his helmet. He gagged and heaved, feeling sudden panic over the idea of drowning in his own vomit. He scrambled blindly for the door, his sense of duty forgotten, only the door wouldn't open. Further down, he saw another door and pulled himself upside down, feet dangling toward the great beast, along a steel cable. This door too was locked.

His hands on the cable were tiring and now the urgency to vomit was replaced with a fear of falling upwards and the more he worried over it the more he felt the exhaustion of his muscles. To relieve his hands, he hooked a leg over the cable and from that position, he saw how it ran about the gigantic room in a great circle and he guessed its purpose, but he had no tether to attach to it. However, nearby there was a person with a tether, and one who didn't really need it. His body dangled lifelessly from it, in a perpetual state of falling upwards.

Will heaved himself to the person and

unfortunately was able to see into the faceplate. He screamed at the sight and thrust the body away, but like a balloon, it bobbed and came back, the face still pointing at him. It was a man and his helmet was half filled with frozen vomit and blood. His eyes looked to have exploded in his face and terrible frozen fluid hardened by the cold ran from them.

Cringing at the sight, but desperate, Will kept his face away and released the tether clamp blindly. However, he did look up to watch the man being sucked up the side of Ba'al, before it disappeared in the storm of the demon's body. With shaking hands, he attached the tether and let himself dangle for a minute, resting.

This was what he was supposed to see, he was sure. However, though he saw, he didn't understand, his mind was in a state of shock and even simple things seemed difficult to comprehend. There were questions that ran around his mind. How did Ba'al get here and how did he get so big? Where was this place? Who would do this?

Floating there wasn't going to get him answers, so when he had rested enough he pulled himself upright and looked around for a way to get out. There were more doors, higher up and more bodies. The room was huge, and sporadically about it, without apparent reason or even symmetry, bodies dangled at the end of tethers.

His stomach rolled over at the memory of the last one and he knew he would avoid getting anywhere near these others. He glided along the cable, hand over hand, until he came to another cable heading up and after carefully detaching and re-attaching his tether, he went up. Going up was easy. He was naturally being sucked upwards anyways.

About fifty feet overhead, he spied a platform jutting out from the wall and he aimed for it. He kept his back to Ba'al, refusing to look in that direction, one of the warnings had read, *Remember-Face the Wall!*

Will took this one seriously, wondering if the people dangling from the walls had looked at Ba'al and he didn't want to think about what they had seen. He shivered at the thought and at the dreadful cold. After a minute, he gained the platform and saw that it was enclosed in steel and heavy glass. There was a door opening out onto the great cylinder of Ba'al's chamber and mercifully, it opened as he approached. He closed it quickly behind him and didn't look back.

The room stretched in a thirty by twenty foot rectangle and unlike the rest of the facility, which was spotless, this room resembled the one beneath the chapel. Symbols and runes scrawled in what was obviously blood decorated the room, but there was no skin or entrails dangling anywhere.

However, there were a couple of noticeable differences. Just inside the door, in front of Will, a pair of heavy chains were bolted to the floor and further back in the room near another door, two caskets similar to those that he had seen, sat empty.

He guessed their purpose now. All of the girls in the caskets he had seen were alike in a few obvious ways. One of the girls would be young, a teenager, while the other could be of any age, but with features that Will now associated with *gypsy*. Black hair, black eyes, sallow or tan complexion.

Luke was doing, what had been done to Talitha, but on a greater scale and the immensity of the operation stunned Will and frightened him to the very core of his soul. He had seen hundreds of doors in that one hallway alone and with the thirty-six subterranean floors, there could be thousands upon thousands of girls, lying forever in this modern dungeon.

Ba'al too was greater.

He knew that the great smoking thing in the steel cylinder, wasn't in fact Ba'al, but a portal into the void, but his presence in this world was far greater. And Will worried then about the size of the portal and a new fear came to him: maybe Luke was trying to open it big enough for Ba'al to come forth onto this plane of existence.

Deciding he'd seen enough, Will tried to force himself awake, but couldn't. He even jumped up and down, but to no avail. Feeling clueless at what to do, he went to one of the caskets and sat down and waited to wake up. Likely, he'd drunk too much and as he sat, he tried to figure out how much he had drunk and he vaguely remembered the bottle at one point half-empty.

He sighed heavily and felt a sudden longing to be home in bed with Lisa. Unlike her, he wasn't much into cuddling while he slept, but he would cuddle now, if he could.

For a long while, he sat daydreaming within a dream, when he heard noise from beyond the far door. He felt a thrill of panic and jumped up; looking around he saw there would be no place to hide except for the caskets, which he ruled out immediately. So he strode to the nearest wall and leaning against it, and idled there as if in thought.

People in the space suits, perhaps twenty, marched in as if on parade and they didn't seem to notice him.

The room's lights were switched on as were heaters attached to the ceiling, they bathed the room with an orange glow and Will felt the wonderful heat baking through his suit.

A woman, Will could tell by her voice, barked an order and the two smallest people came forth, one slowly.

"Ok, it's time, take off your suits." The woman commanded, she had imperial voice, which brooked no argument, and the one who had seemed quicker, stripped down; she was a girl, maybe sixteen, black hair and dark eyes. She wore what looked like a soft white jump suit and she was nervous. Her eyes flicked around the room, taking everything in but Will, who seemed invisible to them.

The other girl was Asian and young as well and she acted as if she had been drugged. Two people helped her remove her clothes and she too wore white, but she wasn't nervous, she simply stood, staring at the floor listlessly, until a moment later she was walked to one of the large symbols drawn upon the floor. There she was pushed to her knees, but still she only stared, seemingly unaware of what was going on around her.

The gypsy girl, Will considered her such, went to the symbol also, and knelt in front of the Asian.

"This is very simple. Just read the top part, like you've been taught." The imperial woman commanded, handing the gypsy a thick-yellowed piece of paper. The gypsy became more nervous, licking her lips repeatedly, but when the rest of the suited people stepped back away from her, to the wall, her fear grew and she looked like she was ready to bolt out of the room.

"Do it now or we'll find someone else who will," the woman said with a dangerous tone.

The gypsy took a deep breath. "Ok...ok, I can do this." She then read from the paper. It was a demonic language, of that Will was certain. It grated on the ears, but it went deeper than that, and sent a discordant ringing throughout his inner being. Thankfully, it was over in moments and the gypsy knelt, swallowing hard and breathing harder, as if it had been a physical trial to speak the language.

"The blood, quick!" the woman screeched.

The gypsy seemed to come alive at the voice and pulled from her white outfit a small curved dagger. Her hands were shaking and it took her a few moments to do it, but she finally cut open the palm of her left hand. She was much quicker at cutting open the Asian's hand and when she had, she grabbed the girl's hand in her own and squeezed.

The gypsy squeezed hard and the Asian clearly felt pain from it. She fell back writhing on the ground and still the gypsy squeezed, her face contorting into an evil mask, but then there was a sound from Ba'al's great cylinder room. It was like the striking of metal on metal and it vibrated through the building.

All eyes went to the windows and the black swirling mass of the portal of Ba'al seemed to be growing at an alarming rate.

"Don't just stand around, chain her, damn it!" The woman pushed at the nearest suited men and they jumped at her command.

The Asian was no longer listless, but neither was she all there mentally. She seemed terribly confused, as if she had woken from a bad dream only to find it still going on in her waking life. She struggled against the suited men, but they moved her easily forward and put her in the chains that were bolted to the floor.

The girl screamed endlessly and no one cared but Will. A part of him wanted to go to her to help her, but he was deathly afraid of Ba'al, and when the others fled the room—and that is exactly what they did, running for the door like children, Will ran too. He stayed near the back of the group and he kept looking over his shoulder at the expanding black cloud.

The door closed almost on him and against his better judgment, he turned and looked through the thick glass windows. Only one other person looked, the woman in command was just to Will's right, the rest stood huddling against the wall.

The Asian screamed on, yet now she was unheard, she struggled against the chains that bound her, only it was in vain and in moments Ba'al's form had filled the entire outer room, and that was when Will saw Ba'al, not all of him but too much of him.

The smoke swirling and eddying cleared for half a second, long enough to see that the impenetrable black at the center of the portal, wasn't impenetrable any longer.

Eight years ago, the portal had been a pinprick. Now in his dream, it was many feet across and Ba'al strained against it. Will stepped back in fear, thinking to run, thinking Ba'al would come through at any moment, but though the beast struggled against the gaping black maw, the opening was still too small.

"Damn it! Damn it! We're almost there." The woman next to him cried out. Will had a better look at her now and he could see that she was older, in her early fifties perhaps and her hair, what he could see of it, was black as were her eyes.

Gypsy.

She sighed behind the mask that hid most of her face and then nodded pleased at something. Will looked back into the room and saw that a portion of the black storm of Ba'al had slipped into the room through special vents. The Asian stopped screaming, her eyes on the death cloud as it grew in the room, and then silently it swept over her.

Seconds later, the swirling retreated and the black mass of the portal began to regain its prior size.

The woman turned to the group against the wall and said to the younger gypsy. "You did well and you are to be rewarded as I said you would." The girl nodded and then danced a crazy uncontrollable jig, as she was tasered from behind.

"You know what to do, Pablo," the woman said casually and with that, she walked off.

Will was torn between following her and finding out what they were planning next and he chose to stay with Pablo. It was a bad choice.

The men bundled up both girls and put them in the caskets; they then attached leads and began running tubes into their noses. He knew the girls would next be placed in one of the many rooms and left to rot until the end of time and he realized he should've gone with the woman.

She was the key.

Will took off after the woman, jogging as best as he was able in his heavy boots, but she was gone and soon he became lost in the maze of hallways and gave up hope of finding her.

And just then, he felt a tug.

It was a stirring of air around him and just like that, Will knew his dream was over.

Chapter 23

The Second Sight

Will came awake with a start, feeling mild alarm jangling his nerves, and sitting up, his eyes roved around the room, taking in the darker corners, looking for shapes, looking for movement. There was nothing.

He lay back with a heavy sigh. The dream hadn't been anything like what he expected and he spent a few moments replaying it in his head. Right then, he made the decision; he would see into the future to find Luke no matter what the consequences to him or to his family would be.

Except, he was afraid to.

With all of his soul, he was afraid to look. The vision of the boy and his box had been like psychic torture. It hadn't affected his body, but his brain felt branded and scarred by the vision and going through that again was the last thing he wanted to do to himself...however the idea of Ba'al in his real form, his true nature exposed for all to see, lose on earth...that would be worse.

He would look, just not by himself.

Perhaps it was hereditary, or maybe it was a sense of duty, but Will tried to be a brave man, however there was no way he could do this alone. The very thought terrified him and even if Talitha and Jim couldn't be in the vision with him, they could at least look after his body. He remembered then, how he had hit himself after the last vision and he knew he would still be hitting himself right now if Jim hadn't been there to stop him.

He got the shivers.

Feeling suddenly lonely, he kicked off the sheets, got up and pressed his ear to the adjoining door to his sister's room. He could hear water running, but no voices. A glance at his watch and the orange glow told him, 11:48pm. This was an odd time for a shower, he thought.

Still a trifle uneasy, he opened the door and the uneasiness became near panic. The place was chaos. The desk was turned upside down and thrown across the room, leaning against the door; chairs sat awkwardly kicked over, lamps laid about on their sides. The bed's sheets and blankets were tangle in a mass and Jim Anderson lay asleep naked half under them.

Will's feeling of near panic shifted gears quickly and he slipped into outrage. He had point blank *begged* Jim to stay awake and the man had lied right to his face and said he would.

"What the hell is this?" Will didn't scream it. He was holding back his fury by only the smallest of threads. It came out instead in a terrible growl.

Jim barely budged, but did emit a low groan as if he were suffering from a hangover.

Will kicked him.

He kicked him hard too. Right on the big man's thigh and this got Jim moving a little more and groaning a second time. Will thought about Talitha allowing this and his rage increased. How many times did he go out of his way for her? Countless!

He stormed to the bathroom and without knocking, he barged in. He had seen her naked so many times; it almost didn't matter to either one of them anymore.

"Talitha! What..." He stopped in mid-yell.

She sat huddled under the shower, still fully clothed, her black dress soaked and clinging. Steaming hot water poured off her, but she didn't seem to care.

Never had there been a more wretched girl.

The water from the shower couldn't hide her tears and when she looked up, he plainly saw the misery in her eyes. There was only one explanation as to what had happened and he turned to wreak vengeance on Jim.

"Will!" she called out to him, but it went unheeded. There was a red veil in front of his eyes and black storm clouds in his mind. He left the bathroom and Jim was standing there, right in front of him, naked, his face already caked in blood.

Will was big. Jim was bigger, but Will had an unmatched fury and Will's balled fist struck Jim hard square on the nose, crushing it. The punch sent Jim reeling, tripping backwards and he fell over the edge of the bed.

"Will!" a voice called from behind him.

He ignored her a second time and as Jim was struggling to his feet, Will took a page from Talitha's playbook and sent a roundhouse into Jim's ribs. There was a satisfying crunch as he felt his foot break bones.

Jim's mouth opened, to perhaps groan, yet no sounds came out at all. His eyes bulged and he fell back down fighting for breath. Will went to grab him by his hair, and that was when Talitha jumped on him. It wasn't an attack or he would very likely have seen it coming. Instead, she leaped on his back and hugged him hard, pinning his arms to his sides.

"It's not his fault! Will, you have to listen to me, it's not his fault!" Talitha spoke rapidly into his ear. He heard the words, but they came to him from out of a fog and he paused as his mind tried to understand, then oddly, he over balanced and fell sideways onto the bed.

Like a bull rider, Talitha leapt off before she was pinned beneath him. She righted herself faster than he could and as he made to get up, she chucked a pillow into his face.

"Will, stop it," she cried, then ironically threw another pillow.

"You stop it! That hurt." The first pillow had struck him full on the face and his broken nose, which he had suffered at her hands that afternoon was still extremely sensitive. He knocked the second pillow aside with ease, and as he advanced on her and she hopped toward the bathroom.

"This isn't what it seems," she pleaded in a soothing voice.

"What? I know what I saw!" Will cried, his anger cooling, only slightly.

"What happened was..." her face collapsed back into misery and she couldn't go on and for a moment the room was quiet except for Will's heavy breathing and the sound of the shower still going full force in the bathroom.

"I raped your sister, I'm sorry." Jim was on his hands and knees, bleeding into the carpet.

"Sorry!" Will's fury was back in an instant. "How can you say sorry? Was it a fucking accident?" He roared at Jim, who refused to look up or defend himself in any way. Will began to head toward him, but Talitha ran in front of him and put up her hand, stopping him.

"It was the other Talitha." His sister explained without force in her tired voice and her face became blank and staring.

It reminded him of how the Asian girl looked in his dream and he blinked then, slowly, feeling odd. "You couldn't tell the difference?" he demanded of Jim, dumbfounded and feeling a little woozy.

"How could he have?" Talitha asked. "I started it. I kissed him...I don't know, I guess I shouldn't have. But that's what brought Evil T out."

"Evil T?" At the sound of the stupid name, Will had to suppress sudden maniacal laughter welling up huge inside of him, and he realized then, that he was still drunk.

"And really I didn't know, I swear. She was very quiet, she barely talked or anything...until the end." Jim tried to explain, apparently to the floor. He still wouldn't look up.

"I know," Talitha said, figuring he was talking to her.

"I'm sorry," Jim spoke again to the floor.

"I know." With that, an uncomfortable silence laid a hold of them. No one moved a muscle, not even to look around. For the next minute, the motel room was like a piece of modern art, the kind that would be featured in a magazine, but no one in their right mind would ever own.

Finally Will declared without emotion, "I dreamed about the end of the world."

This animated the scene.

Jim crawled to his clothes and began pulling them on, while Talitha took a step toward the bed, had second thoughts and then went and sat on the floor against the wall. Will sat down heavily on the bed and told them of his dream, leaving off the part about Lisa and the flowers, as well as the frozen vomit and blood mixture he had seen in the tethered man's helmet.

He tried to recall every important facet, still Talitha wanted more information from him, asking many insightful questions, few of which he could answer. Jim only sat glumly holding a towel to his face and didn't say a word.

At first Jim's silence and haunted expression grated on Will; the man acted as if he was the one who had been raped. But it sunk in slowly that in fact, he had been raped, just not in the violent way that people generally think of when they hear the word. And what's worse, he'd been turned into rapist at the same time he had been raped himself.

Will wanted to reach out to him and comfort him in some way, but he couldn't, not with his victim sitting right in front of him.

For her part, Talitha refused to look anywhere near him, acting as if he wasn't even in the room. "So you didn't see Luke at all?" she asked. This wasn't one of her insightful questions, though it was the only one she had repeated.

"The answer is still no."

"Ok, so you try to dream into the future to find out what Luke is going to do and you see Ba'al Zubel instead...they have to be connected. One leading to the next...right?" She was unsure of herself. And Will was definitely unsure of himself and he only shrugged. "So where does that leave us?" she wondered aloud.

She knew where it led, he could see it in her eyes, only she didn't want to come out and say it. And neither did he. There was now the old familiar pain, the toothache behind his breastbone. His fear made him ache.

"I'm way too sober," he suddenly got up, heading to his room. To his dismay, he saw the bottle of Wild Turkey lying, keeled over on its side. It was like seeing a dog hit by a car.

"Oh God!" He raced over and picked it up gently, and mournfully looked at the tiny amount of amber fluid left. He let out a long slow breath and then upended the bottle into his mouth.

"Crap!" He was angry with himself for having spilled the bottle and he was angry with himself for being such a wuss. Mostly he was afraid. "I should've done this right when I woke up." This he said quietly and to no one in particular.

Talitha came in then, followed a few seconds later by the now mute Jim, who seemed resigned to be hated.

"I'm out," he held up his bottle to them, wagging it about but then he looked at it solemnly. It was like a totem to him, one that had lost its magic. Tears sprang to his eyes and he laughed with unconvincing gaiety. "Ha, ha, ha...oh jeez."

Talitha sat next to him, making his side wet with her clothes. "You don't have to do this...maybe Luke and Ba'al are unrelated."

"Right," he said sarcastically and then rubbed his face up and down vigorously, ending with hands covering his face. "I'm too afraid. It's like asking someone to jump off a building. I'm looking over the edge and I can't bring myself to do it." His leg started bouncing, jiggling a mad uncontrollable dance.

"Of course you're afraid, only a fool wouldn't be,"

Talitha commiserating with him.

Will gave her a look. "Wait, you've called me a fool like twenty times in the last week. Does that mean I should or shouldn't be afraid?"

"Exactly," she agreed.

He laughed out more tears. "Maybe I'm a stupid fool."

"What can we do to help you?" Her sincerity was so genuine, that it made his heart break a little and he remembered then, how only a short time ago he had wanted to kill her. It took his breath away and he clutched her to him hugging her fiercely all the while crying.

"Maybe you shouldn't do this," she whispered through tears of her own.

"No. I'm doing it, I'm doing it!" He punched his fist into his left hand three times, trying to pump himself up and he took a couple of huge breaths. "Don't let me go over thirty seconds! Wake me or shake me, whatever you got to do, but no more than thirty seconds, ok?" He waited until she nodded and then continued, "Here we go, on the count of three...1-2-3!" He took another big breath in and...nothing.

He couldn't bring himself to do it.

"Ok this time for real, but I'm not going to count," he laughed, embarrassed and nervous and scared. "I felt like a kid doing it that way." Talitha smiled and nodded, concern infiltrating her eyes.

Will became quiet and held his hands to his chest so they wouldn't shake so badly. He stared at the floor breathing, trying to relax and finally he closed his eyes, though it was still a few seconds before he allowed himself to look.

...She looked through the peephole, but there was a peach colored glow blocking it. However, it was moving and she guessed he was fingering the crest that the peephole sat within.

"Who is it?" Terry figured it to be Father Luke, he had just called only an hour before. Still she liked to be sure especially at this time of night.

"Father Luke," he replied pleasantly. He had been so cryptic and urgent on the phone that this pleasant voice caused her to pause for a second before opening the door, but it was a short pause and she undid the heavy bolt.

"Hi, what's going on?" she asked cheerily as was usual for her, but upon seeing him, she became concerned. "Is everything ok? You look like, you got in a fight." The priest sported a number of small bandages about his face, and there was a very large one across his neck, which she eyed with a feeling of misgiving.

"This is actually the reason I needed to see you so urgently. Can we talk inside?" She had only opened the door so much; she was a cautious girl.

"I'd rather not, it's so late."

He moved in a little closer and spoke in a conspiratorial whisper, "These cuts...this has to do with your brother, Frederick. It's not something you would want overheard."

"Rick?" Terry opened the door and took a quick peek down the hall, hers was a garden level apartment and kids sometimes hung out on the stairs, but no one was around and she let the priest in. "What's going on with Rick?" she asked once the door closed.

He punched her in the side of the head. It landed so fast that she didn't see it coming.

She didn't really feel pain, not then at least, she was too shocked and confused and numb. Her legs buckled and the next thing she knew, she was on the ground and he was on top of her, hitting her again and again in the head. How many times she hadn't a clue, but she knew she didn't pass out. However, it was a very near thing.

After a while, he stopped and peered into her face.

Her apartment swam in circles around her and she couldn't figure out what just happened. Her brain felt like mush and for a moment, she wondered if she had fallen off a ladder or a chair. She vaguely recalled being punched, but she couldn't connect it with anything, certainly not with the face leering over her. Her eyes started to focus on the face, it was full of concern or so it seemed, but he struck her again on the temple.

Terry's head spun to the side, her cheek slapping the floor and now she could barely focus on the linoleum just in front of her. Her body felt miles away and far beyond her ability to control, though she did feel rough hands yanking hard at her pajama pants, pulling them down. For a second, there was a cool breeze between her legs and then she felt his fingers in her, wiggling about.

Even then she didn't struggle or fight back; she was too weak and bewildered. The best she could do was to put her hands down there and push feebly at the fingers exploring inside her.

"Good...good everything is still where it needs to be." The words floated into her head and she heard, yet did not understand.

Father Luke, who befriended her over a year ago,

who had always treated her with such respect, had a knife in one hand and a picture in the other and helped her understand what was going on. He tapped her lightly on the face a few times until she began to focus again.

"Can you hear me, Terry?" he asked softly. She was weak and could do little, but nod her head and that was when pain started to drift in on low thumping waves within her skull.

"Listen carefully," he continued, "if you scream, I'll cut your throat. Do you understand?"

It took a few seconds for the words to be interpreted and in those few seconds, she felt the pain washing through her head growing and she realized her fear. It had been there from the first punch waiting patiently to express itself and now it took command of her body and she felt it more than she did the pain.

"Y-Y-Yes. W-What do..."

"Sshhh, no talking. Just listen," he said, still calm and deadly. "When I show you this picture, you will want to scream, but don't. I want you to remember something. This is your fault. I wanted to meet at Roger's park, but you said it was too late. So now, since you couldn't walk five minutes..." he left off angry and cryptic again. Her terror grew even more intense and her brow knit in fearful expectation of what the picture would show.

"If you do exactly what I say, nothing will happen to him. Do you believe me?" he asked. She didn't know what he was talking about, and she surely didn't believe him, but felt she had no choice but to nod and he continued softly, "Remember, no screaming." He showed her the picture. It was of a boy. He was bent

over a high backed chair, tied to it with kite string, and the string dug deep into the boy's soft flesh. It was her brother Rick.

Will split at that point.

He had been Theresa "Terry" Brabec, age 19, catholic, freshmen at Boston College, and still a virgin.

However now, Will was Fredrick "Rick" Brabec, age 11, catholic, 6th grade at Eastmore Elementary. Deceased.

Rick woke up to the sound of a glass breaking and a crash of some sort from downstairs.

It wasn't a clunk that you would hear if a chair had tipped over, but a crash. For a second he froze in bed, slightly nervous, however when no other sound came, he relaxed and discovered that he had to pee quite badly. He knew he'd never get back to sleep, trying to hold back this much pee.

So he slipped out of his bedroom, heading for the bathroom that he once shared with Terry, but now thankfully, had all to himself. Sharing the bathroom was the one thing he didn't miss about her. She had been so messy, with her ten thousand cases of lipstick and her curling irons and her blow dryers and the rest of her girly junk.

All Rick had ever needed was a bar of soap and a toothbrush, both of which he kept in pristine condition, using them as seldom as possible after the fashion of most boys.

What he missed most about her, something he wasn't prepared for when she moved out was her reassuring presence, especially at night. The house seemed much, much quieter with her gone and in the last two months he had become a little afraid of the dark. Not a lot. Just enough to make him nervous.

Therefore, it became his habit at night, to move a trifle slower, with a little more caution, to casually glance down a hall before moving down it. He made a game of it, playing of all things, secret service and that night, was no different.

"Termite, this is falcon. The hallway is clear, but we have information, the Ruskies are after the president. Be advised," he said quietly into the imagined microphone attached to his pajama top. With that, he padded down the hallway, keeping to the wall, his gun: the fingers of his right hand, held out in front of him.

The bathroom was at the top of the stairs, and as always he took a peek down them before going in.

"Termite this..." He stopped in mid broadcast. His mom was at the bottom of the stairs, kneeling, looking out of a window—the low one that afforded a very good view into Tish Hannigan's back yard. She was an eighth grader and had recently been classified as "Hot."

Rick Brabec had a paradigm of his mother, how she moved, how she talked, what she did on day to day basis, these things defined her in his world. However, her kneeling, sticking her head out of the window at ten thirty at night didn't fit into that pattern. And thus it was a moment before he realized her position was odd and that the window wasn't in fact open, but broken.

"Mom? What are you..." A shadow moved across her body and Rick jumped back.

"Hello Fredrick, I'm Father Luke." The man, a priest by his attire and introduction, had appeared from their dining room and casually stepped over his kneeling mother and started up the stairs toward him.

[371]

The priest's face was bandaged in places and his blue eyes were hard as steel.

Rick became instantly afraid, however he had been taught from a very early age that priests were to be respected. With that in mind, he didn't flee as every nerve in his body demanded, but instead forced a small smile onto his mouth.

"What's my mom doing?" he asked attempting to peek around the priest.

"Praying of course. Tell me, do you have a camera?" Father Luke had a nice voice.

"Yeah, it's in my room, right...phoooo." Father Luke hit him hard in the stomach and all the air went out of him. Even as his eyes bugged and he doubled over, the priest scooped him up and set him on his shoulder.

He was carried down the hall and thrown on to his bed.

"Where the hell is it?" the priest demanded. However, Rick wasn't in any position to answer. His face was a terrible red and his chest was hitching in a jerking motion as he desperately tried to suck in air.

"Fuck. Why does this happen to me?" He heard the priest say angrily.

Rick, lying on his bed, had balled up in pain from the punch, but now the man yanked his legs down roughly and then laying over him, pulled his arms up, stretching him out.

Terror overwhelmed Rick, the instinctual terror of suffocation and he would've screamed if he could, but his lungs were closed to him. He struggled to breathe, trying to force his lungs to pull in air, but he only managing a tiny repetitive hih, hih, hih, sound high in his chest. *The man produced a knife; it appeared out of nowhere and like a magic trick it had the amazing effect of relaxing the muscles in Rick's diaphragm.*

He forgot for the moment that he couldn't breathe; his whole focus became the knife.

It was a familiar knife, one that he'd handled many times. It was one of their three remaining steak knives, part of a set that his family had from before his earliest memory.

It was a dull knife. It had lost its edge years before and when Rick ever had to use it, it would be with a saw like motion, even on tender meat that still bled warm juices. However, it still had a fine point. It was a dull silver-grey and just then, it took up most of the vision in his left eye.

The priest had it extremely close, and Rick pushed his head back into his mattress as far as it would go, but the knife still seemed horribly near.

"This may sound odd, but I hate lying," the man said, and Rick could make out his face, beyond the point of the knife. The face didn't look angry as he had expected, but seemed blank, emotionless.

"I didn't lie, it wasn't me, it wasn't me," Rick began blubbering, crying without moving. He held perfectly still as the tears ran down his face and his chin quivered uncontrollably.

"Sshhh," the man hushed him, but it wasn't his voice that shut Rick up, the knife came closer and when he blinked, Rick felt the blade with his eyelashes. He had a new panic flash through him then. His neck was straining, pushing his head into the mattress, but it was weakening, and he feared that he wouldn't be able to hold it back much longer and that when he couldn't, he

would drive his own eye onto the dull silver-grey point.

"You said you had a camera," the man interrupted his dreadful thoughts. "Do you have film?"

Rick almost nodded, almost sending the point of the knife into his own eye, instead he whimpered high, but weak, "Y-Yes, it's in my desk...in one of the drawers."

"Good. Now, I meant what I said about lying. If there's no camera, this is going in your eye and if you scream..." he left off and Rick had no intention of screaming.

The man went to the desk. "Excellent." He seemed happy as he pulled the camera from the jumble of the second drawer. Rick felt a few seconds of relief and laid there on his bed trembling, and hopeful that this was all over.

"Say cheese," the priest pointed the camera at him, but saying cheese was beyond Rick and his only reaction was for his eyes to widen as his relief left him. The priest no longer resembled anything like a priest. His clothes were the same, but it was the eyes. They were the eyes of a dangerous creature. At eleven years old, Rick only partially understood the concept of insanity, but he was still new enough in this world not to have unlearned the concept of evil.

And those eyes were evil.

The flash of the camera blinded him for a moment and when he could see again, the man was right above him staring down, looking at him in a way that made Rick begin to pant in fear.

The man looked for a long time.

But then he smiled, shook the Polaroid a few times, and glanced at it. "No, this is all wrong." The man knelt down and showed the picture to Rick. "Can you work with me here? You barely look afraid."

"I am afraid. Please don't..."

"Shut up!" Luke yelled savagely and Rick cringed back, fresh tears adding to the ones wetting his pillow. The flash went off and he let out a half scream and suddenly the knife was back. He closed his eyes hard, but his left one was rudely peeled open and he was forced to stare up the serrated edge of the knife, the line of dull metal teeth echoing in sameness along its length.

"I told you not to scream! What's with you and your family? First your dumb ass sister won't leave her apartment and then your idiot mom wouldn't..." He gave a little laugh. "You know, your mom wouldn't give me the camera. I thought she was being so stupid, trying to protect it, as if it was sooo valuable. But she was trying to protect you. Good for her."

The knife withdrew, as did the fingers holding his eye open and Rick closed them, hard. He didn't move, except to ball up again and he felt a sudden urge to suck his thumb. His hands were tucked just under his chin and he gave into the urge.

The man moved about the room opening and closing the drawers of his dresser and desk, searching his things, and all the while Rick laid, rolled into a ball, unmoving, save for the shaking of his arms and legs. He kept his eyes shut tight, afraid to open them, afraid of what he would see when he did.

Rick tried his best to be small, to be inconsequential, to be something easily missed and forgotten, but he failed at this.

A moment later, he felt the man standing over him again and his fear became everything. It settled into his bones, deep in the marrow and dug in anchors. Despite *all of his attempts not to, he began to cry harder, though he still kept his eyes clamped shut with manic intensity. He kept picturing the knife there, poised just above his eye.*

However, the man didn't stab him. He hit him hard in the side of the head with his fist. The blow was so unexpected and delivered with such force, that all of his muscle relaxed immediately, and he went limp almost fluidly so, but he was still conscious.

His eyes came open and the bedroom spun about, literally. He was picked up, turned around, and dropped heavily onto the wood chair that had come with his desk. He hadn't felt much pain before, only shock, but now the pain was huge. With his every breath, it raced across his chest, and again he felt the panic of suffocation. He tried to push himself up, but the priest was there, kneeling in front of his face.

"I can't breathe," he said to the man in a panicky half-breath.

"If you can talk, you can breathe," the man responded, and then grabbed Rick's left wrist and tied it to the back of the chair. He was using a spool of Rick's kite string and he cinched it down very tight, it pinched the skin and the pain was sharp and nasty, and for a moment, Rick forgot about the pain in his chest.

He watched as the priest struggled to cut away the string with the dull knife and a little voice inside of him, prayed to die right there. His other hand was tied just as cruelly and then his ankles as well.

The man stood behind him for a few moments and Rick felt terribly exposed, unable in any way to defend himself or even to squirm. His tears rained down in front of him, but disappeared, swallowed up in the old shag carpet.

"No, you don't have time for this," the man said it quietly, to himself. He then moved to Rick's side and paused until Rick looked up at him. That's when he took the picture.

"Perfect," Luke said, smiling at it. But then, he smiled down at Rick and his eyes were like pools filling with wickedness, deeper and deeper. He knelt to face Rick and grabbed up a pair of his socks. They were balled up, something his mother always insisted upon, something that had been important to her, Rick had never understood it.

"I've decided that we do have time after all." This caused a fresh stir of panic in Rick, he looked up into the man's eyes and saw raw evil in them, and even at eleven years old, Rick could see his own death there.

"Open your mouth wide...wider!" He brought the knife up and Rick's mouth went open its widest, the sock was shoved in, far back, too far, and Rick lost control of himself. He couldn't breathe and he struggled horribly around the sock and this time he felt he would certainly suffocate and in desperation, he whipped his head back and forth.

But he didn't suffocate.

However, the agonies of the sadistic atrocities he'd suffer in the next few minutes, culminating with that cruelly dull steak knife, sawing at his neck, had Will wishing he had.

Chapter 24

The Search for Terry

Around the time that the brother and sister had been discussing looking into the future, Jim decided that he would burden them as little as possible with his presence. There seemed to be no reason for him to speak and barely any reason for him to even think, and he kept in the doorway that adjoined the rooms, where the possibility of escape from his tremendous shame was only a few steps away.

The darkened room where his crime had taken place beckoned him, tempting him to hide there, amidst the wreckage that a giggling girl had wrought.

However, Jim was too principled, too much of a man to hide from his sin. He had apologized and it had not been accepted. This was a good thing in his mind. He deserved to be punished; what he had unwittingly done had been too much for a simple, "I'm sorry" to fix. It didn't matter that it had been...an accident?

Could he honestly call what had happened an accident?

No, it wasn't an accident; he'd been played as a fool perfectly. The other Talitha had used his amazing stupidity and his obvious love to destroy any chance he'd ever have with the one girl that seemed so right, so perfect.

Just then Will punched his own hand three times sharply right in a row and Jim smiled. He wasn't smiling at poor Will, who was trying to get himself mentally prepared to look into the future, he was smiling at his last thought. It was a bitter smile, full of self-loathing. Who was he fooling? He never had a chance with Talitha, not in a million years.

A long sigh, heavy with emotion and weariness, slipped out of him then. It was loud, but seemed to go unnoticed as Will spoke.

"Ok, this time for real, but I'm not going to count," he laughed, embarrassed. "I felt like a kid doing it that way."

Now Will closed his eyes and seemed to relax and Jim tensed, expecting the same fireworks as had occurred earlier that afternoon, but nothing happened. At least, not right away. He simply fell back onto the mattress, as if asleep and his eyelids fluttered every few seconds. Very quickly, it seemed, the thirty seconds that Will had wished to be his limit for seeing into the future, were up. Talitha checked her watch and then his pulse.

"Should I wake him up?" she asked Jim, but her face never left her brother.

Jim poured out his soul: *Talitha, you have to believe me! I would never have done that to you, had I known. Never in a million years would I do anything to hurt you and you don't have to say anything or even forgive me, but I want you to know, I'm truly sorry.*

This is what he wanted urgently to say above anything else, but instead, he whispered, "I dunno."

She sagged at the two words and then turned toward him; still she didn't look up into his face. "Jim...we've gone through something that would normally take some time for us to come to terms with. However, I don't think we have that much time." Here she paused and finally looked at him, but now it was his turn to glance away. His shame was too great to meet her eyes.

"Jim, look at me," she commanded softly. He did and saw that her face was pinched and strained, but also hard. "For now, let's put what happened behind us and deal with my brother, ok?"

"Yeah," his voice was still a whisper.

She turned away again. "This," she indicated her brother, "isn't how it was this afternoon was it? Your description of his actions is completely different."

"Yeah...he was talking to me and...you know, seemed more aware. Then he went crazy, like I said."

"Right. That's why I am loath to wake him just yet. Perhaps he hasn't come to the portion of his vision that has relevance." She said this slowly with calm reasoning, but her anxiety was mounting and she rechecked her watch.

After another long minute of silence dragged out between them, with Will still only lying there with an occasional twitch, she said nervously, "It's been long enough. Will...hey Will!" She shouted at him. He didn't stir and she then climbed up on the bed next to him and shook him gently at first, but then with more energy as he failed to respond.

"Will, wake up!" she yelled into his face, but then turned back to Jim and there was a hysteria written across her features. "Something's different, you have to tell me what it is."

Jim saw nothing different except for the location and he didn't think that was the issue. "I don't know," he blurted out.

"That's not good enough. You have to..." she

stopped in mid-sentence as air exploded out of Will in a rush and the man's face went bright red.

"Will...Will?" Talitha's eyes shot wide in alarm. "Oh my God, he's not breathing." She gave him a quick violent shake that had his head flopping about and then peered into his face, but only for a second. She then dragged him off the bed and onto the floor and it was then that they noticed he had begun breathing again. It was light and high up in his throat, but it was still breathing.

"Will?" she asked with a little hesitating voice, there was no response. One at a time, she peeled back his eyes, holding her hand close and then pulling it away again looking for a reaction, but if she got one, Jim didn't see it.

"Fill that coffee pot with cold water," she commanded. He rushed for it and she called out, "Please think. What's different?"

This made Jim crazy with frustration and he gripped his head in both hands. "I don't know. He looked into the future, that's all I know." Leaving a wet trail, he brought the pot to her and she poured it over her brother's face, slow and deliberate.

His body reacted, coughing weakly, but he was still gone mentally and Jim forgot his own troubles for a while as he stared down at the comatose man. "Should we call an ambulance?" he asked.

"No, this is beyond them." Talitha looked up at him then and set her face into an odd smile, one that pleaded with him, and she spoke soothingly, "This may not help at all, I don't want you to feel any pressure. Did he say anything different? Did he speak in another language at all before looking?" Jim slowly shook his head at her and she went on, "Ok, how about you go down, who, what, why, where and how. Take your time, think slowly."

Slowly was his only option when it came to thinking.

He had always considered himself smarter than anyone around him ever believed he was, not that he felt he was a genius, instead at least average. But not around Talitha. When her eyes shown his way, it was as if a piano had landed on him, which is to say he felt his mind filled with hundreds of discordant notes and half notes that lingered, thrumming loudly. It made for difficult thinking.

"The who is different. Before he was looking for you, not Luke," he said and she nodded encouragingly at this. "The uh, what...what, he didn't have a what this afternoon. He was all about finding out where you were going to be."

"But now," she reasoned, and her eyes shot back to her brother. "He does have a what. He said he wanted to know what Luke was going to do."

"Luke is a monster," Jim cried in dismay. "You saw what he did to those boys." The hideous memory came back to him, making him go weak and he went to the bed and sat down, staring at nothing.

Talitha looked down at her brother appalled and suddenly cried hard, sobbing. "No, please no," she moaned repeatedly, and Jim longed to comfort her in some way, but felt he would make it worse if he were to touch her.

Another minute passed, it had now been six since Will first closed his eyes and it was then that the air shot from his body again, it was less forceful, but equally as startling and Jim jumped a little at the sound.

Talitha leaned back over him, dripping her tears across his face, "Will? Please come back, please. Don't leave me, please." Her begging shook Jim up and he had to choke back tears of his own and resist again the urge to go to her. For the next ten minutes, she knelt that way, over the still breathing form of her brother and those minutes stretched out in helpless misery as visions of the bound boys kept invading Jim's mind.

Eventually Will began to twitch and make choking sounds deep in his throat, and this ended Talitha's tears. She no longer looked upon him helplessly, and now seemed poised for action, but there was as yet nothing for her to do.

Will's choking became more pronounced with his Adam's apple working its way up and down, spasming under the skin of his neck so rapidly that it didn't seem humanly possible. His high rapid breathing changed as well, it now more resembled the ragged sputtering of an old car's engine, and it would start and stop in an erratic manner.

"Jim, the lamp on the desk, unplug it and give it to me." There was no denying her authority when she spoke like that, and he hopped from his sitting position and got it for her.

With one hand on her brother's neck, checking the pulse, she took the lamp with her other and then did the oddest thing: she took the lamp's cord in her mouth, and pulled the lamp back sharply leaving the cord dangling between her teeth. It had been quite a bit like a soldier in a war movie, biting the pin from a grenade.

Casually, she tossed aside the ruined lamp and took the end of the cord that still bore her teeth marks and bit it again. She then pulled the cord slowly from between her teeth and he saw an inch of gleaming copper at the end of the cord.

Spitting out the excess rubber coating, she ordered, "Pull the desk back, and when I tell you to, plug the cord in."

"What? Why?" Jim asked, taking his end of the cord and pulling back the desk.

"Just in case his heart stops. I'll try to jump it back to life," she said and then bent her head to his chest, listening.

"Will that work?"

"Probably not," she stated matter-of-factly, still listening to his heart. Jim was more worried about Will's breathing: the intermittent hitching had become a little bubbling gurgle. And soon, that ended as well in one tiny lonely sigh.

Talitha was obviously worried about his breathing also. "Will!" she yelled into his face and gave him another of her heavy shakes. "His pulse is weakening, get ready to plug that in." The cord had sat limply in his huge hands as he knelt at the outlet waiting.

There was a pause as she waited to see if his chest would rise on its own. When it didn't, she bent down and plugging Will's nose, tried to blow air into his lungs. However, there was something wrong and she looked instead to be blowing up a balloon. Her cheeks were puffed out and red and she sat back with a gasp.

"Huh?" She seemed for a moment perplexed and then she ran her hands along his neck. "Layrngospasm," she said to Jim and before he could ask what that was, she bent to breathe again. This time her free hand went to Will's neck and she squeezed it firmly and as she breathed, her brother's chest rose.

She paused, her hand on his neck slipping down to his carotid artery to check for a pulse and her eyes widened with a touch of excitement. "He still has a pulse; it's light, but still there. We just have to find away to get him to breathe on..." She stopped talking, Will's chest had raised a tiny amount on its own.

Talitha then began to gently massage his neck and his breathing became heavier, "Will? Hey Willy J sleepy head are you in there?" she asked with hope.

A few seconds later, his eyes fluttered open, he immediately began to choke, and stare about in a half confused panic. He then kicked back away from Talitha, hacking and coughing.

"Will, it's Talitha, the good Talitha. Jim is right here too, ok? You're going to be alright." Understanding came to him in slow degrees and he wilted back onto the carpet still holding his throat and breathing in long exaggerated breaths.

Talitha and Jim went to stand over him, looking concerned. "There you go, just try to breathe normally. We'll wait until you are ready to talk about what happened..." she began.

"No!" He had to force the word out and it was low and raspy as if he were struggling with a terrible cold. He swallowed, which looked to pain him. "We have to go now."

Talitha gave Jim a surprised look and as she helped her unsteady brother to his feet asked, "What's going on? What did you see?"

"Not yet, I'll tell you in the car. Jim, my coat please, it's right next to you." Jim went to hand over the garment and that was when the black pistol slipped from the inner pocket and clunked heavily to the floor.

There was then a moment as all three of them eyed the thing and considered the many implications that it represented. With sudden moves, they all went for it, but Talitha was smooth and quick and she had it in the palm of her hand in a flash.

Jim's breath caught in his throat and he cast a quick eye at Will and saw alarm replacing the last dregs of the fear from his vision, but Talitha seemed innocently unaware of the two men's feelings and without a pause, held out the gun to Will.

"Thanks," he said shakily and smiled at her just a little. He then took the coat and left, hurrying to the car, leaving Jim and Talitha to catch up.

As they came up to it, Jim asked, "Where are we going?"

Will paused and with a puzzled expression, gazed out through the drizzle, at the cars parked around the motel.

Talitha looked askance at Jim before blurting out, "You don't know?"

"Sshhh." Will held his hand out to her to shut her up. "She went to Boston College...and lives five minutes from Roger's park."

"Who are you talking about?" Talitha asked giving Jim another look, a wide-eyed one that told him she was worried where this was going to take them.

"She's my sis..." Will's eyes opened wide for a second and then said, "Uh, a girl that Luke has kidnapped, not just a girl, but a virgin," he added ominously and then squinting into the low rain asked. "Is it a full moon?"

Jim looked up, but Talitha didn't need to. "Yes, and

we can rule that out as a coincidence," she said quietly. "He's going to try to bring back Ba'al tonight, is an easy guess."

There was a pause and then they all scrambled hurriedly into the car, with Jim driving and Talitha in the passenger seat. Jim headed for the highway that would take him to Boston College.

"Where too?" he asked looking into the rear view mirror.

"All I know is that it's an apartment building that's five minutes from Roger's Park. Do you know where that is?" Will voice was still raspy but getting clearer.

"There are a couple of parks near the college and I'm pretty sure I know which one it is, but there are a lot of apartment buildings down there. Do you have an address or the name of the place?" Jim asked.

"No," was all he said. Talitha turned to stare at him in shock and Will protested. "It's not my fault. All I know is that it's five minutes from that park."

"By car or on foot?" Talitha asked.

"On foot...definitely on foot," he responded.

She waited for him to continue and when he didn't, irritation crept into her voice, "Please think, what else was in the vision? Was there mail lying around? A credit card statement? A post card on the fridge. Was there a view from one of the windows?"

He hesitated before answering, lingering over his vision and he paled noticeably while he did so. "My sis...damn it! Terry lives below ground, what do you call that?"

"In a basement," Jim suggested.

"He's referring to a garden level apartment," Talitha explained as if there could be no other answer.

Will became excited, "Yes exactly. And there was something on the peephole, a crest..." He went on to describe the vision in detail.

"You keep wanting to call this girl...Terry, you want to call her your *Sister*. I've heard it twice." Talitha stated. It wasn't a question, but it still seemed to demand an answer.

"When I'm in my dreams and visions, I become the person totally. So for the time I was Rick, Terry was my sister, not you."

"You have bad luck in sisters," Talitha spoke sadly.

"Not totally." He gave her a reassuring smile and when she smiled her thanks back, he added, "I still have Katie."

"Hey!" Now she smiled in fake indignation and the moment was a light one, but it didn't last and slowly all of their smiles faded into grim looks.

Jim was slightly confused about what happened and when, but was too embarrassed to say anything. Part of the reason of his confusion was that his mind kept straying to Talitha. He kept thinking about what had happened, trying to figure out at what point the other Talitha had shown up. But it was all a blur to him and it only left him with a sick guilty feeling.

"Jim? It's going to be soon," Talitha prompted him.

"Which part, the boy or wait... I'm confused," Jim finally admitted.

Talitha patted him on the arm. "Will looked into the future and saw Terry being kidnapped by Luke. Luke showed Terry a photograph of her brother, which he took earlier this evening in order to keep her quiet and that photograph triggered a second vision by Will, but this time it wasn't a vision of the future, but of the past. He saw Luke attacking Terry's brother...are you following me?"

"I think so. Will saw Luke attack Rick, take his picture, and then kill him. That happened in real life, about an hour ago. He also saw Luke attack Terry and kidnap her. That hasn't happened yet, but will in the next ten minutes or so." She nodded and Jim rubbed his head. "That's confusing."

"I agree, but our job is simple. Find the apartment, stop Luke, save the girl. Now, can't you go any faster?"

Jim shook his head. "I can't. I've had it floored this whole time." The old station wagon was dreadfully slow at top speed, but what was worse and they would find this out in a few minutes, was its acceleration rate.

"Down there, those buildings all lit up. That's the campus. I think the park is just beyond it about a mile." Jim pointed, turning off the highway. A half a mile from the park Talitha had him turn parallel to it and they began searching apartment buildings.

"Will, what about those coming up on the right?" Talitha called out as they came up on the first. A tall brick building, which seemed dark and broody, lit only sporadically on its front. "Never mind, no garden level; go Jim," she added with a little touch of anxiety.

He didn't need the encouragement, he had already floored the gas pedal, but the car was so sluggish, it barely chugged along and picked up speed slowly.

Again, it was Talitha who spotted the next apartment building, "There's another one, a block down." She seemed to see well past the range of the headlamps and even the thick misty rain didn't limit her vision noticeably.

This apartment turned out to be a bust also, as were

the next three they found, not one having a garden level. However, the one after that did and they raced from the car like television cops, Will completing the image, running with the pistol in his hand. They found the doors locked and just as Talitha made to kick it in, Will told her it was the wrong place. He had been peeking through a window and saw there were no crests like the one he had seen on the any of the doors.

Without a word, they ran back.

Jim began to feel like a fading yo-yo. With every new building, his hopes would rise within him and with every bust, they would sink back down. But after fifteen minutes, the highs didn't get to high and the lows were getting lower.

"We're too late," Will spoke dejectedly. "I know...I can feel it. He's got her now."

"There's still a chance," Talitha said. "Keep going, Jim, but circle closer."

They found the right place ten minutes later—*The Camelot*. They hurried in, but with a lack of urgency and Will kept the gun hidden. The front doors of the building were flung wide, as was Terry's apartment door.

There was nothing to see.

Terry, despite a messy bathroom back home, was overall a neat freak and the apartment was spotless, she even had floor mats on both sides of her front door. They searched anyways.

Actually, Talitha searched, while Jim kept out of her way and Will stared, tears leaking from his eyes at the refrigerator where Terry had stuck pictures. Some were of friends, but most were of her brother and mother.

After twenty minutes of meticulous searching, Talitha gave up. She gave Jim a sad look and then they both looked at Will.

He felt their eyes on his back as stood in front of the pictures. "I can't do it. I can't look into the future anymore. This time for real, I'll go crazy, insane, cuckoo for coconuts. I feel myself slipping away even now...it was worse in the car, when it got quiet. I could hear their voices, and see their faces..."

"Will!" Talitha spoke sharply to focus him. "I don't want you to look into the future, ok? I'm sorry now that I even considered it. We'll find another way. Do you believe me?"

"Yes," he whispered and a moth had stronger voice that he did. She went to him and hugged him with a soft but fierce love and he sobbed for just a second before he fought to control himself.

"There you go, Will. Dad would be so proud if he knew what a man he had for a son," she said, still with his arm around her brother. "Now this is going to sound weird coming from me, but I'm clueless. How do we find Luke?"

"You think I'm supposed to know?" he asked in disbelief, his features rising only enough to show his surprise and then they sunk back down again.

Jim had an idea, but he was nearly too embarrassed to bring it up, "We could check into the fortune tellers around here, you know, gypsies? Lisa said gypsies were behind the last possession and you had that weird dream."

"Smart thinking, Jim." Talitha gave him one of her smiles that were so precious to him.

"We'll start there, but it may be a dead end." Will

said. "He may not need a gypsy. After all, he was working some sort of incantation on his own."

"Maybe," Talitha acknowledged. "But in the dream it wasn't him, it was a lady."

"Either way, it'll be too late for Terry." Will glowered at this, showing some iron in his spine. Jim felt it too, an impotent fury, which he had a strong urge to vent.

"We'll start in the morning," Talitha said taking Will by the arm and leading him out of the apartment. "You two look like you're the walking..." she paused. "What is that?"

Talitha stopped and her eyes flew wide. Moving in a blur, she shoved Will into the hall and then spinning, she sent a back kick into Jim's stomach. The air blasted out of him and he reeled, stumbling into the apartment.

Chapter 25

Reunited

Jim had nearly forgotten the dull ache in his ribs from the blow Will had dealt him, however Talitha's spinning kick not only knocked the air from his body, but it brought that pain screaming back. It hurt so bad that he had trouble getting to his feet.

Will didn't even try to get up.

From his position on the ground, he yanked out the pistol and had it aimed straight into Talitha's butt. Jim gaped at the strangeness of her position. After kicking him, she had done the oddest thing possible in that situation; she dropped to her hands knees and bowed low to the doormat as if in prayer.

"Did either of you wipe your feet on the mat?" she asked in a voice, loud with excitement.

Jim couldn't answer, he was still struggling at finding his wind, but Will spoke and there was sudden dangerous steel in his voice, "Playtime's over Talitha. I will shoot you in this position, but it's going hurt more than I want it to. So sit up slowly and put your hands behind your head and I'll make it quick."

"What? I asked if you..." she looked back now and saw the gun. "Will, it's me, the real Talitha. I was with you when you had your vision of Rick and Terry, ok?"

"No, it's not ok. Why did you just attack us?" The gun hadn't lowered, it still aimed square into her backside.

"I'm sorry if I hurt either of you, but I was worried

you would step on the mat. I think Luke wiped his feet on it."

Jim groaned in a tortured voice, "I didn't wipe my feet, at least I don't think I did."

The gun came down. "I don't remember," Will stated flatly, but his eyes were still hard. "What does it matter?"

"The mat has the same smell as the factory, but there's also the smell of burnt wood on it, like the ash from a campfire. It's very faint. It may be possible that Luke went back to the factory before coming here."

"And he may be going back as well," Will said getting to his feet and without another word, he turned and headed to the car. Jim and Talitha followed him out into the night.

It no longer rained, but there was a mist in the air and cold settled on Jim. He pulled his coat tighter about him and noticed then, that not only was Talitha not wearing a coat, her dress hung still quite damp from when she had sat in the shower.

He stripped off the coat and put it out for her to take; she refused. "I'm fine really. You need it more than me."

"Please take it," he insisted, but when she opened her mouth to refuse again, he opened the coat up and physically put her arms through the sleeves. It felt good to touch her skin, even in the innocent manner that he just had and it felt even better when she couldn't stop smiling.

"A fool and his coat are soon parted, as the saying goes." He held the car open for her and she dipped her head in thanks and climbed in. Jim jogged around the car, pretending not to see the glare that Will gave him from the back seat.

Jim set the slow station wagon on a course to the factory and turned up the heat in the car as high as it would go, it wasn't very high.

"Take the coat back, I'm fine," she said resolutely.

Will had stopped glaring and instead was actually smiling. "She is fine, Jim. She doesn't feel cold anymore."

"Well that's not entirely true. I feel cold, I just regulate my temperature so that it doesn't bother me," she responded.

"You're keeping the coat until you get dry clothes or until you point a gun at my head." Jim growled playfully. "I've wanted to ask you since I met you, how do you do all these things? You can smell as good as a dog; you stay warm when it's raining and cold out. How?"

"I'm going to assume you meant my sense of smell is equivalent to a dog's, unless you think dogs smell particularly sweet?"

"Just answer the question. You know what I meant." He wanted to give her a glare, but he felt the little flare of happiness that always accompanied his talks with her and he could only purse his lips at her.

"The human body, yours or mine is an amazing instrument, with capabilities far greater than any person, myself included, has ever discovered. When I came back from the void, I was able to enter my body as a stranger would, and explored it, not in the limited fashion of a newborn, but as a person fully formed and mature, and as a person who had not had a body in hundreds of years.

"It was this exploration, or rather experimentation,

that showed me how I could control my body if I willed
it. Take for instance my body temperature that you
asked about. We both can raise our body temperatures,
but you can only do so, involuntarily in response to
certain external stimuli, such as the presence of
bacterial or viral infection. In other words, when you
are sick, you get a fever. I on the other hand can
regulate that part of my brain, the hypothalamus to such
an extent as to raise and lower my temperature at will.
Now of course there are limitations, I can't walk about
at the North Pole in my underwear and expect to live
for more than a couple of days."

Jim nearly missed what she said next. He was
picturing her walking around in her underwear.

"Regulation is also key to many other attributes of
mine, which you might find extraordinary. Let's take
my sense of smell, as another example. Humans have a
very insignificant number of receptor cells compared to,
say a dog, but that isn't their most limiting factor." She
paused for a moment and then asked herself, "How can
I put this...let's say you walk into a chocolate factory,
what you'll smell and only smell is chocolate. The
reason for this is that you cannot control your receptors,
which will become quickly overloaded, while I will
allow some receptors to smell the chocolate but leave
some free for other purposes.

"So you and I and a dog enter the chocolate
factory. You will only smell licorice, the dog will smell
mostly licorice, but since it doesn't really care for
licorice, it may smell body odor and a turkey sandwich
if there's one lying about. It can't control its receptors
either, or it's brain, so that unless it's highly trained, it
will now smell that sandwich above all else. Lastly, I

will smell everything, albeit without the same intensity as the dog would, but certainly with more purpose. I will keep freeing up receptors as I analyze the different smells, so in this way, Jim, you might say I smell better than a dog."

She stopped speaking for a moment and looked back at her brother and then to Jim. "Hopefully, I'm not boring you. Science is usually fun only to those who are interested in it."

"For me every subject in school was only good so long as I had a good teacher," Jim said. "You should go on, I'm learning a lot."

"Well, what else would you like to know?" she asked Jim, but Will spoke up from the back seat.

"How do you heal so fast? That's a trick I'd like to learn."

She gave Jim a look and he nodded indicating he would like to know as well. "The easy answer is that I heal the same way anyone does, but just at a faster rate. It's control again. When you scratch yourself, your body gets the signal that there is an abrasion and it sends out its little maintenance crews to fix the problem. However, your maintenance crews are busy fixing a thousand other problems you may not even be aware that you have. In addition, there are finite recourses available, such as vitamins, minerals proteins, fats etc. These are going everywhere throughout your body and may not go where you think they should.

"I heal fast merely by concentrating my bodies recourses on what I deem important and putting on hold those that I don't. For instance, because of the break in my arm and other lighter injuries, my hair and nails haven't grown at all, and my bones are about six percent behind in their reformation cycle...do you want to hear about osteoblasts?" she asked hopefully.

"Osteoblasts? Are they a kind of..." Jim started to say, but was interrupted by Will, who had a peculiar greenish tint about him.

"Excuse me? Jim? Can you pull over at that Liquormart?" Will's voice was tight with a hint of his earlier choking. Talitha looked back at him in concern.

"Have you seen something?"

"Nothing new...nothing I didn't know already...thanks Jim," he slid out of the car and hurried inside the over-bright liquor store. Talitha and Jim watched him walk up and down the aisles taking short fast steps.

"I guess we will find Luke tonight for certain," Talitha's face was tight with worry for her brother and her eyes followed him about. "Do you think it's smart to go after someone as dangerous as Luke, with Will being drunk?"

"There's no saying he'll be drunk and after his night, I don't blame him if he were. I could use a drink myself." Jim actually felt a different need, but Talitha beat him to it.

"I'm sorry I punched you in the face," she said looking at him as a little girl would, with her pointy little chin down, barely meeting his eyes. "I reacted on instinct, without thinking. And I know what happened...the thing...wasn't your fault and I'm sorry that I've been acting as if it was."

Jim felt like he had been punched a second time. He was even slightly light-headed. "You don't have anything to apologize about. Certainly not the punch. And the other thing...the r-rape." The word came out with difficulty, and in nearly a whisper. "That was my fault. I fooled myself into thinking I ever had a chance with you. I led myself down that path and all your other self did was open the door a crack and I walked right in."

She glared at him slightly. "I'm not as superficial as you would think, Jim." His brows came together with confusion and she went on, "It means, I don't judge the book by the cover, rather I judge it by its merits. I was always this way, but the void instilled it deeper into me. Sometimes the cruelest creatures would appear to be a fine handsome man or an innocent little girl in pigtails."

"Oh, so where does that leave us?" he asked. Jim's heart was filled with such astonished hope, that it felt feather light and instead of beating with its usual steady bass drum, it fluttered like a rabbit's.

She put on a confused little smile. "I don't know. I do know that I like you more than I thought that I would have, or even more than I thought I could have. And I know you like me. I can tell by the drool. You have some right there."

Talitha pointed to the side of his mouth and with embarrassment, he brought his hand to his face, but there was nothing there.

"Just kidding, *sucka*!" She giggled in her carefree way and he laughed as well, unable to restrain his happiness. There was a pause then as they looked at each other and Jim's heart still fluttered like before, but now it was a fluttering bass drum. He could feel the heaviness of his pulse washing through his ears.

They were going to kiss.

If any moment was made for kissing this was it and the fact was cemented as she slid across to him, but he hesitated.

"I'm worried."

"Are you worried that my breath will smell like a dog's?" she asked giving him her most impish of looks.

"No. I'm worried that you'll remember the rape when you kiss me," Jim said, trying to be as honest as possible.

"Then maybe my confession wasn't complete enough. Part of the reason, I held onto my anger for you, was that I was also angry with myself. Not only did I kiss you...but when you were knocked out, I could still feel you in me and my muscles still thrummed with...pleasure. I tried to hate myself for my feelings because...there was another boy."

"Brian?" Jim prompted gently.

Her smile was sad but sweet at the name. "Yes, Brian. You see I have this great guilt when it comes to him. I also have this huge knowledge deficit when it comes to love. I don't know if I'm allowed to love again, if that would be ok. And I don't know if I'm being disloyal...or hurting him or even sinning. But now, I don't have time to waste on worry. I'm not going to let anything happen to you or Will, so that means our time is short."

"You're too late. I've *vowed* not to let anything happen to you and since you can't break a vow, it looks like you're going to have plenty of time for worrying," Jim said. Her words of dying for him had the odd effect of putting him in a happier mood.

Her smile had slowly slipped away as she talked about not knowing about love, but it came back at his words and she said, "Is the vow in writing? Contractually, if it is not in writing..."

He kissed her then.

It was the only way he'd ever win an argument with her. The kiss was fantastic and frantic as well. It was like two rivers coming together. The waters were turbulent and full of energy at first, but then became smooth and calm, intertwining in such a fashion as to appear seamless.

The windows of the station wagon fogged in a ghost like fashion to start with, and soon nothing could be seen in or out and still they kissed. Jim kissed her not only with passion but meaning as well. He didn't think he would ever be able to express his feelings for her in any better way than this kiss, but he didn't try to be the world's best kisser, he only tried to show her the depth of his emotions. And though his penis was fully erect in seconds, the kiss was less about sexuality and more about love.

But as with all things, it came to an end, but unlike most things, it ended with a smile. "That was good...but we're being stupid. We may have to face Ba'al and we're acting like a couple of teenagers."

"How should we be acting? Remember our pledge to be happy?" Jim said wiping at his mouth.

She leaned him and kissed him again, a briefer kiss, as if this one was just to remind her lips of how he tasted. "I don't know." Her smile faltered slightly. "I just wish Will could be happy as well."

"Should I kiss him too?"

She punched him playfully and Jim kept his face neutral, holding back a grimace of pain, until she leaned over him to wipe away the fog from his window. The punch, like a hammer, had gone right to the bone in his upper arm and it got Jim thinking.

"Talitha, your other self can't read your mind or your thoughts right now, can she?" he asked.

"No, it's only the thoughts right at the change over," she leaned back, still looking through the window. "I believe it has to do with what's called working memory. The brain is much more active, dynamic you might say when it stores working memories, which it does on a continual basis..."

"So your answer is, no?" he interrupted.

Her eyes glared at him, but a ghost of a smile played behind her lips. "I ought to powzer you, but I saw how well you handled my last punch. You think I didn't notice, but I did." Jim raised his hands in mock surrender and she said, "Why do you want to know?"

"I'm afraid that your worse half might show up tonight and I won't be able to tell you apart. So I came up with a plan...if you think it's stupid, we can go with another one."

"Let's hear it. I'm tired of doing all the thinking around here." She couldn't conceal her impish side when she was happy.

"We have a code word...or a phrase, something simple that only we would know."

"That's a good one, it's smart. You pick the phrase, since it was your idea."

"Ok, but you may not like it," he said and she scrunched her face at him in puzzlement. He continued, "I ask you: *who am I* and I'll know if it's you when you answer: *You're Spider Man.*"

She glared at him with more bogus anger and then she launched herself into his arms and they kissed until a knock came at the window several minutes later.

"Are you two done in there? It's getting late," Will

said from just outside the car door.

They jumped apart like teenagers getting caught necking in the woods.

Chapter 26

Will Becomes William and the New Name

When Talitha said the word *Osteoblast*, a word Will had never heard before, he saw perfectly the vision of a black barreled pistol—the same one that lay heavily inside his coat pocket. It flashed a very bright lick of flame and from the angle he saw this, looking dead into the deep bore of the barrel, he knew he'd be on the receiving end of the bullet.

There were two curious aspects of the very brief image that had him puzzled. First, was the great sharp pain that exploded in his chest at the end of the vision and second, was the faint feeling of hope that seemed to hang around the edges of it.

The excruciating pain had him more worried than curious. In the movies, people tended to slump over in a quick manner after being shot in the chest and they never seemed to linger in pain, much less even groan. But, he knew he would feel great pain. It would hurt right through to his spine and it frightened him. It was this agony, even more than his upcoming death that had him heading into the liquor store where he purchased his second bottle of Wild Turkey of the night.

He had it open and drank straight from the bottle even as he paid, earning a dubious glance from the clerk. Feeling an urgent need, he looked about, but there wasn't a bathroom in sight and only a single door behind the register.

"Can I use your bathroom?" he asked the clerk, but

the man hesitated until Will dropped a ten-dollar bill on the counter.

"Right through there," the clerk was all smiles now and cocked a thumb at the door. The bathroom hadn't been cleaned, ever by the looks of it, but Will touched nothing other than his own skin and the bottle. However, even when he was done he didn't leave the foul smelling little room. He leaned against the wall and sipped at his whiskey, looking into the dirtiest possible mirror that could still cast a reflection. There was a need deep within him to rub at his chest where the bullet would strike and he indulged the need between sips, wondering how that little spark of hope could keep him going.

That hope was the other intriguing thing about the vision.

It was mostly curious because hope wasn't a normal feeling for him. The last time he could remember feeling that wonderful sensation had been on a Thursday morning, seven months previous.

Stepping out of the shower, he saw Lisa, still in a jumble of sheets blinking at him from the bed. She had yawned and stretched, never looking more like a sleepy kitten than at that moment.

She is pregnant and the baby will be girl.
He *knew* it.

"I hope she has Lisa's eyes," he had thought.

That was it. His last hope. That hope had lasted the thirty seconds he took to climb back into bed with her, whereupon he saw his daughter's blue-green eyes in a quick simple vision and fell in love for the second time in his life.

Now, he breathed a heavy sigh and the smell of

urine got past the swelling in his nasal passages making him grimace, but still he didn't leave. That feeling of hope nagged at him. There was no meaning to it. No explanation. It was just there within him, buried under a great avalanche of icy fear.

It wasn't a magnificent hope either.

It felt more like Hail Mary pass from deep within his own end zone, or a gambler's hope at pulling an inside straight with all his money on the table. But what it felt most like was some sort of a trick to keep him heading to the factory.

Without that little glimmer of hope he knew he would never go—he would just drive home in that jalopy of a station wagon and let the future take care of itself.

"You're a liar," he said to the man with the broken nose and black eyes and the swollen face staring at him from the other side of the dirty mirror. There was another reason that kept him going. Obligation, a sense of duty.

"Craapp," he groaned and went to see the clerk.

"I need to make a phone call, long distance to Maine. Ten dollars should cover it." Will said and handed over a twenty.

"I don't know..." The man was trying to bargain and Will fought a strong urge to pull the gun out, but instead glared at the man with a ferocity the clerk had seldom seen. "The phone is right here."

The clerk stood there for a moment while Will dialed, until he saw the glare hadn't left Will's face and then he moved off to give Will some privacy.

The call was painfully brief. Will wanted to linger there on the phone listening to the best part of his life tell him about her day, about when the movers were arriving in the late morning, about how the baby was kicking like mad, but after five minutes he started to feel the urgency, the demand of the future. It was like having the warden come to his cell, telling him that it was time and that the Governor hadn't called.

He forced himself to say his goodbyes and didn't start crying until he hit the cold of the night air. Squatting on the curb next to car, he let the self-pitying tears silently fall for a few minutes and he remembered the day eight years before when his own father had cried out his frustration just as he was doing.

His father would be dead soon. The thought struck him like a gong and it reverberated all through his body. It dried up his tears and he did just as his father had done after his long cry. He tucked away his fears and his sorrow in a deep part of himself and hardened his features.

Climbing to his feet, he called out softly to the fogged window of Father Alba's old station wagon, "Are you two done in there? It's getting late." He smiled at Talitha and Jim's reaction and gave them a few seconds to arrange themselves in a decent manner before getting into the car.

"Hey Bro, what's up?" Talitha asked trying to appear as if nothing had been going on. She was a laughably bad actress and Jim sitting as stiffly as if he was in the front pew at church was even worse.

"It's time to get going," Will said simply.

Her face lost a little of the pink she had high in her cheeks, but she nodded, "I think we're ready, what about you?"

"I have hope." His cryptic answer caused her eyes

to narrow and even Jim craned his head around to eye him.

The big man gave him an odd look. "Would you say you had high hopes?" Will thought he was serious and was about to give him a straight answer when Talitha giggled and began singing.

"*Will's got high hopes, he's got, high hopes...*" She broke down laughing.

"You guys are weird," he said it good-naturedly and took another swig.

The two of them, Talitha and Jim chatted lightly for part of the ride, but as the minutes ticked down, their mood became somber, as Will knew it would.

When they finally quieted, Will said, "I've got good news: if we can kill Luke it means you two will live."

"What about you?" Talitha asked.

Will lied by way of a shrug. "One way or another we're going to find Luke tonight. I want us to have two rough plans outlined depending if Ba'al has been summoned or not. In a perfect world he hasn't been and we only have to deal with Luke and a gypsy...and more than likely evil Talitha. If so Jim takes care of Talitha and I try to neutralize Luke. That scenario actually frightens me the most, since it will be three against two and Luke is crazy and Talitha is even crazier."

"I think it would be wise not to view her in that way...or me for that matter," Talitha cautioned. "We're not schizophrenic, but separate entities."

Before yesterday, if asked, Will would've said she was suffering from multiple personality disorder, but he'd never really talked to her other evil half for more than a few minutes in all of the last eight years. Now, however he'd talked to her enough to know there wasn't a shred of his sister truly in her and he could believe that she was indeed a separate person.

"I'm sorry, Sis. Calling her crazy or schizo means I'm calling you that as well, right? I won't do it anymore," Will said honestly, but immediately went back to his planning, which was coming to him on the fly. "I want Talitha ahead of us the entire time, that way she can sniff for traps and if she were to switch over, we'll have an extra second to react."

Talitha and Jim nodded in agreement at this, but Will expected a little more trouble at what he planned on saying next.

"If evil Talitha makes an appearance, she'll likely try to take another hostage." Will paused a moment to gather his thoughts. "If the she does we have to kill her even if it means killing the hostage."

Silence greeted this.

Jim shook his head, as he drove. "No, there's another way. We can chain her up and leave her in the car, or maybe get handcuffs, or..."

Talitha patted his arm. "Not at two in the morning. And if we wait, Luke will have moved the bodies. I'm afraid it's now or never and Will's plan is sensible. Talitha and Luke count on us not harming the innocent, but in order to save many more lives we have to be able to sacrifice them as well as ourselves."

There was a pause—Will began to see the flash of the gun, and the boys tied to their boxes, the visions overlapping. He gritted his teeth and shook his head. "Talitha is right. I need to know, both of you, that you'll kill me if it comes down to it."

"I will if I have to," Talitha said without hesitating. Jim however was silent and she gave him a poke. "I would if I were you, Jim. He really messed up your nose."

"It's not funny," Jim growled testily.

"And it won't be funny if Luke gets away and sacrifices a thousand girls," she retorted.

"Fine! I'll shoot your brother." Jim slowed down and took a turn into the neighborhood; they were getting close.

Will got a funny chill at the way Jim had spoken. "This is all *just in case*. Ok? If I have to die, so be it. But if I do, one of you had better get Luke." They both nodded and he went on, "Scenario two: Ba'al is summoned already. I'm hoping that Talitha, good or bad will challenge Ba'al. If that happens we'll have a tiny amount of time to kill the gypsy. We can't hesitate. Kill her and be done. This will send Ba'al back and leave us with only Luke and Talitha to deal with."

"But what about Terry?" Talitha asked. "She won't be able to make it back to her body if we don't."

Will closed his eyes feeling sick of himself. "If Ba'al is there, we won't be able to save Terry. We don't have a sword or even a knife to form a connection. Terry is going to have to make it back on her own, if she's strong enough."

Talitha looked glum at this and the corners of her mouth came down. "We can only do our best, but if you can save her, please do," she added quietly.

"There it is," Jim pointed at the building looming up out of the mist. "Wow, maybe they're someplace else."

Will leaned down to get a better view and saw that half of the factory had basically disappeared and the rest looked like a great black pile of rubble. At the sight

Will felt a foolish hope that he was mistaken about how the night would end, but the re-occurring vision of the gun told him otherwise.

"He's in there. Don't get your hopes up. Drive past it about a block, I want to be able to sneak up on them if at all possible."

Jim did this and as they were getting out of the car, Will had a stupid idea, one that he wished he had thought of before. "Tal, check the glove box."

It was right there.

Perhaps the one thing that might have saved Father John: a flash light. Will looked at it guiltily, but it gave him another idea. "Look for a bible or some crosses." They searched, but they found nothing and only Will wore a cross, the heavy pewter one that Father Alba gave him.

The vain search seemed to have taken the steam out of all of them. Jim looked like he was sweating despite the cold, while Talitha's face was pinched so tight with worry that she was almost unrecognizable as his beautiful sister and Will didn't dare check his own reflection in one of the mirrors, afraid of what he would see.

"Let's say a quick prayer, ok?" he asked. The others nodded and waited for him to begin and he went with the Our Father. The one Jesus had taught.

The prayer was over in less than a minute and his mood of fear hadn't been improved by it. Will sighed heavily. "Let's go, Talitha first."

Jim and Talitha paused and after a sheepish look at Will, they kissed. It wasn't a romantic one, but under the circumstances, it couldn't have been. It did look tender though and Will felt a moment of jealousy.

Pulling the black gun from his pocket, he waited for them to finish, letting his fear chew away his insides. He didn't have long to wait and when it was over, it sadly reminded Will of a kiss goodbye.

"Who am I," Jim asked when their lips separated. A question Will found very odd.

"Spider Man." Talitha answered brightly and then with a shy look to her brother, said, "We can go now."

Will shook his head in wonder, as Talitha walked forward, ducking under some yellow crime tape. She led them to what was left of the front of the building. It now appeared as a great, blackened skeleton; walls without rooms formed its ribs and the entrance, still with some shape, its head.

Talitha walked slowly, her steps lighter than a cat's and she barely disturbed the ash-covered parking lot. Near the entrance, she paused and studied the ground.

"Luke's been here recently; see how this impression has held its shape. And this one as well." She pointed at the soot-covered asphalt and with the night as dark as it was, Will didn't see a thing until Jim shown the light on it. She then bent low and sniffed over the prints. "I smell Luke and Terry, but there's another woman with them. I guess he has a brought a gypsy along."

"Then it's official. From here on, no talking unless we need to," Will said.

Jim now shown the light on the entrance and they could see that the doors had been pulled off and the foyer was a scorched and smoldering mess. It looked like one of the thousands of dungeons in the void and this was mainly because the walls were black and peeling like the skin of a burn victim. Many demons skin their prey and leave the rotting flesh hanging, where it will eventually turn black.

Seeing this gave both Will and his sister a pause; she turned back to him, even in the dark, her eyes were wide. Will gave her a quick nod to go on, but her hesitation drew so far out that Jim finally stepped forward to give her a nudge.

She moved then, but slowly and carefully as before and now Will could hear the faint sound of her near continual sniffing. He gave the place a tentative sniff himself, but it smelled just like a fire pit from a campsite.

The trail she followed was quite obvious to Will, but only when Jim chose to shine the light towards the floor, which was infrequent. Jim was nervous and this was plain to see by the way the flashlight swung in every direction, especially if there was any noise. Of course, with the bones of the place still smoking in spots there was plenty of settling and shifting, and the light seemed more like a spotlight searching for an escaped convict than a device to help them find their way.

Talitha was just a head of Will and as they came to the stairwell door, she stopped and sniffed at the corners and edges of it with a great deal of concentration. Perhaps thirty or forty seconds went by before she opened it as quietly as she could. However, once it was open, she stopped in the doorway and despite two little shoves from Will, she wouldn't go forward.

"What's..." Will started to whisper the question, but then he knew what was wrong. He could now feel the bone-chilling cold seeping up from the deep blackness in front of him.

Ba'al was near.

The thought sent an electric surge of fright through him and he turned without a word and snatched the flashlight from Jim and shown it down the stairwell. Again, just as in the entrance, the walls were black and not smooth as they had been, but were torn and gouged in spots, but also rippled from the heat in others. Thankfully, there was no sign of the smoking body of the demon, however the cold slowly intensified the longer they stood there.

He remembered the advice from his father, not to stop or there was a chance they wouldn't be able to get going again and so he gave Talitha a bigger push. She resisted at first, backing into his hand, but then she started edging forward.

Even though Will kept a hold of the flashlight and used it to peer as far down into the darkness as possible, she still went with exacting slowness, part of which was due to the slippery conditions. Water trickled in from every direction and mixed underfoot with the ash and Will found himself slip on more than one occasion.

He walked with a hand on her shoulder, not just to keep from falling, but also for reassurance, both for his own sake and for hers. The control she had over her body was not complete; under the large coat of Jim's, her muscles were vibrating wildly in fear and her breath was quick and light.

Will wasn't immune to this mounting fear either and his own heart rate had escalated to an amazing degree, however he felt an odd relief that he was to die with a bullet in the chest. It was a comforting thought just then to know that his death would at least be natural. Remembering the death of Adrina the gypsy sent a spasm through him and he paused to cling to the rail for a second. When Ba'al killed, the deaths were the most ghastly things—beyond imagination.

After a moment, he was able to walk again and they had almost made it to the first sub floor when Will, shining the light over Talitha's shoulder, saw the great figure of the demon on the landing at the bottom of the stairs. The brother and sister froze in place at the same instant. Will's first action was not a smart one—he raised the gun to shoot the creature.

His hand came up in a slow motion blur and even as he sighted down the length of the barrel, he saw that it was in fact not Ba'al, but a huge pile of the old furniture burned and melted into a strange exotic shape. The effect was uncanny and had fooled them both. He was just relaxing, bringing the gun down when Jim, who hadn't seen them stop due to the fact that he couldn't help looking back over his shoulder, barreled into him.

Will in turn stumbled into Talitha and his body reacted instantly, putting out his left hand to stop his fall. The flash light struck the rail and was knocked from his grasp and bounced away.

For the second time that day he was plunged into absolute darkness. Everyone froze in place and Will, who was caught between Talitha and Jim, could feel both of their heartbeats against his skin. Talitha's seemed fast, but less so than his own, while Jim's was downright alarming. It was almost as if Will could hear it beating through the man's thick chest.

For the span of only a few seconds they stood that way, gripped in the natural fear of the dark as well as the unnatural fear of the proximity of a demon. "Get the flashlight," Will said to his sister, giving her the smallest shove forward so as not to unbalance her.

"I don't know where it is." Her reply confused him. How could she not know where it was?

"Why are you being like this?" he asked snappishly. "Ba'al could come up here and we won't know it."

At the mention of the demon's name, she pushed even further back into him and again Will was sandwiched. "You get it, Will." Her voice shook, tremulously.

"Calm down, ok," he used the most soothing voice he could manage, that is to say he snapped at her, but tried not to. "I can't see it or I would."

"I can't see it either," she hissed at him.

"Of course you can," he hissed back. They had stayed in one place far too long for his liking and what he had said a moment before about Ba'al coming, began playing on his imagination. He started to see eyes sprouting in the darkness. They would form themselves and dissipate with unsettling randomness. The odd false glows came from all sides and he even put out his hand to touch one, but struck the wall instead, and was so startled by the nearness of it that he jumped a little.

"I can't," she insisted "I need at least some light to see, but this is complete darkness."

"Just feel along, it bounced down to the landing," he said.

"Please, you go get it," she turned, trying to switch positions with Will. It felt odd the way she did this, the stairs were not particularly narrow, but she acted like there was no room at all.

Will wanted to argue with her, however her voice had an edgy quality that was shrill and so unlike her that he feared she was close to true panic. What's more, Will had done this before. When she squeezed behind him, he bent down to feel the first step below him. It was clear of obstacles and he stepped down onto it. He then gently waved his arms all about the air in front of him, still nothing, so he repeated the process of bending down again, but froze as Jim spoke.

"Talitha, who am I." His voice was so startlingly deep and loud, and came out of the darkness seemingly from high above them. It made Will, for just a second, think that it was the voice of God.

When she didn't respond Will felt the hairs on his neck stand up. He had been tricked again by the evil Talitha and he felt sure he would feel a blow coming from out of the darkness, but none came and there was only silence for another second.

"Talitha!" Jim's voice was sharp, bordering on anger and again God like.

"I'm sorry, you're...you're Spider Man."

"Ok good, good," Jim said soothingly and Will could hear them hugging, and suddenly, he was jealous again. It added to the stew of his other emotions and the net result was that the slow simmering anger over his terrible situation began to come to a boil.

It made him apathetic about dying by some diabolical trap and standing back up, he walked down the stairs holding the rail in one hand and feeling the wall with the other. At the landing, he waved his hands in the air until he found the great twisted pile of furniture and then he bent and scrambled around in the muck, finding the flashlight relatively quickly.

He hesitated only a second before trying to turn the thing on. He had pictured flicking it on, only to find Ba'al looming over him, but he shook that off as silly, there was no way the demon could be so close without his knowing. Nonetheless, when he turned the switch on, he took a quick glance around, but there was nothing. He did however get to see both Talitha and Jim age twenty years in a second, just not in the way one would normally think.

When the light came on, he could have sworn he was looking into the faces of a couple of frightened six year olds. They hadn't budged, but were gripping each other tightly. The light dispelled their fears, at least their fears of the dark and they hurried down the stairs like moths to a flame.

Will wanted to be angry still. He didn't like how they continued crowding him, despite the light and how Talitha now refused to go first, or even the fact that they were all covered in black ash, as if they had rolled in it. But his anger had departed and so had most of his fear, and it was with an odd sort of elation that he realized he was now truly his father's son.

A few seconds earlier, while he had huddled between Jim and Talitha in the dark his fear had been very great, but a little thing like his anger had managed to push it aside, or so he thought at the time. Now he realized that one emotion couldn't push another one about, unless he allowed it. It was such a simple thing, but one that could never be taught, only experienced.

Right then he knew his fear was his to control, and what's more, he knew he could go on and face Ba'al and then face his own death. He squared his shoulders and made the conscious decision to die just as his father had lived.

Of course conquering fear didn't mean he would be less cautious.

He shined the light down the next flight of stairs a long time, checking every corner and tumbled piece of furniture before he started. The feeling that he was descending a stairwell in one of the void's many dungeons grew with each slow step down. And it wasn't the way the paint peeled off the walls, or how the debris began to look more like hunks of charred flesh than anything else, it was how the darkness began to overcome the light of the flashlight, squeezing the energy from it, making it seem feeble and dim.

But more than that, there was the cold.

It was the dreadfully familiar cold of Ba'al, which could be mistaken for nothing else. Each step down marked a greater temperature drop and it wouldn't have surprised Will to see the end of the stairwell encased in black ice. However it wasn't. That final set of stairs, were slippery with quickly freezing ice sludge, but at the bottom, there was a pool of black water, which it hadn't yet frozen over.

The water couldn't have been more than a few inches deep, but it gave the impression that it could be of any depth and Will hesitated before stepping down confidently even as his father would have. He turned out to be right, the water being barely two inches deep, but it was shockingly cold and it gave him a jump.

"You ok?" Talitha asked from a few stairs above him. She and Jim held hands, like a couple of lovers in a coalmine or so they appeared as covered in filth as they were.

"I'm good, the water is just cold is all," he

responded and then waved her down. "Check if you can smell out any of those traps of Luke's."

Talitha came down and made a great show of sniffing at the edges of the door, even squatting down in the puddle to sniff lower down. Just as she did Jim slipped. The big man came down hard on his butt and Will swung the flashlight back to him.

"What is it?" Talitha cried softly in alarm.

"I just slipped, it's nothing." Jim whispered to her as he tried to get to his feet. However, his foot slipped out from beneath him again. "Damn," he grunted still quietly.

"Huh?" Talitha said from the blackness below. He shown the light at her, but it blinded her and she held up her hand blinking into it.

"It's nothing Tal. Did you smell anything?"

"Naw, I'm having a little trouble. The cold is freezing the mucus in my nose," she turned back to the door. "Also I can't catch the scent of another gun, because of that." She pointed to the pistol. "It's overpowering. Put it away or..." she struggled out of Jim's heavy coat, "Better yet, wrap it in this for a moment."

She held out the coat for Will to take, but Will's hands were full; the flashlight in one and the gun in the other, so she laid the coat out for Will to put the gun into.

He paused, not just because the girl in front of him wasn't his Talitha, but also because he didn't know what to do about it.

At some point in the last minute or so, they had switched, the good Talitha for the bad. He knew this not as part of a vision, he just knew it as her brother. It was how she had said, "Naw." It wasn't her style. She disliked using language in such a casual manner.

But now that he knew, he had to very quickly come to a decision. His choices were limited, in fact it seemed like he had only one choice and that was to force her at gunpoint into the presence of Ba'al, and then...he didn't know what. He hoped they would fight it out, but he came to the sudden realization that they wouldn't.

It was only a guess, but Will figured that Ba'al would orientate on him as his primary opponent strictly due to the gun and if he did, Will wouldn't last two seconds. However, if she held the gun...

"Here you go," Will said, placing the gun in the coat. She didn't play around and simply took the gun in her small hand and casually tossed the coat aside. Will felt a ball of ice form in his belly, but ignored it.

"Thanks for this." She smiled sweetly.

Jim watched this for a moment with his mouth open, but finally figured it out. "Who am I?" he asked in a hoarse whisper.

"Is this a trick question?" She looked like a cat eyeing a mouse, while chewing on the neck of a bird. For her it was a happy look.

"Jim, don't bother, this isn't our Talitha. This is Ba'al Fie-ere; she doesn't deserve the name Talitha." Will explained calmly, eyeing the girl.

"You bet I don't," she said bringing the gun up for a quick sniff. "It means 'Little Maid' and those kind fellows at the hospital took care of my maidenhood a long time ago. And speaking of maidenhood, Jimbo what happened to your face? Was Talitha not happy with our little surprise?"

"Go fuck yourself," Jim growled with a hard edge to his voice.

She brought the gun up, pointing it at him, something that was actually not at all noticeable in the dark, with only a very flimsy light shining across her. "Go fuck myself...very original. Your wit is certainly not as developed as your dick. This would be a compliment if you knew what to do with it."

"Ba'al, why don't you leave him alone," Will stepped closer to her. She brought the gun to his chest and started to slowly pull back the hammer—he ignored it.

"Because, I don't want to." She shoved him back with the barrel of the gun. "Do you even know what this guy did to your poor little sister? He raped her, Will. Rape is clearly defined as any act of sexual intercourse that is forced upon a person."

"Actually it was you who did the raping." Will's anger was an emotion that he was having difficulty controlling, so he forced himself to breathe as slowly as he could and it went from boiling to a low simmer.

She suddenly smiled wistfully. "Yeah you're right, it was genius. And Jim, you played your part, the part of the fool, so well. It gives me the tingles just thinking about it." She sighed dreamily.

"When you're done with your tingles, we have a problem." Will said in a high voice, one he hoped would be mistaken for fear. "I'm sure you're aware that Ba'al Zubel is near. We should get out of here quick." Jim's eyes flicked to Will, uncertainly, but Will made sure to ignore him completely.

"Yeah, let's run!" Talitha mocked him. "Will, your plan is transparent. You willingly gave me the gun. You want me to go out there and kill Luke and send Ba'al back to the void, why don't you just say so."

Will deflated so much so that he sat down on the slimy steps. "You're right," he said in a depressed voice.

"What are you going to do?" Jim asked the girl.

"I'm going to go talk with them. Isn't that what you wanted me to do when you thought that putz, Luke was really Ba'al?"

"Then I guess we can wait here for you?" he said knowing there was no way she'd allow that. It was so ludicrous that she even smiled.

"No, dear brother. You and Jim are going to be my bargaining chips. You see, I know for a fact that Ba'al hates you with such an amazing passion that he may be willing to give up anything to have you. Even some of those incantations or maybe something more." Her smile was terribly diabolical in that light and Will's new found victory over fear felt at that point to be a hollow triumph.

"I'm not going," Jim glared down at her defiantly, but Will shook his head.

"She'll just shoot you and make me drag you along and I'm too tired for that. And besides, this is what we came to do."

She giggled and the sound was creepy; a snake giggling would sound more human than she did. "You two came here to die?" she asked.

Hearing her say that reminded him of his vision, the *knowing* that two of them would die, and now the ball of ice was growing, numbing his hands and feet. "I guess so." Will said without much hope and stood to face her again.

Talitha reached back and not taking her eyes from

Will opened the door. It was a door onto a frozen hell.

The air all around them whipped up and shot through the opening of the door making a high keen sound as it raced into the burned out remains of the building. Replacing the air was a cold that made the staircase feel like a June morning and Will who had just stood up felt the strength ebb from his shaking legs.

He meant to take a deep breath and follow Talitha out, but the cold stung his lungs so badly that he ended up coughing weakly and heard Jim doing the same thing. His coughing was uncontrollable and for at least a minute he hacked, but finally Talitha yanked him into the destroyed atrium.

The feeling of descending into the void while on the stairs had been nothing compared to this. No human could have wrought the crazed and malignant shapes that the consuming fire had created in its desire to destroy. The building he had been in earlier was now twisted into a perversion and blackened by greedy flames; it was slick with ice and silent as the far side of the moon.

Standing there, Will's coughs dried up, and now he barely had the strength to even breathe. But it wasn't the cold and the horrific landscape that sapped him, it was Ba'al. Will felt that horrible buzzing in his head that he had known before and his eyes went in different directions for a few seconds before he was able to control himself.

Jim took longer to begin thinking clearly; maybe two minutes more and during that time he could only moan softly as if in great pain. As he waited for his friend, Will stole glances at his sister, wondering how he could get the real Talitha back in time to deal with

Ba'al.

In truth, he didn't have any faith in his sister to actually win a confrontation with the demon. Will himself had tried and in a matter of seconds had been crushed to the size of an ant. He started to get the shivers at the thought, but he remembered his father and he gritted his teeth against the onslaught he knew would be coming

At length, Jim stopped moaning and gave a sniff and Will turned to see that he was actually crying slightly. He turned away and Talitha rolled her eyes at him.

"Jeez, the two of you. It's just a demon." But even though Jim seemed able to go on, Talitha still hesitated wearing a hard look on her face. She turned to her brother. "Have you felt the eye of the demon on you yet?"

"What do you mean?" He tried to sound innocent, but her glare was so fierce he answered, "No. I think you would've noticed." He knew what she was referring too. The last time, eight years ago, Ba'al could almost drive a person insane with a just glance.

"Neither have I, but you know it's coming. In fact..." She cocked the pistol and put it to his head. "Don't worry, this is only insurance."

It unnerved Will terribly to have the gun pointed at his head, since the demon could look upon Talitha even through walls. "Don't do that or your plans will go out the window as soon as he looks on you," he counseled.

"Don't be such a wimp. I'm not like you and besides, I have faced him before you know."

"Did you win?" Will knew the answer to that; there was no way she had.

"Hell no, but I held my own, at least for a while."

She didn't realize it, but she had just opened his eyes to that one little bit of hope that had skated around the edges of the vision. He felt it then, it was a tiny thing within him, just the whisker on a mouse. Talitha really could stand against Ba'al and longer than the two seconds he had—perhaps long enough for him to kill the gypsy.

Her eyes were upon him and they were lit with a strange light and Will realized the hope must have shown on his face. He stared back and her eyes narrowed and suddenly he knew what she was feeling; she was the slightest bit nervous. He almost smiled, but cast his eyes quickly down instead.

"See the prints, follow them." Her tone was cold.

But not nearly as cold as the carcass of the building they were walking through. The atrium and parts of the walls had fallen at some point and the five poor dead children were now buried beneath it all. With the opening above his head larger, there was enough ambient light for Will to follow the tracks without the use of the flashlight. The tracks ran on, weaving around great piles of blackened rubble, and bent piping. The basement was completely unrecognizable, but through it, unerring the tracks lay, and finally, Will saw what could only be the red orange glow of a fire. It came from a room whose walls were still mostly intact and the light flickered from its open door.

Through the wall, Ba'al looked upon Will then.

A great rushing sound filled his ears; black vile torturous thoughts raced around in his mind; pain drilled into his every pore. His vision went grey growing quickly darker and darker...

"Enough!" Talitha roared. "He is mine! I have come to barter with his soul, but if you try to take him, I will kill him here and now and you will get nothing."

Ba'al was gone then and the first thing Will saw was the dark bore of the pistol. It was a foot from his face and seemed huge as if it would shoot a cannon ball rather than a bullet. Looking past it, he saw the dark clouds of the night and this made him realize that he was actually flat on his back.

"Get up," she demanded harshly and when he only blinked stupidly at her, she kicked him hard in the arm. Jim came over and struggled to pull Will up, slipping frequently with the icy conditions. Will felt sorry for Jim then. His face was as pale as death and his hands were so cold that Will worried Jim would lose his fingers to frostbite.

It was then that they heard the voice of Luke. It was a truly repulsive sound, in that it had the effect of making Will want to crawl away and hide.

"THese are THE worDS of Bay ALLLL Zoo BuLLL."

It was similar to human speech in much the same manner as a cat walking along the keys of a piano is similar to music. The demon was speaking through Luke and was having difficulty controlling the simultaneous aspects of breathing and speech. The result was ghastly and made Will clutch at his throat.

"Bring to Ba'al Zubel Will Jern," the voice cried in the same terrible manner. It took a moment to translate, but when he did, Will could feel his hands begin to tremble. However when he tried to force them to stop, he found his new mental toughness went only so far.

Talitha's face was a study in concentration. "Yes,

Lord Ba'al Zubel," she called out. In a lower voice she said, "Will, go the doorway, but do not enter. Jim, stand just to his left and pray your ass off that I don't need to use you as part of my negotiations."

"What are you..." Jim began, but Talitha pistol-whipped him across the face. Blood sprayed from a long gash that opened up high across his cheekbone. The big man staggered and Will caught him, barely holding up under the man's colossal weight.

"I hear another word out of you or if you try to interfere in anyway, I'll give you to Ba'al as well. I'll even gift-wrap you, by turning your skin inside out. See if I don't," she snarled this into Jim's face.

Jim was dazed, but defiant and glared at her as best he could. She ignored it and only snapped her fingers, pointing toward the doorway. Will and Jim, still hanging on to each other for support, sliding as they walked, made their way to the entrance and stood blinking as if they were blinded by the demon's presence.

They weren't of course. Ba'al wasn't bright in any way. It was dark and hideous, and in fact dampened the light from a small fire that burned in silence a few feet away. To Will, Ba'al was unchanged. It was a tremendous column of swirling black and grey smoke, with hints of something more solid, yet more sinister beneath.

They blinked strictly because of the affect that Ba'al had on their minds. The buzzing that they had felt before was now a great rushing noise and it was a few seconds before they could think clearly.

"You are wise to bring this offering to Ba'al Zubel." Luke said, still wheezing in and out, as he spoke. Luke stood just in front of the demon, if stand was indeed the correct word. Even though his feet were planted on the ground, he seemed to hang nonetheless like a puppet on a string. He appeared unconscious despite the fact that his glassy eyes were open and staring off. Will, revolted by the sight, flicked his gaze over him, and took in the fire.

Even fire was unnatural so near to the demon. Its flames bent over, leaning strangely toward the creature and its smoke seemed to rush happily to join in the storm. It was a cold fire as well and did nothing to warm the room, but perhaps the oddest thing concerning the fire was that it was dead silent. There wasn't a single crackle, fizzle, or snap, nor was there the wush sound of the flames dancing about. It was as if Will was seeing a silent movie of a fire.

It was disconcerting, but mesmerizing as well and his eyes hung on the bent flames a moment longer than he had meant them to, but finally he tore them away to see something more real. The girl, Terry Brabec, still in the clothes she had been kidnapped in, lay as if dead on the ice, Will felt a hitch in his throat at the sight. At that moment, he knew a touch of brotherly love toward her and with it came a natural need to protect.

It was a wonderfully human feeling and lit a fire under his anger which flared within him. There was another girl in the room, a woman actually, black haired and black eyed, kneeling over Terry.

Her demeanor was of a person listening intently, she had her head cocked to one side and in her left hand, she held a knife, the blade of which curved wickedly. Her other hand was empty and she held it just above Terry's face and from a small cut on her wrist, blood dripped into the girl's mouth.

Will felt an instant of fury and without thinking, he started forward, but Talitha held him back. He went to glare at her, however saw the pistol just to the side of his face, it was no longer pointing at his head, but at Terry and there wasn't a single quiver along its short black length.

Talitha held it steady as a rock.

"Will Jern is not an offering!" she called out in a loud voice, or so he assumed it was. It came to him in the muffled way that he had expected. The void truly was just that. It was a great emptiness, similar to that of space, except there were no stars there, no possibilities for new worlds or new life. It was just a greedy sucking blackness that echoed with fear and it pulled everything to it, including sound.

"Then why do you parade him about in front of Ba'al Zubel?" Up and down went the words, loud and then soft, but not muffled, Ba'al had control of the opening to the void.

"I will trade Will Jern for my name!" she called out.

"Ba'al Zubel cannot give you a name, fool! You have to earn it."

"I already have! However, Ba'al Zubel can witness me earn it again when I kill your virgin." The hammer went back on the gun and Will's hopes skyrocketed, but Ba'al Zubel made a strange noise that caught his attention.

"Bruagh, bruagh, bruagh," the puppet, Luke spat out and Will realized the noise was something like laughter. "Ba'al Zubel can kill you in a half a second and then you will be with Ba'al Zubel in wrath."

Talitha called out, "And I can kill your virgin in a quarter of a second, and Ba'al Zubel will no longer have his path to this world! And Will Jern will kill your witch and this thing." Talitha nodded toward Luke.

During this conversation, Will's anger slipped away from him, leaving him with only an anxious confusion. He was being bartered, but for what he didn't know. "What's going on," he asked his sister.

"If Ba'al is smart, he will say my name, if not," she shrugged as if to say it was no big deal, but Will knew better. She was the gambler now and her soul was in the pot, along with his.

Ba'al seemed to be taking a lot of time to come to a decision and Will asked, "What's the deal with the names?"

"In the void, having a name symbolizes power. You see, only demons have them." She was right behind him whispering in his ear and her breath was the only warm thing about her. "In order to become a demon you have to force another demon to say your name. It's quite simple and nearly impossible, especially..."

"Ba'al Zubel has conditions," Luke announced in his see-saw voice, interrupting her. "Ba'al Zubel will name you, but with a name of his own choosing. Second, my servant tells me that you are afflicted by the presence of a creature residing in that body. In order to ensure that Ba'al Zubel is in fact naming the right being, you will kill Will Jern now."

Talitha didn't hesitate a second and brazenly retorted, "I have already chosen my name, Ba'al Fie-ere, denier of Ba'al." She paused as if for reaction, but none came, the hideous black smoke only circled and flared in its usual manner. She went on, "And I will kill Will Jern, but only after I am named." His sister seemed to pause oddly and Will could no longer feel her breath on his ear.

"You must hand over your other servant as well," Ba'al Zubel spoke through Luke.

"I will."

"Then Ba'al Zubel names you the demon Ba'al Fie-ere, Denier of Ba'al," Ba'al said through his meat puppet. "Kill Will Jern and depart."

When Will heard the words, his skin flashed hot for a small fraction of a second and then went numb. His body seemed to be dying even before the bullet struck. His limbs felt heavy and lifeless and instead of hyperventilating, he couldn't feel himself breathe at all. Even his vision was going grey around the edges and his hearing became more muffled. His sister said something and he looked back.

She was celebrating with triumphant arms raised over her head. He expected her to look different, like some sort of hideous creature, but except for the eyes, she hadn't changed. Her eyes were blacker than ever and held the greatest malevolence, there was no sign of his sister in them, she was now all Ba'al Fie-ere.

"Get on your knees, before Ba'al Fie-ere!" she commanded waving the gun toward him. Her face held black joy and he couldn't look on it for more than a second before turning away, sickened. When he did, he saw the huge frame of Jim Anderson, it tilted slightly.

The next thing Will knew he was laying face down on the black ice. He had fainted and he looked around blearily, before strong rough hands gripped him by his heavy coat and yanked him upwards. He stood swaying, held up only by Jim.

"On his knees, you idiot," Talitha screamed. Jim pushed downwards gently and Will collapsed.

When Jim stepped back, Will said, "Thanks." It felt weird to say, but nothing else came to him. For his part, Jim didn't say anything, but just looked at Will with a face that was drawn long with lines of fear running up and down it. His brow had curious beads of frozen sweat dotting it and even as Will watched, one fell off. It bounced when it hit the black ice.

"Look at me," Ba'al Fie-ere demanded in a soft voice, that was still so much like his sister's.

Will turned and the vision he had earlier was moments from occurring. The bore of the gun ran perfectly round and the small black hole was inches from his face. He stared for a second and then hung his head. He no longer felt the slightest hope; he was going to die just as he knew he would, but without any purpose. He wished it would anger him, but he had no feelings whatsoever, not even fear. The closest thing to a feeling within him was exhaustion, and he knelt waiting for the bullet.

"Well?" Ba'al Fie-ere asked.

Will didn't look up. "Well what?"

"Any last words? Aren't you going to pray?" The tone of the voice was friendly but there was cruel mocking laughter just beneath it.

"You want me to pray? Why?" When he didn't look up she squatted down in front of him, her black dress crackling where it had frozen stiff.

"As a favor to Ba'al Zubel, actually. It would be poor form for me to kill you without giving you the chance to pray." She looked him in the eye, but he only shook his head in confusion and she continued, "It's just so much more fun to see a new soul, especially a sweet one like yours, look around the void, shocked at the lack of angels and fairies and all that crap. It's a big turn on."

"Well, I don't plan on making the void my home. Free will you know," Will said and now he was starting to get some feeling back in him, anger.

She smiled wickedly. "I love being the one to say this to you, but the void is going to be your permanent residence. You would normally have a choice, but you are dying in the presence of Ba'al Zubel." She worked hard to keep his blue eyes on her black ones. It seemed important to her for Will to know of his coming confinement in the void. "He'll scoop you up so fast your head will spin clean off your shoulders...I know because the same thing happened to me. In fact I kinda wish I could be there to see it."

"Give me the gun and I'll make sure you have a front row seat," he hissed this at her and she only smiled broader.

"How bout I just give you the bullet instead." The gun came up and Will didn't flinch at the sight of it, but glared around it and started praying.

"Our Father, who art in heaven...what are you going to do with Talitha?" Will felt suddenly sheepish about having forgotten the terrible plight of his sister, now that she was sharing her body with a demon.

"Don't worry about her. I'll drive her out of me somehow, and there are ways of storing souls until they are needed. I'll force her into a gem or some such." She actually went on talking, but Will wasn't listening.

In a blink of an eye his faint hope had been

restored, kindled into life by an accidental combination of words. His mind raced down a thousand avenues searching for the simple sentence that he hoped would make a difference, but he was coming up empty.

"Will? You ask a question and you don't even have the courtesy to listen to my brilliant answer." She seemed genuinely angry and she stood back up, bringing the gun to bear on his face.

"Wait! Uh...one prayer!" Will cried in sudden anguish. She paused as she was pulling the hammer back and now there was evil joy emanating from her. This was what she was really after. She wanted him to beg and plead for his life. Instead, he found the words that wouldn't save his own life, but maybe they would save Talitha's.

The words came to him just as he had read them eight years before. In the days after his confrontation with Ba'al Zubel, the concept of demons had weighed heavily on his mind and he had read everything he could concerning them and more importantly how to get rid of them.

All that he had read had shown that there were two versions of exorcisms, the long and the short. The long one could last days, involved endless prayers, and lengthy rites. All the paraphernalia was needed, Holy Water, Crosses, Rosaries, even the proper vestments, right down to the correct kind of stole. He had none of these things, except a cross and he didn't even have time to fish that out from under his shirt.

The short version involved being Jesus Christ, or maybe one of his apostles.

Will had about ten seconds. He decided to go with the short version. After all, the power for an exorcism was not centered around the right color robe he could wear, but rather it was in the Lord. And God would either hear his plea or not, and act on it or not.

And Will, who had felt the power of God once before when he had needed it most, leaned forward so that only the demon wearing the skin of his sister could hear: "In the name of the Father and his son Jesus Christ, and the Holy Spirit... I command you, Ba'al Fie-ere to leave this girl at once, return to the void, and never come back."

He didn't shout the words to the exorcism melodramatically, or even wave his cross, which was still only a fantastically cold lump against his chest. He just stared her into the eyes and spoke with all the confidence in the lord he could muster.

For a second he didn't think it worked. She leaned back as if she had been slapped and looked confused as if his words were not at all what she had expected, and Will was most certain they weren't. But with a suddenness that startled him, her face screwed up, twisting into such a gruesome mask that he was sure the skin of it would split down the seams. Her expression was of a hated being that had been cheated, but it lasted only a second and it cleared like the parting of clouds, revealing his sister, Talitha underneath.

She blinked slowly in confusion, but her heightened senses told her all that she needed to know about what was going on without turning her head. Her eyes found Will's and it was all he could do not to smile at her.

"Thank you, Lord," he said, quietly relishing that one moment, perhaps the last touch of happiness his soul would ever know, but it was short lived and his mind raced. Ba'al Zubel would demand his death any second and a delay would very quickly reveal the fact that the Demon Ba'al Fie-ere was no longer with them. His only hope was that Talitha would turn in that one instant and shoot the gypsy.

He flicked his eyes in the gypsy's direction, and Talitha in a show of steady casualness gave a look into the room and Will saw the muscles of her face clench, but only the slightest. Just then, as Will had guessed, Ba'al Zubel spoke through Luke.

"He has prayed enough, kill him now."

Will looked over at the demon and saw that Luke was advancing toward them, a knife in his hand, but worse, he now stood between Talitha and the gypsy. Will was at a complete loss; to hesitate would invite an attack he didn't think they could win. Luke looked for all the world like some sort of zombie puppet and with Ba'al Zubel pulling the strings, he might already be dead and thus unkillable in a normal sense.

At that moment, his vision from earlier came back to him, complete with that tiny fringe of hope.

Will unzipped his jacket in a quick motion and then tore open his button-down shirt. The cold instantly attacked him, but he ignored it. His plan had already sent a shiver of ice down his back. It was actually quite simple, Talitha would kill him and when Ba'al Zubel was relaxed or wasn't ready, she'd shoot the gypsy.

"You have to kill me, then her. There's no other way," he whispered, but didn't dare say anything else, Luke was very close now.

Still she hesitated and he was forced to give her a glare. "Take care of business," he warned.

Finally, she brought the gun up and Will was so

proud of her to see it steady in her small hand. She aimed it square into his chest and fired.

The pain was a shrieking terror and just as in his vision, it was surprisingly so, but when Ba'al Zubel looked upon him, greedy for his soul even before he died, the pain got worse. Much worse.

Chapter 27

Death and the Eternal Void

When Will yanked open his shirt, a button kicked loose and skittered on the ice near Jim's foot. It looked like a piece of plastic trying to masquerade, as a piece of wood, there was even imitation wood grain running through it. It had four little holes and in two of them, a tiny filament of white thread ran.

There was nothing else to the button, but he kept staring at it nonetheless. The alternative was to watch a man, a friend actually, die in front of him.

Jim hoped it wouldn't hurt him too much.

His own death was also a certainty. Will had foreseen it and Jim believed it wholeheartedly, he only wished to kill Luke before it happened.

He hated the man.

This was the only feeling that he could commit to. Everything else seemed far away, buried beneath the heavy strength-sapping lethargy that surrounded him. He figured it was his exhaustion, the numbing cold, and the closeness of Ba'al, looking out from his black cloud, that caused this lethargy, but also it was Talitha.

He had seen the girl he loved for the last time; of this he was sure and that knowledge left him unable to do anything but stare at a stupid useless button.

One would've thought that his hatred would've been toward the female demon, after all the trouble she had caused. However, in Jim's eyes, this was what demons did. Not that he liked her in anyway, far from it, but he would've sooner blamed the sun for being too warm.

Luke had no such excuse and neither did the gypsy, who Jim had sworn to kill as well, however that was more out of necessity. With Luke, he expected to feel just a little bit of satisfaction.

Suddenly, he noticed something new about the button. The exterior of it was raised...

Bammnn!

...relative to the interior. It looked like a poorly constructed bowl.

Will's hand came down on Jim's shoe and gripped feebly at the laces. There was blood between his fingers, it wasn't a lot, but it was very wet looking and the freshness of it bothered Jim. So did the rest of Will for that matter. The problem was that he wasn't quite dead, he was making a horrible choking noise, and his body twitched and jerked about as it lay face down.

It made Jim a little sick to his stomach and he looked up from Will expecting to see the gun pointed at him. However Talitha stood looking with ill-disguised shock at her brother. It almost seemed that she was horrified by what she had just done and was trying not to appear so.

Weird for a demon, he thought.

She even looked into his eyes and he was shocked to see a guilty sadness there, something he would never have expected from a demon.

She's trying to trick me.

It wasn't going to work; he had been played for a fool once too many times. He suspected that she'd try to make him think he was going to live, and then, Bam! Right between the eyes. At least he hoped it would be between the eyes, Will was still twitching gruesomely, and the idea of being shot like that gave him the willies.

He decided right then, he was no longer going to play their games. Will had been biding his time looking for an opening to do something and he had bided all the way into a grave.

Not Jim.

Throwing off his lethargy as best as he could, he stepped around Will's twitching body, expecting at any moment to be shot by the demon. However, she only stood there eyeing him with a strange expression on her face and Jim made a point to keep his head turned away from her, ignoring her. He walked past her and two steps into the room he found Luke.

Jim balled his mighty fist and punched Luke square in the face. It turned out not to be as satisfying as he had hoped.

For starters, Luke acted like a puppet and felt like a puppet. It was like hitting a frozen body rather than a man and what's worse, Luke didn't moan or whimper or cry as Jim had secretly hoped. Instead, he only took a few steps back and gaped at Jim with an odd blank, glassy-eyed stare, ignoring completely the fact that his nose had been crushed and was now a bleeding misshapen blob.

Jim paused a heartbeat at the oddness of the situation and then went to hit Luke again. Right then Ba'al Zubel looked at him.

It was beyond excruciating. It felt as if flames had been poured over his body. With pain like that thinking was impossible and he flung himself to the floor, rolling, kicking, screaming. The pain felt endless and he had no clue how long he endured it, but suddenly two gunshots echoed in his mind and just like that, he was released. The flames disappeared as if they had never been.

His eyes went wide, staring all around him and the room was a dizzying place, swirling about, and for a second or two nothing made sense. When he could, he sat up and felt his skin, afraid it would be crispy and black, but it was surprisingly smooth. He was just touching his face when another gunshot rang out and he felt the wind of a bullet caress him gently just beneath his ear.

This was neither alarming nor curious to him. It simply was. His mind was in a state of shock and it was only then he realized there had been two earlier gunshots. He looked over to where the sounds had come from, and saw Talitha standing rigid, gripping the gun in a tight little fist, her eyes rolled back in her head.

Clearly, Ba'al Zubel was attacking her in the same manner as he had been attacked. For a span of three seconds, he watched this blankly and uncaring, without a thought, but then he realized this was the scenario that Will had described.

A tremendous urgency overcame Jim.

His one job, *and* the only way he had a ghost of chance at getting out of there alive was to kill the gypsy. He dragged himself to his feet and turned to kill the gypsy who stood watching everything with wild eyes.

However, she wasn't going to cooperate with his plan so readily and just as he turned toward her there was a flash of an arm and Jim looked down to see the gypsy's knife sticking out of his chest.

The woman stepped back grinning wickedly,

eyeing her handiwork, but that was a very stupid thing to do. The knife's blade was five inches long, but curved like a small scimitar and barely three inches of it had been driven into Jim. Though it looked nasty, it hadn't even scraped against his ribs and was stuck in the tremendously thick muscles of his chest.

It didn't even hurt a lick, especially not after the pain Ba'al Zubel put him through. The gypsy let out a squeal of terror as he leapt forward, far faster than she had ever expected him too, and he grabbed her by the arm and pulled her roughly into him. She fought back, but it was a useless gesture and his great hands squeezed her neck with a force few could withstand. A few seconds of this and she'd be dead, but just then Luke attacked Jim and his knife proved far more capable than the gypsy's.

A wild murderous pain shot down Jim's spine and a moment later, he felt the individual teeth of the serrated steak knife running along a bone in his back as Luke withdrew it. The villain pulled back his arm to strike again, but he hadn't count on Jim's quickness either.

Most people, when they see the enormous leviathans who play the line on football teams, assume that men that big aren't very fast. Those people are dead wrong. Jim released the unconscious gypsy and spun in one move, bringing an elbow around as he did so. The blow caught Luke flush on the side of the head and cranked it around far to the right.

Jim then went to punch the man again, only just as he did he felt a crippling pain lance down his back, all the way to his tailbone.

With a cry, he sank to one knee, reaching around to find the cause. For a second, he thought the gypsy had attacked him again, but his hand came back wet with blood from the same wound that Luke had given him. There was a hole in his back that seemed to go directly through to his vertebrae and for a moment he feared that his spinal column had been injured. However, he had no time to worry about it, because Luke attacked, swinging his knife at Jim's face.

The blow cut him across the forehead as he ducked, and blood ran like water into his eyes. Jim was now practically blind and didn't see the next blow coming. He saw Luke's arm heading in and tried to pull back, but the knife sunk deep under his collarbone, but luckily stuck there. It was only lucky in the sense that he couldn't be stabbed again, but just then another shooting pain in his spine collapsed Jim completely and he fell back with Luke on top.

Luke went to pull the knife out and Jim grabbed him by the wrists and he now had a view of Luke that sickened him. The two gunshots he'd heard less than a minute earlier had both found their mark. Part of the right side of Luke's face was shorn clear away, leaving a grizzled valley running along his cheekbone all the way to his ear. In addition, there was a second wound—a hole the size of a nickel—dead center in his chest, which should have been fatal.

For a moment, Jim could do nothing but stare with words like ghoul and zombie running through his mind, but then his situation became even more precarious when unbelievably, Luke started bending Jim's great arms down.

Jim began to panic.

There was no way a man this small could do such a thing, but nonetheless it was happening and his left arm began to hurt with the terrible strain. The arm held out only a second longer and when it came down, Luke slammed him in the head with his elbow, sending stars across his vision.

Luke struck him again with the same elbow and the blow was like a kick from a horse and suddenly there was no more fight left in Jim. His head swam and he was dazed to such extent that he was seeing things, because another person who should have been dead came up just then.

Will stood behind Luke holding a partially charred wood board in his hands; this he slammed into Luke's head, sending pieces of wood flying in every direction.

Luke flopped over but immediately struggled to his feet.

"What the hell?" It was the choked whisper of Will Jern. He stood swaying, his hands in a fighting stance, eyeing with revulsion the creature that was once Luke.

Jim's eyes went to Will's chest, expecting to see a gaping bloody hole, but instead saw only a dreadful bruise and an odd shaped bleeding cut, but also, swinging back and forth, still on its leather string was the pewter cross that Father Alba had given him. It could hardly be called a cross now, because of how it bent inwards forming a shallow 'C'.

Joy and excitement raced through Jim and he wanted to yell out to his friend, but he was too woozy, besides which, Luke attacked Will. It was a lunging attack, a grab for Will's waist, but the man dodged back, very nearly coming into contact with the smoking demon behind him.

"Look out!" Jim tried to call out, but he lacked the strength in his lungs for anything more than a loud whisper. However, Will didn't seem to need his warning and managed to step aside in time not to touch it.

"Get the gypsy!" Will yelled back.

Grimacing at the shooting pains in his spine, Jim sat up and saw the gypsy lying as if already dead. Her body lay stretched out near the fire. He couldn't walk, so he crawled to her, casting looks at both Will and his sister as he did. Will lurched about clutching his chest, dodging this way and that; however Talitha was on her knees, her hands straining at her head as if she were trying to crush her own skull.

She couldn't last.

Jim had no time, seconds maybe. Certainly not enough time to choke the gypsy to death, something that could last two or three minutes. So instead, as he came up to the gypsy he yanked the curved knife out of his own chest and plunged it with all the force he could muster into hers. With his strength the knife sheered away bone like butter and plunged deep into her heart.

In an instant, Jim became part of the connection— the connection that linked a demon, a gypsy, a virgin and his Talitha.

It was the strangest feeling. He could sense the gypsy and knew her name, and knew as well that she would live out an eternity of death in this shadow land. He could feel Ba'al Zubel as well. It was a monstrous horror that lurked behind everything, a creature of gluttonous appetites without equal in the void.

And he knew and sensed Theresa Brabec as if he were an old friend of hers, which was strange, because he now knew she had no old friends and very few new ones either. She stood far from him, deep in the void, but despite the distance, he could still feel her fear. It was rich and a delight to the fiends that flocked around her—few of which dared to stray to near because of the proximity of the horror of the shade, the tyrant.

Then there was Talitha Lynn Jern. She was a part of the connection as well and there was an intimacy the two of them shared in the fraction of time that the connection lasted. It was the same love that he'd always felt for her, but now he could feel her love in return, it was unhesitating and it was no small thing.

He could sense, in a way, all of them as soon as he crossed into the void. The void itself was inexplicable; indefinable beyond the simplest terms, which in no way can give it meaning. To say it's cold, or dark, or drowned in a caressing fear means nothing until one stands within it.

For James Anderson the most definable aspect of the void would be the fear. It was the air he breathed and it grasped at him, trying to choke him with itself. It sought to bath him in its foul purity and it left him feeling blemished and slick with its texture.

There was darkness as well, but it was not all consuming as the fear. Shadows layered on shadows gave the darkness a nightmare quality that pure blackness never could have. Moreover, the darkness wasn't absolute, there was actual light spoiling it.

The light was dim and far off, but it was real and it beckoned to Jim. But in order to come upon the light, he would have to leave the path that he stood upon, something his soul cried out against. He turned and saw he could leave the void and return to the world, if he so wished, simply by walking back up the path.

However, his heart cried out for the light as well,

and he knew the distant glow was not a trick or a will-o'-wisp designed to lead him astray, but it was the light of the souls that he knew and they were in mortal peril.

Leaving the path, he flew to the small lights on winged feet, and the darkness gave way before him. In time, not time as is counted on the planes of the living, but as counted in the void, Jim found the lights of three souls and now his heart quaked in real fear. The great Tyrant of the void had stepped back and in essence had given up his claims to the light, and now a multitude swarmed over them in an effort to devour their light, that is to say their souls.

The lights of his friends were dimming quickly, there was first Talitha, she glowed brightest of all and battled with a desperate ferocity. Then there was the girl, Terry. She had already lost her battle with fear and lay as a feast for the many creatures that dined upon her light, sullying it and diminishing it. Finally, there was the gypsy, whose name he knew, and whom he had killed in the world, but still looked upon as a person. She foolishly searched for a patron among the demons of the highest rank, resigned to deceiving herself in the belief she would be safer with one of them.

Jim saw this from afar and came as a hurricane in his wrath and he felt a great power within him, and he wished to unleash it on the hordes to save his friends. He drew himself up and the darkness slunk back for a time, all save a single shadow, which stepped forward brazenly.

It was Ba'al Fie-ere.

"Save your breath James Anderson," it said, forming its shadows into a pleasing form.

The form was that of a wickedly sensuous Talitha

Jern, who shined black as jet.

Jim turned away from her saying, "Don't talk to me, I cannot trust you."

"You have no choice. You are far from the path back to the world and you will never save Talitha without my help."

Jim became troubled not knowing the truth and beckoned the demon to follow and he approached closer to the souls.

He wanted to rejoice, even in the crushing darkness, at the sight of Talitha, and he went to her and made to kiss her, but the feeling of the void, which was everywhere, intruded, fouling the pleasantness of her lips.

"Jim you should not have left the path," she said holding him to her.

"That couldn't be helped, I came here for you," he answered and looked at her light closely. It was dimming slightly and he worried, for the swarms of creatures had not retreated far and were becoming bold. "I'm afraid I may not be able to find the path again," he said. This was an unfortunate truth, he had looked back for path almost as soon as he had left it, but it had been swallowed up in the endless void as if it had never been.

"I know where the path lays." Ba'al Fie-ere stepped into their light. Talitha and the demon glowered at each other.

"The demon is composed of nothing but deceit. We cannot listen to it." Talitha cautioned.

"Then none of you will return to the world. Is that what you want?" They were silent and the demon continued, "I am offering you a choice, no tricks. I will see that Talitha is freed...but I will have your soul and that of the girl as payment."

Talitha shook her head as if to say, no.

Jim said, "I can feel the power of the life in me, I can hold out against these creatures."

"But for how long? Not very I surmise and then what would you do? I have seen the power of the *Word* and it cannot be denied, but it is not limitless. Do you feel what is behind these shadow creatures? It is the Tyrant. He learned from his mistake the last time and he is waiting for you to do battle and when you are weak...he will take *all* your souls."

"If what you say is true then in good faith, show us where the path lays," Talitha said and Jim could see her plotting, but Ba'al Fie-ere was cunning and he worried that this was a trick of the demon's to ensnare all them.

"Talitha, please, no," Jim pleaded. "I'm willing to give my soul to save you, as I have vowed, but there has to be another way." Still Talitha wanted to see the path for herself, and she took his hand and followed after the demon, with Terry and the gypsy in tow.

As they travelled, the horde of demons kept pace, and some of the greater ones darted in, attempting to carry Terry off. She did nothing to defend herself save move closer to Jim, which had him puzzled.

"I feel the power of the word in me, but it is not in Talitha or Terry, or even the gypsy, why?"

"These two came into the void kicking and screaming, forced against their will," the demon answered pointing at the gypsy and Terry. "And Talitha came only because she was connected through the demon by their battle of wills, but you had a choice and you came with love in your heart."

"Speak no more to her," Talitha warned him. "She is too great a liar."

The demon, Ba'al Fie-ere gave her a patient look. "I only lie for a purpose and I only tell the truth for the same reason. I seek what benefits me. Helping you benefits me. I will receive two souls where I would have none. You will see." She was silent for the rest of the journey and they did see.

The path, red against the black was held against them by battalions of loathsome creatures and still more demons crowded in their wake. Hopelessness began to fill Jim's heart and when Ba'al Fie-ere saw this, she fretted.

"Do not despair! It will eat at your heart and weaken you, and then these Ghushkaz will have you... all of you. *Know* that you will save your beloved." Jim nodded and kept his eyes on Talitha. Her nearness swelled his heart and made him feel strong again.

Ba'al Fie-ere then turned to Talitha. "Do you see now, sister? Jim may be able to defeat these creatures for a time, but the power of the *Word* will ebb and then he will fall to the Tyrant and all will be lost. You know I am not lying about that."

Talitha nodded grimly, seeing the truth of the demon's words and Ba'al Fie-ere went on, "You would be fools to trust me, but I can trust you. So I will save Talitha first, if Jim will give me his word to come with me willingly and be my slave."

Jim did not hesitate, "I promise." Talitha was silent and he could see her mind working at their problem, but he knew there was no solution, but this one.

"I don't make that promise," Terry cried. "Take me instead!" She rushed to the demon, but Ba'al Fie-ere threw her down and stepped upon her carelessly.

"We must hurry," the demon said, as she pressed harder onto Terry.

Talitha grew angry at this. "Stop. I will not go with you. Take the girl in my stead."

Before Jim could speak the demon replied, "I can't. As much as I want you here, I can't. You are the only that I can save, watch." She stepped toward Talitha, who stood firm, showing no fear, but then Ba'al Fie-ere stepped *into* Talitha and they merged as if one, black, deadly and beautiful.

She then stepped away again. "You see now? I will take her with me through the ranks of Ghushkaz opposing you and release her at the gate. And when I get back, you will send forth the power of the word. This will disrupt much of the void near to us and in the confusion, I will cloak us in darkness and take you and Terry with me. I will leave this one here to attract the attention of Ba'al Zubel," she said referring to the gypsy.

Jim's heart wavered at first, but he pictured Talitha stepping into the light, smiling and happy at long last. Talitha seemed also to finally recognize that this was their only option and she began to cry, her tears were white pearls, and they grew larger as they fell from her cheeks.

The demon, Ba'al Fie-ere, eyed them hungrily and laid out a part of her, to catch them.

Jim kissed a tear of Talitha's from her cheek, it was of pure water, and it washed the oily black fear from his lips, so that now he kissed her truly. His heart swelled even greater with love, but hers swelled in sadness and he rebuked her then and told her to find love in the world.

"It's time, we must hurry," the demon said with urgency and handed the tears she had collected to Jim. "If the demons gather to close, throw one of these at them, but do not waste them!"

Jim gave Talitha a final look and the demon merged with the girl and took her. He watched them a long while and saw that they indeed passed through the formation, unhindered and made their way along the path. Finally, from a great distance a light came to him that he recognized, it was Talitha and she paused for only a second before slipping out of the void.

He felt the void become less at her passing.

The void, when Jim first entered it seemed like a huge thing; endless, but he realized then that it was actually a very small lonely place. Terry grabbed at his arm and had been for some time and finally he looked around to see the swarms drawing near and so he tossed one of the tears, which had swollen to a great size.

He thought it might act as a weapon and explode, but it didn't. It only bounced against the nothing of the void, and as it did, the demons, all of them near to the ball, charged after it and fought for it. He was forced to do this over and over and he had just two left when Ba'al Fie-ere returned with a triumphant look lighting her evil features.

"I have done my part, it's time for you to do yours. Release the word on these fiends." She was dark and beautiful, so much like his Talitha that Jim hesitated a second.

"Tell me who I am first," he ordered the demon.

"My slave," was her response and her eye gleamed—until she saw that his did as well.

Epilogue

When Jim killed the gypsy, the change in the room occurred as if a switch had been thrown and Will's first act was to cast an eye on the great hideous column of smoke, curious to see what would happen.

It was far from dramatic.

The smoke simply dissipated. It eddied about as if in confusion for a moment and then drifted away, leaving behind a black sludge, pooled upon the floor.

The change in the creature that had once been Luke was also far from spectacular. It just stopped moving, froze in place for a second, still staring at Will with its sightless glassy eyes and then it toppled over and didn't again stir.

With that, a warm breeze, at least warmer than the frozen room, drifted in and Will felt his hearing pop back to normal and he could now perceive the small sounds of the room; the snapping of the fire, the steady dripping of rain water cascading down from the partially destroyed roof, his own labored breathing.

For seconds nothing happened and he looked around him dazedly; Talitha knelt with her hands to the sides of her head, Terry lay as dead looking as she had when they first saw her and Jim lay across the body of the gypsy. His body's position looked strange to Will, who got up and went to him.

Jim was dead.

Will pulled him off of the gypsy, heaving him over, despite the pain flaring throughout his chest and felt at the man's throat for a pulse. He *knew* there wouldn't be one, but he checked anyways.

Suddenly he heard a great sob from Talitha and he saw her running, in a staggering drunken manner toward him. She pushed Will aside with considerable force and threw herself on top of the man's huge chest and cried many tears.

She wept for a long time and was at first inconsolable, but at length, when Will finally got up to check on Terry, she wiped at her face and said with heavy bitterness, "Don't bother, she's dead too."

"What happened?" he asked, and from her empty look he didn't figure he would get an answer, but she described everything she had seen, crying constant tears as she did. When she had finished, Will felt such complete exhaustion that he could have slept there on the fading ice.

"What did we come here for? Everyone we've tried to save has ended up dying," he said dismally.

"I've been saved, twice." Talitha whispered and then bent to Jim's lips and kissed him gently, before she stood. She eyed Will with red-rimmed eyes that held a mixture of relief and sadness. "I'm glad you didn't die...when I shot you that is. I aimed for the cross, but I had no way of knowing if it would stop the bullet or not."

Will touched his chest, gingerly, realizing only then what had happened. The pain of the gunshot had been like a fire in his chest, but what Ba'al Zubel had done to him had dwarfed it to such an extent, that only now was he truly feeling it. He took a deep breath in and felt the pain radiating throughout his bones and muscles, it hurt, but he also felt strangely comforted by the pain. It meant he was alive.

"I'm glad I didn't die as well and I'm glad you didn't either. But what about the other Talitha? Is she gone...for good? Can you feel her at all, inside you?" Will felt as if he was on the verge of passing out and swayed as he spoke, but he needed to know.

"She's gone all right, thank you for that. I feel so alive, but poor Jim..." Talitha cried again and he went to her, holding her until he began to reel on his feet. She kept him steady and gave him a sharp look through her tears. "Are you ok? I've never seen anyone so exhausted looking.

"I don't know what I'm feeling," he answered and his head began to swim. He lurched over then and she held him up.

"I'm going to take you back to the hotel. In the morning we'll figure out what to do." She gestured to the grim room and the four bodies.

Will remembered none of the details of the next twenty minutes, other than his sister getting him back to the hotel and putting him in bed. His only thought now was to call Lisa and tell her that he loved her, but the clock read 3:32 am, and he didn't want to wake her, so he slept.

It was a deep sleep, unmarred by dreams, or even worry and it was with a far lighter heart that he woke with light shining into the room. Talitha lay asleep in the next bed and he smiled seeing the great black mess she had made of the sheets from the soot that covered her clothing. Since he hadn't bothered to undress either his own bed was a mess as well.

He went to let out a long sigh of relief, but his chest throbbed and he cut it short. Slipping out of the bed, he went to call his wife, but just as he did he realized that Talitha was asleep. She had slept and he hadn't had any dreams.

He should have been elated, instead he felt a sudden coldness sweep over him. A fear like a dagger drove into him and he was suddenly sure that she was dead in the bed beside his. His fear, a metallic taste in his mouth, mounted quickly within him as he hurried over to her, but just then she snorted in her sleep.

He jumped at the sound and then leaned back, smiling for a moment. Shaking his head in amazement at how quickly his fear had exploded inside him, he turned back and went into the adjoining room. Ignoring the overturned lamps, chairs, and desk, he called his wife and as he waited for her to answer, he raised his hand and saw it shaking, he still had the fear.

"Hello, Will."

The voice coming out of the phone wasn't his wife's.

The End

An Illusion of Hell is dedicated to my wife Stacy. She is all over the pages of this book.

*

Author's note:

Thank you for putting up with me during an Illusion of Hell. Opening the door to hell is not for the weak of heart or the squeamish. I tried to give the readers a simple taste of what it could be like and it was very difficult to pull back on the descriptive or the imagery since real hell would likely be a thousand times worse.

On a self-serving note, the review is the most practical and inexpensive form of advertisement an independent author has available in order to get his work known. If you could put a kind review on Amazon and your Facebook page, I would greatly appreciate it.

Peter Meredith

Hell Blade: The Trilogy of the Void Book Three is now available:

And he lived happily ever after. For just the briefest time Will Jern thought there could be a chance at the perfect fairy tale ending, but then he discovers there's a stranger in his home and that his wife is being held captive by a witch bent on vengeance and who is desperately in need of a soul.

And she lived happily ever after. For Talitha Jern it will never happen. When her demon was banished back to the Void, it left behind the gift that keeps on giving: memories. Her mind now rings with the screams of those her evil side tortured and her hands bear the scent of their blood. Soon she can't tell which memories are of her making and which came from the demon. It's enough to drive a person crazy.

And they all lived happily ever after. Not for a moment did Katie Jern believe this; she knew her family was good and cursed. At the age of six she saw the demon and peered with innocent eyes through the gate unto Hell. Those eyes are innocent no more. They are guarded lest anyone can look past her perky features and see the raging paranoia beneath. But at least she gets the answer to the question that all paranoids ask: Am I paranoid enough? Not nearly.

Fictional works by Peter Meredith:

A Perfect America

The Sacrificial Daughter

The Horror of the Shade Trilogy of the Void 1

An Illusion of Hell Trilogy of the Void 2

Hell Blade Trilogy of the Void 3

The Punished

Sprite

The Feylands: A Hidden Lands Novel

The Sun King: A Hidden Lands Novel

The Sun Queen: A Hidden Lands Novel

The Apocalypse: The Undead World Novel 1

The Apocalypse Survivors: The Undead World Novel 2

The Apocalypse Outcasts: The Undead World Novel 3

The Apocalypse Fugitives: The Undead World Novel 4

Pen(Novella)

A Sliver of Perfection (Novella)

The Haunting At Red Feathers(Short Story)

The Haunting On Colonel's Row(Short Story)

The Drawer(Short Story)

The Eyes in the Storm(Short Story)